The shining splendor of
the cover of this book re...
the story inside. Look fo...
you buy a historical romance. It's a trademark that guar-
antees the very best in quality and reading entertainment.

BRANDED BY DESIRE

"Say my name," he demanded in a voice rough with emotion.

She felt the heat rise between them, catching like tinder. "As you wish, Nicholas."

His fingers followed her lips as they shaped the words. "Say it again."

"Nicholas," she whispered, and it seemed like an admission, that when she voiced his name, he then became real. And when he was real, he was not the enemy she was fighting with her very soul.

His fingers moved, feeling the texture of her lips, the sensation of his name in the sound of her voice, testing the pliant shape of her mouth.

And then he bent toward her as he moved his hand from the exploration of her mouth to her strong-willed jaw; he cupped it, and raised her lips to his.

He had kissed her before, but not like this, with no acrimony between them, no duel of provocation, with the light so low and tender, and somewhere, caught between them, the burgeoning of something tenuous and strong.

He melted into her, his heat defining her, his hands entwined now in her hair. And still they kissed, hungry for each other in this place where there were no boundaries, no strictures, no ties. The fire was glowing, the embers burning low and strong, banked like the passion between them . . .

PASSIONATE NIGHTS FROM

PENELOPE NERI

DESERT CAPTIVE   (2447, $3.95/$4.95)
Kidnapped from her French Foreign Legion escort, indignant Alexandria had every reason to despise her nomad prince captor. But as they traveled to his isolated mountain kingdom, she found her hate melting into desire . . .

FOREVER AND BEYOND   (3115, $4.95/$5.95)
Haunted by dreams of an Indian warrior, Kelly found his touch more than intimate—it was oddly familiar. He seemed to be calling her back to another time, to a place where they would find love again . . .

FOREVER IN HIS ARMS   (3385, $4.95/$5.95)
Whispers of war between the North and South were riding the wind the summer Jenny Delaney fell in love with Tyler Mackenzie. Time was fast running out for secret trysts and lovers' dreams, and she would have to choose between the life she held so dear and the man whose passion made her burn as brightly as the evening star . . .

MIDNIGHT CAPTIVE   (2593, $3.95/$4.95)
After a poor, ragged girlhood with her gypsy kinfolk, Krissoula knew that all she wanted from life was her share of riches. There was only one way for the penniless temptress to earn a cent: fake interest in a man, drug him, and pocket everything he had! Then the seductress met dashing Esteban and unquenchable passion seared her soul . . .

SEA JEWEL   (3013, $4.50/$5.50)
Hot-tempered Alaric had long planned the humiliation of Freya, the daughter of the most hated foe. He'd make the wench from across the ocean his lowly bedchamber slave—but he never suspected she would become the mistress of his heart, his treasured sea jewel . . .

Available wherever paperbacks are sold, or order direct from the Publisher. Send cover price plus 50¢ per copy for mailing and handling to Zebra Books, Dept. 3794, 475 Park Avenue South, New York, N.Y. 10016. Residents of New York and Tennessee must include sales tax. DO NOT SEND CASH. For a free Zebra/ Pinnacle catalog please write to the above address.

THEA DEVINE

TEMPTED BY FIRE

ZEBRA BOOKS
KENSINGTON PUBLISHING CORP.

ZEBRA BOOKS

are published by

Kensington Publishing Corp.
475 Park Avenue South
New York, NY 10016

Copyright © 1992 by Thea Devine

All rights reserved. No part of this book may be reproduced in any form or by any means without the prior written consent of the Publisher, excepting brief quotes used in reviews.

If you purchased this book without a cover you should be aware that this book is stolen property. It was reported as "unsold and destroyed" to the Publisher and neither the Author nor the Publisher has received any payment for this "stripped book."

First printing: July, 1992

Printed in the United States of America

Prologue

Paris — January, 1807

"Let me assure you, Jainee, M. deVerville will be here. I expressly asked for him to come tonight, and I know the Emperor will not refuse me," Therese Beaumont said with more confidence than she felt. She turned away from Jainee then to examine herself in one of the many looking glasses that decorated the parlor walls, but she could hide nothing from Jainee. Behind her, Jainee stood, the living embodiment of herself when she was young, reflected like an echo of passing time and an indictment of the present.

She sniffed and pulled her mobile face into an expression of disdain. "He never has, you know."

Jainee said nothing. Therese fiddled with a lock of her hair. "Refused me, I mean," she added, as if Jainee did not know this as well as she. It galled her that everytime she sent to deVerville, Jainee reacted with the same vehemence and more, the same inexplicable anger.

"Still, his tokens of affection have increasingly diminished," Jainee retorted, without caring whether this spiky little truth inflicted any pain, "and still you have not learned to control your passion for the cards."

"A friendly game now and again," her mother snorted dismissively. "Just to lend a little pleasure to life. After all, they did say he was good to the women he had loved, but look at how stingy he has become with the passing years. Ah, men are fickle, Jainee. The best way to love them is to strike a bargain with them

5

and ultimately come away with something, because it is always women who must pay the price."

"It seems to me that our dear emperor has been made to pay the price, *Maman,* and not only by you," Jainee said with no small edge of malice coloring her words.

"And was it not wise?" her mother demanded. "Do we not have this conversation *every* time I send for deVerville? Truly, did you expect me to raise you *and* the emperor's bastard without a husband or any means of supporting myself? And then, when your father stole the boy away, did you really expect me to relinquish the income to which I was entitled? It is easy to spend grief, Jainee; I squander it daily. But you cannot spend what you do not have and so I have made sure that we *have,* and it is just our great good fortune that the emperor has no desire at all to see his son and that deVerville wishes to discharge his duty to the Emperor as quickly as possible.

"And so, you will await his arrival as usual, Jainee, and you will kindly give me the money as usual, and we will continue on as usual."

"Unless you gamble it all away tonight," Jainee said tartly. "Or if this is the one night that M. deVerville comes and refuses to pay the money. Or, if he brings word from the emperor that he wishes to dispense with this obligation to you. What happens then, *maman?* What will you do? What if he gets wind that you want the money to feed to the cards, what then?"

Therese shrugged. Therese always sloughed off the little lies. "It will be simple," she had said in her artless way. "I will merely write a note pleading the urgency of the situation . . ."

"The only urgency is the fact that you haven't got a thousand francs to put on the card table at the end of the week," Jainee pointed out stonily. How she hated this, begging charity from the man to whom her mother had willingly given her body and who, worse still, probably barely remembered her.

She was desperate, Therese had written. Oh yes, desperate for one more bloody game with that scoundrel Le Breque.

But Therese was never moved solely by the event of the moment. She needed money, she had access to a ready source, she had only to write a note and enhance the truth of the matter to achieve results.

"He will not refuse me," Therese said with childlike certainty. "This money supports his only living son."

"Until he finds out there is no son, that your demands are a lie, that you suffer not except in your excesses, and that you care little or less about the child you bore him," Jainee shot back in anger, and perhaps a little fear.

Therese's expression turned to stone. "And *who* shall we tell him handed the child over to her father willingly, despite all my precautions against even letting the man into my house?"

She watched Jainee's defiant expression crumble with great satisfaction.

"And *who* shall we tell him broke her mother's heart? Who mourned the most, Jainee? And who finally was able to find solace in an occasional harmless game of cards? And tell me then, *who* begrudges her mother *any* recompense in spite of what she did to her?

"Yes, I think you now see the wisdom in assuming that things will remain as they always have been, and you will meet M. deVerville tonight, Jainee, and that will be that."

Jainee turned her back on her mother as she finished speaking. It was one thing to be reminded of her great galling sin. It was quite another to let her mother see that she too still grieved the loss of the baby and her own innocence in the matter of the man who was her father.

"The double-tongued devil," Therese called him, "so slippery and fine, *du meilleur rang* — aristocratic, so elegant, so *English* —"

And yet Therese had not been able to resist him, so what could be expected of a fourteen year old girl who had not seen him in ten years and who had made him into some kind of hero?

"A Judas," Therese spat any time Jainee wanted to know about him and she never would believe everything negative Therese said of him. In her heart, she believed — she had to believe — he had had a reason for taking the boy. But the fact remained that Therese had not been home and Jainee had allowed Luc to go, and it manifested itself in the tight guilty hold that Therese wielded over her.

That, and her conscience. Such a delicate, binding chain, a conscience.

"Make sure," she began in a muffled voice, "make sure that there are no open curtains, no obvious lights, no noise."

"Of course not," Therese said, and it was as if the previous conversation had never happened. "I am never careless."

Nor, she thought smugly, *am I ever wrong.*

The clock in the hallway struck the hour. Nine. Nine-thirty. Ten. Jainee waited in the dimly lit library, pushing away the fierce feeling of dread that washed over her with each passing half hour.

"Jainee—!" Therese cried in a querulous voice.

Jainee eased open one side of the sliding doors and shook her head, not liking at all the desperate note in Therese's voice and the scent of disaster that seemed to hover over her.

Therese bit her lip and waved Jainee back into the library, and she waited—ten-thirty. Eleven . . .

"Jainee!" Therese's desperation had turned to panic and Jainee hardened her heart against the terror in her eyes.

"Nothing, *maman.*"

"Dieu," Therese muttered, her expectations dying a fast death as she went down another rubber at picquet against the ruthless Le Breque.

Jainee could not bear to watch. She sat behind the sliding door listening to the silence, the thick, edgy, deep silence that was broken only by the faint sound of one card slapping against another. She could not stop the game, and she never could stop her mother who was like some light flittery moth, always racing headlong into the singeing flame to be consumed by it and an appetite for gambling that never could be satisfied.

All she had ever been able to do was lull Therese into thinking that their comfortable and somewhat fraught mode of living would go on forever.

And steal from her.

Oh yes, and steal from her half of every purse delivered so punctiliously by the patronizing deVerville.

That she had been able to do very well.

The clock struck again—midnight—the last gong modulating down into a palpitating matte stillness underlaying the ripe

8

atmosphere of calamity that emanated from the room beyond.

And then she heard the thunderous banging beyond the door, the clatter of scrambling feet and furniture as the front door crashed in, and Therese's voice, edged in raw horror: "deVerville!"

And his voice, booming above the sound of receding footsteps: "So, Madame—No food, is it? Sold all your furnishings to make rent, did you? Starving, Madame Beaumont? Penniless? About to be thrown in the street? I think *not*, Madame—no, *stay*. That's better, Madame. Now tell me—*where is the boy?*"

Jainee cringed at the sound of Therese's quavering voice. "I—"

deVerville's voice again, harsh, commanding: "Don't move. You, Durand, make sure she does not move one step from where she stands."

Jainee froze as the sound of his footsteps echoed up the stairs at the front of the house and pounded down the upstairs hallway from room to room above her. "Boy, come out *now*," he shouted and tossed furniture every which way and slammed closet doors in the resultant silence.

She didn't know which way to move as his footsteps veered to the back of the house and the rear stairwell so close to the library where she stood her ground. In five steps, she could be out the window and free—and leave Therese to pay for her follies.

"Where is the bloody boy?"

And then there was no choice whatsoever. Just as deVerville burst into the library, she flung open the sliding doors and darted into the parlor.

"Jainee!" Therese, folded into a chair, cringing in fear, dissolved into helpless tears. The masked man beside her wheeled and trained his pistol on Jainee. Behind her, deVerville's voice: *"The boy . . . ,"* and she whirled to face him and the deadly pistol in his hand.

"There *is* no boy," she said defiantly, even as she began backing away from his menacing figure inch by inch.

There was no getting away from that pistol. He held it steady as a rock and she knew he could hit her a hundred feet away, let alone five.

"The boy is not *here*," deVerville amended smoothly. "Where *is* the boy?"

9

There was another heart-stopping silence, and then Therese said suddenly, desperately, "He's gone."

"Gone? Where, Madame?"

Jainee made a movement, almost as if she thought some physical barrier would deflect her mother's pointless confession. It didn't matter to deVerville where—as the right arm of his Emperor, who had thought he was supporting a son all these years and not a vain and capricious woman, the fact the child was not in the house was enough reason for him to mete out punishment.

"His father took him," Therese said finally, and was emboldened to elaborate at deVerville's polite, attentive silence. "To England. Where in England, I cannot tell you, but he took him to England, of that I am sure."

Ever rash, imprudent Therese. Whatever he expected to hear, deVerville's expression did not change. "England, Madame? The blood of the emperor resides in *England?*"

He motioned with his head almost imperceptibly, and Durand moved away from Therese, and toward the front door, as he himself backed up against the sliding doors so that Jainee and her mother were between him and Durand.

His face hardened visibly as Therese wailed, "His father stole him away," and Jainee reached out to take her hand.

And the first shot rang out—deVerville surely, and Therese's bosom stained with blood.

"Maman," Jainee screamed, throwing herself at her mother's body; the second shot ripped through her arm as she fell onto Therese's lap. A third, a fourth . . . she had to have died, there was only blackness . . . and footsteps, a curse, a door slamming . . . and a thick, blood-letting silence.

And pain, indescribable, soul-tearing pain. Dear God, her mother . . . "Therese! Therese!" She couldn't see . . . she was blind, panicked; no—blood congealing on her face, she couldn't even cry. *"Maman!"*

Her mother's body, lifeless under her own, and she was so tall, so heavy, she could be hurting her, making it worse . . . she held her breath and reached out her hand: Therese felt warm still, her arm, lifeless against the side of the chair.

She dragged a limp hand across her face. It came away wet, sticky. Tears streamed down her cheeks. *"Maman!"*

10

Now she could see . . . her mother's face, white, drained of life, so beautiful, heedless Therese, covered in blood, defended by a body as limp and mortal as her own. There was nothing a daughter could do for her now.

"Maman!" Her anguish shrieked up from the earth. Her mother was dying; *she* was dying. She felt the blood draining from her, from places she could not feel, could not touch, and the blood of the mother and daughter mingled, became one, had always been one . . .

". . . Jainee . . ."

It was the faintest of whispers.

"Maman," Jainee cried brokenly.

". . . better thus," Therese breathed. "Listen . . . find the boy."

". . . I'm dying," Jainee cried.

"Live, and find the . . . boy. Promise me, promise . . . They'll kill him. Repay me . . . the gold you stole, Jainee. Find the boy . . ."

"I'm bleeding," Jainee sobbed. "How can I promise?"

"Swear it to me, on my dying body . . ."

"Oh, *Maman,"* she whispered, wrapping her arms around Therese's limp body. "I swear, I swear . . ." Oh, what did it matter what she promised when her lifeblood was trickling out of her, a rivulet of red to flow with her tears. She felt weaker, she felt Therese's body shudder with the effort to say more, to keep awake, alive to tell her more, more that would not matter fifteen minutes from now.

"Shh, *Maman,* shhh . . . I will find your son, I promise, I promise," and she chanted the word like a litany over her mother's dying body until she surrendered to the promise of the light and the night beyond her pain.

Chapter One

Brighton, England: January, 1809

This was the part she hated the most, the moment when she paused in the doorway at the top of the stairs, her body silhouetted against the light, her damped-down underdress molded tight to her curves like a second skin, the moment when all conversation stopped and every man in the room turned to look up at her and then the sibilant sound of her name rose up to enfold her like an undulating wave: "Ah, Jainee, Jainee, Jainee," they murmured, the word passing from one to the other as if with her arrival the real event of the evening had finally begun.

"Jainee," they whispered in one voice as her hand firmly gripped the icy marble bannister and she began her descent into the main reception hall of the *Alices*.

"Jainee," they begged, reaching for her hand as she made her way into the room through the small select crowd. "Jainee," they smiled at her and she smiled back, hating the so very English pronunciation of her name — Jen-ay, and having to act so very pleased that all these fine and fashionable gentlemen had come yet another time to game away the evening with the coolly elegant Jainee Bowman at the *Alices*.

She was an attraction now, and she took some enjoyment in the irony that just a year before she had been but another emigré desperate for a roof over her head, willing to do anything, even handle the tainted cards, in order to find a place where she could retrench, learn the language and find some means to fulfill her impossible promise to Therese.

The memory of Therese haunted her by night and by day; her guilt sometimes overwhelmed her, pushing her when she faltered, and when the ever pragmatic side of herself whispered *why go on? Who would know?*

But she knew: Therese would know in that haunted heaven she believed in so firmly. And *she* would know.

"Ah, Jainee," a fluty voice called over the muscular noise of the crowd.

"Dear Edythe," Jainee acknowledged her, even though she couldn't see her for a moment. And then a small knot of exquisites bowed and made way for the woman who stood just beyond them, and then commented loudly and wittily on her forceful stride as she joined Jainee in the middle of the room where, together, they made a picture of slender grace and dominant determination.

"I was hoping you would come," Jainee murmured.

"My dear, I told you I would help you if I could. You were ever wise to choose me as your confidante."

"I have thought it was more likely that *you* chose *me*," Jainee said tartly, edging a glance around Edythe's shoulder. "Tell me, is there anyone likely tonight?"

"Better than that," Edythe said, softening her voice to a whisper. "Southam is in town."

"Truly?" Jainee said artlessly as the mention of *his* name sent her senses skittering. "I cannot recall the name." She marveled at her great aplomb: she was sure not one jot of emotion showed on her face when in actuality she felt an overriding desire to attack something. But Southam was nowhere near, nor would he remember an obviously trifling incident from a year before when she was green and untutored in the ways of elegant gentlemen in places they considered their purview. She learned quickly enough that women too were objects to be fondled and played with as discreetly as the cards or dice, and Southam had taught her that hard lesson.

"He is the perfect plum for you to pluck," Edythe Winslowe said meaningfully. "Listen to me, Jainee: here is the way. You could never ask for the favor you could command by merely offering the one thing the most wealthy of men cannot refuse."

"And what is that?" Jainee demanded through gritted teeth.

"A challenge, my dear."

Jainee's face set. It was almost time to man the tables, and she really had no time to think about how to skin one top-lofty aristocrat out of his last farthing. "I cannot do that," she said finally.

"Hear me out, Jainee. Southam has all the wherewithal you require. He travels in the right circles—Prinny has just taken him up, what could be better? But more than that, he can afford you."

"I cannot listen to this," Jainee said obdurately, making a quick movement toward the gaming room.

She felt Edythe's hand at her elbow and slowed reluctantly.

"Do not rush to judgment, Jainee. This is a powerful man who, by all accounts, has only just discovered the world beyond his estates and his banker. Never was he a gamester until he was jilted by Lady Emerlin. They say he went right into a tailspin and never came out. They say he is bloodless at the gaming table, but he loses as much as he wins. They say that no one has fixed his interest since. Now here is the point, Jainee: you have been scheming for a way to get to London and to enter the higher circles in society.

"Now, I have never questioned your reasons or motives, nor do I now. I have offered what aid I can give, and in this last year, you have succeeded remarkably well, both from my tutelage and by your own native shrewdness and beauty.

"But this is the test. This is the point: we have talked about this very plan and here, marching into your web like a fly to the spider, is one of the richest men in England, a man who is unattached and unnaturally disinterested in anything but his most basic wants and needs.

"It is up to you, dear Jainee, to take this information and to make use of it—to take your opportunity if it should present itself. Or to make it, if it does not. Vengeance is sweet, Jainee, and who should know but I? That is my advice. Women such as we are never afraid of expediency. We just make sure that others are afraid of *us*.

"No—do not escort me, Jainee. Take your table. There is nothing, after all, to say that Southam will even show up tonight."

* * *

15

And so, because she was keyed up to the possibility of seeing him, she was both elated and disappointed that Southam did not put in an appearance that evening.

Over and above that, she was alarmed at how quickly Edythe Winslowe's suggestion took root in her mind, and how she relished the thought of provoking one such as Southam—and coming away the winner.

There were ways to do that, and she had learned them all at Therese's knee. It truly was no wonder that she had found her place at the *Alices* once she understood the nature of her gift and her mother's curse.

The *Alices* had been good to her, and fate had been kind. She believed in it now—luck, fate, fortune—whatever the goddess was that her mother had worshipped. It had brought her safe and sane across the water and delivered her into a kind of destiny which, once she had accepted it, she knew she never could have escaped.

Now it was all a matter of how she chose to use it.

She had conceived the plan not long after she had come to the *Alices* and months before she had picked out Edythe Winslowe as the knowledgeable courtesan that she was. Southam's callousness had only cemented her determination.

Then she had watched and sewed, along with the little maid whom Murat had insisted on sending with her, until she learned enough of the language to communicate that she was as able as any of the women who played at the *Alices,* and that she wanted to take her place among them.

Even that would not have been possible had she not possessed a remarkable degree of beauty, intelligence and *sang-froid:* she rather thought herself that her coolheadedness was valued more than her looks. Nothing shook her, she who had dealt with Therese and survived a murder attempt, turned down an emperor and traveled a continent and a world away from everything she had ever known.

And then Southam. Here was a world of experience encompassed in one steely, coldblooded man who commanded enough wealth so that he could choose and be certain no one would refuse his demand.

Even she knew better now. The innocent she had been could

16

never have played games of chance with him. She had needed this year of seasoning to hone her senses and her language, to focus her intention and set her goal. She had needed time to learn the ways of the gentlemen of the English cloth, and to understand how to flatter them and tease them into falling for the traps she so cleverly devised.

She had needed this year to fine-tune the skill that she had inherited from Therese, and to understand there was but one way to achieve her ends.

That was the simplest comprehension of all: she must use anyone and everyone at her disposal, no matter what it cost, no matter what she lost in the process.

And so the thought of Southam gaming at the *Alices* began to take on the delicious aspect of a farce: she envisioned herself leading and him following until she had him finally under her fragile kidskin slipper, on his knees where she wanted him.

Who was Southam, after all, that his name should send a shudder through her? Oh, she had made a monstrous mistake betraying her revulsion to Edythe, even to herself. She had spurned him that other time, yes, but then she had been a negligible waif in the garments of servitude, an emigré, unknown, unknowable, an object for his use only. To him, she had no face, no life, no duty other than submission.

Nor had she thought of him in nearly a year; no wonder she had at first rejected the idea that Edythe Winslowe proposed. (*Stupid, stupid for being so vocally stubborn about it . . .* she could never undo that *faux pas*.) Now she would just have to go on as if nothing had ever been said.

But that was the way with the English: everything was judged by appearances and what was said as well as what was ignored.

Southam would judge her on her appearance as well, should he ever enter the portals of the *Alices*.

It pleased her to ruminate on the specifics of such an encounter as she played the night away at the green baize gaming tables at the *Alices*. It piqued her interest to wonder how much she had really learned in a year about the vices and vagaries of gentlemen, and whether she could even handle such a one as Southam as easily as she did the exquisites who invariably crowded around her at the tables every night.

17

It was a matter of maturity, she decided, and time; when the challenge presented itself, she would be ready to meet it.

He paused in his minute scrutiny of the intricate folds of his cravat as he heard the imperious rap on the door to the grand salon. This was followed by the immediate appearance of his hostess, the Dowager Duchess of Tazewell, Lady Waynflete, and he watched her progression across the long length of the room through the mirror with a faint smile curving his finely defined mouth.

Lucretia always amused him because she was diminutive; regal, dressed sumptuously as a queen, for some reason she assumed that because of her height, she could be outrageously outspoken and never suffer the consequences. Even now, he could see by the tilt of her chin that she was ready to engage in some combative discourse with him and there was no way he could escape.

She nodded her head exasperatedly as he turned to acknowledge her and she caught a flicker of wariness shadow his devil black eyes before he could school his expression, and it pleased her to see him look for one brief moment like a mischievous schoolboy caught in some prank.

"Just so, Southam."

"Ma'am," he murmured coolly, betraying nothing.

She rapped his arm with her fan. "I did not like it above half when you went around betting against that chit you got engaged to crying off, but to haul us down to Brighton at this time of year to maunder away in gaming hells with Jeremy and Prinny's set is outside of enough."

"Why then, you needn't have troubled yourself to come, madame," he said mildly.

"Oh, that would have suited you and Jeremy just fine, Nicholas. Not a shred of sense or conscience between the two of you. Of course you wanted me here so I could pull the reins a little when you two got out of hand. Besides which, Arabella Ottershaw always spends Yuletide here and you know very well she is my bosom friend. Well, be that as it may, Nicholas, I assume you are accompanying me to the Cardleigh's rout."

18

"I mean to put in an appearance, yes," Nicholas agreed.

"Cool as ever, my boy, but I can see right now you fully intend to strand me there and go to hell at the card tables."

"You mistake me, madame. It is the excellent supper at the *Alices* that I seek."

Lady Waynflete slapped her fan against the back of a nearby chair in frustration. "Nicholas—you cannot continue this way."

"My dear Lucretia, I am merely going on in the way I always have."

"Nonsense. You never went near a card table before that Charlotte woman jilted you."

"Truly? Never? How little you know of gentlemen, madame."

"And Dunstan stands by, I suppose, and never says a word."

"But it is none of my uncle Dunstan's business," Nicholas said gently. "Come, Lucretia, do not ring a peal over me. The Southam fortune is still intact. And Jeremy makes me mind my manners, I promise you that."

"Jeremy is a fribble," his mother muttered ungratefully. "Nicholas—"

"You mean well, madame," he interrupted ruthlessly, "but you have no cause for concern. I know what I am about."

Lady Waynflete stared at him for a long moment, gratified to see that his expression hardened and his eyes shuttered against her knowing gaze. Dear Nicholas. She saw him still as a forlorn child who held onto his emotions so tightly he could not bear to give or receive the affection of even his closest friends.

She offered him her arm, finally, as the clock struck the hour of departure. "Dear Nicholas," she murmured, "I daresay you do *not* know what you are about, and I truly hope someday you may find out."

It had been four days since Edythe Winslowe's momentous disclosure, and it was now the week's end and Southam had not put in an appearance at the *Alices*.

That Saturday night, everyone prepared for a late evening, for it was common knowledge that the Cardleighs were entertaining and even the most inveterate gamester could not in good manners or good conscience leave the party before eleven of the clock.

To that end, the mistress at the *Alices* directed that everything be prepared and ready one half hour before the expected arrival of the guests.

She, who called herself Lady Truscott, and who was an intimate of Edythe Winslowe, was reputed to have been a fashionable impure and fearless at the gaming tables, and had eventually accumulated in winnings the small fortune which she had used to open the *Alices* some fifteen years before.

She had, in addition to that, wisely chosen and trained her own hostesses, seeking them from the gentry as well as from the ranks of the illegally emigrated young women so as to insure their loyalty to her. She believed she had a gem of the first water in Jainee Bowman, who seemingly had been born knowing all there was to know about the tables, and who had only to mature from a somewhat defiant and scared waif into a beautiful, sensual and dangerous young woman to fulfill the promise of her usefulness to her.

Alice Truscott did not believe that Jainee Bowman would spend the rest of her days at the *Alices*, but she did believe that the take of the house had increased ten fold since the day Jainee had taken her place at the gaming tables. And she was absolutely certain that once Southam and his set got wind of this new treasure, she would welcome them to the *Alices* every night until they all took off for London and the beginning of the Season.

She discounted completely that Southam had once disrupted her poor house just after his disastrous engagement to that horse-faced Charlotte Emerlin had been broken off.

It was merely that Southam had not been himself on the occasion of that visit, and had demanded wine, cards and women in that order, and had played with a reckless abandon that had swollen her coffers and her heart with great affection for him. She proudly dated his newfound predilection for the cards from that evening, and never remembered that she had almost sacrificed Jainee into the maw of her greed. She told everyone that the play at her establishment was so above par that Southam had positively caught the fever and had been seeking that ultimate experience ever since.

And now there was Jainee to add interest to the audacious play of the gentlemen. Of course, Southam would come back to the

Alices; she made book on it, wagering that he would not appear before midnight, and was forced to act gratified nevertheless when he strolled in at half past eleven in the company of Waynflete, Ottershaw, Fox and Chevrington.

And did he not stand out among them, as they waited for her to greet them and suggest a menu of play. He was taller than most, and finely fitted out in black which, with his proud carriage and harsh face, made everyone else seem overdressed and over*stuffed.* His voice was deep, his eyes black as night and guarded as a vault. He had no other expression in company but that polite and disdainful impassivity which was at once frustrating and challenging, and she knew from experience that the best tack was to ignore it completely or rise to the challenge.

His overwhelming attraction was that his pockets were deeper than most, and that most satisfactory thought warmed Lady Truscott's greeting to an unaccustomed effusiveness.

But she saw immediately that his attention was caught elsewhere, and she had a fair idea exactly where his gaze rested. How could he help it?

She had made sure to display her jewel in the best setting possible—the best room, the center saloon just off of the reception hall which was framed by an elegant carved and gilded door molding, the best furniture, the costliest rugs, and elegant satin draperies. In the middle of this luxury, Jainee, dressed as always in diaphanous blue the exact color of her eyes, held court.

The table over which she presided was made of a rich polished mahogany, inlaid with green baize, and surrounded with a set of twelve matching chairs upholstered in bottle green silk, six of which were occupied by overdressed fawning young men, serious players all.

The walls were painted in a rich cream color which, under the soft flame of a hundred candles, enhanced the dreamlike setting against which Jainee's soft, faintly accented voice invited her guests to continue to play.

Southam stood back from the room, just outside the door, admiring the set piece that Jainee, the saloon and her hangers-on presented. He liked nothing better than a woman who knew what she was about, and this one, for all her beauty, had a look in her eye which attracted him beyond all reason.

21

It was almost as if she were amused and it was that, rather than her obvious and rather blatant beauty, which fixed his interest.

"She *is* beautiful," Lady Truscott murmured unobtrusively beside him, having directed his companions to the rooms which catered to their various vices.

"Is she?" Southam responded abstractedly, "I hadn't noticed."

Lady Truscott let that out-and-out lie pass. "Beautiful to watch as well, my Lord. She knows just how to play the high flyers, don't she?"

"Indeed," Southam said noncommittally, not caring to pursue the way in which the perceptive Lady Truscott had echoed his own thoughts. He felt bored already with his preoccupation with this woman's face.

But still he did not move from the doorway, and he watched intently as she cracked open a new deck of cards and shuffled with cool and practiced hands.

Yes, there was something in her expression that positively arrested him and for one moment he felt a violent wave of antipathy, as if he could dislike her intensely even though he was certain he knew her not at all.

And she looked up just then, her melting blue gaze unerringly settling on him, and she smiled, and it was the smile of the siren; she spoke, and her voice was like a caress. "Join us, my lord."

It was not even a command, and still he moved forward into the room on the strength of his curiosity and the look in her eyes and took his place at the table with only a cursory glance at the order of cards embedded in the baize.

She in turn placed the freshly sorted deck into the beautifully gilded mahogany box beside her, and then looked up once again, her imperturbable gaze resting once again on Southam. "Your wager, my Lord?"

Nothing more, nothing less, and still he felt such a jolt of antagonism toward her, he was hard put to concentrate as the others set out their bets and she put the cards into play.

He went down quickly on the tide of his inexplicable animosity, and left the center saloon shortly thereafter to seek out Jeremy Waynflete as he was sliding into oblivion at the E.O. table.

"I swear, Nicholas, it is you who are leading me down the path to ruin," he greeted Southam ill-humoredly.

"I collect you are down a few hundred," Nicholas inferred calmly. "Never mind that." He helped himself to a glass of champagne from a tray offered by a passing manservant. "Come; look at this Greek goddess instead. She positively fascinates me."

Jeremy grabbed a glass of champagne and followed Southam through two card rooms to the reception hallway where they could mingle with a number of other guests taking a respite from the rigors of play.

It was perfectly plain from the crowd gathered around the doorway to the center saloon just where the goddess of the Greeks held court, and Jeremy made his way among them without any direction whatsoever.

Nicholas, however, held back, feeling another inexplicable surge of hostility as he watched the fawning exquisites who were vying for a seat at her table.

He could just see her quite lovely face and those intelligent, amused eyes. (*Scornful eyes, lightning bolt eyes wishing him dead* . . .) resting with great confidence on each and every man who took a seat around the table.

Lying eyes . . . She said a word to each, her expression reflecting a warm, seemingly personal interest that had to have been faked; she could not possibly have known them all. And yet each looked flattered, and more than that, wound up and ready for a round of spirited play.

Nicholas turned away in disgust; Jeremy joined him several moments later in the dining room after accurately deducing where he had disappeared to, and found him seated at a window table with a tray full of cold meats and another glass of champagne.

He looked up at Jeremy with his familiar insolence. "Well?"

Jeremy took a chair and sat down emphatically next to Nicholas.

"Your wits are addled, man. Do you really not know who the goddess is?"

"I do not, nor do I care," Nicholas said, making a show of wiping his mouth with his napkin. *Did he know? Maybe he didn't believe it* . . .

23

"Good God, Nicholas, that woman is the wench you took to bed last Yuletidemas, the witch who poured a decanter of the house's best claret over your head and ruined your new coat and top boots and then threatened you with a candle and fireplace poker."

"Did she really?" Nicholas murmured. *From guttersnipe to goddess in the space of a year, with those knowing eyes that now would never stoop to such crudity with a paying guest? Such a fascinating transformation; almost worth a coat, a pair of boots and a half hour of humiliation. And Jeremy, damn him, would remember every last detail; while he—he never would forget.*

He shook his head. "Do you know, I can't seem to remember anything like that happening at all."

"I believe the bedclothes caught fire," Jeremy amplified helpfully. "And of course, the incident did nothing to add to your consequence, Nick."

"What a shame," Nicholas said mildly. "I do hope the gentleman in question got out in time."

"I believe there was great damage to his pride. But then, it was bruited about that he had been drinking, something quite unlike him, and the whole was laid to the door of some broken engagement. Apparently a man will be forgiven anything in the name of drowning his sorrow."

Nicholas sighed. "So it seems. A man could be thoroughly foxed and have no memory at all of passing events. The thought is diverting. I believe I must have another long look at this goddess. I am sure she will never give me away."

"The trouble with you, Nicholas, is that you have too much money, too much time and too much inclination, and you take great enjoyment in testing my patience. You surely don't mean to take revenge at this late date."

"My dear Jeremy—you talk in such violent terms about an incident of which I have no memory whatsoever."

"Exactly, my lord. You never saw the chit. She never jammed the poker perilously close to your unmentionable. You were never here. I was never there. It's all of a piece, Nick. You have been furious for a year that she took you that time around, and, come to think, she probably took you at the Faro table this very evening, and you are probably furious about that as well."

But Nicholas, as was his wont, said not a word in answer to this upbraiding, and Jeremy finally threw up his hands. "You are being thoroughly dislikeable, you know."

"Never," Nicholas said with feeling.

"In any event, you would be better served if I returned to the Cardleigh's and attended to my mother."

"Perhaps not," Nicholas said, rising to his feet and dropping his well crumpled napkin onto the table. "Come now, Jeremy. I merely wish to ascertain if the goddess is worthy of my mettle."

"I know you, Nick. You will gnaw at a thing until it's nothing but bone. But the goddess has backbone, I'll wager, and I'll even bet who comes out the better in any encounter between you two."

"Done," Nicholas said, as they walked together into the reception room. He motioned to Lady Truscott. "The betting book, if you please." It was, as he knew, ready to hand. "A hundred pounds, Jeremy?" He wrote it in the book and handed it back to Lady Truscott. "I bid you goodnight, Jeremy."

Jeremy smiled. "But how could you think it, Nicholas? That I would leave you to the goddess's tender mercies and not stay to rescue you as the occasion arises."

"Foolhardy of me," Nicholas murmured, damning Jeremy for his perspicacity and the way in which he had been manipulated. He was a little off the pace this night, but that didn't signify. He viewed these little unforeseen surprises as one of the things that made life so amusing. His demeanor in that respect never changed. Nothing threw him, and he always presented a calm and collected appearance, and it was one of the many things for which he was both envied and despised.

He motioned now toward the center saloon. "Do join me, Jeremy."

"I wish you well, Nick," Jeremy said. "And may one or the other of you be fully done up by day's break."

Chapter Two

She had barely a moment to study Southam's face as he entered the center salon and proceeded to elegantly and somewhat ruthlessly remove every obstacle in his path to her table.

He was a wonder to watch in his severe black evening dress with that implacable, harsh-featured face which gave over nothing to either excess politeness nor the exigencies of fashion. Still, he was the most refined and noticeable man in the room and it was obvious that this anomaly was the thing that set him apart from everyone else, and more, that he deliberately cultivated it.

But she would have known him had he been clothed in satin and a powdered periwig, and it was plain from the careless glance he gave her as he settled himself into the chair opposite her, that he remembered exactly who she was as well.

Yet, she could have sworn the half hour previously there had been no recognition in his eyes at all.

She looked up at him from under thick, long lashes. Not a muscle moved in his face.

Yes, that was the thing they said about Southam. He never betrayed a thing, his feelings always locked in the attic, never to be exposed to the light of day.

Formidable opponent. It would not do to show a moment of weakness to this man, but still, as she turned away from his mesmerizing black gaze, she felt a little tremor of uncertainty.

She would definitely be out of her depth if she tangled with this man. She wasn't sure at all that she wanted to, given his languid disregard for everything save his own comfort. There were others besides Southam who would serve her purpose equally as well—that elegant and plainly dressed man beside him, perhaps, who had a much nicer face and a quirky smile.

Or this next man to the other side of her, who was perhaps a shade overdressed and did not present as *comme il faut* an appearance as did Southam . . . but what difference was that now to her plans and schemes?

The pressing urgency she always felt to comply with Therese's deathbed request was obliterated now by the very presence of Southam and her sudden, latent, and very fierce desire to face him down, to take up the challenge of his play and to strip him bare before his peers.

She didn't try to analyze the urge or even the anger. It came from some deep place within her, and it vented itself, as they began play, in some reckless wagering that seemed to shock him and sent the players of lesser skills careening from the table.

Only the glint in his eyes betrayed any feeling: it was the cold hard glitter of the predator matching wits with its prey, finding unexpectedly that he was being led instead of leading. But then, at times she did not know either if she were the hunted or the hunter. It was the most exhilarating moment of her life to find that she could hold Southam, of all people, in the palm of her hand with the turn of a card.

Back and forth it went, a dance of vengeance—she knew it for what it was finally—a duel to the death, eye to eye and hand to hand.

"Your skill is commendable," he said at one point.

"I salute yours as well, my Lord," she answered in kind.

The crowd around them grew with each passing wager. Lady Truscott hovered around the edge of the table, counting pounds and feeling near to fainting as the amounts began to total astronomical sums.

An hour went by, two. There was no polite table talk here; they were adversaries, equals, antagonists on a battlefield, nothing more, nothing less.

"Your play, my lord."

"Your turn, madame."

Another hour passed.

"You are excellent at probabilities, my lord."

27

"Do not be too careless at stringing your bets, madame. A word of caution solely."

They played on, with each new commencement of the game marked with a fresh set of cards shuffled, cut and placed within the box, and the win-lose cards drawn immediately and placed beside.

A half hour more elapsed.

"It is a mistake to play the colors for win-lose, my Lord. I believe you are whipsawed," Jainee said as she pulled from the box the last in a series of three cards by which he had wagered.

"Then I will call the turn at the last, madame, and we will have done for tonight."

"As you wish, my lord. Will you play numbers or colors?"

"Colors again. I will see them Black, Black, Red."

"The wager is laid," Jainee said as he put his counter down. She pushed the first card out of the box. "It is black." She felt the tension rivet the room; behind her, every last man and woman toted up the number of counters that now lay between them, win or lose.

She looked squarely into Southam's matte black eyes. It was a moment that would break a lesser man than Southam. But nothing showed in his eyes except that predatory glitter and his expression remained as impassive as ever.

"Proceed," he said and there was no hint of anxiety in his deep voice.

She smiled faintly; the man's nerves were encased in ice. It was rather interesting to watch his face as she slowly slid the next card from the box face up. "It is red, my lord."

He nodded, and she saw not a quirk in his expression as she laid the card on top of the pile next to the mahogany box.

"I make it ten thousand pounds, my lord."

Nor did he protest the sum. "The house must ever win in Faro," he murmured, and snapped his fingers to call for a pen and voucher.

Lady Truscott delivered these to his hands with almost obsequious alacrity and watched hungrily as he filled out the voucher and handed it to Jainee.

"My pleasure, madame," he said politely.

"And mine, my lord. We will perhaps meet again."

"It is possible," he agreed noncommittally, levering himself upward with that same languid grace that characterized all his movements. "Jeremy? Lady Truscott? I bid you good evening."

Everyone around the table stood transfixed as he made his way out of the room.

Lady Truscott moved first, reaching out to snatch the voucher from Jainee's hand. She smiled complacently as she read the figures once again, and then she turned to her guests.

"But it is still early, my friends. Come, let the games continue!"

She was feeling agitated beyond all reason when Edythe Winslowe came to call the following morning.

"My dear Jainee, calm down," Edythe said dampingly as she took a seat near the fireplace in Jainee's room. "What on earth has put you in such a pelter?"

"That damnable Southam is what," Jainee spat. "Do you know, do you realize . . . he did it deliberately and he did it knowing full well only *I* would realize, only *I* would understand. Oh, he is a cold cub, that one, and a master at maneuvering others to do his will. No, I did not see that yesterday, but today my eyes are clear. I see him for what he is, damnable man!"

"Well, it is all very fine to be in rage, Jainee, and you do it very well, I might add, but the audience has no idea what the plot is, so why don't you just lay that out for me before you start throwing things," Edythe said pragmatically as she removed her hooded cape and gloves with great care and delicacy.

The movement of her hands arrested Jainee in her tracks. "The man is a monster, and did I not know it from last year's encounter? I should have realized . . . I should have known . . . he lost to me deliberately, madame, calculatedly, intentionally."

"In spite of the cards, you mean?"

"He used them, he used me. I tell you, I cannot live with myself for being taken in by him," Jainee said vehemently.

"Of course you won't; why should you? Better gamesters than you have been taken in by Southam. Don't despair. No one else will ever know. I, for one, will never tell."

Jainee turned on her heel and stormed to the window which

overlooked the rear courtyard of the *Alices*. "I wish you would not take this so lightly, madame."

Edythe Winslowe shrugged. "Perhaps we have different perspectives, Jainee. We have talked often of all the possibilities that could be obtained if you were to remain at the *Alices*. Last night, I hear that the foremost of these, the appearance of Southam, has indeed come to fruition, and I make haste to ascertain if you are not in transports over the event, and here you are in a rage and *not* thinking clearly."

"I am thinking *too* clearly," Jainee growled. "I must have my revenge."

"Your theatrics find no sympathetic spectator here," Edythe said dampingly. "You must consider what is best to do."

"I know what I am going to do. I am going to play his lord almighty again—and *I am going to lose!*"

Edythe clapped her hands. *"Of course!* This is perfect, my girl! How else to put yourself into his power! It is irresistible!"

Jainee turned from the window. "What are you talking about? I merely meant—"

"You merely meant that you are trying to avoid the issue," Edythe interjected. "The moment finally is at hand for you to take the opportunity you swore to me that you craved. It is the crowning touch to all you have planned and all we have talked about this year. You must indeed lose to Southam, and if you can do it in a private way, so much the better. Do you take my meaning?"

"It is impossible not to, madame. I am to deliberately lose to Southam and to offer myself in place of my voucher."

"Indeed, my dear Jainee. Your vowels must be but one—'I,' just as you have planned . . . *if* you have the fortitude and the will to carry through—and *if* your desire to breach the stronghold of society is cast in stone . . ."

Jainee shivered and folded her arms across her chest. Edythe Winslowe was right, of course. She had worked diligently for a year to come to the place where she would have the advantage of all the nobs who frequented the *Alices*. And now she was point to point with the situation and the reality of it was, at best, a little sordid.

But then heretofore there had not been such an eligible candidate for her scheme as Southam.

She had conceived the framework of the plan shortly after Lady Truscott had admitted her to the floor to take her place among the attractions of the *Alices*.

From there, it was easy to see that the house was full at any given time of the year with the bored and the wealthy who would come in residence at select times of the year, and particularly when the Prince of Wales chose to come to town on a whim.

It had simply been a matter of comprehending what was necessary to achieve her ends. By herself, she had no chance at all of going up to London, and she had known this even before she had embarked on the arduous journey from Paris.

So it had been built into her thinking at the outset that she must devise a way that would accomplish both the event of her presence in London and give her the entree she needed to the strata of society in which she believed her father moved.

She supposed, later, that since both of those conditions seemed almost to be an impossibility, she might never have had to keep her promise to Therese, and then she had met Edythe Winslowe. Edythe had arrived one evening surrounded by a phalanx of admiring men who had set her to playing at the tables, funded solely by their generosity.

Instantly, she had perceived that men were always generous to Winslowe and that here was a woman who could tell her exactly how to get on in this very perplexing world where style was everything and substance meaningless.

She had chosen exactly right: Edythe was a Fashionable, and to be seen with her added immeasurably to a man's consequence. She had long line of attentive escorts begging for her favors, and when it all got to be too much, she invariably took herself down to Brighton and spent a few days squandering the money of one beau or another.

It was deadly simple to become a Fashionable: one had only to flout convention and not be mealymouthed. One had to dress with distinction and preferably in an ostentatious way—which meant flaunting the body as well—and one must act as if *nothing* were amiss and accept all accolades and snide gossip with cool equanimity.

"It really comes down to this," Edythe told her, "if one *acts* self-assured, everyone will believe one *is* self-assured and will try to emulate you. *Everyone* is scared, my dear. When someone acts forcefully, he becomes the new paragon. And that is the secret. Always act as if you know what you are doing, even if you don't — and even if you are unsure of the consequences."

Of course the consequences were the troubling part; Jainee was tutored in the implications of *that* as well: that Winslowe had many lovers and it was nothing to her how many men occupied her bed or whether they gossiped or not.

"The fact is, the more they gossip, the more people pay attention to you," she elaborated. "One's moment in society is as brief as a throw of the dice, and how one gets along is equally as chancy. You make your moments, my dear Jainee, with style, dash, elan and some good nature, and you try to have some fun and some pleasure and not hurt too many people along the way."

It sounded so easy — but Edythe had always made it sound easy, even from the first, and Jainee had taken all of her good advice, including a surname change to make her more acceptable to the patrons of the *Alices*.

And since all the components of her somewhat nebulous plan were mere theory, she had never, barring her one unnerving night with Southam, had to deal with any problem like it since she had come to the *Alices*.

On the other hand, she would be the only one involved should she find a way to implement her plan. *And* the only one hurt.

But to take on Southam, especially in light of her previous experience, would be like taking on a monolith, a man equally as immovable and unknowable as any primordial statue.

She was not afraid of him. No, she didn't *think* she was afraid of him. She had had her trial by fire and she had successfully vanquished him. And now she had seen him again, she could see that it was just as Edythe Winslowe had said: he was held in such esteem because he presented himself as a man to be respected and because no one knew what, if anything, went on in his private moments. He was powerful, always correct, ever honorable in all his dealings, it was said, and he was not a man to topple heel over head into any undertaking, either of the heart or the mind.

The affair of the Emerlin girl was the sole exception and said to be the case of a man of a certain age becoming desperate to set up his nursery. In truth, that had seemed to be the only answer for his uncharacteristic behavior. Or at least, so it was said.

In any event, he was not an easy man to fathom; she could take no measure of the man from his presence at her table. He was as everyone said he was—cool and unflappable.

And he had deliberately gone down ten thousand pounds to *her.*

She felt suddenly as if fate had taken control. The thing was out of her hands completely. She knew, with no concrete evidence to support her feelings, that she had piqued Southam's interest, and that the moment was at hand to take control and make her decision.

She turned to face Edythe Winslowe. "You are right, of course. Southam is the one. The plan will proceed."

"You feel confident to take him on?"

Jainee's eyes glittered at the thought. "A wonderful challenge of my abilities, madame. Your taste is impeccable as always."

"I have never steered you wrong," Edythe Winslowe said, not without some satisfaction. She rose up to take her cape and draped it artfully around her shoulders. "Be guided by your good common sense as well, Jainee. Vengeance is sweet only when you do not have to grovel."

"But no, madame," Jainee protested. "I plan only to kneel at the feet of a master and offer myself as the prize."

Chapter Three

He came again three nights later, and the first thing he saw as he entered the reception room was the tableau of the goddess dressed in gauzy blue presiding at the table in the center salon. She looked luminous, unearthly, and altogether too seductive.

Seductive. He brushed away the sensation and handed off his greatcoat and deliberately sought the stairway to the upper floor where a variety of games were in play in the various rooms.

He chose to sit in at the E.O. table where the wagering did not require the concentration of a card game, and laid a quick bet on the unlucky red number five, and lost that and ten more rounds in quick succession.

Seductive. His reaction confounded him. Women were nothing to him; he could not afford to give away his heart or his emotions. Women were an evening's companion or an overnight convenience, Charlotte Emerlin notwithstanding.

Women had tried their wiles on him; every well-heeled and pushy mother had displayed her daughter for seven ongoing seasons in the hopes of her attracting the reclusive and reluctant Southam.

That Charlotte Emerlin seemed to have succeeded was due solely to pure calculated necessity on his part, and eventually, sooner than later, he had handed her the ammunition with which she could — she *must* — in good honor break the engagement. It had been a well done ruse and it had worked well: his reputation had not suffered, it had gained a new luster as he proceeded from the clubs of London and their excellently stocked bars and rash play to the more sedate environs of Brighton where a gutter urchin turned goddess now resided in a hell of her own making.

It defied comprehension, and he wondered why he needed to understand it at all.

"You like everything neatly pigeonholed," Jeremy had told him. "When everything is lined up just so, like ducks on a shoot, *you* then have the power of deciding how to proceed so that all the advantage is on your side."

"Truly?" Nicholas had murmured, staring into the amber lights of the liquid in his cut glass goblet. "Then how do you account for the fact I paid out ten thousand pounds to the *Alices* last night?"

"Not to mention my hundred quid," Jeremy reminded him. "I don't explain anything about you, Nicholas. You are a creation unto yourself. And you *don't* like to lose. Yet you spend hours of an evening deliberately losing. You never seek the company of women, yet you are planning to go back to the *Alices* to engage this woman once again. She is the only one I know who has bested you at least once, but there is something more to *that* story, I wager. No, Nick—no denials. I am not asking. I know what I know."

"You are a damned good friend, Jeremy, but you must be guided by the principle that sometimes things are not what they seem," Nicholas cautioned him ever so gently.

Jeremy's eyes flickered. "Don't try to smokescreen me, Nick. You are the most consistent person ever, and you are fallible as most men. This past year has proved it. You made a mistake with the goddess, you made a mistake with the Emerlin, and you have run amok at the gaming tables as well."

"You have caught me out," Nicholas agreed smoothly, and too quickly, he thought on rethinking the evening later, "and for that reason I plan to spend another evening at the *Alices*."

That bald statement of intent left Jeremy with nothing to say, as he knew it would. Jeremy was too perceptive by half; it was damned wearisome taking Jeremy by the leading strings and pulling him off the path.

But the die was cast and he was back at the *Alices* for that very reason. And the goddess was the furthest thing from his mind, now he was immersed in play.

"Do you know who is here?" Lady Truscott demanded in an undertone against Jainee's ear.

"I saw him, madame. He made to go upstairs, but I am sure the Faro table will lure him before the evening is out."

"Perhaps you should lure him," Lady Truscott whispered, and then discreetly withdrew from Jainee's side before she could respond to this outrageous suggestion.

But she did not give Lady Truscott the satisfaction of detecting any visible movement of dissent. Nevertheless, her heartbeat accelerated and her limbs felt just a tremor of weakness at the thought of approaching Southam and tempting him into a game.

But which game, she wondered, as she delicately slid the cards from their compartment and placed them one-two on the piles beside the box.

She had dressed herself over these past nights with the express intent of captivating his interest and to advance her own program. Still, in the abstract, she did not feel any sense of danger. It was easy to sacrifice oneself to an idea, a promise. To do it in reality was another matter altogether and one she had wrestled with for these three days and nights.

But now Southam had put in an appearance, there seemed to be an electric excitement in the air. It weighed on her. She felt it and she knew that in a very short few weeks, that atmosphere would dissipate with the oncoming London Season. The *ton* would depart Brighton and everything would slow down until the next time the Prince took it into his head to come down when he felt bored.

And then she would be bored, and she didn't want—she didn't want . . . a rebellious little thought snaked its way into her mind. She didn't want to be there when the fashionable crowd had gone.

No! The notion was positively mutinous, especially because of what she felt she owed Lady Truscott. She didn't know where the thought had come from; she almost missed pulling a card because she was so distracted.

How ungrateful would she be just to walk away from the *Alices?*

You want to be in London this season coming, the traitorous little voice pursued her. *You do not want to be here.*

But the real truth was, she didn't know where or what she wanted to be and she was so annoyed with herself for letting the idea get a grip on her thoughts that she motioned to another hostess to take her place because she could not concentrate on the game.

Lady Truscott nodded approvingly from across the room as she relinquished her chair, and she motioned subtly toward the upper floor, as if to indicate that Southam had not returned downstairs since he had entered.

She lifted her chin and went in the opposite direction, toward the dining room where supper was laid out. A small crowd of hungry pleasure seekers were helping themselves to the tempting array of viands on the tables.

Everyone knew her. It took but a week for those who became instant habitués to form an easy relationship with her. Everyone was aware of the tacit rules and everyone complied, except in the rare instance when Lady Truscott was the arbiter of a situation and someone like Southam was involved.

Oh, but best not to think about that. She would not pursue Southam. She would wait until fate put him once again in her hands. She could handle him, cunning as he was. *He* was a true example of how the English revered outward appearances. It was even easy to enumerate why society fawned over the man—he had a great deal of countenance, forbidding though it was, a great deal of money, and an overall touch-me-not disdain that could only provoke society into wanting to do the exact opposite.

But she, she was not of this society, and she could not be fooled more than once either. She even thought there was a small part of her that wanted a little revenge for the shameful way he had sought to use her the time before.

Swear to me . . . on my dying body . . . The words were engraved in her consciousness and came to mind when she was most stressed, most in anguish. Therese had provided her with a clear mandate and no way to escape the ramifications.

Southam it must be, and she knew she had decided this three days before, despite her initial trepidation. But it had occurred to her that this plan of offering herself to Southam was no more or less iniquitous than Caroline Murat offering to intercede for her with her brother, who had made it abundantly plain that he wanted her to share his bed.

And Therese's words haunting her once again: "The best way to love them is to strike a bargain with them . . ." It *was* true; in this year of her arrival in England she had seen the evidence of the fact that a woman must not lose her heart and must keep her wits about her at all times.

Within Lady Truscott's shelter, no less than three women over the course of a year had fallen in love, desperate love, unrequited love, punishing love. One had followed her lover-soldier to war; the other had not been able to make the lord of a noble house take notice of her and pined for him till this day; the third had been abused by a lover who had abandoned her and left her with a woman's price to pay.

Wise Therese. A woman must pay. No man ever nursed a broken heart; there was always someone to pick up the pieces. How had Therese known that? It was not possible she could be so shrewd and so foolish.

Her daughter was not foolish. Her daughter, Jainee often thought, had managed her mother and their life together very well. And she was not going to throw it away.

Nor was she going to ignore her deathbed promise to Therese. She had gotten this far, and now the means were at hand to put her in a position to begin the search for her father and the child who was her half-brother.

She smiled at a gentleman who had kindly offered to procure a plate of cold meat for her and nodded her assent.

It struck her that life was a circle, a roulette wheel, if it came to that. One spun out one's life and one took chances and wherever the wheel stopped became the place from which one had to begin anew.

Everyday there was a new chance and a new decision.

Now she must take hers and make hers. Behind her, as she accepted the plate of food she did not wish to eat, she heard a stir, and whispered wash of sound, a name—*his* name.

She set down the plate—she would be at a distinct disadvantage with something in her hands—and she turned slowly.

There was Southam, tall, forbidding, dressed in his habitual severe black, framed in the doorway, his incisive gaze slashing through every last person in the room and finally coming to rest on *her*.

She was nothing less than Circe. For one infinitesimal moment, he was utterly transfixed by the sight of her.

She was all in blue, as usual, gowned in evening dress that consisted of a silken tunic draped over an underdress of silver blue sarcenet that was caught between her breasts with a small round silver pin. Her hair was piled in artful disarray on her head and in her curls she wore a silver diadem with a blue stone embedded in the center point. Two broad silver bracelets surrounded her wrists to give her the contradictory aspect of a woman bound.

His sense of that was emphasized by the fact she was no pocket venus. The goddess was unfashionably tall, a fact not obvious at the gaming table; the top of her lustrous head would graze his chin, and he could drown in those amused and knowing fiery blue eyes if he even gave into the compulsion of his curiosity.

But he was never a man to do that. The woman, impressive though she was, was negligible to him. He had come for an evening's play, nothing more, and he disliked the bold look in her eyes that told him plainly that she, in spite of their brief past history, was not afraid of him.

"Good evening, my lord."

Yes, her head came right up to the underside of his jaw. Damn it.

"Madame," he said dismissively.

39

"I profess I am surprised you have returned so soon to the tables, my Lord."

"You need not be," he said, and the reproof was that much more stinging for the mild tone of voice in which he uttered it.

She was taken aback for a moment by his rudeness. But it was meaningless to her: she was the only one with nothing to lose. And he, from his guarded expression, did not wish to pursue any further conversation, and his insolence made her all the more determined to have at him in any way she could.

"Then perhaps you would not be averse to another contest between us," she suggested, not backing off one inch as he expected she would.

"I think not," he said curtly, hoping that this set-down would remove her from his path.

She smiled and looked around at the small knot of people who were pretending to eat and covertly listening to this juicy exchange.

"Well, I can perfectly understand that, my lord. You did sustain an amazing loss for an evening's play," she said kindly, her voice dripping with innuendo. She saw this tack take him by surprise. He had not expected retaliation, nor that she would turn the tables on him so neatly that he would look churlish.

"I wish you luck this evening, my lord, and I hope you will do me the honor of playing at *my* table again—sometime." She gave him her most benign look, and she was overjoyed to see that her hesitation was not lost on him, nor the implication of what she was saying.

The English were ever so—she could see he was intensely aware of those in the room and the fact that they had most likely and impolitely overheard the conversation. In that one moment, he had seen himself reduced in their eyes because of his reluctance to commit himself to play with her.

And so, because appearances meant everything, he protested, "You mistake me, madame. I am always willing to play, even when I seem to be at a disadvantage."

Oh, how he weighed his words for the eavesdropping dinner guests. He was a clever man, Southam; he hadn't expected to be backed into a corner by anyone, ever, least of all someone who had thwarted him one time before.

But she had still another arrow to pull from her quiver. This was the optimum moment—there would never be another, and her heart started pounding wildly as she considered in the space of a deep breath everything riding on the sweetness of her draw and the accuracy of her aim.

"Well then, my lord, may I suggest a private game between us?"

He was stunned by the brazenness of her counterattack. She was a worthy opponent, the goddess. She was a damned huntress, looking for prey, and she had played with him fearlessly and lunged in for the attack.

He felt the teeth of her cleverness in the back of his neck. He bowed slightly. "At your service, madame."

Her heart dropped to her feet. But outwardly, she coolly and efficiently called for the cards and for Lady Truscott to assign a room.

"My dear, that was brilliant," Lady Truscott whispered, as she led them to a small anteroom on the second floor which was set up with a table, two chairs, a side table and a branch of candles.

"It is the house's money, madame. I hope I may serve you well," Jainee told her, almost choking over her sin of omission.

"The fact that Southam has returned serves me very well indeed," Lady Truscott murmured as she motioned them into the room. She laid down several unopened packs of cards on the table and bustled about for a few minutes adjusting the light and the position of the table before she turned again to Southam and inquired: "My Lord? May I get you a glass of wine, or perhaps something to eat?"

Southam waved her away and pulled out a chair for Jainee and then seated himself opposite.

"Your choice, madame."

"I defer to you, my lord," Jainee responded in kind, but her heart still pounded and her hands were icy cold. She couldn't handle the cards, not yet.

But she seemed composed and nerveless to him. Then again, a woman who worked the gaming tables at Lady Truscott's would have to be. He just could not square the two pictures of her: gutter brat and goddess.

Which side of her was real? Or did it matter? The only real thing was the cards and the game at hand. He picked up one deck and set the others on the side table, and then he cracked open the new package with a violent whack on the table that startled her out of her abstracted expression.

"We are but two, madame." He shuffled the cards thoughtfully for a moment. "We will play at *Quinze*."

"As you will, my Lord," Jainee said. "You will find counters in the drawer of the table." She pulled out the drawer on her side and removed a box of wooden discs. "And your wager?" she added lightly.

Southam handed her the thoroughly shuffled deck, rooted out his own box of counters and stared at them consideringly. "Twenty pounds per round, madame."

She made a split second decision to make another bold stance. *Quinze* was a game of rapid rounds where she would have little or no control over the cards, and she could win as easily as she could lose. But his choice was canny: it would allow him to accept her challenge while dispensing with the obligation in as little time as possible.

For that reason alone, she wanted to up the stakes, and so she said briskly, "You need not be kind, my lord. I make the wager at fifty pounds round unless you cannot afford to lose it. We will play for one hour." Now *she* had dictated the terms.

Again he was taken aback. There was nothing genteel about this goddess, even in a situation where a man's best instinct was to try to act the gentleman. "Agreed, madame."

She pushed a counter to one side and he did the same. She looked up and smiled at him. "We will commence."

She dealt them each a card and he found he could not keep his eyes from the movements of her hands and the glowing silver bands that circled her wrists.

He lifted the card. "Draw."

She looked at hers. "Stand." She dealt him a second card.

"I am fourteen."

"Ten." She pushed the stake to his side of the table, and the play began in earnest at breakneck speed, with intermittent punctuations of "Stand," "Draw," and, on her part: "I am *crève,* my Lord," when she wished to give him the trick in spite of her cards.

Periodically, when they tied or both drew over fifteen, she made certain that the succeeding stake went to him, doubled, to incur further losses for herself.

But still, it was damned hard to lose to Southam, particularly at this game. His grasp of the possibilities was impressive, and his memory of passing cards was complete, equal to her own.

They were at a stand-off by the half hour, with each side piled with counters.

"Perhaps you weary of the game," she suggested to him to prod him into a moment of reckless anger.

"On the contrary," he said mildly, "I am endlessly fascinated."

She dealt the next cards. There was something in his tone she did not like, almost as if he suspected that the odd overdraw on her part were a pretense—as it indeed was.

She needed to slap him down and she went at it with great determination. She dealt him a second card before she lifted her first. "Draw." The second card put her over again. "I am *crève,* my Lord."

Something kindled in his eyes. "I believe I must see the evidence, madame."

She smiled cagily, and turned the cards. "It is nothing, my lord; too much is at stake for me to hoax you." And on that, she was most sincere, so much so that he gazed at her oddly for a moment, and then swept the stake to his side and motioned for her to begin again.

He could not make her out. Nothing in her manner harkened back to their encounter of the year before. He would have wagered, in fact, that she was rather enjoying the fact that he had realized who she was and that *he* had chosen not to refer to it. And she was equally amused about his choice of game and the procedure by which they played.

His suspicions mounted as the counters piled higher and

higher on his side. But her expression remained intent, faintly amused, wholly involved; when he asked her to show cards, she did not back down. And as this was a game which did not involve reckless play, he could not fault her audacity with the cards. She remained cool, level-headed, a little brazen in her table talk, and he felt himself veering off the pace again.

It was the eyes, as fathomless and eternal as the Mediterranean, cradling secrets and some kind of life of which he had no knowledge. It was the eyes and those fine-boned hands enslaved by the bracelets of yore.

Suddenly he knew just what it was about the eyes that so bemused him: they were no longer the eyes of an innocent, and she would never be at anyone's mercy ever again.

That was the secret behind her eyes and the surety of her hands. He was so caught up in his notion that he missed her soft words: "I am *crève,*" and he did not ask to see her cards and he only became aware of his misstep after she had folded her hand into the deck.

"The coup is yours, my lord," she said softly, her eyes glowing with that same impertinent light. "I believe that makes it one hour we have been at play."

He looked at the pile of counters on his side, which was considerably higher than hers, and he felt as though somehow she had bested him once again. The feeling was engorging; he was choking on it.

He began the count and she followed suit.

"It seems you are indebted to me to the tune of ten thousand pounds, madame," he said finally, with every last sense in him clamoring with distrust at the coincidence of the same sums wagered and lost between them.

It therefore was not as easy as accepting a voucher to have done with the matter. His bold black gaze raked her serene face, seeking any sign of fraud, but how could there be? She had lost.

Still, he trusted his instinct, and when she made no sound of protest at the sum, he wondered at her *sang-froid.*

But then, that was her stock in trade. He should not expect her to be like other women; these things were all in a night's work for someone like her. Doubtless she now had a variety of duties to perform, and presumably she had become as adept at those as she had at handling the cards.

It was merely a matter of testing her skill once more, to be sure that something vindictive did not underlay the reason for her challenging him.

But she had lost. That was the thing that totally threw his reasoning.

"I'm of a mind to make one more wager, madame."

"As you wish, my lord," Jainee answered him instantly, her guard immediately up and assessing him. She could tell nothing from his expression, but his hesitation in calling for pen and voucher told her volumes: he did not trust the outcome of the game.

A wary man, Southam, but he was still having a hard time of it, she guessed, trying to fit the pieces of the puzzle—her loss, her incredible transformation, his sense of not controlling the situation . . . yes, that must bother him the most of anything. He was off-balance because he could not figure out why he felt something was wrong when she had gone down ten thousand pounds in practically the blink of an eye.

She wished she could have controlled the amount of the loss, but such things were chancy. It was her bad luck that the amount turned out to be the same. Nevertheless, he wished to buck fate and his sense that she somehow was manipulating events, and at that, she thought, she would be perfectly happy to get him to a gaming table where in fact the probabilities *were* in her favor.

For her now, it was more than just a contest between equals. It was a pure out-and-out battle for the upper hand, and she *must* win and he must be the means by which she accomplished her goal.

The more she sat with him, the more she wanted to evoke some emotion in the set expression on his face. She was close enough to him to see the wear his years had wrought on his face in the web of lines around his mouth and eyes. And she could see that even he, despite his reputation, was not immune to feeling.

45

She had caught a flash of response deep in his eyes twice, maybe three times in this brief hour of play; she had noted his deepening vexation in the minute shifting of his body as he had gotten more and more exasperated with the play, and finally, in the set of his mouth as he realized she might be faking the declaration of *"crève."*

But all that was over now: he was renewed by the thought of taking her on once again, and with witnesses this time.

"What is your pleasure, my lord?" she asked him impudently, bending her head to hide the sparkle in her eyes at the audacity of the question. She was on such thin ground here, but she could not let him master her, not when she almost had him to the wall where she could claim victory.

Once again her direct question caught him off guard. He was not used to a woman speaking her mind, but then, a goddess should not have to mire herself in verbiage.

"One more wager," he said evenly, "the loss riding on the outcome."

"I agree to that," Jainee said, matching his tone, thinking furiously. She had to put herself in his power somehow; he could win just as easily as lose at any banking game played in the house. The problem was that the house money put her in no risk whatsoever, and she had to get the bet in the book in order for him to honor it. It had not been enough to lose ten thousand pounds of house money to him, and he knew it. But he didn't know why or how she had done it.

"With two provisions," she added, knowing this counterpoint to his proposal would arouse his suspicions still further. "The first is, the wager goes in the books. And the second is that I must use my own money. I cannot commit the money of the house to another possible loss."

He hesitated but a moment: her demand was not unreasonable, but he was totally baffled by it. He had no choice. "Agreed. Mine must be the choice of game."

"Agreed."

"One round."

"Agreed."

He came around to pull back her chair for her then, and as

46

they proceeded down the steps to the reception room, Jainee called for the betting book.

"Here it is, my lord: we will say ten thousand pounds against the outcome of the turn of the cards on one play of the game of your choice. You have but to name it."

He watched her write the particulars on the book which she had replaced on its lectern, with all the fluttering exquisites gathered around her, tittering over the boldness of the wager. He watched the sweet curve of her mouth, in profile, as she listened to the commentary, and the slight crinkling of her eyes when something really amused her. And his unwilling eye was caught by the fullness of her breast against the taut material of her tunic and the graceful bend of her body as she leaned over the lectern and completed the details of their wager.

"Your choice of game, my lord?"

She was looking up at him now, her blue eyes blazing with amusement and confidence, and he heard her voice as if from afar. He focused in on it, and her and her downright cocky attitude, and his need to always win.

"One round of Blind Hookey, madame, and the results will stand."

"As you wish, my Lord," she said evenly, writing his choice down in the book, closing it and then gliding over to join him. "It seems we will have an entourage, but perhaps it is better that we do." She slanted a speaking look up at him. "Please permit me to lead the way."

In this, he had no choice, and he had another distinct and uneasy impression that were she let, she would always lead the way. He was but a pace behind her as she threaded her way through the already overcrowded center salon where an active and noisy game of Faro was in progress.

Two rooms beyond that were set up with the smaller banking games: *vingt-et-un* and baccarat; on the lower floor, the roulette games held sway, and more card games, and on the third floor, the private rooms and the dice games, with one large front room devoted to Hazard.

The dining room was on the reception floor, and next to that the second card room where a dealer was just commencing a round of Blind Hookey when Jainee entered with Southam and a trail of gossipmongers.

There were five players at the table as the dealer placed the shuffled deck in the center of the table. The player to his right cut the cards and reunited them, and the player beside him cut the first stack and set it beside the deck. The next player cut and then the next so that there were altogether six stacks of cards made from the deck, all of varying sizes, in the center of the table. The player to the right of the dealer selected one packet of cards and pushed it toward the dealer and the wagering began.

As the last colored counter was laid win-lose against a package of cards, the dealer turned the whole of his stack over to reveal the bottom card, a queen high.

The first stack tied it, and the dealer took the tie. The second was lower, the third lower, the fourth, a tie, the sixth a king to take the dealer's bet.

The dealer took the cards, and Jainee called out to him: "We have the next round," as she made her way through the crowd around the table.

"My lord Southam and I will play one round," she said to the dealer, keeping her voice as neutral as possible. "We will play a fresh deck."

"As you wish," the dealer said. He opened a drawer in the table and removed a half dozen wrapped decks of cards and invited Southam to choose the one with which they would play.

Southam selected one and the dealer swept the others away, and then opened the deck and shuffled it thoroughly, after which he placed it in the center of the table for the first cut.

Southam made the cut, the dealer closed the cut and motioned for Jainee to make the next cuts.

Southam brushed aside her hand. "I will make the cuts— three of player's stock and one to the dealer," he said, his hard black eyes boring into Jainee's, daring her to gainsay him.

"It is your choice, my lord," she said, shrugging, and her indifference to his upsetting the rule infuriated him all the more.

He watched her as closely as a cat as he felt out four varying sized packages of cards. "You may choose the dealer's stock."

"I have no wish to," she said, thereby throwing the odds back to him. Or was she? He could detect no movement in her toward the dealer, no sign of collusion. And yet he still was possessed of the sensation that she had everything in hand and he had no chance, no choices whatsoever.

Grimly, he pushed one thin stack of cards toward the dealer.

"Lay your wagers," the dealer said.

"We will have one counter apiece," Jainee said, producing a box from a drawer on her side of the table. "My lord, choose your betting piece," and, as he took one, she chose another from the opposite side of the box, and said, "This shall be mine. Each piece is worth ten thousand pounds and we will wager on one stack of cards only against the dealer."

She heard the audible gasp behind her as she announced the terms, but Southam appeared as impassive as ever. "Place your bet, my lord."

"I would defer to you, madame," he said in kind.

She smiled then, that cat-lapping smile that he was growing to hate, and she laid the counter down on the thickest stack of cards, the one in the center.

Carelessly, he put his counter on the stack to the left of hers, on the dealer's right, and he watched *her* as she signalled to the dealer to upend his stack.

The dealer's card showed nine.

Jainee motioned for him to turn over her cards. Her bottom card showed deuce.

Southam waved off the dealer's hand as he reached for his cards. He turned his own stack to reveal queen high, and he shot a fast hard look at Jainee and caught her out, just this one time, as she was schooling her features into an expression of complete disdain to hide the small quick smile of triumph that had lit her face as he turned over the queen.

Chapter Four

The course was set, and again she had the full impression that her actions had not instigated events at all. Nor could she convince Lady Truscott that there was any benefit to her losing such a large sum of money to Southam. Lady Truscott was not pleased in the least to have Southam recoup his loss and to have another ten thousand pounds added on top of it.

She was only slightly mollified when Jainee disclosed that she had wagered her own money, and went away scolding Jainee that she could not take chances with every sharp who walked through the door.

And yes, she would send Southam to the receiving room so that Jainee could make arrangements with him. Perhaps Jainee should withdraw from play for one evening to rethink where her loyalties lay.

Poor Lady Truscott, Jainee thought as she edgily paced the room waiting for Southam. Somehow she had been deluded into thinking that her protegés felt themselves beholden to her like biblical slaves who traded years of servitude for a chance at life.

Of course it was true that Lady Truscott had taken her on when she was just a scared and rather witless French-speaking emigré; out of the goodness of her heart, Lady Truscott had hired her to clean and sweep and to serve her guests as the occasion arose. She knew an apt pupil when she saw one, but more than that, she knew exactly what would entice the jaded and the bored well-to-do in a provincial town in the dead of winter.

So it had been a mutual trade: Jainee received room, board, found coin and a small stipend for her services, and the little maid, Marie, who had accompanied her from Italy, was taken on as a seamstress and helper for room and board only. But then, Marie was not attractive; Marie was hired to stay behind the scenes.

It had been fairly obvious that Jainee would not. Almost immediately she bartered her handful of shillings for lessons in the language, certain that once she had command of that, the rest would be easy. But it became plain to her fairly soon that the only way she could get what she wanted was to take to the tables. That had been the hardest decision of all, with the spectre of Therese and her obsession with the cards firmly rooted in her mind.

However, she had chosen Brighton and she had chosen to apply to a gaming house because Brighton was the place and gambling was the amusement of the wealthy when they habituated the town in summer and winter.

The fact that she was now awaiting the appearance of Lord Southam surely attested to the shrewdness of her judgment, if not the efficacy of her plan.

Here she had no prearranged signals with which to work, no preordained outcome, no confederate who could rescue her. She was on her own here, and she was girding herself to go point-to-point with Southam and not much relishing the thought.

Not that she would *ever* allow him to intimidate her. The man was vulnerable—she had seen glimpses of it deep in his eyes—and he could be taken by surprise, and that was her strongest weapon of all.

If she were ever allowed to use it—

"I will be very happy to accept your voucher," Southam's deep voice said behind her, and she wheeled around from the window to find him standing just inside the doorway.

Well, now she was at a disadvantage, not even having heard him enter the room. She had not one word to marshal to her own defense, nor could she see immediately how she was going to play her distress in order to win him over. He did not look as if he wanted to win any much more than he had already.

For one looming instant, she had a great warm feeling for why he was considered so formidable. But she could not let that stop her.

"Thank you, my lord," she said as graciously as she could, still playing for time to try to figure out how she was going to approach him about her supposed insolvency. "That is most honorable. But I'm afraid—" yes, perhaps this was the tack to take, "I'm afraid that I have not been quite so honorable."

He closed his eyes in pure exasperation. She could see it working, and then the condescending politeness: "Do tell, madame. And how can that be?"

"I do not have ten thousand pounds to pay you," she said bluntly, but the statement did not shock him as much as she thought it might.

"Yet you wagered it," he said evenly, and she felt like a child caught out in some costly prank.

Still, she was ever Therese's daughter, and she did exactly as Therese would have done. She shrugged and waved her hand and said, "I am a gambler, my lord. Surely you understand the chance was half and half that I could come out ahead."

"And so we must deal with the half that didn't," Southam interpolated, acid dripping from his voice.

"Well, I believe so, my lord. What else can we do?"

"That is for you to say, madame. It is hardly a debt that can be forgiven, since you chose to make it so public. Nor should it be, because the amount is so excessive."

"Exactly," Jainee said before she even considered how this would sound to him. And, in fact, he reacted to it and she had to turn away before she got herself into deeper trouble before she could play the rest of her hand.

"I am all ears," Southam said, and the very lack of expression in his voice alerted her to the fact he would almost certainly feel distrustful of any suggestion she might make.

She plunged into it. "Perhaps we can come to some kind of accommodation, my lord."

He refused to help her. "Well now you have intrigued me, madame. Just how do you mean?"

She felt like stamping her foot. Another gentleman would have taken her meaning completely, but then, she should have grasped that Southam was not just any gentleman, in *that* respect at least. She lifted her chin and looked him straight in his fathomless black eyes. "I offer you that which is most precious to me—myself."

There, that was as brazen as she could make it. Surely no other woman had ever stood up to him and virtually told him to take her.

"Gammon! Do you take me for a fool, madame? One year ago you were ready to dismember me and burn the damned house down. What has changed so drastically that now you are ready to share my bed?"

"A heavy debt," she said candidly, and that was no lie, but he obviously would not be gulled by her willing and bald-faced desire to sacrifice herself.

Every warning signal went off in his mind. The goddess had sought him out, the goddess had lost, deliberately perhaps, against a bet she must have known she could not pay in order to offer herself to him after previously having tried to throttle him for the very same offense. It was a sweet irony, one of those unexpected surprises that amused him, and because of that, he was willing to hear her out and, concurrently, watch her squirm.

But he had not reckoned with her determination. The glimpse he had seen the year previously was to him merely the response of an emotional woman who did not understand her place or duty.

The woman she was now did not seem emotional or particularly enamored of him. He felt a small curiosity to know exactly what it was she wanted of him.

"A heavy debt *is* enough to corrupt the virtue of any woman," he countered mockingly, "but you were in dire straits

53

when first we met and you resisted body and soul a liaison which could have enriched you with little effort on your part."

"But I spoke very little English last year," Jainee retorted, "and so, perhaps I did not understand."

There was chance-taking; not even he could be fooled into thinking that she had mistaken his intentions that horrible night.

"My dear goddess, you understood perfectly well. But do try to see my point. I couldn't possibly risk burning down the townhouse, and possibly the whole of London."

"This is a grave consideration," Jainee concurred, "but I assure you, I have gained some sophistication in the matter since then." Goddess? *Goddess??* Oh, thank the fates—here was a point in her favor. He was not exempt from the baser feelings of men; here was an advantage, pure and simple.

"Yes, I can well believe you have," he said dampingly, "but how is that of any moment to me?"

"I collect there *have* been instances where honor has been satisfied in exactly the manner I have chosen," Jainee said carefully, pushing, pushing gently because it was quite evident that if he agreed, she would have to come to the point, and in her heart of hearts, she did not want to. She only knew she *would,* if it were the only way to advance her plan. Her practical mind would not let her think in any other direction.

"Indeed," Southam murmured, his flat black eyes just boring into her. *The goddess in sacrifice . . . laid out on the altar of her greed—or her vices; goddesses were ever notorious for their capriciousness . . .*

And she never avoided his eyes all the time he paced around her thoughtfully. She felt as if she were a piece of horseflesh on display at Tattersalls.

The man was intractable; she couldn't tell what he was thinking or even if he were amenable to her proposition as any other *gentleman* would have been.

All the details would have been arranged by this point, she thought sourly. Southam had her very off-balance, and she resented that mightily. She was very used to assessing a person instantaneously: she could almost tell to a shilling how high a man might fly and where he would draw a line.

But Southam—she had badly underestimated him. She felt like kicking him but such behavior would not give her the advantage of him.

And then he shocked her again.

"Well, madame, let us get down to cases. Tell me exactly what you want and why, and perhaps we may deal together."

That was plain speaking, she thought, standing her ground under his harsh scrutiny. All the feminine blandishments would not work with him. He could not be enticed by the thought of having her at his mercy, that was clear. Yet she could see that something about her fascinated him or he would not be here parrying words with her.

She needed to get the upper hand and quickly, and she toyed for a moment with the notion of telling him the truth.

But what truth? Everyone had a truth—her mother, her long-gone father, the brother who might never remember his past given his youth, herself—even Southam had a truth, but with him, she decided, she could not cave in. The best method was attack.

"My lord, I believe it is true that it was *you* who chose to lose to me three nights ago."

And how neatly she turned him about. She understood already that he was someone to be reckoned with, but he was a little amazed that she could still surprise him.

And now he had to dissemble. "I do *not* like to lose, madame."

"Except when it suits your purpose," Jainee countered sweetly, seeing her perception prick him in just the faintest movement of a muscle in his jaw.

"I would have no reason whatsoever to want to lose to *you*, madame. You would hang a man out to dry."

"Thank you; I take that as a compliment, my lord. Then you can see that I too play to win and would have no reason to forfeit deliberately to a man who takes pleasure in crushing women under his heels."

"Yes, I rather thought my reputation had preceded me. We are at stalemate, madame. I do not believe you. You are too anxious to sully your own name, and that swears with what occurred between us this past Yuletidemas."

"Your consideration of the delicacy of my feelings is appreciated, my lord, but totally unnecessary. I chose to remain with Lady Truscott, and I knew full well what that decision entailed. I play by the rules, my lord. I wish only to discharge my debt to you in the most honorable way possible."

It was a pretty speech, but she saw immediately it did not play at all with him. He leveled that malevolent black gaze at her and he said gently:

"But my dear goddess, you are far too eager to offer yourself to me."

Oh, the clever man. Clever, clever man. She could barely see beyond her nose as a fine roiling rage began to build in her. She would *not* allow him to turn things topsy-turvy. She had made her choice and she intended to follow through on it, whether he willed it or not. Her blue anger subsided as she considered her purpose and her need.

Southam was perfect, and it was he who would capitulate.

"But I am no green girl who swoons at the mere mention of a liaison, my lord. I am also a woman of an age who, if she were properly raised and nurtured, would either be married now or considered on the shelf. I am not *eager,* my Lord Southam. I am merely sensible."

"And *I,* madame, am fully sensible that you are not telling the truth. So we come to that again," Southam said, "and we will get nowhere until we discuss the ripe reasons for your disastrous luck at the tables."

"I owe you ten thousand pounds, my lord. That reason alone should suffice," Jainee said brazenly.

"And you look very ready to trade your heart and soul for that debt," Southam retorted. "Try again, madame."

"Not my heart, my lord," Jainee said tartly, and something in her tone made him look at her with renewed interest.

Not her heart . . . He felt the jab keenly for some reason,

56

and he thought perhaps that he believed she ought to be *begging* for mercy rather than trading quips with him. It struck him that he wanted her to beg, that a goddess should not get to have things all her own way, that she was too pragmatic by half. What kind of woman would barter herself for a debt which she had coolly and deliberately incurred?

And why would he not settle for what she had offered?

But he knew—it was too easy and she was too sure and every instinct within him shouted that there was something more. He meant to find out what that was.

"There never was a gambler who bargained with his heart," he said finally.

"And my mother taught me always to strike a bargain and never to give my heart away—advice that has much merit, my lord," Jainee said. "I believe gentlemen subscribe to that tenet as well. Perhaps it would make things more palatable for you if *you* were to be my *Cyprian,*" she added with malicious kindness.

He choked. What audacity—and what style. She was truly something, this bold-speaking Circe; she blew smoke-rings around the truth better than any circus performer he had ever seen and she stood her ground like no man. Nevertheless, he could not give in to his bemusement with her, nor allow her to twist things all her own way. The fact remained that she had created the situation in order to use him in some way, and he meant to know what it was before either of them left the room.

"It is a ravishing thought, madame, but I refuse to be at anyone's beck and call."

"So you understand perfectly my very own feelings on the matter."

"We are in accord on everything but the reason you so precipitously threw your money away, madame." He watched her face closely as he brought the discussion back to the main point of his questioning, and saw a little flicker of wariness touch her steady sapphire gaze.

"It is time to come to the mark, madame. *My* honor is not

at stake here; I can refuse your payment and put you at the mercy of moneylenders—you do recall that *you* called for the book?—or I can discharge your obligation altogether, which will kill your reputation. So now you must decide which is the best course for you."

And so he had come in for the kill. She recognized the superior reasoning and all the ramifications instantly, and she shrugged and said, "Very well, my Lord. It is as simple as this: I wish to go to London."

No, she was not easy, he thought, waving off her bald statement. She was very adept at misinformation by omission as well. For one fulminating moment, he felt as if he wanted to encircle her somehow, to contain her and all that intelligence and amusement that would not bow to his authority.

She really didn't understand how simple it was: he would accede to any story because she amused him. He had never met anyone like her. She was no home grown English miss; she had no airs, and once she had had a veil of innocence, but that had been replaced by this rather shameless and hardheaded confidence.

He would have staked his life that she was not worldly in any way, and the fact that she was ready and willing to submit to him on the strength of this conspicuous loss said much about her determination.

She did not only wish to go to London, and he told her so. "London is mere hours from here, madame. You could travel up by mail-coach any day you have the means to do it."

"Well, then—it is obvious I don't," Jainee murmured, hoping still to put him off the scent.

"Except that you wager with the most reckless of the boneshakers, and I would lay odds you know exactly what you are doing at all times."

"Thank you, my lord," Jainee said impudently.

"We will strike the bet from the book," Southam said, out of patience with her at last. "You have provided me with an hour's entertainment, madame, and I count that worth ten thousand pounds to me." He strode to the door, leaving

Jainee just a little stunned by his about-face.

She had been so sure he would give in on the basis of her inability to afford that which she sought from him. Women had bargained their lives away on less, and here he felt he had a right to claim more.

Well, it could not hurt matters now, she thought, and she called to him as he reached the door: "Lord Southam!"

He wheeled around in his graceful way. "Madame?"

"Perhaps you are right," Jainee conceded, measuring the effect of her words against his expression, which still did not change. There was no triumph there—yet—of his having made her bend to his will. There was nothing but polite attention. "It is no easy matter to talk of things that have been private with me for many years."

Southam came back into the room and motioned her to a seat at one of the many card tables around the room, and he took the opposite from her.

"You may begin by telling me where you come from."

She smiled faintly. First things first, and after all, as she phrased it, she was not telling a lie. "I came from Italy, my lord."

He slammed his large hand down on the table. "Do you *never* tell the truth?"

She bit her lip. "Only when I must, my lord, and I can see you are no fool."

"Neither will I count you one if you stop trifling with me," Southam said trenchantly. "You have eloquently proven the thing you wish to hide—you are no provincial simpleton, madame, and you are most proficient at parrying your opponent's thrust. So which shall it be—a lunge? A jab? A sidestep? Divert? Repel, perhaps?"

"Your *wit* repels, my lord," Jainee interposed through gritted teeth.

"And yours is most diverting," he answered in kind. "So shall we proceed to the endgame, madame?"

Jainee threw up her hands. "I will tell you what you wish to know. It comes to this: I seek my father."

She didn't expect an explosion of understanding, but surely there was something righteous about that, even to someone like Southam.

"And I am to be the instrument of this search?" he inquired very gently.

"You have the wherewithal to ensure my presence where I might most efficiently search for him."

"In London?"

"The season is about to commence, is it not? So everyone will be in London, will they not?"

"Including your father?"

"I assume so, but I do not know for sure. I gamble, my Lord, that the set of facts I know about him will fit the description of someone who travels in the circles *you* frequent."

"Well, now we have the whole of it," Southam said in an awesomely mild tone of voice. "Very good, madame. Very good—you are a complete hand. A whole concocted story and ten thousand pounds odds-out that you would persuade me to give you entree to the best circles." He stood up abruptly and pushed at the table. "A doxy's virtue in exchange for a voucher to Almack's is no small price to pay. I salute you, madame. You are too clever above half, and with any other man you would have succeeded beyond your wildest dreams.

"The debt is cancelled, madame. I bid you good evening."

And at that, he wondered at how calm he felt, and why the streaming disappointment he felt somewhere in the back of his mind did not come exploding to the fore as he strode to the door.

"Monsieur!"

He froze, and then he turned just as she covered her mouth in dismay.

"Yes, madame?"

Her fine-boned hand slid down her neck and came to rest just at the swell of her breast. "There is more."

He marveled at her talent for facile understatement. But still, in spite of her gaffe, she remained composed and watchful, and that interested him. He shifted his body so he could lean against the doorjamb, and folded his arms across his chest. "I am all ears, madame."

She hated him at that moment; all the power lay in his hands. She resented it, and she refused to prostrate herself before him, even verbally.

"You are all temper, *monsieur,* and it is not a pretty sight," she said waspishly.

"And you *are* a pretty sight, madame, and you have a temper to boot. I take it you are French."

"I am. I came to England by way of Italy as I have told you. I search for my father who is English. Many years ago, after he had married my mother and she had borne me, he abandoned us and left her to the mercies of the French court. The emperor pursued her, won her, and got bored with her in very short order."

She stopped as she perceived him visibly stiffen to attention. That could not bode well for her. The French were not loved, less so since the war on the Peninsula had begun and everyone of foreign extraction was presumed to be a possible spy.

It was one of the things that made Brighton and the cloister of the gaming house so unusually attractive to her. Brighton swarmed with emigrés; it had been easy to lose herself here and then to emerge when the time was right. But how did one explain that to Southam, whose face was like stone and who said nothing to encourage her to go on with her story.

She clenched her fists and continued:

"The emperor's generosity was very well known, my lord; even so, we had no recourse as to whether to try to find my father, and certainly not money enough to pay our fare to England, even with the stipend my mother received. I was told that my father was a diplomat and a gentleman who moved in the first circles, and that surely he was devious as well, as a gentleman of foreign affairs must be.

"I last saw him some ten years previously and . . ." And . . . how *did* she explain the gaps, and Therese's death?

61

" . . . and my mother and I—" she could *not* tell him about the money—"got on reasonably well until the time she petitioned the emperor for more money. She was a gambler, my lord, and ever after the next game of cards. The need was severe and it caused her death. The Emperor's emissary came and when he found that"—*Oh, Therese forgive me for lying!*—". . . her destitution was a charade, he made sure that the emperor would never have to pay her another centime."

No, no—he believed none of what she was saying: a lie would have been preferable to the half-truths that tripped so glibly from her tongue. A lie would have been more coherent. She could have embroidered a lie.

The truth, or what she had told of it, was a sinkhole of mud and she was fast being sucked alive into it.

Doggedly she went on: "I was wounded myself, and my mother pleaded with me, on her deathbed, to find and go to my father, that her dearest wish in heaven—" dear heaven, what melodramatic nonsense! But it sounded good—it did, it did and she could see it affected him as well—". . . was to see us reconciled."

She ended her recitation there, not trusting herself to embellish further. Nor did she wish to lay herself open to questions which would require filling in the blank spaces: it was enough that she had obliterated her half-brother for her own purposes.

She lifted her chin as she boldly met his flat black skeptical gaze.

"And your father's name, madame?" he asked silkily.

"He was called Charles Dalton."

"Never, madame. There is *no one* in service by that name."

Immediately she felt her temper rising. "And how would you know, my lord?"

"Let us say I am connected in that area, madame, enough to know that your story and the name are components of the same lie."

She shrugged. "Believe what you will, my lord. Whatever the truth of the matter, my debt to you still stands and my

62

sole motivating force remains that I am honor bound to find my father."

"You are bound to no one but yourself, madame, that is evident, and you are bold as brass to present me with a name that is pure fiction."

"My lord, you did not say that you were to be judge and jury of the truth," Jainee retorted. "I believe you said you only wished to hear it." She took a deep breath to calm the storm of anger she felt. There was never a more difficult man to deal with. But she had to make him see, she had to convince him to take her to London.

"You *must* understand, my lord—*I need to find my father.*"

And she had no idea where that wellspring of emotion exploded from: in her heart, in that moment, she felt a seizing yearning to know and be known by the father who had used her so badly, to have him answer questions, to have him say that all of it was nothing to do with her and he would have done it differently if he could.

Or was that some festering dream she had had a long time ago and had buried in the recesses of her mind?

Her eyes welled with tears and she blinked them back. She had never in her life thought this way about the man who was her father.

Why now?

Or was she so jaded that she would use any trick at her command to sway the judgment of the intractable Lord Southam?

She had no *need* of her father.

So where had this keening cry of yearning come from?

The man had betrayed her, purely and simply, and in retribution, she would betray him. She had promised Therese, she had sworn on her mother's dying breath.

I need to find my father.

Those words might haunt her, and yet they were the only real words she had spoken to Southam from the moment she had set out to ensnare him in her scheme.

And he knew it. He heard in those six words the soulful

cry of something broken and wounded.

He understood it.

Something in the flat black of his guarded gaze glittered with recognition. But he would not let her off that easily.

"The man does not exist, madame. Where do you propose to find him?"

She swallowed down the knot of anger and tears that blocked her throat. She hated him for asking the right and reasonable question, the one she had considered over many months of anguish over Therese's death and the difficulties of her own flight out of the country.

"I can only suppose that he does not go by this name in England," she said finally, reluctantly, "and that I would know him if I saw him."

He smiled then, a small unpleasant little smile that sent a shiver through her. Clearly he couldn't, or wouldn't, make any decision on the basis of what she had told him. Nor would he be gallant or kind.

After all, what had he to work with but a fantastic gothic tale that resonated with her easy familiarity with "the emperor" and "the French court" and how singlemindedly she had pursued her course. It sounded far-fetched, even to her ears, and worse—she had portrayed herself as an adventuress.

But an adventuress *was* a gambler, and she sat right on the edge of her most audacious play; she felt no romanticism about it—she was asking him to take her story at face value, not probe any of the details, then take her to London all on the strength of a tainted bet and some long buried emotions.

It sounded unimaginable.

It sounded like a ruse.

And she didn't like the speculative look in his eyes. He was looking at her like she was a chameleon, scuttly, furtive, changing color whichever way the light played. Too clever by half, she was, dangling half-truths in front of his nose and expecting he would be led by them.

She was like a hunter, following a faint but discernible trail. The goddess on the prowl—a regular Diana, with all the grace, cunning and volatility of an all-knowing who manipulated events out of capriciousness, need and pleasure.

And then there was the story—the lies-by-omission story about a phantom father and life on the rim of the French nobility. It was good, it was very good, and it presupposed a layer of further explanations which she was obviously not prepared to give.

But he could wait, and he could play her game and eventually he would discover who she was and how she fit into the puzzle.

"Tell me your name," he said abruptly, startling her out of her thoughts. But he could not shake her composure. She looked up at him inquiringly, her expression calm, serene, almost as if she had been following his thinking and could predict what his next words would be.

Nonsense! Fanciful—he was not a man given over to whimsy, but still he *was* continually thinking of her in these comparable terms. And it was only a step from that to: "No—don't tell me." He slanted a look at her. Whoever she was, she was most definitely a goddess. "I will call you . . . *Diana,* the huntress. For you are on the prowl, are you not, Diana?"

He got a reaction from her then.

On the prowl? On the prowl? Like the veriest cat in the alley! She felt such indignation and for one fleeting moment, she allowed it to show in her eyes. And didn't he like that.

The truth was, *he* was the cat and she was the prey, and he was playing with her as subtly as any stalking predator.

Then he pounced.

"I accept your challenge, my dear goddess. I accept your terms."

And he caught her completely unaware.

"But," he added softly, dangerously, *"you* must submit to mine."

She ignored the undercurrent there. She thought she would wilt with relief. The point was to get there. The rest was academic. "I will comply with your conditions," she said evenly, refusing to even consider the implication of his words as he so obviously meant her to.

"But I haven't set them, Diana," he reminded her in that hateful haughty way of his.

"I am sure you will correct that oversight immediately," she retorted acidly, reacting to an instant flare of hostility, her gratitude stifled by his heavy upper hand.

It was better thus: from the first he would know that she would never be compliant, passive or subdued in any way. She suspected he had figured that out already, and that he would, nonetheless, make her honor any contract between them.

It was evident in the banked light in his eyes as he paced back into the room and around her chair to loom over her.

"Make no mistake, Diana—my demands are exactly what you offered: your precious body in exchange for my sponsorship of you in London." He grasped her arm and lifted her from the chair, savoring the feel of her bare skin in his warm hard grip.

He liked the fact she was not intimidated by this bold move, that deep in her eyes he could see defiance, and a touch-me-not hauteur that belied the woman in her who was begging to be tamed.

"And how will you determine, my lord, when the ten thousand pounds has been amply repaid?" she asked grittily, as he held her tightly against him and dared her to protest.

"I will forgive ten thousand pounds," he said silkily, "but I will not forgive a default. Understand, Diana, that by accepting my terms, you become mine in every way conceivable, any way you can imagine and some that you cannot. That you will be available to me whenever I want you and that you will never refuse anything I ask of you that is private between us. You are no nun, Diana. You know what is expected. And you surely perceive I am a man who will collect his pound of flesh."

She ignored the tingling of her body, the warning chill that coursed through her veins. "This is all very well for *you,* my lord, but what may I expect in return?"

Oh, the hard-headed daughter of France—strike a bargain ... yes, he remembered what she had said, the only way to love is to strike a bargain. She did it without thinking, it was so ingrained within her. Nothing touched her, not his words, not the promise of sensual delights. No, she must be practical and tote the rewards for herself on the opposite side of the board. And he did not like that one bit.

"You may expect, Diana, that you will be housed and clothed in a manner that befits an unmarried woman of age, that you will be creditably sponsored by an unexceptional chaperone and you will have full entree to those places where you might expect to see the man you think might be your father.

"I am equally sure that within two months you will captivate every man in London who is not attached, and some who are vacillating, and you will have a parade of lovers lined up outside your door from the steps to the Tower of London, at which time my usefulness will be debatable.

"But until then, Diana, I will have all of you that ten thousand pounds can buy. If I tell you I want to fondle you, you will sit on my lap and allow me the freedom of your body. And if I tell you I want to make love with you, you will disrobe and await me naked on your bed. And if I demand your kisses, goddess, you will part your lips and give me the wet heat of your mouth."

Oh yes, now it was clear to her; he felt her flinch at his words, and he raised his left hand to touch the naked skin above her bosom and he smiled as she allowed his hand to rest there and then to move upwards to cup the arrogant tilt of her chin.

"Your kisses, Diane," he whispered against her resistance. "I want your kisses," and he lifted her lips to his own and covered them with his mouth.

He almost swooned at the jolt of erotic sensation that shot to his loins. He felt primitive, conquering. Her mouth was ripe, innocent, wet, heated with martyrdom, her body stiff

67

with combativeness.

He moved his mouth a centimeter from hers. "That is not the way, Diana—that is, if you truly want to go to London and hunt down your quarry."

He watched the indecision play in her eyes, and he wondered if she would back down and cry off.

But she was ever practical; in her mind, in that brief moment, she speculated on all the angles. She knew she was merely playing for time, hoping at the end not to have to give herself to him. After all, this kiss would buy her a trip to London and all that it entailed. She did not have to love him—hadn't Therese, always in love, pounded that into her head? And she had no reputation to lose.

She was a gambler whether she willed it or not, and Southam had become her odds.

The light in her eyes deepened as it became clear to her that she could not escape this losing hand. In her mind, she moved on to the next round of play even while she smiled that cat-lapping little knowing smile that he so disliked and said softly, "I am here, my Lord, in honor of my debt. And so, I will try to please you."

"Debt be damned," he growled, enfolding her against him so that she could feel the throb of his desire explicitly. "Here is the truth of the matter," he whispered hoarsely against her mouth, and then he invaded it, the heat of his frustration driving him, and the lush taste of her virgin willing mouth.

He didn't stop to think how that was, because soon enough, under his hot rough tutelage, she was battling him touch for touch, nipping and licking in turn, in pure venom for his treatment of her, understanding finally in this dance of tongues and play between them what it was for a man to wield his power.

And this was only the first dimension of what was in store.

She hated him. She bit his lips, she evaded him, and she attacked when the moment was right, when he thought he had her gentled and quiescent.

And she quelled the furious arousal of her traitorous body,

68

the unexpected spume of liquid heat to the very center of her female core; she ignored the thrust of her breasts against his hard chest and the erotic and unfamiliar chafing of her tender nipples against the gauzy fabric of her gown.

In this contest, mouth to mouth, body to body, they were equals: he could not claim her, she would never submit to him.

Still, a man had a potent weapon in his strength. His arms were like steel around her, he was a wall of molten sexuality; he burned with it and not even she could withstand it.

"So much for honor," he muttered, still close to her mouth, almost as if he could not relinquish the tide of his desire to possess it, to master *her.* "This is the truth of it, Diana. I will have you and your everlasting honor in exchange for your debt and your avaricious wish to conquer society. A shallow thing, honor; it clings to you as lightly as do your silken skirts. And it is breeched as easily, but this is neither the place nor time. This is but a taste of the fullness to come between us. This is but a sample of the bargain between a man and woman that you are pledged to fulfill."

She shuddered at the harshness of his words and at the space-hurling thought that there was no turning back, not now. But she would die before she would let him see her hesitate one moment, or back down one inch from the course she had chosen.

The light of battle kindled in her bold blue eyes as she stared defiantly into his shuttered black gaze.

"I understand, my lord," she said finally, lifting her chin into that arrogant, opponent-be-damned tilt.

There would be no submission here, he thought, refusing to acknowledge the disdainful set of her mouth as she uttered these words.

He grasped a coil of her lustrous black hair and tugged at it so that she was forced to look up at him by his direction and not in that once-removed insolent way she had. This was better.

The light in her bolting blue eyes flared into pure flaming

anger as he forced her mouth open and mastered her tongue once again.

There was no help this time; he was bent on subjugating her and nothing less. Her helpless hands, encased in slave bracelets, beat at the enslaver to no avail. He bent her backwards, and backwards again as he conquered her lips, her tongue, the whole precious luscious recesses of her mouth and made her do his will.

And then, as tightly and intensely as he had crushed her against his thick hard length and demanded that she bow to its potent power, he pushed her suddenly and violently away from him so that she stumbled backward and reached convulsively for a chair before she fell to the ground.

"Now you understand," he said grittily. *"That* is the bargain."

She reached deep into herself to pull her shattered composure into play. *He would not win.* The deed was done, the arrangement was set and bound in contract by all that had just transpired. She was a conspirator now, in willful bondage to a hedonistic libertine.

She shrugged negligently as if the movement relieved the onus of her burden. "I am yours, my lord," she said succinctly and deliberately. And then she looked at him with that combative light in her eyes and he knew he read the message clearly and plainly: *I am yours—but you will never have me.*

Chapter Five

"I swear, Nicholas, ever since you began playing at the *Alices*, you've absolutely gone round the bend."

"I am not crazy, Jeremy; I know exactly what I am about, and I await Lucretia's answer with bated breath."

"I think you must have a screw loose," Lucretia said pungently. "You want me to take in some Aphrodite from the gaming house, set her up as my ward *and* sponsor her this season? My dear, you are short a sheet on your bed if you think I would even consider such a ramshackle scheme."

Nicholas smiled warmly. "Thank you, Lucretia. I knew you would understand that if I requested it, I had a reason for wanting it done."

"As ever, Nick," she grumbled. "How you do work your way around me. I had accounted myself a woman of great practicality and common sense and yet every time you require it, I toss my sensibilities out the window for you. I still cannot understand it. A trollop from the gaming house—"

"She is Diana," Nicholas told her, "Diana of the *Alices*, and she is most desirous of going to London and I am equally desirous of helping her."

Jeremy stared at him. "The goddess, Nicholas? The *goddess?* Oh, well—that explains the whole." He turned to Lucretia who was settled quite cozily next to a roaring fire in the parlor of their rented house, with a robe tucked round her lap. "He handed her ten thousand pounds over the Faro

71

table several nights previously and she handed it right back to him two nights ago."

"It was never so simple," Nicholas interposed, as he seated himself opposite Lucretia and reached for the chocolate pot on the table between them. "She lost it at *Quinze,* which is a damned hard game to cheat at, and wagered the whole on a turn at Blind Hookey. I fail to see what is so amusing, Jeremy."

"Only that she deliberately defaulted, because everyone in this town knows that no one is plumper in the pocket than you. Clever girl, I must say, and somehow she racked up a promise that you would sponsor her as well. Take her to London and she'll set the Thames on fire."

Lucretia watched him as he poured the chocolate into a fair sized cup and wrapped his hands around it. "You ain't a man to be gulled, Nick."

"There isn't a man alive who cannot be seduced by a beautiful face, Lucretia."

"Except you, Nick, else why would you have worked so hard to make Charlotte Emerlin so disgusted with you, she was forced to break your engagement? You don't fall easily, my boy, and I know you well. You are cold and rock steady about this and what you want from me. But if you think you are going to give her *carte blanche,* and under *my* roof, you are crazy."

Nicholas lifted his head and his glittery black gaze bored into her. "That, my darling Lucretia, is none of your business. In any event, you should know I would never disgrace you. Whatever you decide, the goddess *will* come with me to London, and if she must stay with me at the townhouse, so be it. But," and here he took a sip of the chocolate to hide the small smile on his lips, "I daresay you would be loath to ruin the first season of a child of a dear friend of yours, someone your husband met in India? Very outspoken, Lucretia, because those ayahs don't know how to raise a girl to be polite. That is why they need a season in

London—albeit a *late* season. She dearly wants to get married, Lucretia, and her father could settle a nice dowry on her were the right man to come along. You might dispense with Almack's unless she really desires it. She can," he added, still enchanted by his little fiction, "be fairly amusing at cards."

Jeremy choked. "It is time for someone to play the grown-up here," he said stringently, seating himself next to Lucretia and taking her hand. "The woman's name is Jainee Bowman, and she has been at the *Alices* a little over a year . . ."

"Jeremy . . ." Nicholas said warningly.

". . . and she's been a hostess and been at the tables for about six months. No, Nick—I haven't heard anything negative about her at all. She works hard, she's damned beautiful and no one knows if she has made any liaisons since she has been there, or where she is from or even where she is going."

"I do," Nicholas said, forestalling anything else Jeremy had to say. "She is coming to London with me and the rest," he bowed to Lucretia, "is at your discretion, my dear friend."

Lucretia looked up at him. His expression had turned stony, obdurate. This was very unlike him, although he was pig-headed to a fault. But never did he deliberately mix himself up with a woman. The Emerlin was the sole exception and she still had not been able to figure out the attraction between them. Nor was it water under the bridge. By all accounts, Charlotte Emerlin had not reconciled herself to losing him, and was sharpening her image to have one last attempt at him this season.

The thought of it set all her well honed instincts to a razor's edge. Whatever Nicholas was about, she would, even with her reservations, be a part of it. The boy needed her, and she needed to rein in his baser nature; and he knew it, or he would not have involved her.

"I think," she said consideringly, "it was a deathbed promise I made to her mother back in '02—that *was* the last time they were able to make it back to England, wasn't it?—Well, poor Marguerite was ill with—what is it they get ill with in India, Nicholas?—and Diana . . . no, Jainee, correct?—was still being schooled back in Delhi—" She paused and looked up at Nicholas with a mischievous smile.

"Yes, I think we can contrive a very nice story to cover the essentials, my dear. The rest," she added confidently, as Jeremy snorted in disgust in the background, "I will leave up to *you*."

When one made a bargain with the devil, one should expect to be consigned to hell, Jainee thought mordantly as she took her place at the tables the following night. Southam was *nothing* if not thorough, and thoroughly despicable into the bargain.

Well, it was all of a piece; she should have expected the worst when she gave herself into his power. There was no use repining now. Her mouth was forever branded with his kisses and her direction inevitably set. Somehow she would deal with this sense of losing control, and in time, she would gain back the advantage, she just knew she would.

Nor could she express any of this to Edythe Winslowe when she appeared that night. Edythe would hardly understand, but then Edythe was crowing with triumph that her protege had bested Southam, and obtained his support all in one cleverly played night.

"Oh, I vow—there will never be such a hot story as this when he finally takes you up to London," Edythe said delightedly. *"No one* has been able to *move* that man. You must be magical."

"Or a goddess," Jainee murmured, ignoring the effusions. "He is a hard man, madame, just as you have said, and I cannot imagine how we will deal together. He

74

takes what he wants, and damns the consequences."

Edythe smiled in complete understanding. "Of course he does. And you be sure to anticipate what he wants, my girl. Get the most of it. Men are all the same. They want no criticism, just compliant slaves, and that is easy enough to do. You have already vanquished him once, twice, perhaps times three. Now he is intrigued. Nothing could be better. But now you must let him have his way a little. It is the secret knowledge among women that sometimes they must play this little trick. You understand?"

Did she? There was nothing to read between the lines with Edythe: everything was laid out bluntly before her, the rules of life among the gentry the same as those among the sharps: you win, you lose and you keep your opponent guessing.

"I understand," she said, not liking to have to admit it. In a snap, the whole would be nothing if she did not gird herself to comply with the more erotic elements of it. But that she could cope with later as well. "Shall I see you in London?"

Edythe wagged a disparaging finger. "My dear, Southam's set does not follow *me*. Take your lead from that. They will be well nigh bowled over to even see *him* attached, but you cannot count on him squiring you about in the manner of an eligible *parti*. Perhaps . . . perhaps we might see each other in passing, and if we should, I promise you I will indicate how or if we should acknowledge each other. Agreed? For after all, too many tattle-mongers have seen us together here, and one never knows in what form the gossip will follow the bearer to town. Take care, my dear. Win well."

She was gone in a swirl of her elegant cloak and a cloud of scent and Jainee felt for a long volatile instant bereft of all friends, all conscience.

But that was to end within the week, for several days later an odd, endearing and quite diminutive whirlwind showed up at her door, bullied her way in, introduced herself as Jainee's chaperone and proceeded to discuss with her at length and in public everything she was supposed to do, and in accordance with the instructions of her dear mother.

"My dear, I had no *idea* you had been reduced to *this*," the whirlwind clucked sympathetically as she eyed the customers streaming into the *Alices* of an early Saturday evening. "I am horrified. But I collect your father has passed on as well and there was no way to . . . an uprising or something of the sort, wasn't it? My dear, you are not *used* to the cold, I can see that. Do take my shawl. No one understands about being raised in such warm climes as India . . . there . . ."

The woman's name was Lucretia Waynflete, Duchess of something, and she was a friend of Southam's it seemed, sent to arrange things with her and to make sure she understood the "story" so that everlasting appearances could continue to be observed.

And Lady Waynflete was quite clever about it. She paraded through the whole of the *Alices,* exclaiming to everyone she met (except that she *knew* everyone) how extraordinary it was that her dear friend's daughter was working the gaming tables at the *Alices,* and that while she was certain that no disgrace attached to any *honorable* work, she could not possibly allow Jainee to continue on as she had because she, Lady Waynflete, who had made a deathbed promise to Jainee's mother, was now here to put things in proper order.

"Well of course you knew nothing about the promise," Lady Waynflete said to her almost indignantly. "Your mother passed before you were told. And then your dear father lost his life in that dreadful . . . truly," she grasped Jainee's hands, "there are no words to express . . . it is a wonder and a miracle that you survived and that you have been discovered."

And that indeed was the word for it. Jainee felt like a

continent upon which Lady Waynflete had launched herself in an orgy of exploration.

"No one is going to believe a word of this Banbury tale," she told Lady Waynflete plainly at one point. "Everyone has seen me at the tables this se'enmonth, and indeed there are witnesses to the skies that I made a rash wager with Southam and came off the worst."

"Relieve your mind," Lady Waynflete said confidently. "There will indeed be those who do not believe it, but our method is to usurp those who would bring up your past to besmirch your name. You must understand, there is nothing a lady cannot do in the name of saving herself and so, if the story of your past accounts for your present, why—you become a romantic heroine instead of a doxy."

"Nonetheless, I am down ten thousand pounds to Southam and I have suddenly been taken up by the mother of his friend. What accounts for that, ma'am?" Jainee said stubbornly.

"Nothing simpler," Lady Waynflete said airily, waving off her objections. "Your father left—banked in England—or didn't you know? I thought *not*. My dear, when a man hauls his family off to India, he has to prepare for *every* contingency. You have no worries. Southam is one of the trustees. It explains everything. He didn't *know* you, he came upon you, he felt it incumbent to discreetly provide for you ... and when you so fortuitously lost to him, why—his only recourse was to dispatch me to your aid. And the wisdom of your dear father, entrusting everything to Southam. The very best man, honorable in *every* way."

She smiled benignly at Jainee. "Do you see? Everything is covered. And when Southam told me, I came right to your assistance. We have only to inform Lady Truscott. She will be the soul of understanding—" to the tune of a voucher for five hundred pounds, she thought dourly, but it was Nicholas' money and she had no say in *that* matter, "—I assure you."

77

"I appreciate your plain-speaking, ma'am," Jainee said, instantly awed by Lady Waynflete's breezy maneuvering through the treacherous waters of *ton* acceptance.

"Excellent, and now we have only to discuss the details of removing you to my townhouse and when we will travel up to London."

Jainee spent two days packing, all the while with Marie's tearful protests ringing in her ears.

"Oh, you cannot go, Mademoiselle. You cannot leave me. Can I not come with you? It is my dearest wish . . ."

Poor Marie. How *could* she leave her when Marie herself had been treated by Caroline Murat like some inanimate object to be attached to Jainee solely on the whim of her employer?

"Ask the lady," Marie begged her. "Tell her how loyal I am to you, how prettily I sew. I can learn everything else. I am able. Please take me with you."

But Lady Waynflete saved her the trouble of broaching the subject. Several days later, as she was critically assessing the components of Jainee's gaming house wardrobe, she said, "This is excellent—a bit flashy for my taste but . . . you have the most extraordinary eyes, unusual height, a lovely figure—I don't believe we will change a thing. We'll just add some ornaments and accents—hats and shawls and that sort of thing . . ."

"I do *not* wear hats," Jainee said emphatically.

Lady Waynflete looked at her consideringly. "Well—perhaps not. We'll see. And then of course, we need to find you a maid—"

Jainee hesitated, but the thought of Marie spending years sitting in a back room at the *Alices* mending piles of tablecloths and ripped hems prodded her conscience and she said, "I know a woman. She came with me from Italy, and she is not being well used by Lady Truscott—" And then she stopped, wondering at the wisdom of recommending someone who knew *all* about her past.

78

But Lady Waynflete immediately agreed to it. "Yes, I think you are right; it would be wise to have her with you. If she can sew as well as you say, so much the better. The rest can be taught. And a handsome wage will ensure her . . . conscientiousness. In any event, Lady Truscott is not known for *her* generosity. A wonderful stroke of luck to have someone who is not a stranger. I will make the arrangements, my dear. Leave everything to me."

How often had Lady Waynflete said that, and how easy it was to do. She had the energy of ten women and the know-how and wherewithal to conjure up little miracles. Everything was obvious to her: she saw all sides of a situation and could sum up to a nicety exactly what needed to be done in order to pass muster.

Jainee wondered what she thought of her bargain with Southam, but she had an idea that Lady Waynflete had some inkling of what had gone on between them and that nothing shocked her. Just nothing.

She supposed that at this point nothing should shock her either, but she could not quell her turbulent feelings about Southam's domineering possession of her, and her rage to take revenge for his high-handedness.

Oh maman, she thought, speaking to Therese in her mind as she often did, certain that Therese in spirit could somehow assimilate these ruminations, *you would be so proud of the bargain I have made on the fantastical notion that some phantom would want to kill your long gone son, and the deathbed promise that I made . . .*

And in her more retrospective moments, even she had to acknowledge that those two reasons were too flimsy a justification on which to hinge her monstrous contract with Southam.

But the thing was done and in a day she would be on her way. *All for a dying woman's delusion.* She had not yet gotten over the tormenting feeling she had abandoned Therese, even as she strove to keep her promise to her.

It had taken Lady Waynflete but two weeks to order everything just the way she wanted it, and in that time, she had removed Jainee from the *Alices,* soothed Lady Truscott's vanity, usurped the services of Marie (for a fat fee in compensation, Jainee had no doubt), spread the heroic story of the orphan Jainee Bowman who had had no choice whatsoever in her career but now was saved, and had gotten Jainee, herself and her household packed and at the ready to proceed on the succeeding morning.

Money, Jainee thought, was a wonderful thing to have. Even she, with her small cache of francs that she had squirreled away from Therese, had comprehended that wisdom in supplying herself with the resources to keep their household together.

And now, on the morrow, she would be on her way to London, further away still from the haunting images of that awful night when she had buried Therese in a satin curtain shroud and run bleeding and in terror from the burning house that had been her home for so long.

But enough! One could not repine. If she had learned anything over the course of this past year and several months, it was that she could only go forward, and that fate played tricks and sometimes dealt you a hand with which you could actually win a round, perhaps two.

And the rest was a toss of the dice. Surely it was sufficient that she had come this far using her wits and guile and several hundred pilfered francs.

Therese, she thought, would probably be proud.

The next day, wrapped in fur and warmed with a hot brick at her feet, Jainee gazed out at the passing scenery from the thickly tufted cushions of Lady Waynflete's travelling chaise which was eating up the miles toward London with stunning speed.

Behind them, a carriage piled to overflowing with suitcases, boxes, servants and one very wary maid Marie, barreled along at a considerably more sedate pace that was timed for arrival in town about a half hour after Lady Waynflete so that "we can have a comfortable space of time before we must cope with *luggage* and unpacking," Lady Waynflete told her. "But then, of course, the servants will take care of everything. We will ensconce ourselves by the fire and take refreshments. I sent Jeremy up to town yesterday to make everything in readiness for us."

"So kind," Jainee murmured, averting her eyes once again to the scenery, and forbearing to ask just what Lady Waynflete was getting out of her enthusiastic nursemaiding of her.

It seemed to her that she fairly tripped over willing chaperones—look at how amenable Caroline Murat had been to sheltering her after the hideous circumstances of Therese's death. Oh, would she never forget that horrible night—awakening from her faint draped over her mother's lifeless body; determining she must bury her lest deVerville return and wreak more havoc; tenderly wrapping her mother in the lustrous satin draperies Therese had loved so well . . . the feel of her mother's limp body as she lifted it and bore it into the rear garden where she had scratched out by sputtering candlelight a shallow grave . . . then securing the money she had hidden all those years, and allowing herself to sleep for an hour, only to be awakened by the acrid smell of smoke . . .

She gave herself a hard mental shake. She could not *let* herself remember. And while Caroline had provided succor and shelter for her, she had been motivated by a great deal more than just sympathetic friendship for Therese: she saw in Jainee another beautiful courtesan who might make her brother forget the dreadful Josephine.

Had Jainee been willing. And at that, Caroline had been amazingly angry with her when she refused.

"What do you expect, Jainee? That you might someday

fall in love? There is no such thing as love. There are only bargains, and you are a fool if you turn down my brother. He could make you a queen. He is desperate for an heir."

"I am going to England," Jainee said staunchly and in a tone of voice with which Caroline could not argue. "I promised Therese."

"But whatever could be in England that you cannot have here?" Caroline wanted to know.

"I am going to find my father," Jainee told her, annoyed that in the face of Caroline's offer, her quest sounded childish and not a little fantastic.

But then she always felt impossibly young around Murat. She had lived with her for the year or so that her mother had been involved with the Emperor and it had been Murat who had taught her just how to get on in court, even when the women of the court made her feel gauche and ugly.

She still could not shake the feeling even though she had applied to Murat for help. But rather than dismissing her little crusade as nonsensical, Caroline actually seemed to consider it.

"Oh, your father," she said musingly. "I had quite forgotten about him, Jainee. He came from England—I do remember now. And there was something about the boy . . . he took the boy, didn't he? Yes, and your mother was so distraught. Well my dear, of course you should be with your father. We'll have to devise some means of accomplishing that."

It seemed to Jainee in retrospect that just after this, Caroline had stopped pushing the Emperor's suit, and then that he had found another, more compliant mistress, and she had felt a little prick of annoyance that he had fixed his interest elsewhere so quickly and completely.

When she asked Caroline about it, Caroline said, "Perhaps it is for the best, my dear. You are so *young*. And the woman—well, the Emperor has begun to realize he can look elsewhere for an heir and that it needn't be a child of his loins. My husband, for example. Look you, I have convinced my brother to send us to Italy where my husband will reign as King of Naples. It will be a test of his fitness to succeed, do you not agree? And you shall come with us. It is *perfect*. You need a change of scene."

And she needed to be that much closer to England, and so she had agreed to go with the Murats when they travelled to Italy. She had spent several fruitless months in Murat's court leading the life of a pampered noblewoman before she broached the plan of her proceeding on to England to Caroline. Like Lady Waynflete, Caroline had been agreeable and had arranged everything, including the gift of Marie as her maid and travelling companion.

And so here she was, a year and a half later, on the last leg of her journey, accompanied by another amenable chaperone who posed no questions and made light-hearted conversation about the duress of the trip.

She wondered at her luck, and why Lady Waynflete had no personal questions about her *at all*.

"The transition between houses is always tedious," Lady Waynflete was saying, "and of course it's impossible to read with the carriage swaying so violently, and one really has nothing to do but stare out at the scenery, but then, how many times can you see a small village or miles of pasture and have it hold your interest?"

Lady Waynflete leaned forward and tapped her on the hand with her fan. "Do you not agree, Jainee?"

Jainee shook herself out of her trance of memory. "It is all so new to me that it does attract *my* attention," she said politely, avoiding Lady Waynflete's sharp eyes.

"In spite of the fact you have been playing with a deck of cards in your hand for this past hour?" Lady Waynflete asked, amused.

Jainee looked down at her hands. The fortune cards. Yes, she had taken them out and had been fanning them out and closing them almost unconsciously just to give her restless hands something to do. They had been a gift from another of the women at the *Alices,* and while she was well versed in the key, she had never ever used them to tell anyone's fortune.

It seemed, in a way, like courting bad luck.

Still, she had deliberately packed them with, she thought now, the idea of somehow using them to supplant her vice of gambling.

But maybe not. There was something so heady about wagering and the heartstopping moment before a bet was won or lost, she didn't know how she would live without that excitement. She hadn't considered that for a moment in the wake of Lady Waynflete's sweeping expropriation of her life at the *Alices* to bring her to London.

"These are fortune cards, ma'am. Perhaps you would like to look?"

She handed the deck over, and Lady Waynflete spread the cards. "Why look—there is nothing below a seven and each of the numbers has been blacked out on one side. How odd."

"No, no—that gives the card a different connotation when it is *en reverse.* Otherwise, how could one read them?"

"Can you read them?" Lady Waynflete asked curiously. *Amusing at cards*—hadn't Southam said it? She would be a sensation if she could and *would.*

"I have never tried," Jainee said frankly, "but I have been taught the meanings, yes."

"Wonderful—you shall read for me."

"I have never done," Jainee said doubtfully, a feeling of foreboding rippling right through her.

"Then I must be the first. I am *not* superstitious my dear; it is parlor game only, as surely you yourself know."

But she didn't know if she knew that at all, and Jainee's hands turned cold at the thought of it. Anything could come up in the cards; she knew that well enough from dealing them. The thought of reading made her blood turn to ice.

"What must I do?"

She couldn't shake the amusement in Lady Waynflete's voice. "Truly, madame . . ."

"Nonsense. We'll have a bit of fun to while away an hour or so and then we will be in London. Deal me your worst blow, Jainee—I promise you, I have more commonsense than blue, and I am not easily shocked."

Jainee swallowed convulsively. Stupid of her to have chosen the fortune cards when she might have diverted Lady Waynflete with a hand or two of picquet or Quinze.

Or was it luck—a spin of the wheel of improbabilities that had made her take out the fortune cards so that the sharp-eyed Lady Waynflete would notice?

She couldn't give in to that—she continued to protest: "But madame, there is no flat surface on which to lay the cards and the coach sways so forcefully, they would slide all about anyway."

"Well then—I will move to sit beside you and you will lay the cards out against the back of the seat and that should do very well," Lady Waynflete said decisively, suiting action to words.

Fate—surely it was fate once again that contrived to provide her with an expanse of surface on which to play her hand.

"Very well, madame," she said finally. There was no getting away from it, and indeed, it was still early enough that the coach was not dark inside and the sun shone through the door window clearly and cleanly. It was now a matter of shuffling the deck, presenting it to Lady Waynflete to cut—with her *left* hand: very important—laying out the cards and interpreting their conformation.

"Cut the deck, madame, and with your left hand, please," Jainee instructed Lady Waynflete, and she did as she was requested, and then watched with great interest as

Jainee counted out six cards and then overturned the seventh, which she positioned against the backrest of the seat, and then folded the previous six cards into the bottom of the deck. She counted another six cards, overturned the seventh, placed it beside the first, and once again put the six previous cards on the bottom of the deck.

She did this twelve times so that there were twelve single cards laid against the cushion, **and** then she turned to Lady Waynflete.

"There is no card representing you here. These cards are not for you."

"Then we must try again," Lady Waynflete said cheerfully, positively fascinated with the whole rigamarole.

Jainee gathered up the cards and laid them out again.

"Ah . . . now we have it . . ." *Dieu,* she thought with a chill, how facile the cards could be in defining a life. It mattered not which fortune the player sought. The results were the same. The cards always won.

She took a deep breath. "Here you are, madame—" she pointed to a queen of spades, "and so we know the cards concern a refined and attractive widow . . ." She slanted a look at Lady Waynflete who made a grimace.

"The cards truly do not say *that,*" she protested. "Do go on, Jainee."

"Very well. The ace of hearts: this concerns your home; ten of hearts reverse—you may have an unexpected surprise. But I expect you probably have had, my lady, with Lord Southam dropping *me* on your doorstep."

"This is fascinating," Lady Waynflete murmured. "Continue."

"Nine of spades in reverse beside the queen: you have sadly been unsuccessful in love, my lady, and I do not foretell that this will change. There will be a man—the king of spade who will want you, but you must be careful: this is a man you must beware of. There will be no reconciliation. I see prison, a marriage proposal and bad news. I cannot foretell the order of these events, only advise you—and yet I see also some useful person may come to your aid ... does this make sense, my lady?"

"Yes," Lady Waynflete whispered, and Jainee turned to look at her. Her expression was positively set, her pale blue eyes riveted on the cards.

"We are not done yet," Jainee said. "The cards provide that we must check the revelations." She gathered up the cards and shuffled them once again. "Do you cut, my lady?"

"Yes," Lady Waynflete said, her voice stronger and more positive now. She reached with her left hand and cut the deck.

"Now we make four packets of three cards each; these stand for the person, yourself, madame; the house; the future; and finally, the surprise. Now—"

She picked up the first three cards: they were not good. She hesitated a moment before she began her interpretation. "See here, the deceptive widow queen—*you,* madame—perhaps something here is not what it seems. There is or was a quarrel, the news is worse than you expected."

She picked up the second three cards. "To the house now. The queen again. You are represented well, my lady. The queen of hearts is everything desirable in a woman. But I see bad love affairs, a bad marriage."

She looked at Lady Waynflete who was curiously still and then picked up the third packet of cards. "You have a benefactor, madame, but I feel for all his good intentions, he is powerless, and therefore you will have to wait longer than you contemplated for some anticipated occurrence—a journey, perhaps, madame?

"And lastly—" she picked up the last stack of three cards. "What surprises? Profits, madame, money—always good news, and perhaps an unexpected surprise? Or perhaps it may be that unforeseen journey, who can tell?" She folded the cards together. "I am done, madame."

"Most interesting," Lady Waynflete said resolutely, but Jainee heard the slight tremor in her voice; she sounded shaken, as if something in this mystifying party trick were meaningful to her.

But that was nonsense. She reached out her hand to reassure her, and Lady Waynflete brushed it away. "Most informative, my dear Jainee. You are quite far-sighted. Most amazing. You must read for my darling Jeremy. And of course—for Nick. Definitely Nick. Oh—look, my dear, we've come to the outskirts of London—we are almost home!"

Chapter Six

Home.

For one moment, as she stepped from the cab of the chaise, she felt like a fraud. This was not *her* home, and yet it was eerily similar: a stately four-story townhouse fronted by semi-circular shallow marble steps, its pristine painted door framed by four grecian columns.

She felt like a charlatan; the fortune cards burned in her reticule like some devil's apparatus, and she castigated herself for being so ungrateful as to let a party trick turn into something more serious, particularly in view of all Lady Waynflete had already done for her.

But there was always her scurrilous bargain with Southam to prey on her conscience. She could not come away from this confrontation a winner, and she took a deep, spine-stiffening breath as the door opened and light flooded out of the house, silhouetting Jeremy Waynflete as he came down the steps, his hands outstretched to his mother.

"Come into the house—hurry—it is too cold for man or beast out here . . ." Quickly he ushered them into the warmth of the reception hallway, and Jainee stared in awe at the height of the ceiling, which must have reached twelve feet at least. The walls were painted a soft sea green color with the moldings picked out in white, while the floor was inlaid with black and white marble squares and covered over with an exquisite Axminster carpet in the center.

A servant appeared, silent and unquestioning, took their wraps and removed himself quietly as a ripple of water.

"Oh, it is so good to be home," Lady Waynflete sighed. She turned to Jainee. "Have you met my reprobate son? Jeremy, this is Jainee Bowman, late of Brighton, who has come to stay with us for the season."

Jeremy bowed gravely. "I believe I have had the pleasure." He held out his arm to his mother. "Come, it is much warmer in the parlor and Blexter is ready to serve refreshments."

Jainee followed them into a hallway just beyond the reception room off of which there were two doors, front and back, and an ornate staircase which curved gracefully upwards with no visible support.

Jeremy opened the first door and ushered his mother and then Jainee into the parlor. This was a large square room at the front of the house, furnished with elegant and comfortable furniture, not one piece so forbidding, Jainee thought as Jeremy settled her and Lady Waynflete solicitously by the fire, that one felt ill at ease in the setting.

The walls were painted the same soft green which contrasted wonderfully with the lustrous mahogany wood of the chairs, tables, sofa frames and one magnificent, multi-drawered drop front desk which was positioned between the two front windows and which was, in tandem with the beautiful carved white marble fireplace surround, the focus of the room.

Jeremy pulled on a bell-rope by the fireplace and then sat down beside his mother on one of the two red brocade upholstered corner sofas, and fixed his piercing brown gaze on Jainee.

"Nick is no fool, you know."

Whatever she expected, she had not foreseen that he would broach the subject of her being taken up by Southam quite so brashly. It felt almost like a frontal assault. Perhaps it was: he had been the man by Southam's side that fateful evening he had played and lost to her.

Perhaps it was admirable that he chose to defend his

90

friend by issuing a warning practically the moment she stepped foot in the house, but she doubted it.

"I know that," she said stonily. "Neither am I."

The door opened just then, saving her from hearing whatever else might be on his mind, and Lady Waynflete, who had said not a word during this brief harsh exchange, motioned for the servants to set up the collapsible tables directly in front of her and Jainee, and to lay out the dishes on a nearby table which had an inlaid leather top and could bear the heat and weight of the trays.

Jeremy uncovered the salvers while the maids laid out plates and cutlery. The butler served one platter after another of ham, salmon, and chicken, cut into dice for ease of consumption; there were side dishes of rice and mashed turnip, a macaroni pudding, cranberries and olives. There was a pot of chocolate and another of coffee, and a tray of desserts: jellies, cheeses, fruit puffs and small cakes.

They ate in silence, Jainee choosing to pour a cup of chocolate and to warm her icy hands before taking a plate of chicken, cranberries and macaroni pudding, which, little sustenance though it was, was still too much for her overwrought stomach.

But the chocolate was wonderfully hot and creamy and slid down her throat with reassuring heat. She was letting Jeremy Waynflete get to her, as if he were someone who would stand in the way of the course of events.

But in fact, he too knew when he was being swept along by a tide, for when Lady Waynflete bid them good-evening, shortly after the arrival of the luggage and the house servants, including Marie, from Brighton, Jeremy went on the attack again.

"Stay a moment more, Miss Bowman," he invited her as she rose to follow his mother.

She sank back into her seat, and accepted the offer of another cup of chocolate.

"I trust the informality of the dinner did not offend,"

Jeremy began, a premise insulting enough in itself because it inferred she was not used to even this much bounty in this kind of setting.

It was time to play his bluff and gain the advantage of him. "It was tolerable," she said insolently. "But nevertheless, I thank you for your generous hospitality."

Only the faint twitch of a muscle in his cheek betrayed his irritation at her impertinence. He did not like free-speaking women and this one, with her galling blue gaze and her positively arrogant air fairly set his hackles up. She had been blatantly *coming* in Brighton; and how Nick could have been taken in, he never would know. Nor would Nick want him interfering, but Jeremy didn't see *how* he could admit this seductress into his mother's home and *not* ask questions.

"Why don't you just tell me why Nick was so anxious to install you in my mother's house in the dead of winter and we will have done, Miss Bowman."

Jainee smiled faintly. "He must have his reasons," she said noncommittally.

"Indeed, and who would know them better than you?" Jeremy asked silkily.

He was sharp all right, Jainee thought, but he had none of Southam's presence *or* his power. He was obviously going to be a buzzing little fly, and she saw she would have to swat him down more than once.

She shrugged and said nothing and Jeremy went on, "Of course, no one ever knows what Nick will take it into his head to do. But I will tell you what he doesn't do is lose vast sums of money at the card tables and then foist a petticoat off on his best friend's mother on the pretext she is the indigent daughter of some old friend. You have some kind of arrangement with Nick, and frankly, I would like to know just what it is."

Well, that was lethal and straightforward; *his* cards were now on the table, and she still palmed the ace. Whether it was the winning card or not was something else again.

She had to rip into him now or forever be at his mercy because she backed down. She shunted aside every explanation that had rushed into her mind in the space of one second, and recklessly, she decided to play the hand.

"What if the arrangement is exactly what you believe it is?" she asked him, shocked that her voice remained steady, calm, assured in spite of the fact she was as much as admitting she had agreed to be Southam's mistress.

He did not look shocked; he just hadn't believed that Nick would be quite so callous as to set up his goddess as a vestal virgin in his mother's house. He still couldn't conceive of it, even with his mother's own acknowledgement of it.

"I like that one," he agreed easily. "I really do. Even my own mother saw the possibility of it. But Nick don't *do* things like that in a public way. It really makes no sense, Miss Bowman, but—if it *is* the case, Nick will be damned discreet, I assure you."

"As am I," she said instantly, almost without thinking, and she saw him register that tiny moment of surprise.

But he was a gentleman too. He raised his cup to her. "Nicely done, Miss Bowman. I salute you. And I warn you. I will be watching you—"

Jainee forestalled him before he could complete the threat. "And *I*," she said loftily as she rose up to indicate their interview was concluded, "will be watching *you*."

And hadn't Edythe Winslowe had the right of it, Jainee reflected venomously, as she was shown to her room. You couldn't let these top of the trees bluebloods roll over you; they would leave you dead for leather in a trice and laugh about it into the bargain.

Nor could she let Jeremy Waynflete's sensibilities get in the way of things. He hated her already, but he would have to stand far in line behind Southam.

Marie met her at the door. "Welcome, mademoiselle. And

I thank you again for recommending me to Madame Wayn-flete."

"*De rien*," Jainee said briskly, brushing aside her gratitude and pushing her way into the room.

She stopped short at the sight of the bed. The bed dominated the room the way her bargain with Southam dominated her thoughts, and with just the same forcefulness. It was *there*, huge and luxurious, with a mattress to sink into and lose oneself, and a canopy that was shaped like the springs of a glass coach and crowned with a plaster cornice from which draperies of the sheerest silk were appended.

"*Dieu*," Jainee muttered, reaching out a tentative hand to touch the coverlet which was reembroidered satin slipped over a counterpane of cotton and wool. The bedframe itself, the headboard and four reeded posts were painted white and gilded with winding twining vines reaching up to heaven and, perhaps, down to hell.

But that seemed too fanciful, even for her, and besides, underneath this massive piece of furniture was a most reassuring scallop-bordered carpet in a soft shade of blue.

Beside the bed there was a matching night-stand, and Marie had drawn up a similar matching table to the foot of the bed and thrown a red velvet cloth over, with a rosewood side chair beside.

Just opposite the bed, there was a fireplace with a meticulously detailed surround depicting classical figures, and on the breastpiece, there was a luminous landscape painted in oil.

On the far wall there was a clothes press, and drawn up by the fireplace, there was an open-armed upholstered chair covered in the same red velvet as the tablecloth with a small round tripod table by its side.

Everything in the room was beautifully made and on a gracious scale except for that bed. Jainee did not know how she was going to push herself to climb into it, let alone sleep in it.

But she was surprised to find she spent a comfortable night, and she was aroused at dawn by Marie, who had drawn her bath and brought her coffee and laid out a selection of gowns, all freshly ironed, for her to consider.

"Did you sleep last night?" Jainee wondered, and Marie shook her head. She had been too excited, too full of the new sights and sounds, and her head too occupied with the nuances of getting along with the household staff in a way so unfamiliar to her.

Jainee had been consumed by none of these thoughts, but after her leisurely bath and a scalding cup of coffee sipped by the roaring morning fire, she considered what the day might bring.

As she understood it, March was still the time of year that the fashionable set secluded themselves on their country estates and town was notoriously thin of company. Which meant that with any good luck, Southam would not be back in London for *months,* assuming he had a country estate.

Therefore, she was unpleasantly surprised to be greeted by Lady Waynflete's fluting voice when she was only halfway down the stairs: "My dear, the very best thing—Nicholas has come to breakfast! He left Brighton shortly after we did," she continued, and Jainee's step faltered as she caught sight of him lounging negligently against the newel post of the banister, "and he and Jeremy have just come from a ride in the park and are *ravenous.*"

"Yes," Nicholas said languidly, watching Jainee resume her steady pace down the stairs until she reached bottom and faced him directly, "I feel like I could just *devour* something."

"How predatory," Jainee murmured, giving him her gloved hand and never flinching from his flat matte gaze.

"As one must be when confronted by the huntress," he countered in his most reasonable tone of voice as he relinquished her hand.

"Truly, my Lord, you must always be on your guard lest I

95

pounce," Jainee said with just a touch of irritation in her voice.

"And yet," Nicholas answered with an undertone as Lady Waynflete led them toward the dining room, "it will not be long before I can have at *you,* Diana."

"I will sharpen my claws in anticipation," she retorted and preceded him into the room.

Gracefully, he made his way to her chair to assist her in seating. "It is always wise to remember that the huntress lives for the kill," he murmured in her ear before going to the opposite side of the table to seat himself.

Jainee unfolded her napkin and then delicately removed her gloves, finger by finger before looking up at him and smiling her catlike smile.

"I can hardly wait to sink my teeth into the proposition, my Lord," she said smugly as the servants began serving the first round of the meal.

Nicholas acknowledged the smile with a sketchy salute as he accepted a cut of ham from a warmed platter placed before him. "Like as not, Diana, you will still find the end result hard to swallow."

"I would as soon choke on the expectation," she said dampingly.

"If you cross me," Nicholas said, his voice mild and deadly, "you will have none."

Well, there was no mistaking that. He was not stupid and he would be on the lookout for any sign she wanted to renege. It was fair warning, and though her expression did not change, she was thinking furiously of all the ways she would thwart him, given the chance.

She wanted to take the cut glass water pitcher and throw it at him. She wanted to stamp her foot in vexation because he seemed to be one measure ahead of her already.

"Then I will be dead in any event," she said finally, as she helped herself to a slice of veal and ham pie from one of two platters placed before her. "Then how would you count the cost of your expectations?"

"The same as when I began," Nicholas said acidly, ignoring the horrified expression on Lady Waynflete's face, "ten thousand pounds for a diamond in the rough, all sharp edges and changing facets with a tongue that could cut glass."

"And so you have chopped me to mincemeat instead," Jainee shot back.

"Before you so very kindly slice *me* into ribbons," he retorted. "But perhaps what is needed is a gentle reminder as to who should be grateful to *whom,* Diana, and who should cease slinging arrows lest her benefactor bleed to death."

"We will say no more," Lady Waynflete intervened at this point. "Such wrangling sits ill on an empty stomach." And, she thought despairingly, made wonderful gossip in the servants' hall.

"On the contrary," Jainee said ungratefully through gritted teeth, "it positively whets my appetite."

"And mine as well," Nicholas said coolly, "but not necessarily for *food.*"

He watched with covert glee as his shot finally hit home; Jainee's cheeks flushed just the faintest pink, which only heightened her gorgeous coloring. She was vulnerable on the subject of their unholy bargain, and now surely out of countenance that he had alluded to it *publicly,* judging by the viciousness with which she attacked her veal and ham pie.

But that was all to the good; it wouldn't do to let the goddess assume that any of her barbs could pierce him; she was too quick-witted by half and cagey to boot. But more than that, she had no appreciation for what he had done for her, and he meant to make her very aware of that.

Jainee, however, had not relaxed, but none of the turmoil within her showed outwardly except for her one blatant misstep in stabbing her poor pie to death. He had noticed, but that could not be helped with her mind just boiling over with the things she wanted to do to Lord Patronizing Big Britches with his smug, cocksure, overbearing male condescension.

Well, she was better now that she had gotten that moment of rage onto the table and out of her heart, and it didn't matter one whit what Lady Waynflete thought of her or how Nicholas Carradine meant to exercise his male prerogative. She was ready for him, and she would not let him goad her into losing her temper again.

But at that, she thought, she had rather sliced him up and served him rare, and when she was finally able to look up at him with some serenity in her mind and on her face, she saw that he felt exactly the same as she: that the battle was not yet fully engaged, and he could not wait until the moment they might be alone together.

After breakfast they removed to the parlor, where a roaring fire greeted them and still more coffee and chocolate were laid to hand on a table which had been set beside the sofa.

"Here is the plan now," Lady Waynflete said, settling herself comfortably on one of the sofas and motioning for Jainee to sit next to her. "I am informed by Blexter, who keeps tight rein on such things, that we have an invitation to the Westerlys, who are having a select few in for cards in a fortnight, and that will be, I think, our first foray, assuming I can command an invitation for Jainee as well, which I shouldn't think would be a problem since she is now to all intents and purposes *family*. And then—" she rifled through a handful of envelopes which had been put on the table beside her, "there is—"

"I will tell you the rest," Nicholas intervened, stemming the tide of her enthusiasm ruthlessly. "She will receive an invitation, along with yours, to the Tallingers' annual winter dinner and the Ottershaws' return to town party, and I will make sure that the Westerlys welcome her with open arms. You need do nothing more than make sure she does us credit, Lucretia—which," he added blithely as he caught the warning combative light in Jainee's eyes, "I am certain she will. Now, Jeremy, you and I must do our utmost to be sure that she is seen in the most appropriate places around town—"

"You have windmills in your head if you think I will be a part of this," Jeremy said with bitterness etching his tone of voice.

"For God and country?" Nicholas reminded him gently.

"That's pure rot and you know it," Jeremy retorted.

"But we won't soil our soles wading in it publicly, will we?"

"I hope you drown in it," Jeremy muttered. "I will do as you want, Nick, but I don't much like it. And now you will excuse me. Mother will let me know the program and I will play the gallant under protest, and *only* because you ask it, Nick."

He bowed coldly to Jainee, kissed his mother's hand and left the room without further comment. Lady Waynflete shook her head commiseratingly.

"He will come around, my dear. It's just that he *thinks* you are an adventuress who has somehow got Nick under her thumb."

Jainee, whose intense blue gaze still rested on the closed door behind which Jeremy Waynflete had retreated, murmured, "He is right."

"How amusing," Lady Waynflete said uncertainly. "Nick?"

But Nicholas was watching Jainee and her changeless expression that focused on the door and he couldn't tell for one moment what was going on behind her eyes or the brassy verification that made Lucretia look at him so accusingly.

"I believe I need to have a few moments alone with my protegee," he said finally.

99

"Well, Nick—"

"My dear Lucretia, I'm not going to ravish her on the Aubusson, you know. It's damned cold, for one thing, and for another, Diana is buttoned up tighter than a miser's fist and the servants would be laying the evening fire before I could get a quarter of her clothes off of her. Now, do trust me, Lucretia, just as you always have, and let me have a few minutes to speak with . . . Jainee . . . so that we may come to an understanding of her responsibilities while she is under your roof."

"Very well, Nick," Lucretia said, but her voice was cold and her eyes were no longer merry with the anticipation of the winter's events to come. "All shall be as you wish, but I must tell you, I do *not* appreciate your levity or your bawdy humor in the least, and I want to remind you just what a great favor I *am* doing you and *all* because of my affection for your family and your uncle Dunstan. Do you understand?"

"Yes ma'am," Nicholas said humbly, but he didn't look in the least penitent. He did not say another word until Lady Waynflete had exited the room, her face set and her posture positively reeking disapproval, and then he turned to Jainee.

"You had better check that unruly tongue of yours, Diana, and remember just where the debt and the obligation lays."

"How can I forget? It lays squarely in your bed, as you have made very plain."

"And you have heard me keep my part of the bargain: you are under the protection and sponsorship of Lady Waynflete, whose lineage and credentials are impeccable, and you now have entree into four of the most exclusive events in advance of the season. It is time now, Diana, for you to give over."

"Nonsense. You promised you would not corrupt Madame's carpet."

"Did I?" Nicholas considered it for a moment. "No, I be-

100

lieve I said I wouldn't ravish you on the carpet. But there are many other possibilities to contemplate."

"I do not wish to speculate at all on anything you might contemplate," Jainee said testily. "I have been in London less than twelve hours; I have been quizzed unmercifully by your great good friend Jeremy Waynflete and dismissed as wanting out of hand; I have been attacked, by you, at the breakfast table, and now Lady Waynflete thinks I'm some mercenary vagabond who might fleece her, her household and you in some unmentionable manner. And over and above this, you wish to treat me like some servant girl at the beck and call of her libertine employer. This is hardly the finesse I would expect from a man of your experience, my lord."

"Nor is it a love match, Diana. It is a bargain, pure and simple, an exchange for favors with services to be rendered, and I call in my debt now. Come to me *here*."

Jainee backed away. Oh, an implacable look was on his face that said he would get what he wanted and all of her excuses counted as a great big smokescreen in the face what she had agreed to.

"I am not of a mind to," she said finally.

"You have no mind in this matter, Jainee," Nicholas said dangerously. "Your sole obligation is to obey."

Obey? *Obey?* Was there ever a more over-proud, over-confident cock of the walk than Nicholas Carradine? It was always the same with men like these: they bartered in clear colors—there were never any nuances and no delicacy at all. And they needed endlessly to be put in their places.

"My lord," she said, feeling her way into a subtle refusal, "surely a gentleman with refined manners has no taste for back door debauchery."

"Never say so," Nicholas said. "I have a great taste for it; it lends a certain piquancy to the proceedings."

As, Jainee thought trenchantly, she might have expected. One couldn't bargain with a satyr. Everything was up front with him: it was easy to see that their *duello* of a conversa-

101

tion was as arousing as a caress and as pleasuring—up to a point.

And it was obvious that Southam had reached it.

"Enough of this imperious word play, Diana. It is time for more mortal activity," Nicholas went on, pacing toward her now as she continued to back away.

She felt her legs bump into the arm of the sofa closest to the door, and she tumbled into the seat.

"That's better, Diana, much better. You like your comfort—as do I." He towered over her as he came to her side, and bent down to grasp her arms to pull her closer to him.

She jerked away, and rolled out from under him and onto the floor, cursing the long skirt of her kerseymere dress that caught in her legs. She rose up on her knees, and crawled to the table where the coffee and chocolate service were set, and painfully climbed to her feet.

"I will not be taken like an animal in a cave," she said tightly, edging her way around the table as he came closer and closer after her.

"But what is the difference, Diana? It is all play and pay in the lower orders as well—as you should know very well. An animal is an animal—we sniff, we pursue, we catch, we . . . possess—it is over."

"I expect more of *you,* my lord," Jainee rejoined, her hand desperately seeking something to repel him, her fingers lighting, suddenly, on one of the lukewarm fat-bellied pots on the table. "Perhaps . . ." she thought fast, grasping the hinged top of the pot and aiming it full bore at Southam's lower extremities, ". . . some sweet . . . *treat—*" and she heaved the open pot at him and watched in fascinated satisfaction as a dollop of chocolate splattered against the obvious bulge between his legs and dripped down the pristine buff of his skin-tight pantaloons. She dropped the chocolate pot and ran.

"Oh no, oh no," Nicholas growled, and in a second he leapt after her and pinned her at the door just as she had got the knob turned and the thing almost open. "Oh no . . . oh, no!"

She felt him crush her body against the door, she felt the heat of his anger, and the weight of his desire jutting into her bottom, and then one steely hand grasp her hair and pull her head back ruthlessly.

"Oh no, vixen huntress—no, that you do *not* get away with," he hissed into her ear. "Open your mouth, Diana. Let me sweeten it with liquid kisses . . ." and as she obdurately refused to part her lips, she sensed his left arm lifting upwards, and then she saw in his hand the chocolate pot, and that it was tilted to pour the thick liquid all over her face and her mouth.

Involuntarily, she opened her lips to lick away the stream of thick sticky liquid as it flowed on her face.

"Yessss," he breathed as her tongue flicked in and out futilely trying to suck up the chocolate that dripped from her nose, her jaw, her chin and onto her dress, in her hair, in her mouth—he kept the pot tilted so that the last dregs of liquid sopped down onto her face and then he tossed it onto the floor and it landed with a disconcerting clank and a spray of fine droplets all over the pristine carpet.

"And now, my fine goddess," he murmured against her ear, and she felt next his tongue along the line of her jaw heatedly slaking his thirst to have her in whatever way he could.

His right hand, entwined in her hair, held her in an iron grip so that she could not move her head from the angle at which it was tilted, and his body rammed against hers rendered her utterly immobile against his strength.

She could kick him . . . she couldn't do a thing: his heated tongue was coming closer and closer to her mouth as he licked away every drop of chocolate that defined her jaw, and sucked gently on the tenderest part of her skin, coming closer and closer still to the soft cushion of her lips.

She bucked against him then and he crushed that brief

moment of rebellion by simply pulling her around so that they were eye to eye, and framing her face between his two iron hands.

"And now, Diana, the sweet ... *treat—*" he murmured and delved mercilessly into her mouth and the lush chocolatey perfume of her tongue.

Now her hands were free, but her body was imprisoned by the thrusting bulk of his, and her mouth—oh, her mouth: he ravished her mouth without a thought to her delight or her need. He took her mouth the way he would have taken her—with pursuit and trickery, and finally out of pure animal need.

And because she had thwarted him.

Again.

And she would foil him now. She *would;* it would just take every ounce of spleen within her, every pore of her skin, and the all-encompassing power of her intelligence to do it, but she would do it, she *would:* the worst thing, the only thing that he could not expect of her at this moment when he rampaged within her mouth like a drunken sailor— at this very moment, she must, she *had to,* receive and to invite his kisses as if she could never get enough.

It was a thrust in another direction; no gentleman wanted entanglements, or importuning of his favors. She had only to give in this once, and she would show him all about power and involvement, and who would beg from *whom.* He would not get away with this treatment of her.

Her fingers curved around his huge hands like talons as she girded herself for the contest of wills.

Always attack, always go on the offensive. She knew it; it was Therese's advice. Make the bargain. Never surrender.

He had thought he could just roll right over *her,* and his title and his formidable reputation were enough to make her bow down and submit to his will.

She closed her hands over his and deliberately arched herself forward and into his kiss. She felt his little start of surprise, and then his mouth gentle as she started to respond to him.

It was easy. No, it wasn't—it was a fight for domination: he was not readily taken in by her sudden compliance. If anything, he pressed her harder, demanding she give to him, eating at her, nipping, licking, drinking every last drop of the gooey chocolate within her mouth and around the edges of her lips.

"As I said, Diana—" he whispered between thick little sucking kisses down her neck and behind her ear, "I am in the mood to devour something . . ."

He came back to her mouth then and ever so gently slid his tongue deep within, found her and began sucking gently at her, so softly, so intensely that she was caught off guard. Her body felt boneless as a whole new swoop of sensations assaulted her.

She was going under, under . . . under, and all because of his softly sipping pull on her tongue and her body's traitorous response to that moment of tenderness. She felt herself giving in for real and in honesty to the seduction of this kiss, and she had to consciously make herself fight it, like a swimmer battling for air. She couldn't—she just *couldn't* let him take her as easily as some doxy off of the street.

But he was so strong and so velvety as he coaxed her and invited her kisses so that she would cede all that power to him—she saw it, she understood it, and she could hardly withstand it. His seduction was too subtle for her, and she was too inexperienced.

She *had* to fight him, even in the midst of a searching provocative kiss that sent her senses reeling. She held on to him, and held on and felt the strength of the hands that cradled her head and could crush her as easily as he could an egg.

Crush and cradle, crush and cradle—with every last ounce of her strength she wrenched away from him with such unexpected force that he relinquished his hold.

She pushed at him then and simultaneously stamped on his foot and he stepped back, surprised by the attack and the unanticipated pain; she ducked out from the prison of his arms, away from him, away from the door, away from the temptation of capitulation.

He turned slowly, with a kind of leashed in movement as if he were restraining himself from doing something more violent, and she saw for the first time the full brunt of the damage.

She felt a crowing moment of triumph at the sight of him which was quickly squelched by the wrathful look in his eyes as he surveyed himself.

His pantaloons were ruined, with a huge brown splotch right in the most obvious place between his legs, and little droplets of stain raining artistically all over his muscular thighs, and his highly polished boots, and his neckcloth was in disarray.

Jainee decided that this was the moment not to exacerbate matters.

She had fared no better; the liquid had soaked through the thinly woven material of her dress so that there was a dark stain at the exact same spot on her. Moreover, her collar hung limply over one shoulder, and the buttons had been torn from the bodice so that the lacy chemise beneath was partially revealed. Little smears of dark chocolate dotted the whole upper portion of her dress, her shoulders and her arms.

The pot lay on the edge of the carpet, with droplets spattered all over its border and the floor near the door.

She took a deep angry breath and she felt the cloying constriction of some substance on her face. She didn't even want to see what she looked like. She envisioned long streaks of chocolate smeared and dried all over her mouth and chin; she could not see herself walking out of the parlor and facing Lady Waynflete.

"I believe my lord has had all the subsistence he can tolerate today," she said finally in a tightly controlled voice.

"Your *resistance* is *in*tolerable, Diana; I could consider that you have revoked the terms of our arrangement."

She met his steaming coal black gaze insolently. Something was there, something—the challenge that Edythe Winslowe had talked about, or some other program that no one knew about but Southam himself, and she sensed that he would not upend her plans—not yet, but only because it suited him, not *her*.

Still and all, she could act upon that intuition and she said, "You won't."

"Oh, my, my—the arrogance of the goddess. No, I won't relinquish the bargain yet, my dear. I will see you crawl to me first and I will take great pleasure in exacting revenge for this morning's work."

He moved to the bell-pull by the side of the door, and yanked it viciously and then stood waiting for his summons to be answered, his sharp blazing eyes never leaving her face.

She stood three feet beyond him and did not move either, the gall in her throat fairly choking her with anger.

"I would give much to see how you explain this to Lady Waynflete," he added mockingly just as a servant scratched at the door.

He opened it a crack. "My coat, please." And then he turned to Jainee.

"Do not trifle with me, Diana. I am past being moonstruck and your beauty will take you only so far. Your defiance will trip you up and land you flat on your back with less fastidious men than me. Take warning, huntress, and reckon who are your benefactors and who are your enemies. Even a goddess has some discrimination."

"While you, my Lord, have none. You are nothing more than a rutting boar—and a great bore, and I will take great pleasure in bringing *you* to your knees . . ." She stopped there; really, she had to curb her reckless tongue; the look

107

on his face made her knees buckle. He would not take much more from her.

"I will be the last to worship at your feet, Diana. And the first to crush your pretensions." He reached for his coat and waved away the servant whose sole duty was to help him on with it.

"You are very good, Diana. Very good. An adventuress born could not have carried this off as well as you. You do me credit. And you give me none. You will share my bed, huntress, if I have to stalk you, bag you and tie you up."

"You will never share *mine*," Jainee swore fiercely. *"Never."*

Nicholas smiled grimly and reached out across the space between them and tapped her cheek. "You will eat those words, Diana, I promise you, and they will be *sweet treats* after all the punishment I shall unleash upon you. Mark my words, Diana." He flicked her cheek once again and he was gone.

Chapter Seven

The bitch!

He was in such a rage over her high-handedness he could barely stand the short ride from Lucretia's townhouse to his own in Berkeley Square.

The bitch, the sneaky, viperous daughter of a devil—damn her, damn her . . .

He jumped out of the carriage before it jerked to a halt and tore up the steps and into his front hallway shouting, "Trenholm! *Trenholm!* Blast it!"

"Sir?"

Nicholas whirled. Damn the man. He was a wizard, invisible one moment, magically there the next, precise to a fault and never discommoded by anything. He surveyed the damage coolly as Nicholas ripped off his coat, and said without inflection: "I will draw your bath, sir."

"And send word to my Uncle Dunstan that I wish him to dine with me tonight."

"Very good, sir."

Very good sir, very good sir . . . the rigorous conscientiousness with which Trenholm performed his duties was both numbingly efficient *and* overwhelmingly irritating, and Nicholas was in no mood to appreciate how effortlessly all his needs were served.

He took the steps two at a time, his thoughts tumultuous with his spiralling anger: he couldn't begin to count all the ways he was going to show Diana, queen of diamonds, just who would take the trick.

He burst into his bedroom, the front room at the head of the second story stairs, and ruthlessly stripped off his morning coat, oblivious of crackling fire already laid and blazing, and the enfolding warmth that caressed the air.

*. . . the brazen-faced jade—*No woman had ever routed him so thoroughly and willfully; she was a handful . . . a mouthful . . . he paused in the act of untying his neckcloth: he could still taste chocolate, he could still taste *her—*

He licked his lips. . . . *Sweet . . . Bittersweet—strumpet . . . no better than she should be with her quick hands and chameleon heart—just the kind of woman to make a bawd's barter . . .*

But those eyes, those arrogant "make me" eyes, and that smug cat smile . . . she was everything he thought she was and more, and he would make her pay for her insolence and her malice, and ten thousand pounds couldn't even begin to cover it.

There was not enough money in the world to save the huntress from his deadly sights.

He did not relish a midday bath, but the chocolate had soaked through his clothing and dried on his skin, as he discovered once he had removed his shirt and pantaloons. He boots were irreparable, and he contemplated the delicious mayhem that he would visit upon the goddess as he soaked in the steaming hot water. Oh, he would topple her from grace soon enough, when it suited his purposes, not hers.

They were on his turf now, at the mercy of the *ton* where appearances were everything. No one had ever guessed that he, Southam, possessed of estates and townhouses and mountains of money he could not spend in a lifetime, still felt like the scruffy little urchin who had tumbled down a chimney and into a fairyland.

He was an impostor—every bit as much as the goddess, and maybe more. The thought amused him.

The thought sustained him. He never forgot, ever, and sometimes it seemed as if all the water in London could not scrub away the telltale layer of soot. Sometimes he still felt it, matted and grimy on his skin.

He had been four, or at least he thought that had been his age. He knew his first name, Nicky, and he knew all the pretty silvery things in the dining room looked just like *his* house. He remembered asking if he were home yet.

But home was a big warm house in the country with his beautiful mama and swoops of landscaped garden and a wild little forest in which he had gotten lost one day . . . or perhaps he had been taken to get lost, he could never be sure. There had been a woman who acted as caretaker of him. The name that came to mind for her was "Mrs. Mops", but he had been sure that had been his childish nickname, and he really had no memory of whether she had accompanied him that forever day in the woods when he found the road—then a rickety wagon which had either been driving along and stopped, or worse, had been waiting just for him.

The kindly Mr. Slote . . . he would never forget the name, or the ride in the wagon . . . and the loss of innocence and the feeling of utter abandonment. Slote fed on cruelty and the sweat of the helpless, he was unscrupulous and utterly without conscience.

He would never forget the beatings when he demanded to see his mother. He would never forget the stinging scrape of the stone against his hands and legs as Slote forced him down chimney after chimney and walked away with his hands full of money and his slaveys limping, chained behind.

He would never forget screaming for his mother, crying and kicking, inconsolable; he had gone from the light to the dark and he hadn't understood, and Slote was not one for explaining. The nightmare of it, the sunken eyes of the children with whom he had shared the horror; the thin gruel that passed for food, the cold of the barracks where they slept in a cellar beneath a tavern under thin torn blankets; the days that passed where some of the boys remained in the cellar, scrounging around for food and warmth like rats; the sense of helplessness that could never be alleviated by tears or by the unending yearning for his mother.

Where is mama, where is mama—sometimes, even as an adult, he felt a heartrending need for her that was always tempered and washed over by the knowledge that somehow she had let him go, that she hadn't wanted him enough to come find him. Not enough to save him from the terror of the unknown and the beatings and—later, when he understood it—the moment when those children turned into savage animals, ready to rip away a piece of bread or a piece of skin of anyone who got in their way.

He never consciously tried to remember these things; they came to him in lightning bolt flashes when he least expected it: little shards of memory that pierced him with the jagged edge of pain that he thought had been buried long and deep.

But he had inflicted pain as well, and he knew it. He had felt nothing but wariness after his months with Slote on that day he had tumbled down the Southam chimney and into the hearts of Lord and Lady Carradine.

Am I home? Grubby, ash-streaked, in rags, emaciated—what must he have looked like to them as he imperiously marched around their dining room, confiding that his house had pretty silver things just like the ones on the Southam breakfront.

And the pounding on the front door—it was like a gun booming from far away, the frantic Slote, determined to retrieve his property and make suitable excuses to the gentry.

And the fascinated Lady Carradine: *pretty things like what?*

Oh, mama has big silver things just like that where we eat every night. And shiny spoons and pretty plates, only . . . only—only—I don't know where my mama is . . . and he burst into tears just as Slote hurtled himself into the room with a string of apologies and cautions against the Carradines being taken in by anything the boy said.

He remembered . . .

They had been childless, desperate for a boy of their own, someone to love and to hand down a legacy of land and hope.

. . . And his mama had had such pretty things in *their* house . . .

The boy's a liar, mum. You know them boys; they would say

112

anything to get out of a day's work. No appreciation for the likes of earning a living. We take good care of him, mum. You don't want to get involved.

He's so thin, Lady Carradine said. *Look at his eyes. How old are you, boy? What is your name?*

He had to think a minute. He could still feel it, as an adult, seizing up his insides, as if his whole life depended upon what he told her. And he hadn't looked at Slote. He was sure Slote would find some way to interfere, he knew it intuitively, like when an animal knows to go in for the kill.

I'm Nicky. I think . . . I think . . . maybe—I used to be four—

Ahhh, he's older than that, mum. He's been around, he don't know no other life, mum—

I do too, I do too—I want my mama, I want my mama . . .

It was that moment when he collapsed into tears again, the flow of them like an ocean within him that could never be stemmed, never be calmed—that he felt he could never be saved.

And in that instant, Lady Carradine said imperiously: *Pay the man, Henry. The boy stays.*

And in that moment, when he should have felt some keening gratitude that Slote was walking out the door without him, he felt nothing, he felt dead: the lady was not his mama, and he had been too young to understand what she had done. But she had been too wrapped up in her own need to foresee that he would not rush eagerly to embrace her or her husband—not then.

Not ever.

He remembered that all he had wanted in those first years had been his mama, and he remembered all the hopeful questions with which he had bombarded the lovely Lady Carradine: he called her the beautiful lady and she had loved that, but he had never called her mother and it broke her heart.

He was a fraud; he had never been a son and he had never returned their love, and still somehow he had earned a place in their lives and hearts they so willingly gave him.

He had never stopped looking for the woman who had never

113

come to find him.

And he had never let any woman find her way through the labyrinth of his indifference.

The goddess would not be the first woman who got in his way, or the first he slapped down. But she would definitely be the last to provoke him so outrageously without just retribution.

They dined *en famille* in the intimate breakfast room at the back of the house, his uncle Dunstan arriving one half hour late, as was his wont.

"You need a new trick, uncle mine. Fashionable tardiness becomes rather boring after a while," Nicholas said as he grasped his uncle's hand and motioned him to choose a chair.

Dunstan smiled faintly. "I am ever in your debt for apprising me of the situation, Nick, but since no one but you is back in town, I didn't think it mattered." He seated himself with no further ceremony and accepted a glass of port offered by a manservant. "On the other hand, I expected *you* to rusticate until April, at least."

Nicholas sipped slowly from his own glass. "I didn't go down to Southam after all. The company was too good in Brighton."

"And rife with opportunities, I warrant."

"I went down ten thousand pounds with no trouble at all the first night. And a hundred to Jeremy on the side."

"Very good, Nick. Lord, I wish I could watch you in action."

"You will certainly have the chance, uncle. There has been a little crimp in our plans, and I'm wondering what you will think of it."

"It? Come, Nick, all goes well. The only possible hindrance is Charlotte Emerlin and you don't want to hear the *on dit* about her."

"She'll have the wind taken out of her sails soon enough anyway," Nick said thoughtfully. "I've brought a goddess back from Brighton who has an apparent claim upon our family."

"Indeed?"

"Yes. Her well-meaning father, having gone off to find his fortune in India, made provisions for his only daughter and I am the agent of that trust. Oh, didn't you know, dear uncle? Well, it seems her mother died and there was some kind of uprising and her father was gone, and the poor girl was left to make her own way in the world. It was *very* fortunate that I came upon her at the *Alices*, recognized her name, and tried my damndest to covertly provide her with the money she needed."

"This is fascinating; go on, Nick. How *much* did you try to provide?"

Nicholas rubbed his chin. "I believe it was ten thousand pounds, uncle." He looked up as a servant began serving the soup. "Mulligatawny, in honor of my new protegée."

"Excellent fare, nephew. Now, where were you? She was at the *Alices*, you say? Good God, Nick, you're talking about nothing more than a common strumpet. Are you in your right mind?"

"She's French, uncle—"

"Like three-quarters of the petticoats that roam those streets and play the tables. What on earth possessed you? A bit of muslin from the *Alices* pulled you down ten thousand, and you offer her carte blanche in London? She must have very *winning* ways, Nick. Where did you stash her? Sure not *here?*"

"God, no. I put her with Lucretia, but that may change. In any event, if I could continue—" He motioned to the servant who had doled out their soup that he might remove it, and a second servant entered bearing the fish course, a beautifully poached salmon with vegetables and condiments placed judiciously on the sideboard. The servant sliced and served the salmon and then withdrew.

Nicholas watched his uncle thoughtfully pick at his fish. "She's a termagant, if you must know, with not a damned grateful bone in her body. She's also very beautiful, and I have no doubt she'll be off my hands within a se'enight of making her debut—which will be at the Westerlys' card party in two weeks. But until then, her story bears looking into, and I wish you would."

"Of course she has a story," Dunstan said. "Marvelous salmon, Nick. Give cook my compliments. And remember, my

115

boy, *every* woman has a story."

"This is a good one. Her father was English."

"I like it already. An English father and a gaming house demirep. Sounds scandalous to me."

"He abandoned them, she says; never came back. Left her mother to the mercy of the French court and the generosity of the ogre who now seeks to fill his coffers and his mistresses' purses with ill-gotten gains in Portugal. The woman was killed when she made one demand too many. The daughter escaped somehow—I'm not particularly clear on that—by way of Italy. But the point, uncle . . . the point is—an English diplomat in France in 1780 or 90 . . . with a beautiful wife, an eager emperor . . . a few francs here, a few promises there—would a man like that not sell his soul for the right price?

His uncle looked at him oddly, and Nicholas was struck, as he always was, by how different Dunstan was from the man he had called father. Dunstan was taller, darker, leaner; there was nothing comfortable about Dunstan. He was the exact opposite in every way of his brother Henry, and a man difficult to get close to.

Yet he had been the one to give solace when Henry died, and later, a sense of purpose when Nicholas thought there was none. Dunstan was the man he called upon for advice, as did prudent government officials who valued his wisdom and expertise, and he was the one to whom he confided his restlessness. But more than that, Dunstan was the man to whom he gave his allegiance as a family member and like a son.

And Dunstan said, "What is this man's name?"

"Charles Dalton."

"Never heard of him. Ah, here comes the meat."

And once again, the parade of servant entered, this time bearing platters of roast beef and sausages and ham, side dishes of macaroni and more vegetables, more than a man could eat in a week, let alone an evening.

"*Never* heard of him?" Nicholas murmured, pouring himself some more port.

"Let us talk reality, Nick—and do top off my glass, won't

116

you?—that can't possibly be the man's real name. And very possibly, it isn't a real story. Just how desperate was this vestal of virtue to get to London?"

Nicholas didn't like that comment one bit, but Dunstan's bald common sense was one of the things he treasured about his uncle. Dunstan cut to the chase faster than any man he had ever known; and in truth, the huntress had been bold—unseemingly bold, come to that—in the manner in which she chose to proposition him.

It was beginning to look like she had trapped him and not the other way around. "She wanted to come," he admitted reluctantly.

"And *you* wanted her. Ah, Nick. You have shut yourself away from earthly pleasures for so long, it is perfectly understandable that someone somewhere was going to trip you up and haul you down. You don't need an excuse to bring the chit to London, boy. Get her out of Lucretia's, set her up, use her and lose her. Don't muck it up with tales out of the schoolroom about long-lost fathers and the French court. I believe you will find she is exactly what you thought she was, my boy—and all you need do is go ahead and enjoy her, with my blessings if—"

"Nothing will interfere with the program, uncle, if that is what you are questioning."

"Excellent, my boy. Better than excellent. The Emerlin is on the prowl this season and if you've got a bit of fluff on the side, so much the better. Lends itself to the story beautifully. Just make sure to give Charlotte the set-down she deserves. Her damned mama has been pestering me for a month about your plans and when you might return, and the fact that there's been some interest in other quarters. But then Annesley tells me that this year's product is much improved."

"I am consumed with curiosity, uncle. What kind of carrot is Lady Emerlin dangling?"

"The usual, which she knows couldn't buy *you* by half. But the Emerlin is something else. No more shrinking virgin, I'm told. She has acquired a new proportion, a little experience, a lot of wardrobe, a new hairstyle and a dash of brazenness to add to

117

her fortune. She has become a diamond *from* the rough, and this is that year she is playing for keeps, my boy. You can be sure that mama cursed her from here to Shaftesbury for letting you slip through her fingers. She'll be looking to remedy that mistake, I would wager."

"I have no interest whatsoever, but rest assured I will take care," Nicholas assured him as the servants removed the meat course and laid out the dessert which consisted of platters of cheeses and fruits, cakes, coffee and brandy.

"A tot of brandy would suit me, Nick, and then I must go."

Nicholas poured and his uncle took the snifter and sipped appreciatively. "Excellent cellar, Nick. Up to Henry's best."

"You'll be at the Westerlys', I assume?"

"I don't know. Perhaps you ought not count on it. Something has come up."

"Well, we'll see each other soon, in any event. I will be very curious to see what you make of the goddess and her quest for this phantom she has saddled me with."

"It worries me a little, Nick. You have her flying too fast too far already; she's bound to take a hard fall, especially if you remove her from Lucretia's protection. Be careful, my boy—and don't be too naive. Women are so clever. You really were ripe for picking, you know," he added as Nicholas walked him to the door. "Ten thousand out, eh? Still and all, nephew, it's a good couple of days' work, and it won't be long before the gossips bring the whole of it to town. In that respect, you've done *very* well, very well indeed. Till next time, Nick."

"My pleasure, uncle."

But he felt no pleasure at all as he closed the door behind his uncle. The morning had begun wretchedly and ended on a decidedly negative note. But then, that was Dunstan's way. He took nothing at face value, and it was a trait that made him infinitely wise and more often than not smugly virtuous because he had been right.

Nevertheless, the goddess was *his* problem, whether her story were true or not. And at that moment, in spite of Dunstan's warnings, and because of her perfidy, he didn't even think he

118

cared.

What she felt was ungrateful.

Lady Waynflete stood poised on the threshold of the parlor and her knowing eyes took in everything in one haughty censuring glance.

"Miss Bowman—"

"The carpet will clean," Jainee said helplessly. "A little cold water . . ."

"Yes, you would know of those things, wouldn't you? And my chocolate pot, dented beyond use . . ." She moved regally to the side of the door and pulled the bell rope. "Blexter will know what to do about this mess. However, he cannot help me with *you*."

"My lady . . ."

"You will go upstairs and change so that at least when we converse I will not feel like I am talking to a piece of Haymarket ware, and then we will talk, although I have no idea what you could say to me that would excuse both your appearance *and* my floor."

Jainee did not know either, but she was thankful for the half hour's respite: she felt soiled and used, and more than that, she was fuming over Southam's tyranny over her mouth and her body.

It just wasn't fair; he had everything on his side—wealth, respectability, strength, experience—oh, yes, especially experience. A man with experience was a prize, but a woman was scorned. Nevertheless, she would give all the silver she had concealed in her trunk to gain a particle of the experience that would give her the advantage of a man like Southam.

Yes, he meant to initiate her into the *experience*, but that wasn't the same as her knowing and coming to him understanding exactly what to do and how to get the upper hand.

No, his experience she did not want. But how could she have known that in Brighton? Or that she would be throwing chocolate pots at him less than three weeks later? The man was insufferable, and had made her position with Lady Waynflete as

119

tenuous as silk.

She didn't know what she was going to do, or even what she might say to Lady Waynflete that would not aggravate the situation.

And that unbearable Jeremy Waynflete would just love to watch her fall from grace, she thought, as Marie buttoned and hooked her into a fresh dress without a single comment on the fact the kerseymere was ruined. But Marie would fix it; Marie did not need to be told.

"Mademoiselle is beautiful," Marie said in French, standing behind her as she smoothed down the wrinkles in the dress before a looking glass.

Jainee met her eyes in the glass. "Mademoiselle is in trouble, Marie. We must tread carefully here."

"We cannot go home," Marie said.

"No. And now I think we cannot go forward, either."

"Let Madame tell you."

Jainee pinched her cheeks to give them color. "That is wise advice, Marie. I thank you. Who knows but what she will say that chocolate is good for the carpet."

But Madame was not of a mind to talk about housekeeping. She held in her hand a letter written on thick cream-colored paper and she did not look happy. She was also well aware of when Jainee entered the parlor, but she chose not to acknowledge her immediately.

From where she sat on one of the angled brocaded sofas, she could just see Jainee's kid boots and the ruffled hem of her ever blue dress.

Southam's chit was a credit to her at least, she thought dourly, as she tried to align his desires with her own misgivings. Even Jeremy was up in the boughs over this; he wanted Southam's petticoat out of his mother's house and the sooner the better.

She reread Southam's sop to his conscience and the abominable way he had behaved this morning. Nicholas never minced words, but apologies were not his style either. All he would admit was that he had been tactless with Miss Bowman that morning and he regretted the end result: the assault on Lucretia's sensibilities, and that she might harbor ill will toward his proto-gée. Nevertheless, he begged her indulgence still, and expressed his firm desire to have her carry on just as they had planned as a very great favor to him.

Soon, he promised, she could come to value Miss Bowman as not only the beauty that she was, but also as a woman who was forthright, well-meaning and *not* a fortune hunter.

She doubted that, Lucretia thought, but in point of fact she could not renege now: it wasn't good *ton,* especially when a half hundred of your peers had witnessed you taking the chick under your wing and fairly abducting her from the evils of the gaming house.

But then Nicholas knew that as well as she, and she supposed he was counting on that as well as her seeing the humor of the whole thing.

She would have given a lot, she decided, to see the statuesque Miss Bowman chasing Nicholas around the room with a choco-late pot. She didn't think anyone had ever chased Nicholas any-where, and she wondered if he had come out worse from the battle of wits than had Miss Bowman. That surely would explain the contrite tone of his note.

She wished she could have seen him before he left.

Finally, she looked up at Jainee. Yes, the goddess of the game was rigged out in blue once again, her hair neatly bound up and entwined with matching ribbon. Her beautiful face presented a picture of cool, perhaps calculated, serenity, but her eyes blazed with emotion, and the spots on her cheeks were not rouge or a heavy hand pinching.

"Sit down, Miss Bowman."

Jainee sat and folded her hands into her lap.

And she knew when to be quiet, Lucretia thought, an estima-ble quality in any woman. But her hands were tight, almost as if she had confined her emotions as well as her words in the hollow of her lap.

She was not stupid, this little protégée. There was an intelli-gence that radiated out of those startling blue eyes; there was a force of personality, and more than that, Lucretia had a sense

121

that there was a great pragmatism in this woman. She was no frivolous doll who would repine over the least little setback or setdown.

And she knew how to handle people—she must if she had been behind the tables at the *Alices*.

The question was, could she handle Nick?

"I hope you ruined his clothes—and his morning," she said at last, and she was amused by the flash of surprise in Jainee's eyes.

"Indeed, my lady—top to bottom," Jainee confessed instantly, wondering at this tack when Lady Waynflete had been so angry and distrustful not two hours before. But she saw no reason not to tell the truth; something in that letter had lessened her suspicions, and she assumed it was a note from Southam. However, she could not picture him making apologies, and she assumed she would never know what he had written to sway Lady Waynflete's opinion.

"*Are* you mercenary?" the old lady asked next, the words cracking into the air like a whip.

Again Jainee was startled, as she deduced she was meant to be. "I hope not, my lady, but surely in this atmosphere of easy money, it is hardly a great leap to become so."

"Are you an adventuress?"

Even Jainee paused at that one. Was she? She had made the mistake of characterizing herself as one, but even she was not sure there was a name for a woman who sold herself to keep a deathbed promise, and meant to renege on the bargain in the process. A liar, perhaps. A cheat. A gambler. An adventuress . . .

"What I am, my lady, is a woman who has lost her parents; one died, one abandoned the family when I was young. I seek my father, Lady Waynflete, nothing more," she said slowly, carefully. No lies this time. Omissions, yes. Misconstrued motives— oh yes. Southam's part in it—no explaining *that* whatsoever. "I made a promise to my mother when she died. And I have searched my soul endlessly on the question—who would know if I didn't try to find him. There *is* no answer, my lady, except that I would know."

Lady Waynflete cut right into it. "That is a very pretty story, Miss Bowman, and perhaps it *is* true, but where does Southam come into it?"

Canny Lady Waynflete. "You must know, my Lady, I lost an extravagant sum of money to him—" Oh, she hoped Lady Waynflete knew, but what if she *didn't?* "—we made a bargain."

"Yes," Lady Waynflete said drily. "I can quite conceive of the kind of bargain *you* would make."

Well, she was down now: Lady Waynflete inferred the worst. She could not defend that position, nor, she thought, did she want to. Once again, she must attack to circumvent a request for details.

And at that, it was easy. Lady Waynflete was not used to such brass-faced boldness even though she possessed it herself. "You mistake the matter, Lady Waynflete," she said stringently, "and with all respect due to you, I cannot see how it is your business to question an agreement between Lord Southam and myself when you are in the process of putting the proper face on it."

"I'll tell you what, my dear, you had better curb that sassy tongue of yours. I will not be the last to say that you pulled off the trick that no other woman has been able to these past five seasons: you have Nick eating out of your hand and chewing up the most impossibly implausible story I have heard in twenty-five seasons in London, and you do it very well. My own mistake was trusting the boy, and thinking he couldn't fall prey to a body or a face or his inexplicable penchant for gambling. But I won't underestimate him again—or you.

"You are correct: I have no choice but to put a proper face on it and I will do all that Nick requests." She waved the letter at Jainee. "But one misstep, my dear, and I will toss you through the hoop and out the door, and then see where your career will land you.

"Nevertheless, since Nick is footing the bill, you shall have all the fripperies, gowns and entertainment that London can afford you, and we shall see just how fast you connect with this long-lost father of yours, Miss Bowman. If I were a gambling woman, I would wager it will take you no longer to find him than the moment that Nick decides you do not fascinate him any more.

"Don't looked shocked, my dear. The gossips are far more vicious than I. But at least you now know how things stand between us. We will take a light luncheon and I will escort you shopping. Your clothes are all very well to do, my dear, but you cannot bare your bosom in a morning gown—much as you may want to."

And that was just the morning. Jainee had no idea what to expect that afternoon as Lady Waynflete politely introduced her to the manner in which the fashionables shopped—going to one of several wonderful bazaars and roaming from shop to stall, beginning at Grafton's for material, until one found exactly what one wanted; and ending at Lady Waynflete's mantua-maker who would transform the whole into proper and compatible style.

But Jainee saw immediately that Lady Waynflete had something very much in mind: she wanted to present Jainee with an aura of innocence. She wanted the light-colored silks and muslins, always leaning toward the color white, and high necks and over-decorated hats, layers of underclothing that Jainee had discarded years before. And the light of battle flared in her eyes as Jainee rejected each of her suggestions.

"I am no schoolroom miss, my lady. I do not wear hats, nor do I wear patterns. I prefer blue, and the low neck, the round gown without the trains and frills, and something vastly more sophisticated for evening. I do not wear hats, but I will wear ribbons, flowers or pearls in my hair. And I will *not* be made fool of."

"As you say," Lady Waynflete murmured, and held up a length of white sprigged muslin against Jainee's face; she made a noncommittal sound and put back the material and picked up something else.

After several tries, she shrugged and threw up her hands. "You win, Miss Bowman. No matter how hard I try, I cannot make you look insipid."

"My compliments, my lady, but none of this is necessary.

124

Surely there is enough in my own wardrobe that we need not put Lord Southam to this excessive expense."

"You cannot appear more than once in the same dress. And I promise you, there will be two dozen men who remember you from the *Alices,* and can tell you to a nicety exactly what you wore on any given night. Now, shall we proceed, Miss Bowman?"

They proceeded, from high-necked morning gowns to more elaborate afternoon round gowns to the thicker corded muslin walking dresses with their abominable waistcoat bosoms, which only constricted and emphasized Jainee's natural curves, to the best and most beautiful evening dresses of luscious silks and crepes, satins and fine translucent muslins, two of which became her immediate favorites: one a deep blue tunic caught at one shoulder over a flowing underdress of lavender sarcenet. The other was made of thick ivory shot satin with a scandalous neckline that fastened just above a deep oval which bared a good portion of her breasts.

And over this, as she moved from party to party, she would wear an elegant black hooded cape which was lined in fur.

"Which, of course, will be discarded in the carriage before you enter anyplace," Lady Waynflete instructed her as she fingered the material and nodded her approval.

"Excuse me? Do I understand," Jainee interposed, not quite comprehending the rules of dress Lady Waynflete was espousing. "I do *not* enter a place wearing this beautiful cape? What do I wear? What if it is cold?"

"There will be shawls, beautiful matching shawls for each of your dresses, and these you will wear when we ascend from the carriage. It is a mere step from there to any entertainment we will be attending. The cold does not signify in that event."

"My lady, this makes no sense."

"It is the way things are done," Lady Waynflete said with great finality.

Jainee girded herself to protest. "You are telling me then that this society demands that its women be fragile and clinging and then rules we must show our innate strength by freezing to death?"

"That is the way of it," Lady Waynflete said, "and you will comply with the manner in which things are done, Miss Bowman, without protests. Now, let us continue . . ."

She duly commissioned the matching shawls for each of the dresses, several pelisses for morning and afternoon wear, matching gloves for every outfit, silk stockings and matching garters, half-boots for day wear and beautifully worked kid slippers to match each of the evening gowns. And there was jewelry: pearls and gold and silver strands to wind around her throat or through her hair. And there were bracelets, a jewelry box full of them to complement the several she habitually wore, and rings and earrings and little bags strung with drawstrings to hold her handkerchief, her fan (a dozen to match every dress), her gambling money, and each of these reticules would be fashioned to match every outfit.

"Whatever you are," Lady Waynflete said somewhat grudgingly as they finished this go-round of measuring and choosing materials and accessories, "you are a pleasure to dress, despite your somewhat exotic predilection for the color blue. However, it does work well for you with your hair and eyes, and I will go as far as to say you were wise to overrule me on this account. You are no schoolroom chit, and anyone looking at you would know it immediately. Now, come . . ."

Jainee did not know whether she had been insulted or complimented, but she had no time to dissect the nuances of Lady Waynflete's comment.

Lady Waynflete, it seemed, never stood still. She had positively raced through the afternoon's shopping and fitting at her dressmaker's, and now they were embarked on a brief carriage ride around St. James Park while she discoursed on sundry topics that had nothing to do with their morning's discussion or her newfound suspicion of Jainee's motivations.

After twenty minutes, she directed her driver to turn into St. James Square where one of her great good friends, Jane Griswold, resided. Jane was married to a member of parliament and she was a stickler for etiquette and formality.

She, Lady Waynflete thought, would give her an impartial reading of the impertinent Miss Bowman, and if Miss Bowman passed muster with Jane Griswold then she could feel secure in her sponsorship of her.

She wished heartily that Nick had not come to breakfast that morning; then she would not have had the slightest reservation about Miss Bowman at all. But that was Nick for you, ever doing the unexpected and taking his friends along for the ride. She only hoped the carriage would not overturn and crush them all during this caper.

Lady Griswold awaited them, having received Lady Waynflete's urgent note earlier that day and being perfectly willing to accommodate her good friend on such short notice.

Her house, one of a long block of similar such attached townhouses, was situated on a cul-de-sac called St. James Crescent, and was distinguished by its colonnaded front portico and the wide shallow steps that led up to it.

Lady Griswold met them in the parlor, holding out her hands to Lady Waynflete and murmuring, "Lucretia, my dear. She is eminently presentable. You must not worry."

Jainee of course heard none of this as Lady Griswold turned to her. She had the impression of great kindness behind Lady Griswold's pale green eyes, and great rectitude as well. Here was a lady with an iron will that was as unbendable as her manners.

Moreover, she had the same kind of height as Jainee and an imposing presence, due probably to her years and her position in society. Nevertheless, she did not seem predisposed to condemn, at least not at once.

This, Jainee thought, was the first test. Lady Waynflete was trying her out to see if she would win the sanction of her friends.

And all because she had carried on so badly with the abominable Southam this morning. Everything could be ruined, just everything. Southam would pay for the indignities heaped upon her this day by Lady Waynflete who, prior to this morning, had been perfectly amenable to the arrangement. And if *she* had been goaded into being indiscreet by Southam, well, she refused to take blame for it. She was giving up enough to the man, including the outrage of being picked apart by this seeming highest of the high sticklers, Lady Griswold.

Even if she were trying to be kind—for Lady Waynflete's sake.

"Miss Bowman?"

"Lady Griswold."

"Come in and sit down, won't you? This is a ghastly time of year to be in London, don't you agree?"

"Except if one is in good company," Jainee murmured, following Lady Waynflete's lead and settling herself opposite Lady Griswold.

Lady Griswold smiled. "How kind of you to say so." She lifted a small bell on a small table by her side and sent Lucretia Waynflete a meaningful look.

"I'll ring for tea."

From that point on, it was easy. Jainee thanked her stars for the time she had spent with Murat at the French court while her mother played coy games with the emperor, and her several months with Murat in Italy.

She saw immediately that there was no difference in the expectations—all was either *politesse* or malice, and one had to learn to walk the very tricky ground between the two.

Jane Griswold was no threat. She wanted to like and approve of Jainee purely to be able to reassure Lady Waynflete.

And Jainee wanted to like her; she could even feel some admiration for a lady who always did things in the cleanest, most aboveboard way.

Yet Lady Griswold was able able to appreciate the recklessness of youth. "My dear, to have come such a long way by yourself on luck and your wits—" she shook her head ruefully as she fed back the very story Lady Waynflete had concocted and now was assiduously spreading about. "But we mustn't talk of the hard times, must we? We can only be thankful that Lucretia found you in time and you are here with us now."

"I am eternally grateful," Jainee said with all the earnestness she could muster.

"Of course, it was Nick," Lucretia put in with just the faintest

128

tinge of resentfulness in her voice.

"Oh, everything is Nick," Jane Griswold said. "There isn't a day someone isn't talking about something he did or didn't do. And then that Gertrude Emerlin has the nerve to trumpet the return of Charlotte to town as if we had all been waiting for this miraculous news—or perhaps she thought that Nick had been. Oh, but that's neither here nor there. Nick is the most perplexing man I know, and don't tell me about his gambling, Lucretia. I don't understand it either, and certainly *not* over Charlotte Emerlin. So perhaps it is a good thing he has something to distract him in Miss Bowman and getting her launched as her father would have most properly wanted."

"Exactly," Lucretia murmured, her eagle eye on Jainee's mobile face, just waiting, just daring her to make some brass-faced comment that would put Jane Griswold out of sorts with her.

But Jainee understood perfectly the *raison d'etre* for the visit and what her part in it was. She was even a little amused by it, as she always was: the everlasting kowtowing to appearances which involved such verbal contortions were not even considered lies.

She didn't say a word as Lady Griswold served tea and little cakes which would most assuredly spoil her appetite, and then questioned what Lucretia planned to do with Jainee for the next several days.

Jainee was a little appalled that Lady Waynflete even had a program, and she found it hard not to publicly protest an agenda which included everything from going to the opera to visiting museums, rides in the park ("to be seen"), and fittings—one, seemingly, every day.

"But that's perfect," Lady Griswold said, turning to Jainee. "After all, London in March—well, it really is the time to visit all those dusty old places before all the matchmaking mothers descend and pull their daughters around in hopes of improving their minds and, of course, being seen. Although I don't know of anyone who visits the museums in May or June who would do so because he wanted to be seen. But anyway, it does pass the time most agreeably. And the opera—so colorful . . ."

And as they bid Lady Griswold goodbye, she took Lucretia

aside and murmured, "Really, her manners are unimpeachable, and her looks quite spectacular. And with Nick handling her trust, why, I would wager someone will offer for her within a month or less of her debut. Never fear, Lucretia: I will launder the story until it is bleached with respectability if that is what Nick wants. You may rest easy on that score."

But Lucretia Waynflete felt very little rest or reassurance from Jane's words. Jane was naive and looked for the best in everyone, and she believed wholeheartedly in Nick, and never would she credit that he would foist a jade into the household of her best friend.

Well, it was done now, and while Miss Bowman did not look smug (which she ought, Lucretia thought mordantly, at having passed the first hurdle of charming Jane Griswold), she did look undeniably beautiful, and more than that, unremittingly exasperated and not at all grateful.

Lucretia thought a little gratitude would have gone a long way toward soothing her increasingly bad feelings at having done Nick this service; it was no longer a lark. But she didn't know quite what it was. She only knew that wealthy and bored widows like herself did not accept wayward girls into their homes with open arms except at the behest of a rogue like Nick, and she swore that evening as they returned to her home in Mayfair that if anything untoward happened over this misadventure, she would make sure that Nick was ostracized—at least for a week. She did not like feeling powerless, and she did not like feeling gray, but she felt old again, as she and Jainee debarked at the house and went slowly up the steps.

The girl was not what she seemed, and she was not what Nick made of her, and Lucretia did not know what to make of the whole. It was easier, she thought, to just pretend the thing was what Nick said it was. At least that way, she could get some enjoyment out of it. And Nick would never let it explode in her face—he just wouldn't: it was very bad *ton*.

And with that saving grace, she was able to make her peace with her part in the affair, and meet Jainee at dinner with some degree of equanimity, and Jeremy who had come to join them, and discuss the plateload of plans she had made for the succeed-ing days.

Marie became her confidante. It was so likely: Marie had been with her through the worst—the time after her mother's death, the onerous trip from Italy, the hard times before they had come upon the *Alices*—and Marie knew the whole and spoke her lan-guage, and mended her clothes just as if she were as noble as Southam claimed, and Marie never protested her role in Jainee's life except to say she was happy to be on the periphery of it.

She had always had little expectations herself: had she not come with Jainee, she would have remained in Italy with the Murats, serving the emperor's household in one way or another.

No, Marie was happy to be away from that situation and amenable to becoming the wall of silence against which Jainee framed her thoughts, objections and frustrations.

Marie was also the voice of practicality, hers ever so much more sensible than Jainee's because she dealt with the everyday and commonplace realities, and now Jainee was flying higher than a hot air balloon with as much heat and amorphous air propelling her.

Jainee must not lose sight of the fact that she made a bargain with Southam and that she must not renege, no matter what the cost.

"I don't wish to think about that aspect *at all,*" Jainee said, biting her lip with vexation as she surveyed the newly cleaned and repaired blue kerseymere for which she had to thank Marie's clever fingers.

"You must think about it," Marie told her gently. "The mo-ment will be at hand when Monsieur demands what is rightfully his by the terms of your agreement, and you must come to terms with that. Like your mother and the emperor: she was flattered, yes, but she was not wildly in love. She loved the pursuit, the games, and in the end, her good sense made her understand that she could extract much from this bargain that she would not have had otherwise."

131

"How true," Jainee muttered in annoyance. "My mother was a pattern card of respectable greed. Everything is possible in the name of honor or fulfilling a bargain. I was better off in Brighton—and I didn't know it. Who would have known did I not promise my mother on her deathbed to seek out the thing most impossible to find? *No one.* No one would have cared. No one would have been hurt. Therese would not have turned in her grave. *No one would ever have known I had not left France to seek Therese's dream.*

"And yet, here I am, having compromised everything and on the threshold of committing all the same follies as did Therese, and perhaps what I will see for my trouble is a handsome stipend from the scurrilous Lord Southam and nothing else. *Nothing.* It is as if I have been transposed into my mother's life, and I can't bear it—*I can't.*

"This is the very thing I dreaded—the heritage I fought to escape. Now it comes down upon me with the ferocity of a windstorm and carries me with it until I no longer know who I am or what I am doing."

"Nonononono . . ." Marie whispered. "No no no, mademoiselle, you know who you are and what you are about. *You* care, that is why you have made the devil's bargain. *You* care. You will fulfill your promise as the good daughter you were, and with all the love you bore your mother. You will. And you will find the man, and you will find the child, and you will satisfy yourself that all is well and then you will know that your *maman* can rest in peace. That is why you have come so far, mademoiselle. The rest does not matter. The Lord Southam is the means to the end. He will be kind to you because it is his whim to be, and nothing shall hurt you so long as you are in my care.

"Ah, rest easy, mademoiselle. Everything will play out in due time and you will see that all your worries will have been for nought, even the necessity of submitting to my lord. It is all for a reason, all for a purpose, and mademoiselle will make the fates work for her as she has always done.

"Rest easy, mademoiselle, for I will always be at your side . . ."

A week later, Jainee wasn't sure that was enough to make her rest easy, as she donned the blue kerseymere in preparation for an afternoon's outing with Lady Waynflete.

"No one would ever know that Southam had drowned me in chocolate," she complimented Marie, pleased with her image in the mirror as she pirouetted this way and that.

"Neither does Monsieur remember," Marie assured her, smoothing down the line of buttons she had repaired and replaced.

"One would think he had utterly forgotten about me," Jainee agreed. "He has been nowhere around for the previous five days and I am thankful for that. It makes it easier to forget him. Lady Waynflete has kept me so busy I haven't had a moment to think. The British Museum one day, the Tower of London the next. A day browsing in some lending library this last afternoon, as if it were the most important thing to be seen borrowing books. And fittings, fittings, fittings. The dresses! Marie, did you wish, you could become a dressmaker *par excellence* with no end in sight of business. You are every bit as clever as any of these seamstresses, and far less temperamental.

"Today . . . let me see, today we go to see some kind of view of some city in Russia that some painter has made, and apparently you view it in a full circle. The thing goes round the room. I cannot conceive—well . . . I will see. And then, of course, there is another fitting. Thank heavens this abominable card party actually happens this weekend. I could scream with frustration, but at least an end is in sight."

"And your reckoning with Monsieur," Marie said.

"Or his reckoning with *me*," Jainee threw out over her shoulder as she dashed from the room in order to meet Lady Waynflete at the appointed hour.

She had been very careful not to offend Lady Waynflete in any way and to express the proper degree of appreciation for Lady Waynflete's escorting her to the various and sundry entertainments which at least had the virtue of passing the time agreeably.

The panorama, one of several to be seen in the city, was indeed in its fashion, a wonder and a curiosity. That a man had made with his own hands, and in perfect proportion, a lifelike rendering of an exotic city in such a way as to capture all the details and elements of it, was an entertainment in itself. It was impressive, and Jainee, who had never seen anything like it, was dazzled and willing to spend much more time than she would have thought possible admiring the intricacies of it.

This naive appreciation of something that had come to be commonplace for a seasoned city dweller charmed Lady Waynflete out of all bounds, and she was willing to let Jainee draw her here and there around the room to examine the particulars of each figure and building.

But soon she wearied of that, and reminded Jainee that she still must have a fitting that afternoon, and if a dress were ready, she, Lady Waynflete, was considering an outing to the opera that evening.

Jainee hoped not. What was the opera but a group of overdressed, overstuffed buffoons caterwauling on a stage in front of a hundred or more people who had no musical sense of appreciation of the melodramatics of the story? She couldn't think of a worse way to spend an evening, and so, she was very disappointed when they arrived at the dressmaker's and found that the ivory satin was ready to be taken home and wanted only a final fitting.

Still and all, this dress—a luscious thick creamy envelope of a dress with its oval bosom-baring neckline, was the most beautiful thing Jainee had ever seen. The moment Madame Signy slid it over her head, she ached to wear it—even to the opera.

"Mademoiselle is a goddess," Madame pronounced as she smoothed away a wrinkle here, and arranged the neckline just so there. "The slippers—here. A matching turban, mademoiselle, the perfect touch," and she set the folds of twisted material on Jainee's dark curls and Jainee had to hold herself back from laughing.

"Perfect," Lady Waynflete said, once again bending that formidable scolding gaze on Jainee lest she commit some impropriety about the turban which, were she feeling more charitable, she would admit looked perfectly ridiculous on Jainee because of her statuesque height.

"We will take the dress with us," she added, and after, as they were on their way back to Mayfair with all packages delicately wrapped and placed in a fragile pile on the seat beside them, she said to Jainee, "The woman is a fool. She recognizes the elegance of your person and then proceeds to make you look like a clown. I will say this, you are quite right about hats for you, and I predict you will cause a sensation in that dress. Only I am not sure if this is good or bad."

"It is whatever my lord wishes," Jainee murmured, looking for some way to reverse Lady Waynflete's negative feelings about her. "Perhaps he will be at the opera tonight?"

"I expect so," Lady Waynflete said, but even she wasn't sure. Nick always seemed moved by the whim of the moment, and no one was ever able to predict what he might or might not do.

But perhaps he ought to see his protegée in action, she thought. He had taken a particularly hands-off stance since the morning of the chocolate debacle, and he had not come round with either flowers or apologies, and in fact had made sure to meet with Jeremy far from the scene of the crime.

Well, his own perpetration was about to be launched publicly, and he ought to be there, she decided, to see whether this barque of frailty sank or sailed.

Chapter Eight

The Regent Royal Theater was an elegant white marble building crafted in pure classical style, from the columned and pedimented entry portico to its arched doorways and gilded and garnished reception hall.

There were ornately capped columns everywhere, including between the tiered balconies that ascended in three crowded levels from the orchestra. The front of each box was decorated with classical motifs and elegant little paintings of neo-Grecian scenes full of mythical creatures and swooning maidens.

It was a spectacle, and it was obvious that here too one attended to be seen and the event of the evening was purely secondary to that.

Lady Waynflete, by virtue of her ability to pay the exorbitant box rental for a season, commanded a seat to the right of the stage in the second tier.

"One doesn't want to be greedy," she said to Jainee as they settled themselves into their seats that night, "nor does one want to be conspicuous. Actually—" she took out her lorgnette and began peering down at the crowd, "it's much easier to be seen in the second row because the first tier is always crowded with hangers-on and *parvenus* who think they have got the best of things by being so *close*. But then, that is how some people think."

Jainee held herself aloof, a little dismayed by the intensity of the crowd. It was impossible not to look around: everyone else was surveying the boxes and the orchestra to see who had come—and who hadn't, but still, such blatant ogling was at once annoying and intimidating.

But only to her. There was such a gush of greetings and carry-ings-on from the orchestra to the very top tier of boxes that she wondered whether the rules of etiquette were suspended at public gatherings such as this.

And that did not even account for the dozen or so people who crowded into the box to pay their respects to Lady Waynflete, and the crowds of friends who pushed their way into the surrounding boxes.

Lady Waynflete introduced her to everyone, a dizzying array of names, faces, scents, hands and faintly reserved "how do you do's" which were leavened by the covert asides to Lady Waynflete: "My God, Lucretia—what a gorgeous child; where did you find her?" And then Lady Waynflete's glib explanations, which would find their way all around the opera house by the first intermission.

The play did not matter; the company did not even try to match the noise level of the conversation. Those who were interested peered at the stage through opera glasses and followed the score from booklets which they had brought with them.

For everyone else, it was a public party, complete with excellent company, and champagne throughout the first act, thoughtfully served by waiters who passed from box to box with the offering.

Jainee sipped her champagne, which was the best ruse to avoid having to make conversation with Lady Waynflete's intimates, all of whom sounded like dead bores.

The champagne soothed her so that she was less conscious of the staring and the murmuring that surrounded her. The theater was suffused now with a soft glow from one central chandelier which lit the orchestra and surround with just enough light for everyone to see, but not enough to distract the players on stage.

It was easy to pretend after a while that no one could see her and that she could see everything. It was almost magical, a fairy tale of an evening, with a goddess in her heaven and all the mere mortals down below aching and praying for a mere moment's contact.

How fanciful: it was so easy to fall into all the mythologic non-sense, especially in a place like this, with its cloud-painted ceiling and angelic on-stage host proclaiming in soaring C-notes the glory of love and death as some kind of sanctification.

Jeremy Waynflete slipped into the chair beside her. "Everyone is

137

talking about you. You should be pleased with yourself."

"I only wish to please Lady Waynflete," Jainee said sharply, aware just how sanctimonious this sounded, but Jeremy Waynflete was not being kind, and it was hard to tell whether this fact would please his mother or not.

Or maybe that wasn't important after all. Perhaps her mind should be on the main question: was there any man here familiar to her? She hadn't particularly thought of the opera as a place to begin her search for her father.

It was in fact the last place she would think to look for him, but she began to focus with more intention now, if only to avoid Jeremy Waynflete's disapproving look.

"None of this washes," Jeremy said.

"You've made that quite plain," Jainee countered instantly, "and also that Lord Southam's wishes would be yours, so I do not see the point of belaboring the situation. I am here, as he wishes. Your mother has been kind to me, and I have no desire to embarrass her in any way, and *your* displeasure does not seem to enter into it at all."

"I will protect my mother from her own folly," Jeremy retorted, and then he said, "Oh, there's Nick."

Oh, yes—there was Nick: it was almost as if there were some kind of spotlight on him. Jainee did not know how she could have missed him, especially with that opera-dancer on his arm, as brass-faced and flashy as a diamond.

She felt herself girding for the storm. He would come, he would come. He was a master at playing games to please himself. But he had not reckoned with *her*. She was his equal in all things: huntress to predator. They were the same. She saw it in his eyes, the brief flash of acknowledgement.

When she saw him, she would make sure he knew that his games meant nothing to her. And how easy that would be, with a box crowded to full with Lady Waynflete's contemporaries—and Jeremy's.

All the young men just swarming around her, now they had seen her with Jeremy, and demanding introductions and saying all those sweet meaningless things on which she would dine for many evenings to come.

There never was a sincere man, she thought, watching Southam wind his way elegantly through the crowd below. Men were beasts; they would tear the marrow from a woman, devour the best part of her, and leave the rest for carrion.

But not she, not she. Therese, the impulsive, the heedless, the reckless, Therese lived deep within her. Only she would know where to draw the lines and when to obliterate them. Only she would play the game on her terms.

"Miss Bowman."

"My lord?" she said politely. The creature was still with him, as blowsy as an overripe peach.

"May I present . . . Miss Mannion."

"So pleased," she murmured and Miss Mannion muttered something in return, and then disinterestedly moved away to speak with Jeremy.

"Nicely done, Diana," Nicholas said, sitting himself down next to Jainee. "You do me proud."

Jainee smiled, feeling the familiar combativeness wash down her spine. "May I return the compliment?" she asked sweetly, meeting his flat black gaze with a limpid look of pure guilelessness.

"They are clamoring for introductions," Nicholas went on, ignoring the jibe.

"No, that cannot be. It is Miss Mannion who commands such attention."

"I think it is that dress, Diana — very definitely the garb of a goddess on the prowl."

"And yet I sit in the shadows —"

"In hiding, waiting to pounce."

"Well then, let us chew over Miss Mannion for a while. She seems a meaty subject to me, my Lord."

"Not nearly as succulent as you in that dress," Nicholas retorted, as several well-dressed young men elbowed their way into the box and gave him meaningful and faintly lascivious looks. "And here my point is proven. Miss Bowman, may I make you known to Messrs. Chevrington, Ottershaw, Tavender, Griswold — I believe you met Charles' mother this afternoon."

She acknowledged them all gracefully, intensely aware of Nicholas' not disinterested scrutiny. How far could she go, she wondered,

139

how much charm could she lay on to make his lordship understand that she, of anyone, would never fall at his feet?

Ah, but she hardly needed to do anything; his hot black eyes scorched her naked skin, and she felt there wasn't a man within the confines of that box seat who didn't admire the cut of her dress and that oval of bared bosom.

Good, so much the better. Perhaps she ought to give reality to Southam's vision—that someone would claim her within the two weeks of her debut. It would be a fitting end to the adventure, to walk away on the arm of some desirable *parti*.

These men were susceptible, more so than Southam, in any event. He looked anything but pleased at how alarmingly easy it was for her to attract all the eligible bucks within the vicinity.

She liked the feeling of power it gave her: Lord Southam obviously did not. He allowed it, for a while, and she did not like the fact that he was orchestrating the procession of men into the box.

But time would take care of that. The point was they all wanted to meet her, and he was angry enough to chew the scenery at that fact.

"Don't make too much of it, my dear Diana," he cautioned her at one point when he had successfully cleared away yet another crowd of admiring exquisites. "Every new face is a novelty; they tire quickly."

"You must know, my lord," Jainee said, slanting a malicious look at him. Thank heavens for fans—she flipped hers open and he only half caught the sweet malevolence in her expression. He thought he imagined it.

And then he was sure he had not.

He cursed her wicked tongue, but he knew she was no match for him.

"Ah, here is Miss Mannion, come to rescue me for act two before boredom sets in." He rose up and took Miss Mannion's arm. "We shall meet again, Miss Bowman."

"Shall we? I wouldn't have thought you had any interest in doing so at all," Jainee said blandly, forestalling the niceties he was about to heap all around her in the name of keeping up appearances.

"You must never discourage a possible benefactor," Nicholas chided her gently.

"But there have been so many offers, my lord. I wouldn't miss yours in the least."

"When I do offer it," Nicholas said stiffly, containing his anger at her positive impudence, "you will not miss it."

"And meantime, there is *Miss* Mannion," Jainee said encouragingly, just loving the flaming exasperation in his eyes. She turned to Miss Mannion confidingly. "Did he offer to be your benefactor too?"

"What is a benefactor?" Miss Mannion asked, slightly peeved that she could not understand what this unflatteringly tall brazenmouthed *unknown* was talking about.

"It is of no moment," Nicholas said, patting her gloved hand. "It has to do with the generosity — nay, let us say munificence, of those unwitting enough to take pity on those less fortunate than ourselves."

"But then," Jainee put in quickly, lightly, before he could get away with such outrageousness, and before he could steer Miss Mannion out of earshot, "it could be said that *I* might be *your* benefactor, my lord."

Even that positive overstatement did not faze him.

"Were you rich enough," he retorted just so she could hear, "which is hardly likely when you consider the limited choice of ways in which you could possibly accomplish that. But you know that already, Diana," he added for good measure, not hiding the rising wrath in his expression as he turned away from her.

"Perhaps I will be rich enough," she whispered, but he could not hear; her eyes followed the broad set of his shoulders as he exited from the box fairly pulling the bemused Miss Mannion along after him.

Five minutes later, she saw him back in the orchestra, Miss Mannion by his side, and she clenched her hands in frustration and she did not know why.

When the evening was finally over, she allowed Jeremy to drape the gauzy white shawl which matched her dress around her shoulders, and she meekly followed Lady Waynflete down the stairs and into the main reception hall where they would await the carriage.

Jeremy, too, was silent. He was to go with them in his mother's carriage since he had come with Nick and Nick now had to escort the everlasting Miss Mannion back home. He did not look happy about the arrangement and Jainee was keenly aware that his disapproval and her rather rude refusal to make conversation with him did not sit well with Lady Waynflete and those of her friends who stood with them awaiting the carriages.

It couldn't be helped. She was simmering over her encounter with Nicholas Carradine, the high and mighty lord of benevolence, and she was furious that now, in the aftermath, she could think of a thousand things she could have said to him, all of which would have pulled his tether and choked him.

No one knew better than she that there were no second chances. One play, one turn of the card. One wager. One win. One loss. That was the way. She had played this day's hand already and there was no going back.

The only question was how much time Southam would allow her to find her phantom of a father, and how much leeway he would give her before he claimed his rights under their bargain.

She was ever the gambler's daughter, she thought mordantly, as she bid a cool good night to Jeremy. She was always looking to beat the odds and never, in the end, counting the cost.

But there was no cost to count here . . . yet. Southam had opened his purse unstintingly and given her a magnificent wardrobe and a beautiful, proper temporary home with Lady Waynflete, and a succession of elegant parties to look forward to.

Maybe it was too much. Maybe, she thought, her tale of omission did not warrant this much largesse. Maybe she didn't think that Southam was that taken with her to lavish such generosity on her and ask nothing in return.

Maybe the cost *was* too high.

She didn't know, but she had the disquieting feeling that this evening's conversation was a prelude to all his demands. The man was a trader, after all, and she had had only one thing to barter in Brighton. The rules had not changed since just because she had taken on the coloration of his world: he would still want payment, pure and simple, and just in the way she could imagine.

And so, because her thoughts were directly on the consequences of her agreement with him, she was not unduly shocked to see him sitting in her bedroom when she finally opened the door.

"My lord," she said coolly, and he would have been stunned to feel how furiously her heart was pounding when he was thinking what a cold customer she was after all.

There was never a woman in his experience who was not discomposed (or pretended to be) on finding a man in her room who had not been invited there. He could have dealt with recriminations more easily than her calm acceptance of his presense as she slipped out of the little froth of a shawl that surrounded her shoulders and turned to face him.

"You are not suited for the role of the piper," she said, reaching in her mind for something that would clarify why he was even there.

"Oh, I think so, Diana. It must be obvious the time has come when you must pay."

And so here it was, and oddly, she did not feel any shock at the notion that he had come to claim that which she had freely offered him the month before.

Or perhaps her gambler's sense of timing was impeccable, and the discrepancies on which she had ruminated the moment before she entered the room had been so telling the conclusion was inescapable.

Whatever it was, she felt calm and ready and a cool curiosity about what would follow, and she said, "Well—here I am, my lord."

Her *sang-froid* positively floored him. At least he had expected her to beg. No, he *wanted* her to beg, he wanted to wipe that brassy confidence right off her mouth and out of her mind.

He felt a galling rising rage that her composure gave her the upper hand of *him,* when she had already this day given him a tongue-lashing that would have laid a lesser man low.

He cursed himself for characterizing her as a goddess: he ought to have known she would use the appellation against him. No, it was time to teach the huntress that she had been rightly cornered and she had nowhere to run, nowhere to hide.

He could even, did he wish, find some amusement in playing with her, now he had won the endgame.

But his vengeful feeling went even deeper than that. He wanted to master her, ride her, and to ever have her in his power where her viper tongue could not slash away at his very vitals.

"And here am I, Diana," he said finally, "just waiting for you to fall into my arms."

She felt a tremor go through her at his words, and she suddenly wasn't at all sure she could carry off this posture of complete indifference. But to show any emotion at all would be to give in to him, and she could see he was waiting to taste that victory.

She lifted her chin. "Perhaps I am waiting for you to fall into mine," she said with the faintest trace of haughtiness in her tone, and it just galvanized him into wrathful action.

She had known it would. He came across the room in five long strides and grasped her by the hair and pulled her to him tightly so that she could see every movement of his impatient lips breathing the words into her face: "I will reduce you to a beggar, huntress, before you taste freedom again; I will ruin you for any other man for that virulent tongue of yours, and I will pull you from your Olympus of sanctity by virtue of the fact *I* put you there. And *now* do you understand, Diana?" His hand tightened around her curls and the thread of pearls wound through them fell to the floor like a punctuation to his words. *"Now?"*

"I understand," she whispered.

"And you surrender, goddess, do you not, to a higher authority?"

Never! she thought viciously, as she pushed at him and he pulled her even more closer to him. Damn, he was hurting her. "I never surrender," she hissed, wrenching her head in opposition to his inexorable tug toward him.

"You dishonor your bargain, Diana," he said, abruptly releasing her. "You are free to go."

"What?" This she had not expected.

"You may go. Now. With the clothes on your back and with whatever is in your trunk. But you must leave now."

She was tempted, she really was tempted.

"Lady Waynflete will disown you as of this moment," he went on, his voice pleasant with malice. "No one will offer succor: they will to all intents and purposes never have met you. You will be alone, and walking the streets, and perhaps that is as good as you deserve. It's really a choice, Diana. Submit there or surrender here. Only the outcome will be different."

"And what makes you think I will not survive?" she demanded, fighting back the frisson of horror his words evoked. She had her strength, she had her skill . . . if he would wait until morning—no, she had not expected this, not in the least, even after all she had heard of his whims and caprice.

He smiled, a not very pleasant smile at all.

"That is no concern of mine, Miss Bowman—as of now."

He walked to the door and opened it—and waited.

It took her thirty seconds to decide, the gambler in her, the *Therese* in her, choosing the cutting edge of comfort over the cold and wretchedness of the streets and the sure slide to oblivion.

"What do you want me to do, my lord?"

He closed the door slowly behind him. "You are most sensible, Diana."

"It would be a wanton waste of money, my lord," she retorted, ever practical, but that view of the situation neither amused nor pleased him.

Nevertheless, she had not yet bent to his will, and they both were aware of it. Only her pragmatic question lay between his power and her submission, and it took but a step to place him face to face with her where he could read everything she was thinking in her eyes and the quirk of her lips.

The fire in the hearth, always laid early and lit by Marie, glowed against the rich satin of her gown. Two candlesticks on the mantel and two sconces on either side of the breastplate provided a seductive light by which to see her changeable eyes, provocative light by which to explore her mystery inch by luscious inch.

But first she had to learn who possessed the power between them, and who must please whom. That first, the taming of her willful defiance; he felt the urgency of it grip his loins.

He did not feel predisposed to be kind. "You will come to me, Diana."

She felt that strong instinct of resistance, and she fought it. She had made the choice, the reasonable choice. Nothing could be worse than the streets, not even Southam's bed. "As you wish, my lord."

The tone was meek but the eyes, the eyes still dared him . . . in the eyes raged all the defiance that he had forbidden to pass her lips, and he meant to crush the words in her mouth if she so much as made one sound.

But it was the eyes — the blazing blue of her eyes, and the positive antagonism flaming there that goaded him beyond reason.

He reached out and grasped the flap of material that hooked the ends of the oval design of the bodice together and he unfastened it. The flaps fell away and the narrow swell of material that covered her breasts slid downward now the oval did not hold it in place, and he very gently slid the rest over her breasts and her turgid nipples and bared them to his sight.

"Yes, I thought you were naked beneath," he murmured, "and here you are, just a push and a pull away from having exposed yourself publicly to anyone's gaze. What a daring design, Diana. How well you wear it. But my innovation is much more provocative — and for my eyes only, Diana; that *is* understood? Move away from me now and let me look at you."

She thought she would die. She thought she would kill him. Her whole body flooded with raw red shame that he had only to snap his fingers and she allowed him to bare her most intimate secrets without a fight.

No fight in her body, her raw, treacherous, proud body. Oh no. Her body *liked* the idea of him looking at her. Her body liked the ravenous look in his enigmatic black eyes. Her body yearned for a man's touch. Her nipples, heated by his touch, were like two hard hot pebbles, demanding he take them and roll them in his fingers. She felt her body elongating, thrusting itself forward to display her breasts brazenly, wantonly; she watched his face as she moved around the room with candlelight and shadow molding her shape, hiding and revealing, caressing her nipples and throwing them into luscious relief against the colors in the room.

She watched his face; not a muscle moved, only the banked fire in his eyes as she displayed herself with the insolence of a well-paid tart.

Wasn't she?

She watched those flat black eyes with the only emotion that

146

moved in him at that moment: the tormenting provocation of a woman flaunting her body.

She watched his face, and she saw it at last — the unyielding fact that it was she who wielded the power by virtue of his enslavement to her nakedness.

Her feeling of humiliation dissipated in an ecstasy of triumph. Here was the way to deal with the arrogant, worldly Lord Southam, and she was willing, very willing, and consumed by tantalizing luxurious feelings of power and the idea that she could win after all.

She turned her back to him, natively, instinctively, almost as if the thing that was feminine within her knew that she would enflame him by merely concealing her nakedness from him, even for a moment.

And she looked down at her breasts; how odd, how tight and taut and thrusting and round they were, how purely female and excitingly naked. She had never experienced anything like this before; her nakedness against the fullness and formality of her dress was ravishing, even to her. The hard peaks of her nipples fascinated her, and her opulent urge to push her breasts forward, almost like an offering to a god.

Fanciful again. But the power she felt was real and it was connected to the temptation of her lushly rounded, hard-tipped breasts.

"Diana . . ."

She turned slowly, arching her back slightly to push her breasts forward still more, and she saw him lick his lips as she began to walk toward him.

"My lord?" How far could she push him now that the power rested with her? The throbbing bulge between his legs was unmistakable, and she eyed it warily as she walked right up to him and deliberately leaned against him and rested the tips of her naked nipples against the fine cloth of his coat.

She was like a child playing with fire; she was all smoldering heat and latent power, and she had no idea of a man's desire weighted against her fragile, seductive, all-enveloping body.

He wanted to rip away her dress and take her, naked and unwilling, on the floor. He wanted to cup those luscious breasts in his hands and imprint the weight into his palms forever. He wanted to taste the sweet succulence of her hot taut nipples and suck at them all night, all day, all year.

He wanted . . . he wanted . . . "Give me your mouth, Diana . . ." Yes, the hot honey of her mouth would salve his need; she lifted her chin and parted her lips and he took her savagely with the drive of his hunger; he invaded her mouth, and he wrapped his arms around the fullness of her buttocks and rammed himself against her, hot, hard, ready . . . ready —

Her breasts — he needed to feel her breasts . . . he moved with her to a nearby chair and he pulled her onto his lap, and he filled her mouth and took her taut-tipped naked breast into his hand and he wasn't sure that something didn't give in the heat of his pulsating male possession of it.

He held her tightly, he ground her soft buttocks against his hard heat, he took her breasts, he felt them, he stroked them, he fondled them, but he never once touched her voluptuous nipples.

He felt her squirming, demanding he caress her hot hard peaks, and he responded by stroking the curve of her breasts just to, just until the moment he would have touched her naked nipples, and he heard her groan deep in her throat, felt her arch herself and thrust her breasts into his hands, demanding the last exquisite shaft of pleasure.

He held her breasts and assuaged her mouth, sucking at her tongue the way he would have pulled and sucked at her nipples, and he felt her anger that he would deny her the feeling of his fingers caressing her lush hard nipples.

She did not know who was enslaved by whom. If he would have touched her, *there,* she thought she might have given herself to him right then if only to feel the rainbow sensation waiting for release in the nakedness of her nipples.

His hands were hot and heavy on her breasts, his fingers delicate as air when he caressed them, his male instinct as unerring as time when he found the perfect place to arouse her and reduce her to the mindless yearning to submit.

And his mouth, even his mouth — the hot wet ferocity of his kisses goaded her, challenged her, demanded that she open her mouth and deepen the kisses, and give him her tongue willingly to taste and suck in a swirl of torrid caresses. She knew nothing of men's kisses and she knew everything about them now, and she wanted more and more, and it was as if her mind had disconnected from the avid need of her body and she wanted only the deep hard wet possession of his mouth.

And his hands. And the bold thrusting prod of the iron source of his manhood against the soft curve of her buttocks. And the nakedness of her breast and his hot hands stroking, pulling, feeling its contour, every soft luscious inch of it except her bulging naked nipple.

She couldn't bear it, she couldn't. She wanted to take his hand and show him precisely where he must encircle his fingers; and she thought that such a bold move would be tantamount to surrender to the dazzling seduction of his hands and mouth, and she mustn't, she must not—she must be stronger than he to keep the balance, the equality, the power.

She felt his body go rigid for an infinitesimal space of time, and his mouth ease away from hers, and she had but that moment to quell the insanely voluptuous sensations that possessed her and await what he chose to do next.

"Diana, huntress of desire, with just enough guile to capture a man's soul," he murmured. "You are very good, my dear. Most excellent, in fact. Such beautiful breasts, made to be naked and demanding a man's caress. No, Diana, you don't leave me yet. I like the feel of you writhing with pleasure on my lap, and your nipples, swollen with yearning. But I will not let them seduce me, Diana—not this time."

She felt him ease her to her feet and she moved away from him— she had to or surely she would have struck him for his arrogance, for his insolence and for leaving her with the unresolved ache in her breasts.

"This is but the prelude to the terms of our agreement," he said, and the smug tone in his voice was almost killing. None of it was meaningful, none of the feelings, none of the pleasure—oh, and wasn't that a man to a fault. When a woman believed for one moment that lust fell by the wayside, it was the very moment a man was crowing over his conquest.

She would never make that mistake again. His caresses could

never be consequential: he was out to use her every bit as she had intended to use him. The bargain was struck, and everything new and seductive about this experience must be savored but never in surrender.

Looking at his impassive face, she was sure there was no other way. A stain blotted the power between his legs. Without it, he could never be forceful, and she would never be willing.

The first test was over and now she needed the long night to reveal to her what it meant.

"When I see you next, you will be wearing something I will send to you, a gift for the delightful surprise of your potency, Diana. Don't take the chance of not donning it every night until I come. Your compliance is part of our agreement, and I expect it."

"As you wish, my lord," she murmured, hating him.

"Very good, Diana. Turn away now and I'll leave you . . ."

She whirled as the door closed gently behind him. When she looked in the hallway, there was no one around.

The gift arrived the morning of the card party, and she wondered which of the myriad of seamstresses in town had stayed awake all night and all day to cut and sew the confection she removed from the box that awaited her silently and secretly in her bedroom when she returned from a morning's drive with Lady Waynflete.

It was blue, a deep sky blue to match her eyes, and it was filmy and gauzy, and cut so low in front there was no way to cover her breasts and still tie the gown around her. The neckline was layered with ruffles and the robe ended in a deep flounce around her feet, and in ruffles around her wrists. There was but one hook, just below her breasts, to close the edges right at her midriff, and one tie to wrap around her waist.

And when she held the creation up to the light, she saw it was so light and translucent that it was certain that when she wore it, she would no longer have any secrets from Southam.

Your compliance . . . Every night she must wear this harlot's robe until he came, and it and his reaction to it would be the prelude to the ultimate conclusion to their bargain.

If she wore it, her breasts would betray her. Just thinking about

150

it sent a skimming excitement through her. Just imagining the flame in Southam's eyes to have all of her nakedness revealed to him . . .

Just imagining she could bring him to heel with such puny weapons as her body and a fluffy dress of gauze was laughable. She was more sensible than that.

Or was she?

There was something about the power of her nakedness which sat strong and vibrant deep within her. She knew, deep within that feminine resource, that the power was there, that she could wield it, and she could vanquish him.

She knew it.

Her mouth was swollen with it — and on the succeeding day of his nocturnal visit, she had to spend the entire morning in bed with cold compresses to reduce the swelling before she could face Lady Waynflete.

And she spent all of her waking hours trying to determine just how he had gained access to the house without Lady Waynflete's knowledge.

He was a cat, a slinky sinuous tiger, but it was she who knew how to bare her claws . . . and use them.

She dressed for the evening in a slight fever of expectation. Tonight she wore the new tunic dress with its lavender underdress, and she wore silver on her wrists and at her neck, and the diadem in her hair, and she had again the little tussle with Lady Waynflete over wearing the cape instead of a thin wrapper, and once again they compromised by taking the cape and the wrapper with Jainee's promise to leave the cape in the carriage.

The Westerlys were a stodgy middle-aged couple with a coterie of younger friends who were not loath to take advantage of their hospitality when town was thin of company. The food was excellent, the location of the house impeccable, the social strata impressive, and all in all, Jainee thought, all the Westerlys had to do was beckon and the whole town would obligingly come to call and play lukewarm games of piquet, whist and loo at positively frigid levels of wagering, all to pass a boring evening.

She had to hold herself back from making reckless bets just to liven things up. There wasn't a person of interest in any of the three

151

rooms in which the play was engaged, and since she was unmarried and unattended, she had to stay for the most part with Lady Waynflete, and she had to be introduced to anyone, barring Mr. Westerly, with whom she wished to converse.

It was a deadly evening, and she was sure Lady Waynflete was watching her with a jaundiced eye, and so she behaved as prettily as she knew how, minded her manners and closed her mouth when she felt the urge to be forthright.

"Well, I thought Nick and Jeremy would at least put in an appearance," Lady Waynflete said dampingly as the evening wore into a cage of pure boredom. "It would have livened things up some."

"I could read the fortune cards," Jainee suggested with gentle malice.

"Oh my dear, never! Not here, at any rate. Too upright for that sort of thing. No, we will depart soon, I promise. I am impressed with your forbearance."

Oh, she had been so good when her fingers just itched to shuffle the cards and kindle a real round of wagering and gaming the likes of which those people probably had never seen.

Yes, she had been perfect and circumspect, and even colorless, if it came to that, and Lady Waynflete had bleached the fairy tale once again in public and with her respectable face, Jainee had been once again taken into the fold.

"You do surprise me," Lady Waynflete admitted as they headed home.

"I surprise myself," Jainee said, "but look you, madame, I am not without manners or some sense of style. I will not embarrass you, I promise."

"Yes," Lady Waynflete said drily, "I do believe you have that much sensibility at least."

But did she, when she was in a fever to return to the house and lock herself away in her room and languish in the tantalizing existence of the gown that bared her breasts?

Don't take the chance of not wearing it . . .

Was that sensible, that she was even *thinking* of playing this game with him, and submitting to his sensual demands? She was no more sensible than a doorknob, she thought, and twice as hard-

152

headed.

She wanted to . . . try on the gown.

Try it on — or wear it to wait for him?

I expect it . . .

It was a game, a game of minds and wits, she thought, slipping out of her tunic and the underdress and the thin shift which underlay the whole.

Naked, except for her white silk stockings, she reached for the robe and slipped her arms into the sleeves.

It enveloped her body like a cloud of soft silk.

She fit the hook into its closure under her breasts and felt the tightening of the material around her bosom as the shape of the underbodice pushed and lifted her breasts upward and closer together in a compellingly enticing way, the silky tactile ruffles a flirty frame around them.

Her nipples hardened instantly with the unfamiliar angle of the thrust of her breasts, and her body canted to accommodate the sensuous arch of her back.

She felt liquid with the heat of her body and the naked blatant display of her breasts: she loved it. The feeling swamped her, seduced her, possessed her. Every night as she awaited him, she would feel this . . . this power, this potent femininity, this bondage to the greed of her body.

How sensible was that?

She had only to think of his powerful wet kisses and her body became liqueous with the power she could have over him. She had only to remember his seeking hands exploring the contour of her naked breasts, and she knew that if he had fondled her nipples, she would have enslaved him forever.

She knew, she knew, and she was certain he would fight and fight and make the most domineering demands, and in the end, she would subdue him.

If only he would come tonight, when her body was new to nakedness and velvet with yearning . . .

She slept, waiting in the gown as he commanded and he — he whiled away the night envisioning her just that way, compliant and waiting, naked and dressed and revealed to him all at the same time.

For that ravishing moment of revelation, he could wait. He could wait . . . but not for long.

The sensuous night magic evaporated in the morning, and when she awakened, Jainee felt not a little foolish for raising her hopes to a fever pitch and then just falling asleep.

But then, he had to come, and she stashed the gown in the wardrobe case and resolved not to be seduced by the thought of it again.

The rest of the day was spent doing the rounds, visiting, shopping, napping, reading . . . yes, reading was a treat, she had discovered; it kept her mind off of the cold-blooded lord seducer, and it stiffened her resolve to pay him back in his own coin, and so she got through the next two days and nights, even while she slipped into the gown and felt the same overwhelming sense of her feminine source and strength, and the same anomalous hatred of him who had shown it to her.

Defiantly, she went to bed without donning the gown, and she awakened all at once in the middle of the night with the sense something was wrong. And then she knew: she missed the gown and the sweet subtle nakedness of her breasts thrusts forward in that raw enticing way. Instantly, she jumped out of bed, stripped off her nightgown and ran to the wardrobe. Her hand groped for it in the dim ember-lit room and she felt a shuddering excitement as she pulled it from the wardrobe and slid her arms into the sleeves.

And then, and then—the alluring crush of her breasts as she hooked in the midriff and then turned toward the glowing firelight to adjust the set of the neckline and the thrust of her breasts.

And then she looked up—and he was there, his eyes devouring the lush fullness of her naked breasts in the gown he had designed to display them.

She felt like a goddess and he was worshipping at the shrine of her divine femininity. She didn't move. He did not command her.

"You have only just changed," he said suddenly, his eyes still ablaze with heat and desire.

She licked her lips. "I wear the gown," she said, her tone faintly defiant. "I have not reneged."

"If you did . . ." he murmured.

"If I did?" she whispered.

"You would pay the price."

Her body tingled with excitement at the thought of flaunting him, just once, oh just one little time; he might have come just five minutes sooner and found her without her gown and then—what price? She felt herself arching toward him, deliberately trying to seduce him with her breasts. "Would you send me away?"

He didn't answer; he could not keep his eyes from her billowy taut-nippled breasts, and transparent curve of her body through the gown, and the thick tuft of feminine hair so sensually visible. "I would give you a second chance," he said finally.

She moved toward him, one step. "And then?"

"Don't test me, Diana." He did not like her enigmatic smile. Or the way she moved around the room to tantalize and entice him, as if she were in control and not he. But they both knew better. She was testing him already, as she had done two nights before, turning away deliberately, and then letting him see the silhouette of her rounded peaked breasts, and then facing him, to give him a full unobstructed view.

She saw the desire flame to life in his eyes as she moved around the room, arching, bending, exaggerating her movements in order to entice him. She did it out of defiance, out of need. The air was thick with suppressed desire, his, hers, explosive with the combination of the two of them and her lush obedience to his will.

And yet it was a duel to see who would break first.

And she meant it to be him.

"Do you like the gown, my lord?" she asked softly as she flaunted her nakedness deliberately in front of him.

"I gave you the gown."

"And do I look the way you envisioned in the gown?" she went on.

"I have paid you the compliment of the gown," he growled.

Oh now . . . she narrowed her eyes and lowered them to that deliciously telling part of his body. How wonderful were the skintight pantaloons—they revealed every bulge, every thick inch, every throbbing response to her naked breasts. *He* could not hide. That pulsating iron length of him very definitely wanted her.

He watched her eyes and he could have sworn he elongated another inch under her knowing gaze. Only a jade could wear such a gown with such aplomb; that smug smile hid a world of experience.

She was exhibiting her nakedness with no sense of modesty at all: she wanted him to look, to touch, to feel. She loved the gown, she loved flaunting her breasts; if he told her to strip the gown off, she would tear it away in a second and reveal her naked body to him.

She was begging to be taken. She knew exactly the moment to tantalize and tease him by turning her back to him. She knew just when to reveal herself to him again. She did it once—twice now, and he felt like ripping the gown away and riding her taunting nakedness to hell and back.

She was the goddess of naked bitches and he was not done with her yet. He pulled a chair away from the wall with the toe of his boot. "Get over here," he commanded, and she came, twitching her hips and thrusting her breasts, her body streaming with excitement.

He pulled her into his wet greedy kiss and onto his lap as he sank into the chair. He had waited for that mouth, that hot honey of lusty avarice, who played the courtesan's games with such consummate skill. Her mouth was ready for him, eager even, her tongue teasing and inviting him to explore its lush nectar.

Hot wet voracious kisses, deep honey-wet taste of tongue, her body squirming and wriggling with the pure wanton arousal of his thick lush kisses, begging for more, arching against him, her naked breasts insistent against his chest, her bottom writhing enticingly against his iron-hard male shaft.

Her body was liquid with sensation. She felt everything all at once: the thick wetness of his kisses, the rock hard length of his manhood beneath her buttocks, the nakedness of her breasts begging for his touch. She felt his hands on her thighs, on her buttocks, on her hips, grinding her down harder and harder against his jutting length. She wanted to strip away the gown to give him all of her body, hot, naked, willing. But only if he caressed her nipples. Only if he took her there . . . only—

"Listen to me . . . listen," he growled against her mouth. "Listen, goddess of odalisques, straddle my knees facing front now,

156

and hook your legs around mine. Just like that, excellent, Diana. Now put your arms around my neck — as best you can — and don't move. Don't move . . . tilt your head back, just like that, and give me your kisses . . . yes . . ."

She gave him her mouth eagerly, arching her back slightly so that she could take the whole of his voracious tongue into her mouth, aware with renewed excitement that she was wholly revealed to him now, her legs splayed, her gown open, her breasts thrust tightly forward, her buttocks nestled firmly against the heat of his long thick hard maleness.

She savored the moment, the sensation, the lush wet kiss of the prelude to the shuddering urgency of the culmination he desired.

She felt his hand move from her chin to her neck and then to her chest, just above the rounded curve of her naked breasts. His hand was hot, hard with experience, experience of her now, his fingers circling the lush contour of her naked breasts, caressing them each, one and the other, without touching her yearning nipples, and then moving downward to part the edges of the gown and bare the rest of her body.

His hand skimmed her belly and moved downward to the thick bush of hair between her legs. And still downward — and her body shimmered in reaction as he touched so lightly her most intimate source.

She could not escape him. She could not move her legs, her hands; she would not. She pushed herself away from his invading fingers and up against the hard rock of his manhood.

"Don't move, Diana." Now he warned her, and he would have his way. His fingers skimmed her secrets again, combing through her hair, testing, seeking her velvet cleft, finding the sweet moist entrance to her deepest secret, and resting there, just at the moment of decision.

"I can't," she moaned against his lips.

"You will," he told her, and he sought a little deeper into her femininity, and a little more as her body eased back and back to bear down on his invasive fingers. "That's right, Diana. You know what to do. Please us both, vestal virgin. Now . . . and *now*," and he delved back into her mouth as her body began to respond to the stroking of his knowing fingers, began to drive and writhe against

157

them, with them, her hips gyrating wildly as sensation upon sensation built up deep within her, feelings, thoughts, glittering spasmic sensations; they climbed and climbed, going somewhere, nowhere, everywhere — his experienced hand would not let her rest from the feelings; her body pumped against his towering erection and suddenly, suddenly erupted into a gush of streaming silver that just flowed through her veins and down to the center of her womanhood.

"Oh no no no," she moaned, tearing her mouth from his.

"Oh yes yes yes," he whispered, "yes. Perfect. Excellent, Diana. Don't move. Don't . . ."

Dear lord, she couldn't, she couldn't. All she could do was focus on the bed, the huge luxurious bed that had stopped her cold when she had first walked into the room and entertained thoughts about the ramification of her bargain with Southam.

And now she was but a step away from sharing it with him, and she wondered at the amusing twist of fate and whether the gods were laughing because all her instincts, all of her sensibility had betrayed her.

Never explain, always attack, make the bargain and come away with something for yourself . . . Therese's voice, eddying away in her mind from the depths of the past into the spangling pleasure of the present.

Why not? Why not? Surely she had already gained more than she had lost: she had acquired *experience,* she had learned how to maneuver and manipulate, and with every passing night that she entered into the game, she would achieve more and more power.

She saw it so clearly: he wanted to dominate her, and he wanted to bend to her will.

But she didn't know why. He was not obsessed with her, and the farthest from any feeling at all except for his overweening need to wield the whip hand.

And he had utilized it well today; today he had made her into his compliant slave, and she was still a prisoner of that resonating pleasure and the powerful sense of her body's potency, and its potential to subjugate him.

His hand still worshipped at the altar of her femininity; his free hand tilted her mouth back to his so he could taste the voluptuous wet heat of her tongue, and when he had taken it, he moved his hand downward, ever so slowly downward to the tempting thrust of her naked breasts and began fondling and feeling them all over again.

Her body reawakened like a furling flower as he sucked the nectar from her tongue; she shimmied against him, begging those experienced fingers to find her again; she groaned deep in her throat as she bore down on his questing fingers and his ramrod manhood, and his hot hand playing with her breasts finally covered and caressed first one hard succulent nipple and then the other.

The glittering silver sensation poured through her veins again as his fingers played with and squeezed the taut yearning tips of her nipples.

She was ready, she was molten with need, and he — and he was convulsive with his engorged desire for her.

"I want you *now*." His ragged whisper sent the glittering streams of desire flowing through her. She floated in a molten haze of hot lush voluptuous sensation. She never wanted him to move his hands, his mouth, the towering granite length beneath her buttocks.

She wanted time to stop, just there, so that the feelings would go on and on forever, and she would always be on the verge of that shattering culmination.

"Oh no, Diana, this is not purely for your pleasure," he growled suddenly when she did not respond to his primitive demand.

And he lifted her; he wrapped his one arm around her midriff and just lifted her and carried her to the huge enveloping bed, and he lay her face down on the mattress and climbed onto the bed next to her, ripping off his clothes as he positioned one leg against her two to keep her from bolting.

But she didn't struggle; she felt as if this were as inevitable as the dawn, and that everything she had agreed to had been the prelude to this inescapable point.

Her body was ready for him. She felt keenly the removal of his hand, she felt empty and flushed with the shimmering excitement of wanting and waiting.

Here now he was totally, inexorably, hers, at the mercy of his rampaging manhood. She felt his hands lift the thin gauzy gown away from her body and begin caressing and stroking the long line of her back down the saucy curve of her buttocks.

And then she felt him slide his long arm under her belly to lift her and mold her tightly against the stone hard force of his naked male member.

It was like butting up against a rock, and she knew that sensation. The only difference was the feeling of skin against skin, and her dawning recognition that his granite maleness was made of flesh and muscle and towering desire.

And that, whatever the cost, she wanted it. Her body coiled with the voluptuous sense of feeling him naked and hot and hard jammed tightly against her buttocks.

He surrounded her, straddling her whole body and holding her bottom rigidly against his ramrod length.

"This," he growled into her ear, "*this* is what the goddess of Cyprians worships," and he released her middle so that she lay flat on the bed, and then he turned her so that she lay face up, faced with him, facing her fate.

She saw it first, the symbol of his power and virility, jutting at an angle away from his body from a nest of thick wiry hair. She saw the shape, elemental and proud, fleshy and rigid and thick with coursing passion. She saw its pleasure, the way it was made to fit that lush yearning secret place within her.

And she saw its innocence: the primitive mate seeking its home.

And then she saw *him*.

In the dying light of the fire, he looked like the very devil, all of him dark, his skin, the sheened muscles of his arms, the black black hair spread like a shield across his chest and trickling down down down to the very root of his secret source.

But in that ineffable moment, when everything was still and understood between them, she knew the real truth: *she* was his secret source.

She raised herself up on her elbows so that her body was one long erotic line of thrusting invitation from her protruding breasts to her long legs.

She was ready.

But what if she said no?

Oh yes, if she said no, if she denied him, the game would be on again, and the thought of delicious capitulation turned into something dark and coiling and sweet, like the thick chocolate taste of his first intentions.

She began then slowly to slide her body upward and away from him, and away from the fascination of his taut muscled body and his tactile inflexible masculinity.

It took but the time of a blink of the eye between her thought and the action; she caught him off guard, and he grabbed at her foot and she wrenched it away and scrambled to the opposite side of the bed as he pounced after her.

"What game is this, Diana? I will not pursue you."

She shrugged carelessly, her eyes narrowing as she regarded him across the expanse of the bed. "I do not wish to accommodate you tonight, my lord."

"Oh really?"

Oh, his voice sounded dark and dangerous indeed. He climbed off the bed and walked slowly around to where she stood in all her haughty glory with her smug smile and those flashing, knowing blue eyes.

He was stark naked, and the ramrod power of his erection had not diminished; it stood tall, angled and voluptuous between them.

"Tell me again, huntress, you don't wish to *what?*"

Attack, attack, attack; if she bowed down now, he would crush her with one muscular bare foot.

"I do not wish to accommodate you; that is perfectly plain, my lord." She turned away then, because her breasts, her thrusting taut tipped breasts would betray her, that just looking at him made her nipples stiff with desire, and he would see it, and he would know.

But he had seen; he reached out and he hauled her around to face him. "You lie, huntress. Here is what I taught your body today—here . . ." and he reached out and cupped her naked breasts and moved his thumbs over her rock hard nipples until she felt like swooning from the sensation.

"Your nipples want me," he growled, thrusting his blatant manhood against her body as he fondled the hard taut peaks, "your body is hot and wet and waiting for me, your mouth, did it not talk

161

lies, would beg for my kisses, wouldn't it, Diana . . ." he moved in closer still, his manhood like a primitive iron bar between them, "wouldn't it?" and he took her mouth then in a naked, raw display of potency and then he abruptly released her.

"I never wanted a woman so much I would beg, Diana, but I promise you that *you* will beg; you will beg for my kisses, and my caresses, and you will beg me to suck your nipples, and you will plead for my force of life to enter your body. You will pay for this night, Diana, mark my words."

The fury of his anger shimmered between them. *Attack, attack, attack, and come away with something . . . a woman always pays . . .*

She drew herself up and away from him. "Not I, my lord. I will *never* beg, not for your kisses, not for your caresses — *never.* You called me the huntress and it is apt. I am that, and there are times I would accept your favors, and times I would not. And if you cannot abide by whichever whim moves me, then I will find a hundred other men who *would* be willing to accept whatever I chose to offer. And you will not be one of them. Or you will be down on your knees in supplication first."

"I will kill the man who touches you."

She smiled then, the killingly smug smile of amusement that he hated. "How would you know, my lord? While you are out carousing and gambling and doing whatever it is that lords do in town — how would you know? If you have such easy access to this house, why cannot another man? One who would be willing to kiss me and caress me and adore me, and take me at my word if I chose not to grant him my favors? Some men are content just to worship a woman from afar . . ."

Oh, she was treading right over the line: she saw it in his face.

"You are a bitch, Diana, and now, I will not fall down and worship your considerable charms. I would rather leave you to the folly of believing some other fool would."

"It is possible. Jeremy, perhaps . . . ?"

She had almost, almost goaded him too far, with her mocking tone of voice, and provocative erotic images of a parade of men kneeling before her and kissing her naked feet, working their way

162

slowly slowly up her voluptuous body to her woman-essence and her luscious taut-nippled breasts. Damn her!

His manhood was like a volcano ready to erupt as the picture of her, naked, with a line of men just aching to do whatever she wanted and needed, flooded his mind

"I will kill the man who touches you," he said again, reaching for his clothes, for his sanity. "No one fondles your body until I am finished with you."

"And are you finished with me for tonight?" she asked insinuatingly, watching his face, playing with his emotion deliberately, hatefully—she didn't know what she felt.

"I don't beg," he said with heavy finality. "You are the one who must sleep alone—tonight."

Ahhh—he had scored the hurt at last: he could ease his lust tonight, anytime, anywhere that he chose.

She felt an irrational fury that he had such a freedom and she had to quell the spiralling erotic feelings within her—alone.

"We will see who begs who for what, my lord," she said testily, coldly watching him throw on his shirt and step into his trousers which, when he had pulled them up, did nothing to disguise the blatant bulge between his legs.

She turned away from him then, because if she didn't, she knew she would attack him. In her mind, she pictured him leaving the house, driving to one of the clubs and upon leaving his carriage, being accosted by a beautiful woman. She envisioned the moment in her imagination: the woman coming forward, immediately aware of the throbbing evidence of his virility, and holding out her hands, begging him to come with her, telling him she wanted his kisses, his caresses, she would do anything for him; she would caress him, running her hands all over the clothed ramrod length of him. She would strip off her clothes for him and lead him, compliant, pleading, to her bed.

She couldn't bear to think of the rest of it. She would make him pay for this indignity.

"Poor lonely goddess. Up on the mountain it gets cold, Diana. Never forget. Especially when you could be warm with kisses and caresses and the heat of your desire—"

"No!" She whirled to face him. "No, my lord. I would rather

163

freeze."

"You have only to ask, Diana."

"To beg, you mean. To get on my knees to you and I will never do that."

"So we shall see, bitch. So we shall see." He moved swiftly then to gather the rest of his things and he opened the door.

She said nothing; she looked magnificent, with her naked breasts heaving with emotion, and her lush body outlined against the firelight in the transparent gown that he had had made for her. But there was no appreciation for that either, he thought darkly, and he closed the door against her resistance.

She felt numb and naked in the most soul-searing way; she wanted to shroud herself in the neutrality of darkness and banish the insinuating thoughts of the beautiful submissive woman who awaited him somewhere beyond her door.

You wait, my lord, you just wait, she thought ominously, *you will not have it all your own way because you are a man. I will have to teach you, my lord, that the player who holds the winning card does not necessarily win the hand.*

Chapter Nine

And the lessons would begin the very next day, she decided, when a very reluctant and exasperated Jeremy Waynflete appeared that afternoon with a parade of his friends whom she had met at the opera.

"Why, it's Lord Griswold, is it not? And my Lords Ottershaw and Tavender—of course I remember you," she said with every evidence of delight and, perhaps, calculation when she saw Jeremy's face darken perceptibly at her ingenuousness.

Nor was he happy with the way she was dressed. Her dark blue cambric muslin dress had a deep vee neckline which Marie had altered considerably to reveal more bosom than should normally be seen in the afternoon, and Jainee had insisted on an edging of rich lace to outline and frame the obvious changes.

It was very effective. Three men crowded around her like little boys, vying for a smile and a kind word.

It was too perfect. Jeremy rang for tea, pumping at the bell-pull like he was ringing a fire alarm, and Lady Waynflete came running, sure something awful was amiss, and was staggered to find Jeremy sitting to one side like a sulking child watching Jainee play lady of the manor with his three best friends, who had turned into salivating idiots.

Of course she must take charge. Jainee ought to have called her to begin with.

"Oh, but I had no idea," Jainee excused herself prettily. "This is my lady's son and his friends, surely to be considered members of the family . . ."

165

"I think *not*," Jeremy said thunderously, and Lady Waynflete quelled him with one telling look.

"Miss Bowman will not make that mistake again when she realizes that at every stage of her career, whether it be in her home or in public, her conduct must be irreproachable," Lady Waynflete said, not without irony as she eyed the questionable neckline of Jainee's new gown. "I must infer her intentions were sincere, and of course we know she is accustomed to playing hostess in her own right . . ."

Jainee had the grace to feel a wave of heat flush her cheeks, and then a bolt of anger that Lady Waynflete should refer to her disreputable past so publicly.

But then, she had chosen to toss a sop to Jeremy's sensibilities at the expense of Jainee's image: she had no loyalty to her protegée whatsoever, except that she wished to indulge Nicholas Carradine, and Jainee could perfectly understand that and still feel that Lady Waynflete had not had the right to chastise her just that way.

However it was of no moment to the men who could not keep their eyes off of her. Only Jeremy understood, and she met his angry gaze with bland indifference, and then bent her attention to Charles Griswold, who was asking her something annoyingly banal about the performance of the opera she had attended.

The tea arrived, and with it a tray of edibles, a light early afternoon repast; Blexter interrupted the conversation at one point to announce several more visitors: Chevrington and Annesley, who was also an intimate of both Southam and Jeremy, and before the clock struck one, there was a lively little party in progress in the Waynflete parlor.

Jainee was behaving unexceptionally, Lady Waynflete thought, as she monitored her manners throughout the whole of the spirited conversation. Jainee sat demurely in the midst of what amounted to a coterie of the top of the *ton*, eligible men whom mothers would kill to drag to an evening's party let alone a tedious afternoon of tea and tittle-tattle, and she was neither forward nor inordinately attentive to any one of the men.

She spoke with verve and humor to each in turn, and made

amusing observations on the little she had seen of London and its preening society, and she did *nothing* to command the obsessive interest in her except look gloriously beautiful and aloofly seductive.

Lady Waynflete was about ready to throw in her hand and tell Southam he could not make a silk purse out of a silk purse, and she would turn his life inside out and upside down if he proceeded for one more moment with his mad plan.

Of course, he arrived in the midst of the merriment and stood there, after Blexter had announced him, looking murderous as he surveyed the scene.

"Do join us," Lady Waynflete invited, and he moved slowly and irritably into the room, and took a seat next to Jeremy who looked as out of patience as he felt.

"She's a damned siren," Jeremy whispered as he passed a plate of something to him: he didn't know what he picked up from it and popped into his mouth. It was a relief to chew on something, because he felt like biting Jainee, and that would have caused a riot.

But then he hadn't expected to find her in an admiring sea of all his closest friends. He had anticipated that she had come out the worse for wear from their battle of wits and wills. He had not reckoned on her making good on her threat less than twenty-four hours after she had issued it.

He should have known: the huntress would forever be on the prowl and *nothing* would ever satisfy her lust to ravish her prey.

She looked ravishing this day; her skin was flushed with delicate color from her cheeks right down to the tempting hollow of her exposed bosom, and her eyes gleamed with that feral humor he so disliked. She was watching him, provoking him with her cheeky little references to how sweet it was that all these dear men had come to call on her. How kind they were; how they had complimented her all out of hand and just made her blush.

And how they were all just watching her as she bent forward to speak to each and all of them, hoping to catch a glimpse of those pert naked breasts beneath the thin cover of that obscenely low neckline.

167

She was not naive; she knew what she was doing, and most of all, she understood exactly what she was doing to them and to him.

And yet, her manner and her manners were impeccable; she said nothing unseemly to anyone and each of them could not keep his eyes off of her.

It was Lady Waynflete who decided to topple her oh so virtuous virgin from her pedestal. "Did you know," she asked brightly, "that Miss Bowman reads fortune cards?"

Her announcement caused an immediate hubbub and each of her fawning new acquaintances begged for her to read his cards.

"Really, Miss Bowman—I met you first, I believe that is an entitlement."

"Nonsense! She was introduced to my *family* first, isn't that so, Lady Waynflete; did she not meet my mother before we met at the opera? That gives *me* several hours up on you, Chevrington."

"Boys, boys, boys," Lady Waynflete said gently, holding up her hands. She had known them all since practically the cradle, and she had no intention of letting this party trick get out of hand. If anything, she had wanted it to diminish Jainee in their eyes, but they were so dazzled they could see nothing but her pushed-up bosom and her tantalizing cat-eyes. "We'll send for Marie—she knows where you keep the cards, my dear?"

"She does," Jainee said, slanting a coaxing little smile at Chevrington.

Lady Waynflete summoned Blexter who would relay the demand to Marie.

The room settled into an excited silence, and everyone's eyes focused on Jainee's elusive smile until Blexter returned with her little leather pouch, carried disdainfully on a silver salver which he placed before Lady Waynflete.

"Thank you, Blexter." He withdrew, and Lady Waynflete surveyed the scene benignly. They were all like eager little schoolboys, with exception of Nick and Jeremy, who sat slightly apart looking bored and faintly annoyed.

"Now Jainee, my dear, I do believe that Nick needs his fortune

168

told. He has been supremely out of sorts since we returned to London. So come, make room for Jainee and Nick shall benefit from the wisdom of the cards today."

The scramble to give over a seat to Jainee was almost comical, but Nick did not move, thus forcing *her* to come to him, and she was very well aware of it. Chevrington moved a chair so that she faced him directly, and she thanked him so seductively that Nicholas almost reached across the table which Jeremy had set in front of him, and slapped her.

She sat down opposite him in an exaggerated way so that he got a full good view of her luscious breasts, and so did each of the men surrounding her.

She sent him a provoking smile. "Let us begin, my lord."

She took the pouch, removed the cards, and shuffled them. Then she handed them to Nicholas to both inspect and shuffle. He gave them back to her and she indicated he should cut them with his left hand.

He did this and she took the deck and began counting out the first seven cards, laying the seventh one face up and reunited the previous six cards with the rest of the deck. She did this twelve times so that twelve cards were laid face up between them.

The silence, as they all awaited her interpretation, was breathtaking.

Even she was slightly startled at the way the cards turned up and she looked up at him uncertainly, all the *coquetterie* washed from her expression, and set the remainder of the deck aside pensively.

"Pure mumbo-jumbo," Nicholas snapped, irritated by the unnatural silence and Jainee's inordinately solemn expression.

"Of course, my lord," she said lightly. "Magic and sleight of hand; however, the cards come up inordinately negative. Are you certain you wish to hear?"

"How do I know they are *my* cards," Nicholas demanded aggressively.

She pointed to the Jack of hearts. "The eligible man, my lord, and he is you. You have cut the cards. The fortune reads for you."

169

Nicholas leaned back in his chair and looked around at the somewhat anxious faces of his friends.

The woman was a witch: how had she got them all so fraught with worry about what the cards revealed, he wondered. Even he was not immune to her magic.

"Read the cards," he said easily, understanding now that she had woven a spell out of the mystery of the reading and the anxiety of the participants. She was quite amazing, really; it almost seemed like she managed the illusion unconsciously, that she fed on the emotions in the room.

"Very well, my lord. The Jack heart reverse signifies yourself, but it also connotes a person who might have been useful to you. Don't count on it. And here, another warning about someone who will betray you. A surprise, here, unpleasant; perhaps something you were expecting that will not come to hand. But you will have success — in gambling, in speculation, the cards do not specify. I see — I see love affairs, a marriage proposal, but it is true, too, that you will have to wait for your plans to come to fruition. There are three warnings, one of bad news, one a betrayal, and one an unexpected journey. The cards have foretold it, my lord."

They were riveted: she was so sure.

She took the deck and integrated the cards. "We will proceed. We will read for the person, the house, the future and the surprise."

She shuffled the cards again, presented them to him to be cut, reformed the deck and dealt out four sets of three cards each.

"The first pack," she continued, "denotes the person, yourself, my lord. You will be involved in love affairs, but some *one* will become your lover. But still, beware the deceptive one, my lord, for in your house there will be bad news and no success in some future venture. Someone will surprise you, my lord, and so here, in the future, there will be money, illegal profits, perhaps . . . prison. Yet here, in the surprise, the cards show happiness, some discord, and ultimately, my lord, a probable marriage."

She lay the cards aside just as he broke into sardonic applause.

"Wonderful, Miss Bowman. Wonderful. A complete fairy tale, deliciously entertaining."

"But you must read my fortune next," Charles Griswold interposed.

"And mine." This from Chevrington and Tavender simultaneously.

Jainee put up her hands in protest. "Truly, I would *love* to *accommodate* all of you," she said with just a trace of archness in her voice as she angled an insolent look at Nicholas' implacable expression, "but reading the cards makes me *so* tired."

She turned her attention directly to Chevrington, quite powerfully aware that Nicholas was simmering with displeasure, and she told him how delightful it had been to see him again, and he rose and bowed over her hand and got as good a view down her dress as anyone had that afternoon.

And Nicholas watched her blatant playing out of this scene with grim amusement. She manipulated everything, from her ingenuous little protestation right down to the order in which her guests would leave, each stopping at her chair to have a private word of farewell, and each taking his damned time while he stood over her and enjoyed the beguiling fantasy of possessing those nakedly displayed breasts.

Finally it was his turn, but he did not rise up to pay his respects: he waited until, after an uncomfortable moment, she arose and came to him.

"My lord, I hope my reading gave you pleasure."

"You were most accommodating," he said insolently, looking up at her through hooded eyes, liking the fact she knew not what to do in the face of his extremely bad manners and his rude references.

Her eyes flashed, and the cat-smile appeared. "I wish I could have accommodated *all* the other gentlemen, but, well, there will be other times, other places, do you not agree, my Lord?"

"Which you will embrace with both hands in your ongoing effort to give pleasure in all quarters," Nicholas growled.

"I'm sure my new friends will agree that it is a fine thing to give pleasure where and when one can," Jainee said, "and I'm positive they all appreciate a woman who can *accommodate* their various caprices. That is surely what makes one woman more desirable than the next, and the thing that makes a man a willing thrall to her tyranny."

"But who enslaves who?" Chevrington asked coyly.

"Why my lord, I leave that for you to—uncover," she said pertly, and she turned to Nicholas. "I bid you good afternoon, my lord," and she bowed deeply, deliberately, enragingly, and rose up, imperious as any wanton and sailed out of the room like a queen.

She was so pleased with herself: she had vanquished Nicholas Carradine and made him understand fully that any man he knew was as easy to manipulate as a piece of raw material in her hands.

He would not be so complacent about their bargain from now on, she thought as she closeted herself in her room, allowed Marie to help undress her, and then wrapped herself in a chintz robe in preparation for resting before dinner.

It would be early tonight: Lady Waynflete was going out and Jainee was not invited, a fact which actually relieved her. It meant she need not dress formally for dinner and that she would have an evening to herself, although what she would do with all that solitude, she did not know.

Marie bustled in with her dress which she laid on the bed. "All goes well, mademoiselle? The card reading this afternoon? Monsieur was pleased?"

"Monsieur is never pleased and I intend never to give him that satisfaction," Jainee said lazily.

"You have reason," Marie agreed. "When a man is satiated, his interest goes far afield. Do not give Monsieur the opportunity until you have accomplished your ends."

"My thinking exactly," Jainee murmured, fingering the luxurious silken material of the gown.

"Monsieur has been generous, mademoiselle."

"In this respect, yes," Jainee agreed, giving herself over to Marie's experienced hands.

172

Marie helped her wash down her bare skin and helped her into the silken stockings that matched the dress. She wore only the thin underdress of the garment beneath a pleated muslin gown with long banded sleeves.

Marie fussed, straightening a line there, pulling up the shoulder line here, making sure that her breasts were cupped precisely into the bosom line of the bodice which was detailed with satin ribbon edging which outlined the shape of her breasts.

The effect was stunning, and she wore white kid slippers with white satin ties *a la Roman,* and a satin ribbon bound up in her luxuriant hair.

"Madame will not be pleased with the alteration of the bosom," Marie murmured, as she tied another white satin ribbon under Jainee's breasts and fastened it behind so that the long ends fluttered behind her when she walked.

"But we are looking to please Monsieur," Jainee pointed out, turning this way and that in the mirror. "Yes, this is excellent: that Madame Signy did not like to show a woman's breasts, I will tell you. And of course the whole will be wasted on Lady Waynflete anyway. No matter, this is the simplest of the gowns, and meant for dining *en famille,* and I shall be able to wear it again on another occasion."

"The time will soon come when mademoiselle may begin her search in earnest."

"Yes," Jainee said, her expression turning sober. "I don't know what I expected when I made this devil's bargain with Monsieur, but I cannot let myself forget my purpose. It is so easy to be seduced by inconsequentials."

"I do not call Monsieur inconsequential," Marie murmured, as she escorted Jainee out the door.

"Nothing about Monsieur is negligible," Jainee said drily.

"Then do not trifle with him," Marie advised. "At least—not for long."

"I will not, of course, allow them to make you into a party game," Lady Waynflete said over dessert, after a pleasant dinner

173

consisting of two of each course and a stream of trivialities. "Your behavior was almost unexceptional this afternoon, barring the last moments with Nicholas. I cannot understand why you must goad him in that brazen way. It is *not* the thing and surely it made you appear in a lesser light to the gentlemen who witnessed it."

Jainee thought not but forebore to mention it. "I will try to contain my temper," she said meekly.

"And I will try not to comment on the unseemly aspect of your new gowns, which have obviously been remodeled."

"Thank you, my lady. As we have said, I am no green girl and I am proud of my stature and my style."

Lady Waynflete's mouth tightened slightly. "We will leave it at that. I will leave you now before we come to blows over what constitutes style. I wish you a profitable evening, Jainee. I will see you in the morning."

The house seemed cavernous and empty without her, as if the mere force of Lady Waynflete's personality inhabited it. In truth, there was little to occupy her except if she chose to read a book.

There was a room full of them and she wandered aimlessly along the shelves looking for something that wasn't poetry or a philosophical tract, and she settled finally on a novel, and took the book with her upstairs to her room.

"Madame is perceptive," she told Marie, "but she will not fight it."

Marie unhooked the dress, untied the sash and slipped the dress over her head. Jainee picked up the chintz robe which was laying on the bed.

"Not Monsieur's?" Marie asked softly as she hung the dress in the wardrobe.

Jainee stiffened. "Not Monsieur's," she said into the lingering pause, and she picked up the robe and slipped it over the thin underdress.

Marie knew. She hated that, but she should have expected it. She wrapped the robe tightly around her as if it could protect her from Marie's comprehension and Southam's wrath.

"You may go," she told Marie coldly, and Marie withdrew without a word.

She should not encourage Marie to become a confidant, she thought, climbing up into the bed with a candlestick and the book. Did she really think she was going to read? Look at her— she had not bothered to remove either her undress or her slippers and stockings. Clear clues, surely, that she really wanted to be going *somewhere*.

She felt as if it were a night when everyone had something to do except her; she even felt a little rancor that Lady Waynflete had not included her in her plans.

Tonight, the book was boring. Reading was for a rainy afternoon when callers were few and far between and there was a cozy fire in the parlor fireplace, and chocolate, steaming and rich, at her elbow.

And the chocolate pot aimed at Southam's most proud possession. She did enjoy thinking about how she had bested him that afternoon. He had not been able to constrain her yet, and she meant to make it as hard as possible for him to ever have his way.

But why was she even thinking of insolent arrogant Lord Southam who was as high-handed as a judge and jury combined. The next encounter would be soon, perhaps at the Tallingers' dinner, and she would tweak him and twiddle him and make him sorry he ever tried to dictate to *her*.

"I told you that you had better not take the chance of not wearing the gown I had made for you." He closed the door behind him and strolled into the room. "Or did you conveniently forget the terms of our agreement?"

She was sprawled seductively across the bed, and she raised herself on one elbow and turned her head as she heard his voice. Her heart started to pound with a defiant excitement. She hadn't expected him this night. Maybe she hadn't expected him ever again.

"I did not forget," she whispered.

"Then strip off your clothes and put on that gown. This is the second chance, huntress, and I am past patience with you already from this afternoon."

"I am comfortable as I am."

"But I am not comfortable not seeing your naked breasts, Diana. Strip and put on the gown so that I may take my pleasure."

She didn't move. No, she lay there, looking at him with that *make me* glow in her eyes that just begged him to force the issue.

He couldn't wait. He hauled her off the bed and inserted his fingers between her breasts and ripped the robe and whatever it was she wore beneath fair off her body in one violent convulsive tear.

"Get the gown."

She could not argue now; she turned, lusciously naked except for her silky stockings and delicate slippers, and pulled open the door of the wardrobe and took out the gown.

"Put it on."

She turned to face him as she inserted her arms into the sleeves, her breasts heaving, her nipples as stiff as two round hard pebbles, her blazing eyes inscrutable as the sky. Her body quivered as she fastened the undermidriff that lifted and crushed her breasts together, and then lowered her arms and faced him defiantly. "And now my lord has all that he wishes."

"Not *all*, Diana," he contradicted softly. "There is still the matter of your intractability, and the fact that I warned you not to test the limits of my good nature."

"My lord's nature could hardly be called *accommodating*," she said slyly, dangerously. Oh why, oh why did she want to push him and push him, to goad him past the breaking point? His veneer of civility right at this moment was as brittle as ice. Was she deliberately looking to crack it so she could fall into the pond and drown?

There was a thick tense sensual aura in the room: the scent of wanting, one; the other, who would break the ice?

"No, huntress, that is the side of *your* nature which you must acknowledge by the terms of our bargain. I promised any deviation would be punished—" he reached for her once again, grasping her arms and pulling her forward to him, hard against his chest, "and it *will* be."

176

He sank onto the bed with her, and despite her flailing arms and her thrusting legs, he managed to turn her over his lap; the minute he pushed up the gauzy folds of her gown, she quieted.

"What are you going to do?" she whispered.

He stared at the ripe luscious line of her naked buttocks and the sweet secretive fold between. "I am going to exact the punishment you deserve for your disobedience, goddess. Even you warrant a spanking when you behave like a child."

He lifted his hand and brought it down on her plush bare skin, once, twice—she squirmed and tried to shimmy away from him, and he brought down his other hand, hard, on the small of her back to prevent her escaping.

Smack! Smack! Enough to sting, enough to command her submission to his bidding. Enough to make her feel explosive with anger and the desire to turn the tables on him once again because the action of subjugating her was so arousing to him.

She saw the way. In a second, she squirreled her hand under her body and between his knees, groping for the rock hard bulge of his turgid manhood. Oh yes, that was the way; two fingers, three—she could stroke the tight taut sacs beneath his jutting member, and work her way up to the inflexible rod of his male root. And he would feel it.

Smack! He felt it; his hand lay on her naked bottom as his elongating male length responded to the firm caressing touch of her fingers. He felt it: his hand began rubbing and stroking the firm cushion of her buttocks in tandem with her groping, knowing fingers.

His knees parted to give her wider access to his throbbing erection, and she slipped her wanton fingers deep between his legs and began to fondle him every which way she could think of.

He loved it; she could feel his tiny incremental moves of pleasure, his rhythmic caress of her naked buttocks. What a wonder this virile maleness was, how hard and thick and *long* it got; it moved against her fingers, almost as if it had a life of its own. In her mind's eye, she could see it, see him naked as he had been the previous several nights before, with this thrusting jutting proof of his prowess so primitive and *male* between them.

177

And she saw too that with her aggressive move, she had obtained momentary mastery over him.

But not for long.

"The goddess knows everything," he murmured hoarsely, "especially how to pleasure a man. It is a fine thing to give pleasure where and when one can," he added with irony, quoting her. "And to learn how to manipulate your way out of paying for your conceits. It is time to test whether your punishment taught you anything, Diana, besides where to find a man's weakest point. You may rest assured that I am strong enough not to give in to it. Now lay still."

Her body tightened in resistance.

He smacked her buttocks again, lightly, warningly, and she stopped squirming.

He felt ready to erupt, but all he did was take advantage of having her laying compliantly across his lap, plotting her next devious move no doubt, but still and all, for the moment, surrendering to his will.

Her lush curvy buttocks invited his caress, but he knew, he knew, the moment he ran his hands over them, he would be lost to her. Yet he wanted to be lost, and he wanted to give in. But she was not soft, not yielding. She was prickly and combative, and he would subjugate her, and make her plead for his kisses and beg for his favors, and then, finally, his fascination with her might abate.

He gave in to the tempting allure of her buttocks, running his hands all over them and downward, to her thighs and her hosed legs, picking at the knitted garters of her stockings, sliding his hands under the silky covering and feeling the firm flesh of her leg, first one and then the other, becoming unbearably excited by the sight of her stockinged legs.

He couldn't give into it: he couldn't.

How could he not? She was the embodiment of desire, the goddess of temptresses, every inch of her the siren, enticing him beyond his endurance.

Her questing hand became bolder, seeking the most hidden place between his legs; he reacted instantly, almost violently to

178

the feeling of a carnal caress where no woman's hand had ever ventured. He toppled her sideways, onto her back, and climbed up over her to straddle her body.

"No, oh no," she hissed, immediately rolling onto her side to try to wriggle away.

"Oh yes, oh yes," he growled, reaching out to grasp her leg and pull her back under his extended legs. "Don't move, Diana. I am stronger than you, and faster; you will not get away."

She heaved herself up onto her elbows, and watched him through blazing, resentful eyes as he began to undress, stripping off each piece of clothing and tossing it every which way until he was wholly naked right before her insolent gaze.

His huge, bulging manhood jutted out at her like a challenge, an enthralling reminder that it was she who had caressed it into rock hard male-proud tumescence. Her body reacted to it, her nipples peaking before her eyes into stiff taut points of pleasure; and her womanhood reacted to it with hot yielding sensations.

And he reacted to her as he kneeled over her and watched the fertile excitement of his sex envelop her senses. "Your body cannot lie, Diana. You cannot hide the longing of your nipples, or the liquid heat of your need. You have only to ask for what you want."

"I will not ask," she said through gritted teeth, her body shuddering with convulsive tension.

He edged himself closer so that her whole world at that moment was the throbbing hard length of him. "This is the game, goddess. I command, you comply. Those are the terms of our bargain. I swore to have all of you. And you swore you were mine to command." He leaned forward and cupped her lush thrusting breasts. "Beg for what you want, Diana."

Oh, she hated him. He stood over her like some marble incarnation of male passion personified, as hard and as cold as a statue, as distant.

But her body told her differently. Her body felt hot waves of excitement at the thought of even saying the forbidden, of crossing the line between what she was now, and what she would be were she to answer her body's sumptuous pressing desire.

179

"But you will," he murmured with arrogant surety, moving his hands over her breasts to lightly stroke her nipples, gossamer touches, tormenting caresses that sent a thick sensation of pleasure trickling through her.

Her eyes closed, her body quivered. Her mouth did not move. *If only he would squeeze . . .*

Her body writhed with invitation, the transparent gown falling away from her legs, exposing the lush mound of her femininity. Her body, compelled by the gorgeously sumptuous feelings he aroused in her taut hard nipples, mindlessly sought the next step in their erotic waltz.

She could hardly bear the feeling in her nipples; it kept building and building and then suddenly it stopped at the very moment it might have peaked into something explosive and convulsive: he had removed his fingers.

She forced back the feeling of hot resentment she felt; she felt abandoned, she felt desperate, but she would not beg.

His eyes were implacable, flat, the banked desire flaming to life as he lifted one of her bare legs.

"Lay back."

She didn't want to do it; her arms were aching, and she would die before she would obey any command of his. She wanted to see everything, every last expression on his face, every last inch of his rampaging manhood.

She wanted to see his eyes. There was a boiling point in a man of which women had no conception. She wanted to see it, she wanted to use it.

He began to unravel the satin ties of her slipper. His hand shook as he braced her leg against his matte hairy chest and began slowly removing her long silky stockings, sliding them off inch by inch, savoring the feel of her leg under his hands until finally he reached her foot.

And then the other, first the ties and then the slow sensual slide of silk down her leg . . .

And she watched, and she wondered about the nature of a man's arousal and how just the mere act of undressing her leg made him hot and hard with lust.

180

And what if, she wondered as his shaking fingers removed the second stocking from her foot, she wore stockings and ribbons bound round her leg apart from the shoe. What if she wore silk and satin ribbons bound round her whole body? Would his hand tremble so tellingly? Could she, through the means of lacing her body with strips of satin and silk, subjugate him to her nakedness?

The thought excited her beyond anything, and this was the nature of her arousal. When he came to her, as she conceived of the idea and as she envisioned the long snaking trails of satin winding around her naked body, she was soft and yielding, her thrusting breasts like twin does, inviting his hungry mouth, her body moving downward in concert with his.

He surrounded her body, and dipped his head to feed on her succulent nipples and she writhed with pleasure as he took one into his mouth and began sucking it, and then the other, sucking, wetly sucking and drawing its taut tip still further and further into the wet heat of his mouth and the molten sensations in her nipples engulfed her all over again.

His manhood nudged at her body, his knee easing her legs apart so that he could just slide himself gently within the satin fold of her most secret place.

She felt it; she knew it. He had done this before with his hand and she had loved it. She braced her body, waiting for the next thrust when he would settle himself against that pure point of pleasure that sent her into silvery convulsions.

But it was different this time. The thrust of him combined with his avid sucking on her turgid nipples sent hot waves of yearning through her. Her body lifted, of its own volition, to meet the angle of his entrance and with one long plunge, he possessed her, barely noting in his ramrod force the fragile barrier which hardly impeded his way.

And so *this* was *experience,* she thought in the one hellish moment she felt the sharp tear of pain; and then she understood that his thick iron bar shaft was deep inside *her,* and her whole body stiffened and scrambled to get away.

This was possession, this was the overtaking of the whole of a person's body and soul and owning it. *This, oh god, this* . . . she let down her guard for a minute, thinking how she might overpower *him,* and he did this to her: turned her into a vassal enslaved by the mastery of his primitive male invasion.

And she could not get away; his whole weight pressed her down into that thick luxurious mattress. She could not fight him; he held her, he had conquered her, and he triumphed.

It was there in his face, the emotion in his eyes.

"The goddess is mortal after all," he whispered.

"The goddess is a vessel, nothing more, like any other woman," she spat, pushing at his hard hairy chest. "Get off of me. Get away from me."

"But why should I? I have you now, Diana."

"No . . ."

"Yes." He began to move now and she felt a faint rim of excitement begin to expand within her.

What *was* this, that she could fight to escape it, and then suddenly capitulate to it as it moved insidiously within her body?

It crept up on her as she tried futilely to fight his carnal penetration and the pumping possessive movement of his body against her. *It* washed up and over her like an inexorable wave, carrying her with it, never letting her gasp for air. It was a tidal wave of feeling, utterly voluptuous, a cascade of sensation as if there were a waterfall of glittering hot points spangling all over her body and coming to rest someplace in the deep feminine fold of resistance that he held in his thrall.

And it was different from before, and it was the same. She knew it and it was utterly wondrous, and it was all connected to him in this mysterious bonding of their bodies: the summit of *experience.*

And he was not immune to it, either. There was something nascent deep in his eyes as he regarded her from the advantage of his elbow-supported height.

"Goddess of desire," he murmured, "no longer immune to the pleasures of the flesh of her gratification in surrender."

"Nonsense," she snapped, instantly feeling trapped by the betrayal of her body and his "cock-of-the-walk" smugness. "That

182

was not surrender. That was merely the opening of hostilities, my lord. That was *nothing,* purely nothing except your self-indulgence. You have proved it, my lord. You *are* stronger than I. Now, are we finished?"

"By damn," he growled, "it would take a Hercules to deal with your insubordinate temper, Diana, but I swear I am up to the task. Perhaps this is but the fulfillment of the prophecy of the cards. Perhaps you even devised this entire seduction by tempting me to deny the destiny of my fortune."

There was never a man as vexatious as he; she could not even dignify that goading remark with any kind of denial. *"Are we finished?"* she demanded, feeling her patience fragmenting as he did not move and he continued to look at her as if she were something he had never seen before.

"No, Diana. We are but beginning."

He lowered himself so that his mouth was but a breath away from hers.

"We will see whether it was *nothing,* Diana," he murmured, as he thrust himself more tightly within her silken core. "We will see . . ." and he settled his mouth on hers tightly, invasively, commandingly.

But why wasn't it over? she wondered as she fought with him, pushed him, beat at his shoulders, and bucked her body against the inexorable force of his manhood.

But that served no purpose other than to embed his hard heat more deeply within her. It was a miracle how her body accommodated him, how the hard length and towering fullness of him was sheathed by the velvet haven of her femininity. It was unspeakably raw and elemental and she felt the resistance draining from her as his mouth possessed her as intensely and relentlessly as his volatile manhood possessed her body.

She wanted to get away, she wanted to stay. Someplace in the explosiveness of their union, in the erotic fit of their bodies together, in her throbbing embrace of his towering erection, someplace *there,* something changed. Something slipped away from her—her sense of culmination eddied into something different, something devastatingly unexpected: the need for *more.*

It was as if the one fed the other, that having *experienced* that bone-melting pleasure, her body could remember it, recreate it, demand it be fed once again from the well of his sustenance.

She hated her body for its betrayal of her mind, but even that was irrelevant to her gradual and shocking sense of his hot bare body pressing down on hers; his rough haired chest scraping her tender breasts; the nakedness of him deep deep within the carnal heat of *her;* the very openness of her body as it encompassed his lusty possession—all these feelings coalesced into one voluptuous slide of torrid yearning for his driving completion.

Her body arched against him at the ravishing thought, pushing him still deeper into her womanly mystery.

"Ah, Diana, how voracious you are—just like a goddess, taking, taking, taking," he whispered against her mouth. "But this time, you cannot command. This time, you must beg."

"Never," she hissed.

His tongue moved over the shape of her mouth, the very same lips that just defied him. "Soon this mutinous mouth will entreat me to unleash the pleasure of your body. You feel it now, Diana. Your body moves, languid with the heat of voluptuous yearning. You are so hot, so enticing. You have the power, goddess; all you need do is say the words."

"I will *not,*" she ground out; instantly he covered her mouth, muttering, "Silence, huntress; it is *my* game," and his hot wet kisses took her to a lush simulation of the duel between them and showed her just who would win in the end.

And he did not move, except to thrust himself more tightly against her and deep, deep within her voluptuously enveloping sheath. He wanted her to feel him there in all his primitive nakedness; he wanted her to surrender to the torrid sensations of her body as he possessed her. He wanted all of her, he wanted to drain her so there would be nothing left for anyone else.

He wanted her utter and complete submission to *him* and no one else. The very thought of it made him spurt with a torrent of excitement.

But she—she would torment him; she would withhold everything until they both couldn't bear it and then—she *might* capit-

184

ulate.

God, he hated and he adored the mystery of a woman; had he not vowed never to become enslaved because of his deep-seated fear of abandonment? And would she not tromp on him the moment she was satiated and tired of him?

Oh yes; a woman like this, full of vinegar and vengeance, full of the sense of her power of men, a woman like this would kick the dirt of her shoes in his face and think it an amusing trick just as she was turning to the next man for admiration and dalliance.

A woman like her . . .

Her body shifted again, her hips shimmying against the thick force of his virility, a mute demand for its pumping prowess to possess her.

"Oh no, Diana, oh no. Only your words can unleash the power in me to pleasure you. Come down from your mountain, Diana. These feelings are as elemental as the earth. Your body knows it. Your body begs me. See how you move against me; your hips entice me, pleading with me to join your dance. How does your mouth, Diana? Can your lips shape the words?"

She shook her head mutely, her hips jamming against his inflexible erection, imploring him to move, to begin his masterful drive to inexorable release.

"Diana . . ." he whispered hoarsely, clamping his hot hands over her plunging hips.

"Oh God, oh lord, oh yes," she sobbed, hating him, cursing him for pulling at her like this, for denying her; she would get him, she would. If she said the words, she would make sure *he* regretted them. And still, in the throes of her torrid need, she felt the arousal of finally capitulating to him.

"Oh yes, let me feel you, I need to feel you," she begged him, the words almost clogging in her throat. Oh, but not quite. The sense of release in actually saying the thing that she wanted sent a spiraling excitement through her. And a sense of power. She felt his galvanic response to the heat of her words.

She felt like she could use it: words made her free. "Let me feel you," she whispered enticingly, as he reared backwards to take the first long powerful thrust within her, *"all* of you—slowly, my lord, slowly . . . oh yes, oh yes . . ."

Just the words. Words had weight, words created potency; her words directed him now, their life in the air between them arousing her unbearably as he slowly slowly thrust his virile manhood into the source of her pleasure.

"Yes, yes . . . oh . . . ummm . . ." He swallowed her moans with his kisses, deep dark kisses, wet lush kisses that could not quell her deep moans of surrender.

He felt ready to explode; his body took on a motion of its own, fed by her thick hot kisses and her primitive response to the feel of him driving insistently into her.

She wrapped herself around him instinctively, her long silken legs enfolding him, her arms embracing him, her body moving in shimmering counterpoint to his long hard lunges.

Her kisses grew frantic, heated, wet; she drove herself feverishly against his thrust, seeking the point of pleasure, the swell of the onset of the opulent sensation that would begin her molten climb to culmination.

It was there . . . it was there . . .

She felt insatiable, as if it would never come, that his lathered body would collapse before either of them scented sweet release.

And then suddenly, like a container toppling and spilling its contents, it was there, a torrent of sensation, streaming out from her center core all over her body, a deluge that utterly carried her away on ribbons of gushing sensation.

He felt the change in her, he felt her give, he pressed, he pushed, he rammed against her perfectly in time, and he hurtled over the edge of satiety into his own racking, wrenching release that went on endlessly, mindlessly, as if his body needed to fill hers with every last drop of his male juices so there would be room for no one else.

There were no words after that; she could not be cruel after such shattering pleasure. Not at once. But he made no move to leave her; he lay nestled within her, still staunch and hard and strong, his weight heavy on her now, his nakedness intrusive.

"Surely you must go," she said finally, and her tone reflected none of the fulminating passion they had shared.

Courtesan to the core, he thought violently. But what had he expected?

"No, Diana, I must stay. I like having you on your back and begging for pleasure. It may be that you will come to the point of wanting again."

"Never," she retorted, but in the aftermath of their passion and with his full nakedness impressed upon her, she knew her denial had no heat whatsoever.

But neither did her body feel any heat; her body felt saturated with their comingled wetness and a total sense of repletion.

The worst thing she could do, she thought, would be to fall asleep in his face. And she would think about the rest tomorrow.

It would be on his head if Marie found him in her bed in the morning: *he* would have to explain to Lady Waynflete . . . no, maybe she would . . . she felt the lassitude of satiation creep over her.

Nothing mattered then, as the little light in the room crumbled into embers, and the weight of his body became a cocoon of warmth surrounding her.

Nothing . . .

He watched her drift off to sleep, his emotions in turmoil, his sure sense of her perfidy seeded deep within his soul.

Oh, this was a bitch from the very first word; he wasn't even sure that Dunstan wasn't right about it. Every one of his instincts had betrayed him.

He had uplifted a gaming house strumpet and he was being well and amply repaid.

He would take Dunstan's advice: he would use her and lose her.

But he stayed enfolded within her until long after Lucretia returned home; and he finally left in the darkness of the dawn.

Chapter Ten

The Tallinger's dinner party was supposed to have been small and select but, as Lady Tallinger said, "Town was supposed to have been so thin of company, and before we turn around, we have Jane Griswold, and Charles, the Beckwiths, Chevrington, Annesley . . . I felt bound to include *everyone* because I would not slight anyone. It will be lovely to have everyone at table tonight. The more the better, Jarman always says. Dear Lucretia . . ." she greeted Lady Waynflete.

"My protegée," Lady Waynflete said, "Jainee Bowman."

"Jen-ay, Jen-ay? What an odd pronunciation of Jenny. Well, no mind. Welcome my dear. I'm so glad to have you."

"And Dunstan Carradine?" Lady Waynflete asked. "Will Dunstan be in attendance tonight?"

Lady Tallinger shook her elegant gray head. "No, no. Of course, Dunstan—he cried off at the last moment, Lucretia. Business again, although I have yet to fathom exactly what this business of his is."

"Nor have we all," Lady Waynflete murmured as she nodded to Jainee to precede her into the parlor.

It was like a little homecoming. She knew everyone there: her three unabashed admirers, several others she had met in passing at the opera, and Nicholas Carradine, forbidding and formidable in his usual black formal dress, his expression as dark as his eyes as he caught sight of Jainee and her newest blatant gown.

God, no wonder those idiot bucks were throwing themselves at her feet and just begging her to step all over them. She was

188

dressed like a trollop with only the cut of the gown as any concession to good taste. Everyone's eyes were positively pinned on her damped down underdress and on the round low bodice which seemed to be held up by a vee of two silver straps that circled her neck and cut right across the mounds of her breasts to fasten at the center of her midriff with a silver pin.

He could see every nuance of her body beneath the clinging undergown.

And so could everyone else, he thought wrathfully, as he watched her positively *negotiate* the room, leaving panting partisans in her wake.

There were a half dozen people she did not know, but she remedied that lack in minutes: they were all enslaved by her beauty, her body and her flirtatious silvery fan, and he felt like throttling her for her effortless ability to seduce whomever she chose.

She made it look easy; there was something so inviting about the look of her, and the way she tilted her head just so when listening to someone. She always had either a question or a pouty little comment that did not fail to captivate her listeners.

Because they all wanted a long loving glimpse at her shamelessly bared breasts, he was sure, and certain she had dressed so provocatively just to annoy him and command the attention of those present.

He quelled his wrath. There were ways to make Diana of the drabs understand that public display was not good *ton*—if indeed she wanted to remain under Lucretia's protection—

In the meantime, he supposed he could eke some enjoyment out of the way she played with his friends, and with the knowledge that the night before, she had wantonly played with him.

"My lord." Her soft voice, her disarmingly correct and revealing curtsey: she was a consummate actress. He *was* a fool.

"Miss Bowman. I beg your indulgence; my mind was elsewhere."

"It *is* a nice change, my lord," she said tartly. Yes, he understood that reference very well. "Ah, I see Charles Griswold across the room and I have not spoken to him yet."

"Be sure you only talk with your *mouth,* Diana," he said in an undertone, cursing himself, even as he spoke, for demeaning himself to even caution her.

She went off in a whirl of gauzy muslin and Lucretia took her place by his side.

"The chit makes you crazy, Nicholas; I don't much like that," she said, putting a comforting hand on his arm. "I feel very leery about this whole entanglement. Think, Nick—for all you know, she may have some secret agenda."

He looked down at her. Such a tiny lady for such large concerns, he thought, gently removing her hand. "But Lucretia, for all you know, so may I."

She felt properly chastised, and she was surprised that she resented it. She had never disapproved of anything Nick had done—ever. "I just do not like the look of it. I will not renege on my promise to help you. I just hope that she will continue to behave in a way that I can support until you have done with her."

"That is all I ask," he said gently, his burning black gaze following Jainee around the room as she greeted or was introduced to the rest of the guests.

"And Dunstan did not come," Lucretia said, somewhat mournfully, following the track of Nicholas' interest.

"I did not know until I had arrived—" Nicholas began, but he was interrupted by Annesley, another bosom friend, a man of like age, complexion and bearing. They were of a height and coloring as well, except that Annesley's face was less sharp and angular and he was not so fit as Nicholas. His eyes were a soft melting brown and there was some gray in his hair.

But there was definitely interest in his voice as he accosted Lady Waynflete and said buoyantly, "That beauty . . . where did you find her, Lucretia? Everyone is bowled over with desire: that dress, that body, that *mouth* . . . !"

"And still," Lucretia said ironically, "she is every inch a lady."

"Very good, Lucretia. The *lady* of desire. The lady desire.

190

Excellent: we have just named the new incomparable of the season. Griswold! Chevrington! Here—a toast . . . to Lady Desire!" He lifted his cup toward Jainee who was deep in conversation with Lord Tallinger.

"And best of all," he added, nudging Nicholas as if he were a conspirator, *"we* met her first . . ."

It was an interminable dinner. Jainee sat between Annesley and Lord Tallinger and across from Nicholas and Jeremy and she felt as if both of them were monitoring every smile, every movement, every time she looked into her dinner partner's eyes.

Still, she managed very well to give equal attention to Annesley and her host, and she decided she didn't care what Nicholas Carradine thought or felt because there was nothing he could do to stop her from being a triumph tonight.

He needed to be taken down a peg anyway, after last night, after her cowardly capitulation to him. Oh, but the sweet power of the moment lived deep within her and she was beginning to understand that she must always be prepared.

She looked up at one point to see Annesley lift his glass at her and then toward Nicholas and mouth something across the table.

Nicholas' eyes blazed and he sipped his port thoughtfully in the wake of whatever joke Annesley had pantomimed. But his eyes were not on his friend; his eyes were on Jainee and Annesley's close attention to her obvious charms.

He thought he might strangle Annesley. *Lady Desire* . . . the damned sobriquet would be all around London like wildfire by tonight and he couldn't extinguish the conflagration even if he wanted to: it would open the door to too many questions and speculation about his involvement with her.

And wasn't the irony of it that he needed her reputation to be as pristine as possible while she culled the various society events for this phantom of a father who probably didn't exist.

Lady Desire—they would whisper it behind her back and it

191

would arouse them to try to take untoward liberties with her. If there were a name, they would think, there must be a reason.

Lady Desire—it would connect in sibilant whispers at every function to which she would be invited, and she would be invited to some purely because she bore the name.

And she soon would see the folly of her flouting him. She might even beg for his protection at that point, offering anything in her power in order to escape the libertine society into which she had deliberately insinuated herself.

"God, those eyes," Annesley muttered. "Those breasts. That body. Good God, Nick, don't you *see* it? She should add a bit of hot-tailed spice to the season, don't you think? Why don't you pitch yourself at her, Nick—and get the Emerlin off your back? She will positively turn Aphrodisian when she catches sight of the Lady Desire. And that bag-witch mother of hers—she may commit mayhem—"

"And *I* might if you continue in this vein, Max. I admit she's a fetching piece, but she probably doesn't have enough wit to saddle a horse with."

"Hell, man, I would take her on myself if I could afford her."

"Lust and money do walk hand in hand," Nicholas said drily.

"It ain't something *you* have to worry about in any event," Annesley said repressively, "and she will be a fleshier mistress than the betting books at White's, and a damn sight more pleasurable. Just think about sinking your . . ."

"A brutal picture to paint for me in public place, Max, or hadn't you thought of the repercussions?" Nicholas asked lightly as he turned away from the scene of protracted leave-taking to hide his burgeoning erection.

"Oh hell, I feel 'em myself," Annesley muttered. "She is something. I named her right, Nick. Just thinking about her—Lady Desire—just melting for you, begging for you—she's a taker, Nick. You'd be better off with this fancy piece than the next floating faro game. I would take her on myself, I swear. Look at those breasts: she cannot be wearing anything beneath that slip. I would wager you she is naked under that dress, Nick."

"And just how would you confirm that?" Nicholas asked dangerously.

"I would strip it right off her body. She would love it. Look at those hot eyes, Nick. No woman goes naked unless she wants that kind of attention. She's getting it too, Nick. You may have to stand in line to buy a moment of Lady Desire's time."

"You can't pay the price," Nicholas said flatly.

"No, I can't. That's why I want to live vicariously through you, old man. I would love to imagine you fondling that body. I would love to think of you getting the best of her and leaving her begging for more. She has got just that kind of look, Nick. I don't understand why Lucretia don't see it. It's there. Every manjack in this company sees it. They're counting silver in their hands, trying to figure out the going coin for one cleverly fashioned Aphrodite who moves through the fair as one of their own."

"Don't count on it, Max. Your Lady Desire has been coached to have some measure of discretion."

"Anyone who dresses like that has *no* prudence whatsoever, Nick. Does she go to Ottershaws' next week?"

"How would I know? Do you?"

"I wouldn't miss it. No telling who will turn up: look at tonight. Till then, I will spend the week on the delightful prospect of musing on the possible state of Lady Desire's un-dress, should she be fashionable enough to be invited. Au revoir, Nick."

"Max."

Nicholas watched him leave with mixed emotions. Annesley was only saying what everyone else was thinking. It was one of his great charms that he could do so and get away with it in polite company, but he was so inoffensive and took such gustatory pleasure in it that no one was ever offended.

Except, perhaps, himself, but he was supposed to be at arm's

193

length from the lady of desire. *He* was supposed to know nothing about it, and he didn't know how he was going to remain cool if every last one of his friends felt the same about her as Annesley.

Annesley would die if he knew that his lady desire had been moaning with pleasure in bed with him the previous evening.

And she looked quite ready to play coy games with him again tonight.

By then, everyone had departed except for himself, Lucretia, Jeremy and Jainee.

Nicholas called for their carriages, which then pulled up side by side before the Tallingers' townhouse steps.

Jeremy helped his mother in hers, and reached out his hand for Jainee.

"I will take Miss Bowman back to Lady Waynflete's," Nicholas said, motioning to his footman to open the door for her. "Hand over her cape, Lucretia. I promise I won't *eat* her."

"This is very ill-mannered of you," Lady Waynflete said sharply, "and it doesn't look good."

"Who will know?" Nicholas asked dismissively, shutting the door of the Waynfletes' carriage on Lucretia's protests. "Get in my carriage, Miss Bowen, before someone does see *and* comment."

He was very arrogant, just the way she most disliked him, and Jainee felt cornered. She looked at Jeremy, who was about to call for his own gig. "Do I have no choice in this matter? I do not wish to be alone with my lord in his carriage, which I think is proper and correct for an eligible woman."

Jeremy shrugged. "You are Nick's plaything, Miss Bowman. I would not override him."

"Nor would you cut off his legs," Jainee retorted.

"Nor would you prefer to walk," Nicholas put in, "if that was about to be your next threat."

"I know when to give over," Jainee said haughtily, seeing no help from Lady Waynflete either. She held out her hand to Nicholas. "You may assist me."

He did like her air of insolence: it amused him, and so he took her hand and helped her into the carriage, and shot Jeremy a warning look. "I plan to attend Lady Badlington's soiree tonight, Jeremy, if you would care to join me."

"What, go looking for trouble with you once more?" Jeremy said in mock horror. "Well, yes, I think I had better. Who knows what kind of gaming house trollop you'll saddle mother with this time. In an hour, Nick?"

"Sufficient," he agreed, and climbed inside his carriage in the seat opposite Jainee, who sat huddled in the corner surrounded by the warmth of her fur-lined cape, and the consideration of a brazier of coals beneath the seat benches.

"You were wise not to argue for once, Diana," he said as he waved out Lady Waynflete's carriage, and signalled to his own.

"I understand the restrictions," she said dampingly.

"I wish you did," he retorted, "else you would not have worn that dress."

"There is nothing ill-fitting about this dress."

"That, Diana, is my point."

"And very crassly made. But I suppose there have been dozens of trollops for whom you have provided who have followed the mold."

"Oh, *dozens*," he agreed darkly. "I am forever at the tables just hoping to find one brass-mouthed Aphrodite with whom I can spar words and make scurrilous bargains—"

"Those were not *my* terms, my lord," Jainee snapped. "I merely wished to come to London, and you truly have had the best of the bargain."

"Let us take account, Diana. Let us tote up the cost in emotional energy in just dealing with you, and add to that the cost of intruding on my dearest friends to house you and lend you countenance, and then, what do you suppose defrays the cost of clothing you for the season in the manner befitting someone of whom—pleasant fiction—I am supposed to be the trustee? It boggles the mind. You have not nearly begun to repay this debt. And yet, and yet—I have taken it on, out of the goodness

195

of my heart so that you might have the opportunity to find your . . . father."

"Yes," she hissed.

"I am impressed with the activity of your search, huntress. For one who is forever stalking its prey, you seem hardly to have caught the scent."

"It can make no difference to you," Jainee shot back, stung. Surely *he* had gotten all from their bargain he had sought. She understood to whom she was beholden, even though she would never admit it to him. And if she felt a little guilt about her almost *laissez-faire* attitude in commencing her search for her father, she was also certain it was none of his business so long as he got what he expected.

"But it does, Diana," he said unexpectedly. "I am inordinately interested in this phantom father of yours."

She felt unreasonably agitated by this pronouncement, and it took her a minute to pull her wits together to go at him in a different direction.

"Well, so much for my lord's declarations of generosity . . . not to say munificence, and his goodness of heart. Why *should* it interest you?" she added, hoping that she sounded disinterested, even off-handed, praying she did not give away her uneasiness at this sudden turnabout in his concerns.

"Let us just say that it does, Diana, and that your undertaking from this moment forward is to bend all your effort to identifying this man."

"I—" she began heatedly, and he cut her off.

"I believe you were very emotional about your *need* to find your father, Diana. I did not forget and I want you to remember. The delights of the season will pall beside the consequences if this man proves not to exist."

She was stunned; she felt more than that—she felt pure tingling shock that he had had a covert motive for accepting her barter. Or had she thought she was such a tasty morsel that no man could resist?

The tension between them had nothing to do with the intimacy they had shared; in truth, she had been sure this was to have been a carriage ride to carnality, and now she had to contend with the notion that he desired something totally different from her.

She could not make the transition in her thinking; she could not grasp why he would be at all interested in the man who was her father.

However, to confess all of this bewilderment to him was out of the question. If anything, she needed to stand stronger against him than before. If he wanted her father, he must have a reason.

What reason? What inconceivable purpose?

But that was for later, when she was alone and could think things through.

All these contradictory thoughts flew through her mind at breakneck speed; outwardly, she showed none of her apprehension, assuming her habitual, unflappable gaming-table attitude.

It was time to attack, she thought, girding herself. It was time to deflect all this untoward interest in her personal life.

"It is impossible for my father *not* to exist, my lord."

He smiled grimly. "I bow to your superior logic, Diana. I can only beg the question of whether he exists in England; he may well be living in France in the maw of the Emperor's legendary generosity. And you may well be a traitor. On the other hand, you have had ample opportunity to commence your search. The wonder is you have not found him yet."

She bit her lip. To be sure, Southam had kept his word to her: he had provided the entree and she had already attained a status that was not normally accorded to any newcomer within his circle. In her amorphous plans, she had counted heavily on her having changed so much her father might not recognize her as readily as she would him. She had thought to move among the swells, and at some distant future time, entering a room, sighting him immediately and pointing her accusatory finger.

She had never given a moment's consideration to what might happen next. Nor had she even contemplated the horrifying thought that had jumped into her mind at Southam's remark, and leaped instantly from her lips before she gave it her full attention.

"What if he does not wish to be found?"

The question hung in the air between them, full of nuances and permutations that exploded like fireworks in a glittering discharge every which where.

"Your candor becomes you, Diana; or else it is the feral cunning of a creature driven by fear. Whichever it is, huntress, understand that friends become enemies and lovers become treacherous in the blink of an eye. And each will destroy whomever stands in the middle as calmly as he would swat a fly."

The carriage swerved then, and he lifted the curtain. "Ah, we are almost at Lady Waynflete's. I trust I have made myself clear, Diana, and that you will be forthright with me. Have you seen the man who is your father?"

She lifted her chin defiantly, refusing to be crushed by his threats. He knew nothing about her yet in all their battling back and forth, and he obviously did not take seriously all those times she had gotten the better of him.

So be it.

"I have not."

"We will leave it at that — for tonight."

The carriage drew to a halt and Jainee glanced out the window, expecting to see the elegant columns and shallow marble steps of Lady Waynflete's house.

"What is this?"

"This is a shield for your reputation, Diana. Pull up your hood; in a moment, you will enter the rear access to Lady Waynflete's home."

"About which you seem to have an abundance of knowledge; this must be the mysterious way in which you invade her home and my bedroom at night."

"Nonsense, Diana. Look, there is Blexter with a lamp to light your way."

She looked at him uncertainly. He held the power tonight. In some unfathomable way, he had cornered her, and she felt uneasy about what would follow. Still, there was no choice but to continue on, and to submit on her own terms.

And always, always attack, and never leave him feeling as if he had gained a victory.

"I trust you feel you have spent a profitable hour before you go to join Jeremy at—where was it? Lady Something-ton?" she asked, a trifle waspishly. And didn't she feel a jot of envy that he was leaving her to enter the edgy world of brightly lit rooms and fast-paced play? She thought she did; she even felt as if he were abandoning her.

"There is always a Lady Something-ton in town at the beginning of the season who likes to play games, Diana."

"And do all the lords bow to her whims and enjoy playing games with her?"

"I will let you contemplate the thought of that tonight, goddess. It *is* a sobering thought." He gave her a gentle push, and she stepped out of the carriage and onto the brick pavement. Blexter stood at the door, his lantern aloft, waiting patiently for her to cease her word games with Southam; the moment she lifted a foot to step up to the doorway, the carriage moved.

She whirled but it was too late. The shades were down, the night was young, and only a man could prowl the streets in search of pleasure.

Her temper was not improved by a dressing down from Lady Waynflete.

"Never, *never* will you go again with Southam if you wish to continue to stay with me. It was the worst impropriety. In the best circumstance a man could takes the most advantage. I cannot think how you could allow yourself to—it was just a matter of entering my coach. Sometimes you must be strong, no matter what a man wants."

"Are you saying," Jainee said coldly, "that my lord could not be trusted to mind his manners, even in the face of your obvious disapproval?"

"My dear, you have the mouth of a brass-faced baggage. A man can never be trusted to do anything he ought, and I should think you would have learned that by now. Nicholas in particular is always moved by the urge of the moment. And believe me, *my* censure from five miles down the road would dissuade him from *nothing*. Over and above *that,* it is your reputation which must be zealously guarded. Your background is already questionable, and we have glossed over it as much as possible. But I will tell you now, there will be some who will dismiss you out of hand in spite of all my and Jane Griswold's efforts. So you had better not give those tongues anything more to wag about, Jainee. Do I make myself clear?"

"Indeed you do," Jainee said stiffly, "and I tell you again: I am no green girl, and Southam shall never have the advantage of me. However, I will take to heart your stricture about appearances. I understand how much they matter."

Damn them, damn the eternal obeisance to outward impressions! She stormed up the stairs and into her room and just fell onto the bed in a frenzy of anger—against Lady Waynflete, against Southam, against the circumstances that had brought her to this pass, against the fates who had made her a woman and not a free-wheeling man who could go and come and do as he pleased and take whomever he wanted.

She needed to think, but she was in such a rage. Lady Waynflete had made her feel like a child, and Southam had made her feel panicky and dispensible. She felt out of control, and she needed badly to center herself so that she could make some order out of the chaos she was feeling.

She could not let Southam frighten her with his threats and demands. And she would never let Lady Waynflete chastise her like that, ever again. Even if it meant she must leave the house in Mayfair.

Yes, she could do that: she still had some money of her own. She could return to Brighton, she could work her way forward

200

again if need be. She didn't need these lofty aristocrats to house, clothe and feed her. She needed them for exactly what they had provided: the means to move in that strata of society where she might find her father.

And she had paid for the privilege and she considered it a fair exchange, and for Southam to add a condition to the bargain was loathsome and underhanded.

But that die was cast already, from the moment she had told him her story; *he* had palmed the card, and played it too late in the game for her to counter.

As always, she must play to deceive. There was no difference whether she moved in the most elegant circles in London or the most vulgar gaming house in Brighton.

She must protect her interests, bluff her way through and always attack to put her opponent on the defensive.

The problem of her father and Southam's unwarranted intrusion into her search for him was something else again.

Why?

Or had her father been his true objective after all?

But she could see no reason for that. Her father had abandoned France ten years before. Well no, she didn't really know that. She really knew nothing about him at all.

He would have aged in ten years as well. He would not be the man whom Therese loved, and the kidnapper she remembered.

Why on earth would Southam have any interest in his whereabouts at all? It made no sense, and he already expected that she would have pinpointed the man who was her father since she arrived.

He might even feel she was holding back the information.

She had to deflect his interest immediately until she could find out exactly why he wanted the information

And she knew just how to do it.

"Marie!"

Marie appeared, silent as air. "Mademoiselle? You are home early from the dinner. Everything went well."

201

"Very well, although monsieur was *not* pleased with your dressmaking skill. Neither, for that matter, was madame. Hear me—monsieur seems to have developed an inordinate concern over the whereabouts of my father."

"So?" Marie murmured. "Does he seek the boy?"

"He knows nothing of the boy, and I want to make sure he never finds out about him—or my father. I need your help."

"What can I do? What can mademoiselle do?"

"I have *one* weapon," Jainee said resolutely. No backing down now; she knew just how to distract my lord pride of the jungle. "This is what you must do for me, Marie. I need four strips of material, that beautiful thick satin, so lustrous to the touch. Blue, I think, and cut and sewn as you would a sash, as long as I am tall, an inch, two inches thick, no more."

"Mademoiselle?" Marie protested. "For what purpose?"

"Perhaps you had best not know. Let us say for the purpose of tantalizing monsieur and turning his mind to other possibilities."

"I see," Marie murmured again. "Yes, infinite possibilities. I will begin at once."

After she had gone, Jainee paced the room restlessly. There was no other way she could take action, and even then, she must wait on Marie's pleasure until she had sewn the strips with which she would titilate the high and mighty lord of lechery.

What must he be doing now, ensconced as he must be at that Lady Something's home, throwing pounds around with the abandon of a profligate prince.

It enraged her just to think of it: all the men she had met this evening were very probably out doing whatever men did when they left their women at home to sit by the fire. Presumably many of them had followed Southam's lead and gone to Lady Something-ton's. Very likely, Lady Something used beautiful women to lure her customers—she would have wanted from the very outset to attract the wealthy eligible customer, the ones with the most money or the longest expectations.

And if she provided congenial company, deep and reasonable

202

honest play and many other intangible incidentals the jaded patrician patrons required, she would have made her reputation and from then on, she would only have to make a discreet announcement in the right quarters to have all and sundry flocking to her gaming house door.

Everyone except a proper lady who would not know of such things; or a vixen who had been dragooned into becoming one for the sake her mother's misty-eyed dreams.

She wished she were anything but proper now: *she* could be spinning wheels and cutting cards in a gaming house at this very moment if she had not succumbed to the challenge of matching wits with Southam.

She was meaningless to him, except as a means to get to her father. And barring that, he would pump his money's worth of lust from her and cast her out as soon as she was bored.

Yes, she saw that clearly now, especially with the revelation of this mysterious interest in her father. How blinded she had been by both her schemes to lure him into bringing her to London and all the energy she had expended since trying to keep him out of her bed.

Of course it was not so simple: she had been warned Southam was devious—and deep. Of course he had had other motives, other reasons, but she could not now repine on her stupidity over that.

Nor the fact that he had won the battle of her bed. Now it was perfectly plain she had to keep him enslaved there—at least until she figured out what she had to do.

Lady Desire, Lady Desire—the goddamned name had infiltrated the parlor of Lady Badlington's gaming house as surely as it would insinuate itself into drawing rooms and dinner parties, and even Parliament, for God's sake, Nicholas thought dourly as he sat aimlessly watching a roulette table in play.

It was too good to be buried in the entrance hallway of the Tallinger townhouse. It had come with their guests, whomever chose to end the evening in this manner, and it was not from the mouth of Max Annesley either.

Have you seen her? they asked. *There has never been a more desirable woman in the whole of London for years. Her body . . . her mouth . . . those clothes . . . her past . . . Someone saw her at Brighton, with Sedgewick, they say. No, she was at the* Alices *and as fair and square as they come. It was just that all the men got so distracted by those eyes and that body, they practically begged her to take their money . . .*

Is she a lady? Oh, we don't know, but God, she is desirable . . .

She would be a legend by morning, his goddess, his Circe; he did not need to lift a finger to help her now. He should have wagered on his prediction: he would have lost his inheritance.

It had taken but one day of her exposure to the right people. No—the right *men*.

"Well, they say you know her, Nick. They say you're muddled up with some kind of trust fund from her father . . . you found her dealing Faro at the *Alices?*"

"Is she the most beautiful thing you ever laid eyes on?"

"The most desirable?"

They came at him from all sides. Everyone knew, in that infinitely mysterious way that such gossip travelled, that he had been in Brighton, been at the Tallingers, spoken five words to her—they all wanted to know about the color of her eyes, the timbre of her voice, was it true she was an heiress.

He found himself inventing details out of whole cloth, cursing the fact that Lucretia and Jane Griswold had done their job too well.

There wasn't a woman at Lady Badlington's who could compare with her.

"Those dresses—they are talking about the cut of her dresses . . . just a little too *fast?*"

"Oh, but consider—she's not just out of the schoolroom; she's been in Brighton, a world of experience for a woman. I like to see a woman who can behave like a *woman . . .*"

"Stuff it, Farthingale; you like mewling misses who come to you on hands and knees, or courtesans like Edythe Winslowe who will step all over you. What do you suppose Lady Desire would see in *you?*"

The arguments raged all around him until he was sick of hearing the litany of her virtues.

"Eh, Nick? Ain't she just the thing?"

"She is now," he muttered, pushing a coin onto a number to play.

The wheel whirled and damn if it didn't come up his number. He pulled his winnings to one side angrily: he wanted to lose tonight, and lose high.

Damn the goddess, damn Annesley and his fertile imagination.

He pulled in another number's winnings and removed himself from the table and from earshot of the ongoing discussion about the goddess.

There wasn't much amusement to be had at the Badlington's. What was she but a more furbished and elegant version of Lady Truscott. She was smoother, younger perhaps, and had a finer sense of the niceties. Her clientele was always select as far as the gentlemen, and permissive with regard to the ladies.

The more notorious society beldames spent the money they did not have at Lady Badlington's tables and she gleefully extended credit and squashed them under her thumbs. The younger women were always beautiful and fast, ripe and relentless, and inevitably walked just outside the society's strictures.

Such a one was Edythe Winslowe, who was very much in evidence tonight, and obviously looking, but in a haughty and disdainful way. As ever, she was surrounded by so many men that no one could perceive the lay of her interest—which was just as she meant it to be. She was very clever, the Winslowe, and the only thing that Nicholas did not like about the group *en scéne* was that Arabella Ottershaw's husband was among the admirers.

But that was not his business, and the rigid code of honor

among the men and the patrons of the house would be strictly enforced: no one would know of Ottershaw's inclinations beyond Lady Badlington's doors.

He pushed his way out of the lower rooms and upstairs into a fast paced game of *vingt-et-un,* where he began, after fifteen minutes, to lose steadily and heavily to a sweet young hostess who did not have a tenth of the skill and grace of the Lady Desire.

Who might be laying in her bed even now, awaiting his nocturnal visit, her breasts heaving with yearning. What would his cadre of questioners think if they knew, if they even *sensed* that someone had been able to bargain her into his bed?

They would descend like vultures: she would be tantalized into the life of an Edythe Winslowe, forever at the center of a coterie of fawning admirers, forever collecting kisses and kindnesses in exchange for more physical offerings until the day her body betrayed her and her gallants were as old as she and could not tell the difference.

Goddamn the bitch: her eyes would tell secrets and her hands would flash out here and there, enticing this one and that one, secretly wooing him into submission, so that he could refuse her nothing.

Lady Desire, the next goddess with whom every man wanted to be seen. Damn, damn, damn—

"Lord Southam?" The voice was sweet, firm, but not commanding.

He looked up. "I stay."

"Very good, my lord."

And he lost, which was as it should be. He pushed himself away from the table, disgusted that his thoughts were dominated by the one woman in the whole of London who would fight him to her bed.

And he wanted to be there, right that moment, to exercise his right of place and his mastery over the only woman who had ever flaunted his authority and gotten away with it.

206

* * *

She waited. She was sure that he would come; it was the perfect night, the night of her triumph walking among his blue-blooded equals, the night of his unsettling declaration about her father—surely he would want to claim some right of assertion tonight.

But perhaps not. Perhaps the mysterious woman of her fantasies had been given entree to the exclusive gaming hell that he frequented.

Perhaps, just perhaps, she was more accessible, more willing.

And perhaps, just perhaps, she was one of his inamoratas, one of many, by chance, to whom he had given a robe exactly like the one that was hanging defiantly in her wardrobe.

And what if this luscious willing woman were available tonight and made her wishes known to him, what then? And then what if she whispered soft coercive arousing words in his ear, and promised him everything he had ever wanted—what then?

She pushed herself upright in a frenzy of dismay. The dream once again had seemed real—too real. Why should she care what Southam was doing with whom at Lady Something's gaming house?

He could do whatever he wanted, as long as she was still able to entice him to her bed.

No—as long as she could do what she wanted too.

She *wanted* to have the entree to Lady Badlington's house with the same approbation as a man.

She wanted to stop thinking this way altogether. Southam had upset her badly, and she did not like the thought of being at his mercy because of it. She had struck her course: she could not let a sudden departure throw her.

There was a knock at her door. Marie!

"Did mademoiselle sleep?"

"Perhaps a little. Perhaps I had a bad dream."

"It is so; you were tossing and turning. But now you are awake I have come to show you, mademoiselle, to see if I have

207

followed your instructions exactly as you wished." She held up a length of satin that she had folded and stitched up the raw side and on the edges. "Stand beside me, mademoiselle. Let us see if this is the length you require."

Jainee wriggled out of bed and reached over to touch the satin strip.

It was blue, soft, soft blue, and it felt as thick as cream under her stroking fingers. Marie unrolled the rest of it and held it up next to Jainee's body. It came six inches above her head; it was perfect.

"This is exactly what I wanted," she breathed, winding one end of the satin strip around her wrist: around and around until she made a thick sheeny binding on her arm, and she held it away and looked at it with the skeptical eyes of his suspicious, mistrustful lord of the libertines.

She nodded her head. "This is perfect. You will do the three other strips, Marie, and together we will tie up monsieur in so many knots he will fall on his face before he can work himself free."

Chapter Eleven

"I have strict instructions from Nicholas this morning," Lady Waynflete announced at breakfast, eyeing with approval Jainee's very proper blue morning dress of merino cloth with its constricting waistcoat bodice that completely flattened the lush curve of her breasts.

"He says everyone is talking about you because of the dinner at the Tallingers and he would like to whet their curiosity even more so that your notoriety will gloss you through the doors of the highest of the high sticklers."

"His lordship's concern is most gratifying," Jainee murmured into her cup of chocolate. If he had been there, she thought malignantly, she would have tossed it right into his face again. Her *notoriety* indeed!

"Which," Lady Waynflete continued, "putting it simply, means he wishes us to travel out and about a little more during the day; normally I would do that anyway, but he suggests that I include you in my common rounds, a suggestion which I do not embrace with open arms." She looked up at Jainee. "However, if you can keep your comments gracious and your bosom inside your dress, I think I can contrive to tolerate your company."

"My lady's condescension is most flattering," Jainee said mockingly. "I can vouch for my bosom, if not my mouth."

"That will have to do," Lady Waynflete said grudgingly. "Here is the program for this morning—"

Jainee half-listened, her mind on the devious cleverness of his tricky lordship of underhandedness. She was just aching to get her hands on him: she would tie him head to foot with her se-

209

ductive satin strips so that he could never make a move against her ever again.

As if she couldn't infer from all the convolutions of his note exactly what he was up to!

What he wanted was *not* for everyone to see her: he wanted *her* to see everyone.

"I beg your pardon, Lady Waynflete?" she said politely, as she became aware that Lady Waynflete was asking her something. "Oh yes, I am quite ready to proceed." She set aside her napkin, having no idea what Lady Waynflete had proposed for the morning's activity.

She supposed it didn't matter. She had no reason to demur, and in fact, was in crying need of *some* activity to while away the hours.

"Now, here is the time where a cape is perfectly suitable," Lady Waynflete said, as one servant and then another helped her and Jainee with their outer garments.

"I will not argue the case with you again; it goes against the grain to present one appearance when gentlemen are present, and then quite another when we are but two women together. No, *please;* you cannot explain the sense of it, my lady, and I wish you wouldn't try."

"Stubborn baggage," Lady Waynflete muttered, as she climbed in the carriage.

From there, it was a peripatetic excursion around and about the usual places which society frequented: the shopping bazaar, the milliner's, several baskets of this and that in stores from Fortnum and Mason, a half hour at the bookshop (". . . but *never* to Mitchell's, even with your maid," Lady Waynflete cautioned. "The most lascivious young men frequent there . . .) browsing through novels she would never ever read, and then on to Madame Signy, whose business had improved appreciably since their last visit—they were forced to wait with the press of fittings for the Ottershaw party.

After that, a drive around the park, it being almost noon by then and most of the bucks were out, raising up an appetite for dining out and about. Here and there, a carriage passed with some sweet young lady newly come to town, bolstered on either side by a doting mother and a chaperone and many nods and waves to the gentlemen in the passing parade.

It was a show, Jainee decided; it was a circus, all flamboyant presentation done as sedately as possible with the pretense of good manners and some civility. And she could play it as well as any of those blushing *demoiselles*.

Except she didn't think she had ever blushed.

It was late afternoon before they returned to the house in Mayfair, and the carriage was quite full of boxes and baskets and sundry goods that Lady Waynflete could just not live without.

She ordered tea and a light luncheon in the dining room and left Blexter and her servants to unload the carriage.

Jainee followed her meekly into the house.

"I want to see the dress you propose to wear to the Ottershaws'," Lady Waynflete said abruptly, even before she had divested herself of her wrap.

Jainee flushed. The color that washed her face was a reaction of pure resentful anger, and she couldn't hide it.

"My lady, I would never embarrass you."

"No, you have not embarrassed me. You have only created an air of flashiness around yourself. Well, I will not have it this time. Arabella Ottershaw is my dearest friend, and all shall be exactly as she would want it," Lady Waynflete said stiffly, holding back her anger at Jainee's impertinence.

And Jainee sensed that there was a moment not to push too far too fast. "I would be pleased to show you my dress, Lady Waynflete. Perhaps I might put it on for you later this afternoon so that you may see that it does not exceed the bounds of good taste."

"I think that would be quite proper," Lady Waynflete agreed. "Now let us have luncheon."

From that stony silent half hour, Jainee went to her room for a half hour's rest and to pull out the dress for the Ottershaw party to examine its fitness more closely.

This dress was unexceptional except for the glitter of its overdress of silver netting which gave it a little dash. This dress,

211

Jainee remembered, was one of the few on which she had agreed to Lady Waynflete's strictures: it was less revealing, more modest, it bore a train, a particular of more formal dresses that *she* did not like, and all in all, it was a costume with which Lady Waynflete would not find anything to dislike.

What was it about this gown, she wondered when she had been laced and hooked into it, that she had liked so much that she had gone so far as to allow Lady Waynflete to dictate the purchase of it?

She turned this way and that way in the mirror, liking the puffed sleeve of the overdress, and the matching silver net ruffle that edged the bodice. The sleeveless underdress of heavy blue crepe draped sensuously against her body, and she began to see, as she walked backward and forward, that there was something very subtle about this dress: that the fiery glow of the candles glanced off of the silver and enveloped her in a halo of light, and that her body moved beneath that aura in a way that seemed totally independent of the radiance surrounding her.

She looked both ethereal and earthly . . . like a goddess, she thought, lifting her head regally.

She was sure Lady Waynflete would not see that aspect of her dress. She pulled on a pair of blue silk elbow-length gloves, took up the matching silver net fan, and proceeded to join Lady Waynflete in the parlor.

The light in that room was very different from her bedroom. Sunlight poured in through the front windows, while the rear of the room was lit by one branch of candles.

Her dress looked perfectly proper in the hallway mirror, and she entered the parlor like a queen before her court.

Lady Waynflete, as always, was seated by the fire, but on seeing Jainee, she rose up and came to meet her, and then circled around her like a cat, sniffing and sniffing, her fur raised, her claws drawn and ready to spring.

"You'll do," she said finally and a little reluctantly. "All that silver is a little much for *me,* but you can carry it. Just don't damp down that underdress."

"The material is far too heavy," Jainee said, lifting the silvery net and inviting Lady Waynflete to touch it.

"Hmph," Lady Waynflete said, marching back to her seat and sitting back down again heavily. She wasn't sure it was that heavy at all. It clung to Jainee's curves as if it had been sculpted there. But no one would notice unless he were standing very close, and parties like this one they were to attend were always such a crush, one barely noticed what anyone was wearing.

"You'll do," she said again. "Do change now, and come back to me. We will discuss the plans for this evening and for the party this weekend."

The weekend was but two days away, and Jainee simmered with resentment that Southam had not put in an appearance to ascertain whether she and Lady Waynflete were making their rounds or even whether Jainee had anything to disclose to him.

The arrogance! she thought. He assumed his word would be obeyed, no questions asked, and when he deigned to find out, they would tumble head over heels with tales of how they had tried to please him.

And no, she had not seen anyone like her father.

It was a very loose and lax society, she thought, as she and Lady Waynflete kept to Southam's schedule those two ensuing days. Town was crowding up now all with the hibernating gentlemen of society who did nothing all day long except go to their clubs or sporting events, or ride in the park, or lounge at the booksellers or anywhere along Bond Street where *they* could be seen; in turn, the gentlewomen spent their days at the shopping stalls, at the lending libraries, riding through the park, or paying morning visits and afternoon visits, and then hoping to secure an invitation to a select dinner or party until the bulk of the season's events began in May.

And over and above that, they all flirted — overtly, covertly, instantly, constantly, coyly, haughtily, naughtily — and they all liked a good game of cards.

And if they were bored with all that, they went on forays to improve their minds: museums, art collections, antiquities, plays, the Tower of London and all its historicity . . . to be seen in all the right places was as good as an invitation Somewhere.

213

Lady Waynflete made sure she was seen in all the right places.
Which meant places where she might see her father.

Improving her mind was only a secondary consideration.

She understood Southam's concerns only too well, and she could not cry off these excursions without seeming churlish.

How did the man manipulate them so adroitly from afar?

There was no one populating the streets of London, old or young, who even remotely reminded her of her father.

It scared her a little; she had never once thought that perhaps Therese had not told her the truth of the matter. She had assumed that her mother, on her deathbed, would not lie.

But the possibility existed that the man who was her father still lived in France, had never been to England, had raised the abducted child exactly where he belonged — in his father-land.

Her imagination was running away with her, she thought, after their Saturday morning carriage ride around the park.

"The brisk air is so invigorating," Lady Waynflete said, thrusting her hands even more tightly into the folds of her cloak.

She did not mean it.

It was horribly cold the night of the Ottershaw party, and Jainee railed again about not being able to cover herself decently in that kind of weather.

"We do what fashion dictates," Lady Waynflete said righteously, but even she wore her heavy cloak over the thin silk shawl which matched her dress for the short carriage ride to the Ottershaws' townhouse.

By the time they arrived, there was already a crush of carriages and persons lined up by the front door.

"It is always like this," Lady Waynflete said, peering out of the carriage window. "One never wants to be *too* early and yet when one presents oneself at just past the appointed hour, one must contend with *this*. It will take a quarter hour just to get to the front door. I wish it were not so cold."

Nevertheless, when they finally were able to debark from the carriage, she made Jainee leave her fur-lined cape on the seat, and she did the same.

They stepped out into the icy air, and scurried inelegantly up the shallow front steps.

"One cannot make a dignified entrance like this," Jainee said, annoyed that she had listened to Lady Waynflete on this subject. How could it detract from a woman's appearance to enter a party enfolded in warmth, and then let it slide off of her shoulders for the perfect dramatic effect?

But then, she was always looking for the theatrical presentation. Even as they entered the reception hall, she could see in the mirrors placed all around how the overhead lights caught the silver flame of her dress and the silver ribbon wound in her hair in a glittery radiance that enveloped her as she removed her blue crepe shawl, handed it to a servant, and followed Lady Waynflete into the throng.

The house was huge, larger than the Waynflete townhouse, and crammed wall to wall with people who immediately stepped aside as they caught sight of Jainee.

It was almost biblical the way the crowd parted as she and Lady Waynflete made their way to the ballroom.

And under the rustling of movement and murmur of conversation, she heard a groundswell of whispers and she couldn't make out the words.

Across the ballroom, in the back of the crowd, Nicholas Carradine stood moodily apart from the arriving guests, watching them all, picking up a word of conversation here and there, and then, when Jainee arrived, the sibilant sound of his worst nightmare: *Lady Desire . . . look, there she is—they call her . . . she is the epitome of . . . Lady Desire . . . Lady Desire . . .*

Somehow, Max Annesley found him in the crowd. "There she is, old boy. They can't stop talking about her, did you hear? Isn't she something?"

"*You* are something," Nicholas said darkly. "What did you do, send prompts to all the invitees? It couldn't be better if you had staged it."

"Nonsense, Nick. She's a new face and a tasty morsel to boot. The name was apt; it spread like fire."

"Like a disease, you mean. And I know who was the carrier."

"Ah, Nick—don't let's engage in bloodletting. After all, what is the chit to you?"

"A damned nuisance," Nicholas said tartly. "And what is the chit to *you?*"

"God," Annesley breathed, "a damned good show is what. Have you ever known the Ottershaws' parties to be so lively? Have you seen anyone command such attention in recent memory? Look at them—the crowd is five deep; and my dear, look at the line of disappointed mothers on the sides. If there were cutlery to be had, one of them would have a knife at the beauty's throat."

"How thoughtful of the Ottershaws not to have provided food," Nicholas muttered. "On the other hand, the crowd of them look like they might eat *her.*"

"I always thought it was noxious of these nabobs not to serve dinner, myself," Annesley said. "After all, what *do* they provide but space to stand around and look at persons one would just as soon not even think about, let alone have discourse with. I still am trying to understand why I even take the time to *come* to these events."

"You fool no one, Max; it's perfectly plain that *you* want to be seen and you don't give a fig if you don't see anyone."

Annesley smiled faintly. "That is as may be, but the siren of the season over there obviously wants everyone to see as much of her as possible."

Nicholas, to that point, had avoided following Jainee's progress when, in fact, he could map it in his mind. He knew every one of the fawning exquisites who abased themselves at the feet of the goddess: he didn't need to watch the travesty. But he was also sure that Diana was enjoying every foul moment of it, preening like a peacock, elegantly beguiling her unsuspecting prey.

But there was only one man who had entrance to her bedroom, and one man who would share her bed: he would kill the man who challenged his right to possess her.

"She plays games with the minds of those fops," he said at

last. "They have no idea they are being led in circles. And then she will come in for the kill."

"I would love for her to play games with *me*," Annesley murmured suggestively. "Think of it—twisting and turning on her leading strings. She could tie me up anytime."

"That is ever the way with you, Max—never *tongue*-tied, *and* the best footwork this side of Prinny. You are the best at suiting action to words: you do it well, and you never have to move a muscle in the end. It's an extraordinary talent, my friend. You practically have her in your bed and you haven't moved an inch from my side."

"Ah, but look at that smile, Nick. It ain't possible she takes a man of them seriously. And they would all take her in a snap."

Now he looked, and it was there: the smile, the faint, smug smile that had drawn him in Brighton, the one he wanted to wipe off her face, and bury with harsh kisses, the one that no other man would know.

He hated the quicksilver glowing gown that caught the lights and attracted men to her like moths to a flame. He hated her surety, and the regal way she moved through the crowd.

He hated the fact he had feelings about her at all.

"Oh *God,*" Annesley said suddenly in awe-struck tones. "Damme, Nick. *Look—*"

Nick swung around, pulled by the urgency in Annesley's voice.

"Oh dear, Nick—don't say no one warned you. It's the Emerlin without her momma, and she is heading straight for you."

The evening had lost its luster about twenty minutes after she and Lady Waynflete walked into the Ottershaw ballroom.

She had never in her life seen such an assemblage in one place at one time, and for one moment, she had felt like bolting. And then the path opened up and she and Lady Waynflete had sailed into the crowd to be accosted ceaselessly by this one or that one who either knew Lady Waynflete or who wanted a precious introduction to the Beauty of the evening.

She remembered none of the names of those to whom she had been presented; she remembered only a sea of faces and an escort of cajoling adulatory gentlemen bearing her along like a tide against the shore.

"Jainee . . . Gen-ay . . ." she heard her name resonate in soft slurring whispers all around the room. "Jainee . . ." She could have been back at Lady Truscott's, with the same fawning exquisites reaching for her hands, her arms, for any possession of her that she might willingly give. The crowds were the same in the elegant townhouse or the barely respectable gaming house.

She knew what they wanted. They wanted what she had gambled away and lost to Southam, and it was now not hers to give.

The bargain was the bargain, and Southam would kill her if she found some other protector—she knew it.

Still, it was hard not to lose her heart to such flattery as surrounded her as she made her way through the ballroom, and it was easy to see that tonight, at least, she could snap her fingers and command any number of willing men to do her bidding.

This heady feeling lasted only as long as it took her to realize that the whole point of the party was the uncomfortable crush of the crowd: the success of the event was counted solely by the number of attendees and where they stood in the social hierarchy.

There was nothing else, no dinner, no refreshment save a tepid glass of champagne, no dancing, no cards, no music even. The whole of the party solely depended on the wit and conversation and the presence of certain persons of eminent standing. Everything else was secondary.

It was no surprise to her then that Lady Ottershaw was in no way pleased with the way she stormed the ballroom with a convoy of eligible men in her wake.

"My dear Lucretia—you must do something," Lady Ottershaw whispered frantically to Lady Waynflete, and Jainee overheard her.

The blasted nobility, she thought, the precious appearance-conscious rich and mighty. For one minute she considered planting herself in the center of the ballroom, commanding a chair

218

(and perhaps a dais if she felt really imperial) and just lording it over the whole lot of them while Lady Ottershaw's good manners prevented her from demanding that she, the upstart outsider, vacate the premises.

It was a sweet and vengeful little daydream, quickly punctured by Lady Waynflete's urgent hand on her arm. "Come stay with me for a moment, Jainee my dear. These parties with crowds and crowds of faces make me feel faint."

She was then honor-bound to succor her protectress. She could do nothing less, and as she led Lady Waynflete to the sidelines, she saw a rush of older women pushing a host of younger, marginally attractive girls into the center of the room and the circle of men.

"I see," she murmured and Lady Waynflete heard her.

"I believe you do," she said briskly. "Come. There is a door here where we may step out and take some air."

"As you wish, my lady."

They stepped onto a stone walled portico, and Lady Waynflete heaved a sigh of relief. "I think they can stand to be without you for a few minutes."

"Or Lady Ottershaw can, at any rate," Jainee retorted before she considered the import of her words.

Lady Waynflete rounded on her. "*You* are an ungrateful trollop. The *least* you could do is show some manners. It must be perfectly obvious to you that any number of eligible young women would be here seeking to make initial contact with a desirable connection. You have never been invited to number yourself among them, and all you need do is show some grace in the situation and withdraw yourself from their number and leave the gentlemen free to at least make their acquaintance this first evening. *You* are not free to dominate the company of any man, Miss Bowman. You only have leave to attend the affair and then return to the place where, by the grace of my friendship for Nicholas, you have a roof over your head. Do I make myself clear?"

Jainee felt heat wash over her face. "Indeed, my lady, I cannot possibly misconstrue your meaning."

"That is well for you, my girl. And now, I must think about rearranging my plans for this evening. I had planned to stay until the late hours, but I see it might be dangerous to do so. This party is, in effect, the first event of the season, a crucial social occasion for every mother with a marriageable daughter, the predictor of what might come. You will behave yourself, Miss Bowman, and not attract any undue notice. It would be well if you would just station yourself in the shadows and talk to no one."

She brushed a hand against Jainee's dress. "I wish we could undo this dress. How could you have deceived me into thinking it was innocuous? I am out of all patience with you, my girl, and you can be sure Nicholas will hear about this debacle."

She led the way back into the ballroom in a state of controlled anger. As they entered, they were immediately surrounded by Jainee's thwarted gallants.

"But where were you? You disappeared . . ."

"You left us at the mercy of those Friday-faced ninnies . . ."

"Not a jot of conversation among them, and those pushy mothers—"

"Come, Miss Bowman, just walk with us to—"

"Don't let *him* persuade you . . ."

"But—where are you going?" they demanded in unison as Lady Waynflete took hold of her arm and pulled her away.

"I must find Nicholas," Lady Waynflete muttered. "This whole idea is a disaster, and is causing my dearest friend no end of embarrassment. Now, where is that obnoxious man?"

They literally raced along the sidelines where knots of people stood either conversing, or doing an elaborate quadrille from one set of guests to another; they bumped into this one here and that one there with murmured excuses nobody heard.

No one could stop Lady Waynflete from her quest, and she wrenched Jainee away from every detaining hand, and every request for an introduction.

She felt helpless with this seductress on her hands. Men swarmed around Jainee Bowman like bees around honey. They could barely take a step without someone accosting them, and, to be fair, Jainee did nothing to signal their interest.

220

It was frighteningly disheartening. It was the dress, that face, those eyes, her spectacular beauty and unusual height. It was all of those things and none of them; it was something she exuded, mystical, magical, potent.

Only Nicholas had not succumbed.

She hoped he had his wits about him tonight. She hoped she could even find him in this crowd.

Jainee saw him first, guided by some innate sense of feeling his presence close by: she didn't want to think that it was so, but she felt his eyes on her, hot and accusing. She could almost feel the heat of his anger and a depth of some deeper emotion drawing her, pulling her.

Unerringly, she swerved to the very place where he stood with Annesley—and someone else.

Someone female and fawning, curvaceous and willing.

Lady Waynflete saw him then. "Nicholas," she called, barreling into the crowd surrounding him. "Nicholas, you must—"

And then she stopped. "Oh dear, oh dear . . ." She gathered herself together and proceeded toward him again, her hand clamped around Jainee's wrist so that Jainee had no choice but to follow her.

"Dear Charlotte," she purred, pulling Jainee up close to the creature, so close that Jainee could not move without seeming incomprehensibly rude.

"Dear Jainee," she added, "here is Charlotte Emerlin, looking devastatingly lovely. I can't believe—" she broke off and began again: "Permit me to introduce Miss Bowman, who is staying with me temporarily."

Charlotte Emerlin turned and focused her steaming pale blue eyes on Jainee. "How do you do?"

Jainee was stunned. The woman was as like and unlike *her* as anyone could imagine. She was as dark, her skin as fair, her height more the norm, her flamboyance as studied as Jainee's was natural. And still, still, there was something the same, something smoldering and hot, looking to erupt.

Something there—something about Southam.

The woman was a pale copy of herself, and she resented terribly that she was hanging all over his arm.

Nicholas removed Charlotte Emerlin's clinging hand with no compunction at all about her feelings, his dark challenging gaze squarely on Jainee's impassive face.

"You wanted something, Lucretia?" he asked, his voice saturated with irritation.

She didn't know quite how to ask him to do something about Jainee, particularly since he didn't seem to be doing anything about Charlotte Emerlin's ill-mannered display of familiarity. "You must," she began, trying to twist her request this way and that to make it appear acceptable in company. Of course, it wouldn't work, nor would she display bad manners in making the demand outright; her words hung in the air while she sought something suitable to bridge the silence.

Jainee leapt into the breach. "Perhaps it is my lord who wants something," she said cattily, angrily, "or perhaps everything—or even everyone."

His flat black eyes positively bored into her. "I think not, Miss Bowman. I think I can say I have what I want when I want it. Unless you would care to contradict that statement?"

"It may be I would have cause," she countered, beginning to boil with anger at his arrogance. "Perhaps your lordship takes things for granted."

"Only that which is granted to me by virtue of *hard* bargaining, Miss Bowman. Anything beyond that does not pertain to the business at hand."

"And that seems to have the virtue of a new distraction, my lord. And perhaps a welcome one on both sides."

"Never say so, Miss Bowman. Nothing will deter me from claiming my rights in any agreement into which I enter—but my adversaries already know this," he added warily, as he became aware of Annesley listening avidly to this exchange, and Lucretia's puzzled expression. "Do they not, Annesley?" he snapped out suddenly.

"Indeed, Nicholas, they positively quake in their boots when they encounter you," Annesley said smoothly without missing a beat, his beatific gaze transfixed by the malevolent glitter in

222

Jainee's glowing blue eyes. What was here, he wondered, in this incomprehensible conversation which the goddess would not relinquish to the superior jibes of his friend?

"Well, we may consider that my lord has warned us all that he cannot be vanquished," Jainee said, "but perhaps wiser heads know better than that."

"Wiser heads would not have undertaken such public discussions," Nicholas said calmly, and Jainee felt the sting of his anger below his words.

She reacted instantly, intuitively as always. "One cannot be wise in such company," she said lightly, meaningfully deflecting his sarcasm. "It makes one's head turn, all the flattery and adulation. I cannot meet a man but that he is not begging for my favors. Have you not found that so, Miss . . . Emerlin?"

"And that is the point," Lady Waynflete interrupted, forcing herself into the conversation. "You must—no, I must—yes, I find I must leave sooner than I expected, Nicholas, and of course Jainee will come with me. That is what I wished to tell you. And that I hope you will call within a day or two."

"If you wish," Nicholas said indifferently.

"Well . . ." she didn't know quite how to take that impassive tone of voice, "then we'll bid you goodnight. Jainee?"

"My lord?"

"Miss Bowman."

He turned away almost instantly, and Jainee clenched her fists as she allowed Lady Waynflete to guide her away.

"And what was that all about?" Annesley asked insinuatingly, as he appreciatively followed the course of Jainee's figure as it receded into the crowd.

Nicholas shrugged. "I have no idea. The strumpet thinks she has some kind of claim on me, I suppose. But then, so do others," and he turned to Charlotte Emerlin, "when I have explicitly made clear that they don't."

Charlotte smiled nastily. "I won't allow you to say hurtful things, Nicholas. Nor will I go back to the past. I have told you I made a mistake, nothing more, nothing less." She paused, considering how much or little to say next.

Her mother had pounded her skin to the thickness of an elephant's with all her strictures and derision; Nicholas could hardly wound her worse. At best, he might be made to see the error of his ways. He only had to wed her, after all, and join together two great country fortunes. Surely that could not be distasteful to him.

Every man wanted money and more money, and now she had the countenance and polish in her manner to stand up to him. More than that, she was determined to have him, no matter what she had to do: she was prepared to make every sacrifice, even the most sacred one. The thought of it sent shivers down her spine, especially when she remembered just how Nicholas had scared her into breaking off the engagement.

But she had been a mouse to his lion then. He had pounced on her, nibbled away at her resistance all the while detailing every conquest he had made from London right down to Brighton and back, and threatening simultaneously to take her and discard her at his will, and without the wedding to sanctify the deed.

No wonder she had run from him screaming; the shock of it had torn her nerves to shreds, and sent her mother to bed for months at the sheer horror of her allowing Nicholas to terrorize her out of marrying him.

The moment her mother recovered, she had bent every effort to educating Charlotte on how to become a temptress so that she could play on equal ground with Nicholas when next they met.

She had even imported a juicy stableboy or two to round out Charlotte's instruction on the more worldly aspects of men, at a cost that she did not consider dear, even when she knew Charlotte was romping in the hay with both of them. Charlotte was learning to take the measure of a man—and it would be a far different Charlotte who would go to London in the succeeding season, one who would not scare easily, and perhaps would reach out her hand and boldly take what she wanted, and what her mother wanted for her.

All these things careened through Charlotte's mind as she assessed what to say and how to say it.

"Your mistake has already been rectified," Nicholas said

coldly, deliberately misreading her statement. "You rightly terminated our connection. There is no more to be said."

She recognized the tone of voice, but it did not cow her now. How stupid she had been. "As you say, Nicholas. One can only go forward."

"I wish you luck," he said baldly.

"And I you," she returned lightly, fuming at how easily still he could dismiss her. He left no room for maneuvering whatsoever; he had no compunction about any kindness at all.

There was nothing else she could do but leave him then. But she felt the encounter had not been a total disaster. Annesley, that old maid of a gossip, was regarding her with a renewed interest that was most gratifying.

Annesley would spread the word that she had changed, that she had spoken with Nicholas and not come away the worse for wear. It really was an excellent first salvo. The gossips would take it and run with it.

Maybe it would even outdo the latest fashionable flirt, the mysterious one they were calling Lady Desire . . .

Chapter Twelve

"You wicked girl — I think the only proper thing you did tonight was pay your respects to Arabella Ottershaw. I do not know how I am going to explain this to her, nor why I left early, which will be considered a great affront by my dearest friend. And over and above all of this, I do not know whether Dunstan was even there, and I had so looked forward to seeing him."

Jainee, huddled in a corner of the carriage and bundled into her fur-lined cape, listened to this diatribe with mixed emotions which, as always, settled on her practical dismissal of the nature of continually preserving appearances.

It was evident to her that it was solely the duty of women to box things in by the proper appearance, and she herself was getting rather weary of this reasoning.

She obviously was not proper, nor did she give a fig for how things looked. On the other hand, that vacuous Charlotte Emerlin seemed to be distinctly proper in spite of her overt possessiveness toward Southam, and that enraged her most of all.

A milksop woman, she characterized her angrily, and what had she to do with Southam and his self-righteous bargains; what if he were tumbling the milksop as well? She couldn't bear to think of it — that that whey-faced example of propriety and rectitude could even compete with her.

She barely heard Lady Waynflete's next words; they came at her from afar, the tail-end of some comment she had made which Jainee did not hear. Her ears pricked up at Charlotte Emerlin's name.

". . . nerve of that Emerlin, taking hold of Nicholas like that, and in front of dozens of people. No shame, that girl, none at all, and after what happened last winter. I would think her mother would have the sense to keep her away from Nicholas. He went haywire after that, he was never the same. And now he has *you* to contend with, for what purpose I cannot begin to conjecture. Oh! I feel a headache coming on. Thank God we are home."

Home. This was not home; this was becoming a prison with Lady Waynflete as the arbiter of *appearances,* and the cost of compliance was escalating by the minute.

She did not need to be sent to her room, and she supposed she might have exploded altogether had Lady Waynflete even tried to banish her. She shook with rage as she mounted the steps; she turned once to find Lady Waynflete staring up at her, an odd expression on her face.

For all she knew, she thought as she allowed Marie to unhook the dress and remove the beautiful netted overdress, Lady Waynflete was on her way back to the party so as not to offend her dearest friend. Perhaps it was well.

She would be alone in the house and she could sit before a warm fire, drink some chocolate, which sounded deliciously comforting, and sort out her thoughts. She had to calm down. Her very first inclination was to take out the robe with which Southam had gifted her and slash it to pieces with a knife. All she could think about was whether or not the Emerlin had a similar item, and whether or not she too wore it for Southam's pleasure.

She would never wear it again. Oh no, not for anything would she yield to Southam's pleasure. Rather, he would submit to hers. And she would make him pay and pay and pay . . .

Marie brought the fragrant pot of chocolate on a silver tray, along with the delicate cup and saucer and a plate of biscuits which Jainee devoured hungrily even before she poured the chocolate.

"Can you believe it? There was nothing in the way of food. There was nothing except people and more people, obnoxious, patronizing *people* . . ."

"And no one familiar?" Marie asked gently.

"No one," Jainee said, the heat in her deflating like a punctured balloon. "No one . . ." She wrapped herself in her chintz robe, settled herself in the chair by the fire, and allowed Marie to tuck a cover around her feet. "Too many men too anxious to court a stranger. I did not understand it. It was not flattering. And Lady Waynflete, angry as always. And the abominable lord, with some sneering milkmaid on his arm. But no one . . . no one familiar . . ."

Marie withdrew, and Jainee poured a cup of chocolate and contemplated the fire. If she could just set aside the force of her feelings . . . there had been so many people. She hadn't thought she was scrutinizing the crowd at all; there had not been time to even think about that as she was confronted by male face after male face delighting to ask for an introduction.

And yet, as Marie questioned it, she knew that somehow, unconsciously, she had been searching the assemblage for one face, *that* one face, the one that had haunted her dreams since she was a child.

Southam would want to know if she had seen that face tonight.

And perhaps, more than that, he would not let her challenge pass him by, whatever he had intended with the milk wench.

So much the better; she would fight him to the end, now that she had a grim suspicion how it would all come out.

The man who was her father did not inhabit the world of the *haute monde;* her mother had been mistaken.

And all her schemes had been for naught.

Later, Marie came and lay four long strips of satin across the foot of the bed.

"It is both good and bad that you cannot find the man," she murmured. "You must occupy Monsieur so that he will not press you so hard."

Jainee sipped her chocolate and forebore to comment that Monsieur had many ways of pressing her hard, and she meant to use the only one to hand that would give her the advantage, just as Marie was suggesting.

She did not need to map things out for Marie. Marie's understanding was perfect; she could have been kin to Jainee herself — they shared a like mind, and still Marie had never overstepped her place. It was well. She knew exactly what Jainee wanted and exactly what to say in all situations. Marie was clever—she had been trained in the court of Murat and that spoke volumes for the precise way in which she attended Jainee.

Jainee licked the chocolate from her lips as Marie doused several candles and refreshed the fire.

"Monsieur may not choose to come tonight," she said reflectively.

"Monsieur *will* come," Marie said, pulling down the covers on the bed.

Yes, Jainee thought, Monsieur would; it didn't matter when. But if he were servicing that curdle-faced milksop tonight . . . how could she hold him for more than ten minutes?

And what right had he to turn murderous if other men wished to beg for her favors?

What if the whole adventure blew up in her face and Southam threw her in the streets? Would not one of those dear solicitous men grovel for the chance to become her protector?

She would be lost to all propriety then; appearances would not matter, only her will to survive. The boy would be gone forever and history would not record the passing of one base-born emperor's son, nor the rash and impulsive demise of his heedless mother and thoughtless half-sister who debased herself to pursue her mother's dream.

There were nights like this when she was sure Therese had manufactured a lie and that she had risked everything, lost her virtue and all honor on the bed of a promise and a fairy tale.

Some nights like this, for all the weeks she had been in London on the whim of a lord who suddenly turned out to have some obscure ulterior motive for having sponsored her, which had nothing to do with his obsession with her body, some nights like this, she felt frightened and alone.

How did one fight against that, and play him for all the time she could get? And when in the end it turned out that Charles Dalton was a fiction of her mother in heaven, what then? What then?

She had nothing with which to parry; no resources but a small cache of silver and the temptation of her body—fleeting things at best, but surely useful in negotiating another situation . . . somewhere, with someone else?

But not yet. Not until he was finished with her, or she was finally caught in the lie; she was certain of one thing — she would never get away until *he* let her go.

Any other way would precipitate a surer scandal than anything else she had done thus far.

She poured another cup of chocolate and set aside the cover on her lap. The only thing she could do was keep Southam so entangled in her web of pleasure and gratification that he would not demand results sooner than she could possibly produce them.

She touched the satin strips on the bed and sipped lightly of the now cooling chocolate. It tasted thick and clotted on her tongue. It tasted of kisses and impropriety.

She turned and set the cup aside and then picked up one of the long satin strips and held it against her body. The light played off of its texture, infusing it with a slithery iridescence.

She held out her wrist and wound a length of it around her hand and halfway up her forearm.

Her skin was like ivory against the lustrous thong of satin binding her wrist and arm. It made her look helpless and strong both, fragile and powerful, an image of endurance and exquisite delicacy.

She unwound the strip and laid it out on the bed next to the others.

. . . his hands had shaken as he untied the ribbon laces of her slippers . . . and felt for the edge of her stocking . . .

She remembered, all of it, from that moment when she had devised the strips right straight through to his ultimate shattering possession of her.

The deed was done now; in that respect there was no turning back. She lifted the hem of her chintz robe and looked critically at the silky blue stockings that matched her gown.

Southam was unpredictable: he might choose to shun her tonight for some other more enticing entertainment. Or he might choose to appear in her room, mysterious as always, seeking to test her obedience to their bargain.

She felt a shiver of anticipation at the thought of flaunting his express dictates; she would never lay down and allow him to walk all over her. She would trip him up every which way she could conceive before she would surrender any power to him.

It was as simple as that: he might come, he could command, but she would do as *she* wished within the limits of his demands.

She shucked the chintz robe and began removing the thin shift that she had worn beneath the crepe underdress. In a moment, she stood naked before the fire, except for the thin blue stockings that encased her legs, and the knitted silver embroidered garters that held them up.

Her body felt hot and erect at the thought of what she meant to do. She reached over to the bed and took two of the long satin strips, and then she sat down by the fire, and slowly and luxuriously began winding them around her naked body.

Lady Waynflete chose to return to the Ottershaw party. She could not see any way around it. To have departed so precipitously would wound Arabella's sensibilities needlessly. And to have missed seeing her dear friend Dunstan yet another time before the onset of the seasonal whirl would have been foolish beyond permission.

Besides, Blexter had strict instructions that Miss Bowman was to be kept within the confines of the house, and no one had leave to transport her anywhere but back to her room.

She was well-satisfied, in any event, that her dressing down had deeply affected Miss Bowman, but to what extent she could not tell: it would either chasten her or arouse still further brazen behavior. If she had to bet on it, she would have wagered on her protegée's outspoken flaunting of the rules, and because of that, she set her sights on finding Nicholas first and making it plain to him that Miss Bowman was not welcome in her home any longer than it took for Nicholas to find her a new situation.

How he would do that, she did not know or care to find out. Jeremy had warned her, after all, and then washed his hands of the whole matter, saying this was one Nick trick that was going to discharge a scandal that would resonate into their lives forever.

Jeremy was a gloom and doomster, Lady Waynflete had decided long ago, and almost fanatically cautious. He was a perfect foil for Nick, and he had kept Nick hewed as close to the straight and narrow as anyone could. But he had also developed a taste for the cards himself, and for the odd incomprehensible, astronomical wager that had to do with being a man among compatriots.

He would not forsake Nick so readily; he was, if anything, piqued at Nick's preoccupation with the Bowman, and cautiously searching for the underlying reasons. What he could not understand, he set aside until it made sense to him. Nick was not making sense at all, even less so than when he was at his worst in the gaming houses, and so he relinquished all responsibility until the time Nick would confide in him.

Lady Waynflete could do no such thing. She was stuck with the chit and her out and out assaults on Lady Waynflete's good nature. She would most certainly haul Nick over the coals for this; but in the end, she would do for him no less than his sainted adoptive mother would have done. But even her patience would have worn thin after several weeks of the girl's plainspokenness.

She greeted friends she had not seen the first around as she reentered the Ottershaw townhouse, and she immediately sought out Arabella Ottershaw, as she must, in good conscience, do.

"My dear," she exclaimed, grasping Lady Ottershaw's hands, "my guest has unfortunately had to return home. The headache — too much unaccustomed noise and company, I am afraid. I send her regrets and her gratitude for your including her among the guests."

"Yes, of course," Lady Ottershaw said distractedly, patting her friend's hand. "I am so sorry, but then — all for the best. Very gracious of her . . . I do appreciate . . ."

"She will write to you herself," Lady Waynflete interrupted. "Now tell me, have you seen Nick?"

"I thought somewhere in there. Dunstan came, you know. They were talking . . . just inside. I'm sure you'll—"

Lady Waynflete was sure she would too. She relinquished Arabella Ottershaw's hands and practically dashed into the ballroom, looking first for Nick, whose height always distinguished him in a crowd.

Just as she departed, Nicholas strolled into the hallway and intercepted Lady Ottershaw. "Did I just see Lucretia with you?"

Lady Arabella wrung her hands. "Yes, and she was looking for

you, and I said—but then of course, I hadn't—all you need do is
. . . but then perhaps she'll find . . . or has he gone as well?"

All of her friends were well used to Lady Arabella's conversational perplexity; Nicholas knew exactly what she meant to say,
and he touched her shoulder reassuringly.

"No, Dunstan hasn't left yet, and I'm sure she will find him.
There is nothing urgent otherwise, Arabella, so you may rest easily
on that score."

"Oh, I do . . . I mean, of course—and you? But—oh, forgive
me—I didn't mean . . . I must—perhaps I should . . ."

"Please," Nicholas said gently, and turned her back toward the
ballroom. As always, Lady Arabella was overwhelmed with both
the size and success of any of her undertakings, and her yearly
party was no exception, particularly this year.

"There are so many people," she breathed in a replete sigh of
coherency, and she walked into the swell of the crowd without
looking back.

And neither did Nicholas; Lady Arabella's incessant preoccupation with navigating her own course through the eddying tide of
her guests left him deliciously free of obligation to her, or Dunstan
for that matter.

Dunstan had arrived, picked him out, had his say, and was now
engaged in deep and probably edifying conversation with Annesley who would keep him occupied with tales of their mutual friends
run amuck in Brighton (including himself, Nicholas thought
grimly, but then he had forestalled that tidbit of gossip by telling
Dunstan the whole himself), and very probably how he himself had
created the new Incomparable of the moment, Lady Desire.

While he, Nicholas, was going to create havoc with the goddess
queen who dared to taunt his wants, needs, desires and rights in
public and thought she could get away with it.

Gertrude Emerlin saw him go and she went immediately to find
Charlotte. "Southam has departed, you ineffectual girl. Do you
have any idea where he can have gone?"

"No, I don't. He was impossibly rude to me, mother, and he was
positively trading barbs with some gaudy bit of fluff I have never

233

seen before."

"You cannot allow any other woman to outmaneuver you this time, Charlotte. I am warning you—"

"Your spies could tell you more than I, mother dear. You have heard nothing in a year to indicate that Southam's interest lies anywhere else but the card table. This strumpet can only be some passing fancy, if indeed she has engaged his interest at all. He looked fit to strangle her—and me, come to that."

"My dear, you want to appeal to Southam's baser instincts, it is true, but not his murderous ones. What good can have come of such an encounter?"

"Annesley was there," Charlotte said promptly, "and he saw the whole, including the fact that I was as brazen with Nicholas as anyone could be in this setting and that I did not back down. More than that, mother, he probably knows who this lightskirt is. I wager he knows a *lot* . . ."

And in a corner of the vast ballroom, Max Annesley was, at that very moment, regaling the whole to Dunstan Carradine, who had a bored expression on his face.

"D'you know, Max, I have heard nothing but paeans of praise to the Lady Desire for the last four or five days, and I must be the only one in the whole of London who has never seen her. And at this stage," he added darkly, "I do not think I wish to. She can only turn out to be a vast disappointment, neither as beautiful as they claim nor as desirable as they would wish. Tell me no more, Annesley, I cannot take it."

"And you need not—here is Lucretia to entertain you further, Dunstan, and to answer the question of where the Beauty disappeared to."

"Oh!" Lady Waynflete said in disgust as she came close and overheard Annesley's directive, "I refuse to talk about that strumpet. She has caused me nothing but grief since I took her into my house—men falling all over her, Nicholas acting totally out of character, with a mouth like a bawd and no sense of gratitude or place or anything. My blood is boiling—my dear, dear Dunstan— it has been an age," and she stepped into a brief dispassionate hug which she initiated and Dunstan could not politely escape.

"Tell me more, my dear," he encouraged her. "This is the first I have heard that this Incomparable is something more than a disdainful goddess who refuses to grant man or beast the favor of a smile."

"Please—Nicholas shall hear the whole tomorrow. I am up to my teeth with her. She is like honeypot—no drone can resist her . . ."

"And they drone on and on about her too," Dunstan put in acidly.

"And she just refuses to be bound by anything like civil behavior, and I just do not know where it will end."

"But you haven't heard the worst," Dunstan told her, eyeing Annesley warily. "Or perhaps it is the best? In any event, perhaps you should know that all the buzzing bees have bestowed a name upon your beloved."

"I don't want to know," Lady Waynflete said instantly, but she knew that Dunstan was going to tell her; would, in fact, delight in telling her.

"They call her Lady Desire," he whispered, keeping his hand over his mouth so that only she could hear the words. "All up and down Bond Street and Oxford Street, in and out of Green Park, and in the environs of Mayfair and St. James, your little protegée has been anointed Lady Desire, and it will be said that the name tells the tale."

Lady Waynflete felt faint. "Does Nicholas know?"

Dunstan looked at Annesley's impassive face and then turned back to Lady Waynflete. "One never knows what Nicholas knows, Lucretia. You above all should be aware of that. On the other hand, he did have the good sense to select the most unimpeachable mentor in the whole of London, someone whose reputation and standing are impeccable . . . yes—you, my dear, so all this name nonsense *has* to be is high spirited folderol among men competing for something they know they have no chance of possessing."

"She is the most beautiful thing," Lady Waynflete said weakly, "she has masses and masses of coal black hair, and the most glowing deep blue eyes—you should see her, tall she is, taller than most, Dunstan, perhaps as high as your shoulder she comes, and the whole point is you could not mistake her for some innocent girl out of the schoolroom. I knew it immediately, and I tried to make her pass, but she would have none of it. Her worldliness bothers me so—and Nicholas has had me dress her to a fare-thee-well. The money . . . Dunstan, I am worried . . . a goddess, he called her in Brighton when he first met her. I don't know what to do."

She turned to Dunstan, seeking the reassurance he invariably gave her. Dunstan was never soppy, and he never lied either. He always spoke plainly and never had he been wrong.

He said exactly what she needed to hear. "Put your mind at rest, Lucretia my dear. It's perfectly obvious you need do nothing. Nicholas will take care of the whole. And if a scandal breaks, I promise you, it will fall squarely on *his* head and no place else. I swear it, Lucretia—because I will make certain that he bears the blame, and no one else."

He eased open the door of the bedroom, slowly, patiently and entered it with the arrogance of a man who knew he would be expected and would not be refused.

He had imagined the scene as he made his way there: the irksome Diana bound by his demands, dressed to his will, waiting on his whim, ready perhaps to beg his indulgence; he relished the thought even if it was out of the realm of reality.

She would never beg. She only knew how to provoke. And in the end, he might find out she was no better than she should be, and just what he had claimed her, but in the maddening anticipatory moment before his eyes grew accustomed to the dim light of the glowing fireplace, he wanted her. The cost and her nature were irrelevant.

He closed the door softly behind him and stood for a moment absorbing the scene, inhaling with his memory the faint scent of chocolate that permeated the air.

Nothing was as he had envisioned it. Everything was *her* way, *her* stage, *her* direction, and his instant displeasure was overborne simultaneously by his body's carnal reaction to *her* as the focus of her erotic setting.

The firelight danced all over her naked body; she wore nothing but a pair of thin silky stockings banded with stretchy embroidered garters, but around her body she had wound enticing strips of lus-

236

trous material, all around her legs and up between her buttocks and around her arms and wrists, and she lay on her belly, her face to the firelight with her luscious naked breasts yearning toward the warmth.

Her legs were splayed slightly so that nothing about her was hidden from his sight, and as she heard his slight movement behind her, she lifted her head, and those glittery "make-me" eyes acknowledged him, because nothing more needed to be said.

She had deliberately defied his stipulations, and she lay there, bound in voluptuous satin, just begging him to take her to task for violating their agreement.

And his first instinct was to give in to the rampaging demand of his insatiable manhood. And his second thought was to walk right out the door.

The knowing smile on her mouth stopped him, and he slowly began to strip off his clothes as she watched him.

Lady Desire — they had named her well . . . she was the embodiment of all they could ever ask for, and the deepest darkest of their most forbidden desires. And she was naked for him and only for him. She had created this fantasy of subjugation for him and only for him, and he did not know who would surrender to whom by evening's toll.

He kicked off his boots and pulled off his shirt to bare his chest to her insolent gaze.

Her eyes moved provokingly downward to the protruding bulge of his manhood; her eyes narrowed as she waited for him to remove the final barrier to his nakedness. Her eyes spoke volumes, begging him to show her the force she had incited in him.

He dropped his hands in the act of unbuttoning his trousers and padded slowly over to the bed.

Lady Desire wanted everything all her own way, and wasn't it too bad; Lady Desire was going to get exactly what he wished to give, nothing more, nothing less.

He climbed over the bedframe at the foot of the bed and straddled her legs. God, she was something, with her wanton body, her contemptuousness and that imperious challenge in her insolent eyes.

237

It was time to tame the vixen and subdue her defiance, to take what she so willingly offered and master the animal instinct of the huntress.

He grasped her thighs, moving his hands roughly over the erotically charged satin strips, upward and upward to feel the soft cushions of her buttocks and the enticing crease between. And then upward again to the delicious curve of her spine where it joined the small of her back and flared into her writhing hips.

Now it was his power which incited the temptress, his caresses rendering her helpless. He pinned her hands tightly above her head, and pressed his rigid body snugly against the pillowy curve of her buttocks so she would feel the hard hot jutting shaft of his desire.

She writhed her bottom against him, deliberately teasing him and enticing him, determined to show him who truly dominated whom. It was not a matter of mastery; she had only to force him to surrender to her taunting feminine temptation, and she did not need her hands or his deep probing kisses to do it.

She needed only his rock hard male capitulation thrust hard against her body to know that the moment of possession would not be long in coming.

He ached for her: she felt every luscious part of his elongating member. Every move she made, every upsurge of her buttocks against his jutting manhood begged to feel his nakedness. Every twist of her body seeking the close tight conjunction against her pleaded for his possession. Every mindless thrust of his body against hers in response to her deep-throated moans demanded his surrender.

She couldn't see; the lift of her arms high over her head obscured her vision. She could only feel; her body was electric with sumptuous sensations as his free hand roamed all over her, sliding and exploring every inch of her, stroking her satin bonds, caressing the tops of her silky stockings and the silky skin beneath.

She felt him resisting and resisting: he would not give in to her arrogant femininity. And she would not rest until she compelled his homage to her mastery of him.

He shifted, he worked himself out of his constricting trousers and he pressed his towering naked manhood forcefully against her buttocks.

"You will beg for my possession," he rasped in her ear, "for I will never surrender to you."

"You will beg to possess me," she hissed, "because I will never willingly submit."

And now he felt the rage of helplessness: he could not take her, nor bend her to his will. He pushed himself tightly, nakedly against her, his body perfectly aligned with hers, a perfect weight upon her, pressing her deeply and sensually into the heat of their bodies and the bed.

The tension between them escalated; her body demanded she move to entice him to join with her . . . she wanted it, she wanted it, she could not rest with it: her traitorous body demanded it.

She wanted to crawl away from him so that she would not feel the hot hard inviting heat of him jutting into her buttocks. Her breasts, crushed against the soft billowy mattress, yearned for his caresses, her nipples taut with unslaked desire to be fondled and kissed.

Her heart pounded, her primitive need for connection overwhelming her senses. She could hear him above her, his breathing thick and resonant with his suppressed desire, his body slick from the force of withholding his passion to possess her.

"I feel your need, goddess," he whispered against her ear.

"I feel something else," she retorted, twisting her head away.

Surely the potency of his need was greater than hers. She felt his taut little thrusts and the sensuous cradling of his hips against her buttocks.

Soon he would have no choice, the primitive power of his manhood would pull him beyond reason, beyond endurance. Soon he would have to give in to the driving demand of the elemental male within him.

Soon . . .

Her body arched against him of its own volition, and caught his last moment of coherent thought: his free arm slipped roughly beneath her hips and pulled her onto her knees to give him purchase to tempt her with the knowledge of the wet wild delights within her grasp.

He played with her there, rubbing himself against her slick heat, pushing at her and withdrawing from her, to entice her to beg for his carnal possession.

She felt the hot slip of his hard muscular manhood thrust meaningfully just within her velvet fold. And then again, and again, and then the long voluptuous slide of his nakedness against her bare skin. And then again, the tantalizing push of his nakedness into her wet heat and out again.

Deeper the next time, and away again. And deeper still until she moaned with pleasure, and squared her hips so that when his next thrust came, she surged backwards against him so that she fully encompassed every long inch of him deep within her pulsating center.

Who then begged, and who finally submitted? She did not know, nor did she care. The greed of her need could not differentiate anything but the driving pleasure that overrode every other consideration.

And his savage pumping manhood surged deep within her, endlessly, unceasingly thrusting, pounding, braced by his hard hot grasp around her belly so she could never get away, never get away.

His overpowering desire drove him and drove him, his need to master her like a pungent ungovernable force within him. He had never lost control, he would never give in, never, and yet his mind was filled with the image of her voluptuous body bound and enslaved, and he was the one grovelling at her feet. He was the one enslaved and enchained by desire.

He was just on the brink of surrender . . .

Her swamping climax caught her by surprise, the sensation roaring through her and crashing through her veins again so forcefully she thought her heart might stop beating. It came and it came, washing over her again and again, an unrelenting spume of sensation, the same as before and different — wholly different and unexpected, and known because it had come before.

She canted her body against him, reaching for the rest, letting it wash away in a white hot froth of feeling, letting it envelop him so that he would never let her go.

And then he let go; in one long churning moan of capitulation, he lunged into her gyrating body and spilled his seed deep within her shuddering core.

Her body eased down, and he pressed himself against her, still nestled within, and gave in to the radiant silence, and the intimacy of touching skin on skin.

She slept, she must have slept — or perhaps she had dozed in some dreamland where that wrenching pleasure had engulfed her and drowned her; something heavy and forceful weighted her down.

She shimmied her body away from it experimentally and found she could move, that she could easily maneuver her arms and legs out from under the bulk of his body without disturbing him. He rested now on his side, with his legs entangled with hers, the satin strips wound like streamers around his legs as if they flowed from the very source of his manhood.

She pulled herself gently out from under his restraining arms and legs and rolled softly toward the fading light of the fire. There was no warmth there, and she shifted her legs over the edge of the bed and pulled at the satin bonds that were both tangled in her legs and crushed beneath his body, and she finally gave up and just removed the strips from her body.

Her chintz robe was still on the floor where she had discarded it, and she picked it up and wrapped herself in it, seeking the least little bit of warmth, and then she poked at the fire to uncover the embers and added another piece of wood to it. It flared up immediately, crackling to life and light, the scent of burning wood overcoming the faint chocolatey perfume still in the air.

She edged the chair gingerly toward the fireplace and sat down to warm herself in the nascent heat. From this vantage point, she could watch him easily and she could defend herself purposefully.

But there was as yet no need; he slept, a great naked beast lolling on her bed, all legs and hair and rampaging manhood which he could not control, barely quiescent after the shattering culmination they had shared.

It fascinated her: she could not keep her eyes off of it. Or him. His clothes were strewn all over the bed and on the floor, and in his nakedness, he appeared to her both menacing and vulnerable.

The firelight softened the harsh lines of his face: sleep rendered

241

him innocent, perhaps even helpless, but the power of his body was not passive, even in repose.

Everything about him was long, strong and virile. Nothing about him was excess, from his broad muscular shoulders to his well-shaped legs. His was the body that filled out the clothes; his was the body that overwhelmed her bed, and sought to vanquish *her*.

But he would never do that, *never;* at worst he would get tired of their games — or bored. Yes, gentlemen like my lord invariably became bored. Or he would find out he had come to barter on a tissue of lies instead of omissions. All of that was possible, probable even — and then what?

Which of the myriad men to whom she had been introduced would take her on then? Which of them could she even imagine in a setting like this, in the aftermath of passion? Which of them could she outmaneuver so relentlessly?

Which of them would she even want to?

She could not for a moment conceive of where her Banbury tale would finally lead her. She only knew she did not want another protector to supplant lord Southam; she had to focus solely on keeping him totally enthralled by any means possible so he would not abandon her when her fool's quest turned out to be a cheating lie.

Would she never stop operating on the need of the moment? But it had always been thus, ever since she had undertaken the care and well-being of Therese after the boy had been abducted.

She had never stopped planning, never stopped scheming, never had a qualm about stooping to use any means at her disposal to get what she needed.

This was no different, nothing more, nothing less than she had always done; only the setting had changed and the manner of the barter.

She had exchanged the one thing she was truly free to offer, and it had not proved to be a terrible sacrifice, nor had the cost been too dear.

Yet.

The final accounting could be but moments away — or months. Lord Southam was religiously unpredictable — everyone had said so. And so she must be as mercurial, and more. She had to keep him off balance and utterly beguiled.

She had to contain him.

If only it were as easy as binding him up in blue satin and keeping him her prisoner forever.

She would take each tie and wind it around the most symbolic part of him and make it hers forever.

Would that be enough?

Could she . . . ? She knelt on the bed tentatively and listened to his firm regular breathing. One end of one satin strip just grazed her hand.

His manhood moved involuntarily, almost as if it were beckoning her. And if he were awake, she thought, her fingers playing with the sleek satiny tie, he would be trying to subjugate *her*. Always it was better to attack first.

She pulled at the tie and it slipped slickly between his legs, softly, sensually: a breath, a cloud, a kiss between his legs.

And gently, ever so softly, she began to wind her satin bonds firmly around the most potent part of him.

Instantly his manhood surged into her hand, demanding she take it, and she looped the lustrous satin strip on and on around the burgeoning length of him until it girded his erection to the firm ridged tip of him, and then she grasped him firmly and slid her hand down the slick material to the base of his hard male root, and then beyond to the taut sacs below in their crisp nest of hair.

They fit tightly just in the palm of her hand. She could take the long end of the satin strip that bound his manhood and wind it very gently around them . . . and just lightly pull.

She felt the power of having him completely in her hands.

He felt it, god, he felt it—that whisper soft constriction, taut between his legs, encircling him like a collar on a thrall.

And then her hands, working their way up his satin wrapped manhood, pulling those cloud soft bonds until she could loop one of them around the rounded crown of his erection. And then she tugged gently on it so that it just compressed the very tip, just . . . and a tiny pearlike drop of moisture appeared at its thrusting head.

She kissed it away, her hands cupping the upper part of his rigid

243

length between them, and he wanted to put every part of his body into her hands.

He felt boneless, weightless, as if she had absorbed all of his power, and he felt all mighty, as a new rush of vigor surged between his legs.

She was his, he felt it intensely, that no other man would claim her — ever; there was no tomorrow, no stories, no motives, no half-truths or lies. There was only this moment, with her leaning toward him, her hands surrounding him, her mouth possessing him — that was truth, that was reality: in the dark between them, there was life.

It was not love; it was solely the urge to possess, to isolate, to restrain, but whatever it was, it existed between them, in the dark and nowhere else.

He could never let her go, and he could not bear to think of *her* abandoning him. It would not play like that; it would not happen.

But he did not know what would happen except that he wanted her then and there again and perhaps again after that.

He reached for her, across the distance between them, and he stayed her hands. Slowly, he slid his own up to the edges of her robe and gently he pulled them apart to reveal her naked breasts.

"Oh God — Diana . . ." he groaned, and he pulled her tightly against his chest, his erection, his mouth, and he assaulted her lips and demanded her kisses.

She tasted faintly of chocolate and memory, and he felt as if he wanted to drown her in chocolate and lick it all off of her body; and he would — sometime he would. And he would drown her breasts in it and suck every last drop of sweetness from her nipples, he would — as her hands played with the enormous hardness of him between them, unwinding his bonds, enslaving him with her kisses, he swore, he swore, he would, he would . . .

Chocolate and satin, body and tongue, he would, he would.

She offered him her breasts, he guided her over his pulsating erection and pulled her deep into the pleasure part of the night, on her knees, straddling his legs, worshipping him, shackled by satin and desire.

She reveled in the extravagant sense of the connection of their bodies, and the feeling of utter control.

His hands grasped her hips, teaching her the ageless communion of lovers in this way. His mouth dominated hers, drowning in chocolate and dreams.

And instantly his body decreed his culmination: he could not hold back. With one grinding thrust, he took her and his senses went careening over the edge in one long explosive gush of pleasure.

And he couldn't hold on either, it was too much, too too much with satin and chocolate and the hands of the lady desire . . . he toppled her onto her back and sought the nestled point of pleasure before it evaporated and died.

She urged him on and urged him on; the feeling was different and still the same — she was empty and full and the lightning sense of pleasure crackled around.her. Her body reached for it and reached for it, bearing down hard on that amorphous center of her womanhood. A moment later the feeling broke, skittering along her body like snapping bolts of electricity.

She grabbed him, her fingers digging involuntarily into his skin as the lashing jolts of pleasure suffused her body over and over and over, and then swirling away like a wave from shore, pulling with it feeling, lightness, mind-convulsing pleasure and leaving only memory in its place.

She arched her body, seeking something more; but her body would not accept it. She pushed at his hand and he relinquished her, and rested his hand on her hip, as if that action could, in the aftermath, contain her as forcefully as her surrender to his sex.

The heat between them cooled; the heat of his desire was but a memory, and the satin bonds lay limply between his legs, symbols in the distance between them that this was a bargain between them, and nothing more.

He could not hold her: she did not invite an embrace. There was nothing warm about the goddess of the moon, he thought, but he had never been receptive to that kind of intimacy, either.

They were a well-matched pair, he thought mordantly as he watched her eyes flicker and her body melt into drowsiness. They were made for each other.

Chapter Thirteen

Lady Waynflete, feeling exasperated that she never could predict if Nick took her requests seriously, sent around a note to Berkeley Square the following morning, stressing the urgency of her desire to see him in person.

Of course, boy that he was at heart, such a remonstrative command could have sent him out of town for the day, since he took much rebellious pleasure in following no one's path but his own.

But she was amazed and rather mollified to see him present gratifyingly early on her doorstep, immaculately dressed in his usual black morning coat, buff pantaloons and top boots.

Nick wasn't a dandy, she thought admiringly, watching him as he entered the parlor where she sat, as was her morning custom, close by the fire with a pot of chocolate at hand. He wore his clothes simply and never affected the vagaries of fashion. No one dictated to Nick, and Nick, in spite of the fact he did not put himself through the exacting contortions of fashioning his neckcloth or wearing skin-tight coats and breeches, still had style and countenance. Moreover, he always looked like he was a man on his way somewhere, a posture decidedly at odds with the usual languid attitude of most young men of fashion.

Including Jeremy, she thought mournfully. It would have done Jeremy worlds of good to copy Nick's attitude and *not* his habits. But the other hand was that Jeremy had been right to be distrustful of the mysterious Miss Bowman from a Brighton gaming house.

"Good morning, Nick," she said lightly.

"Lucretia." He inhaled the scent of chocolate the instant he entered the room, as it fused with the scent of his sex and Lucretia's uncertainty.

"Won't you sit down? I won't be able to *think* if you pace around here like a caged animal."

Nicholas sat; plainly it would not do to antagonize Lucretia.

"Something to drink? Chocolate? I can ring Blexter to bring us some coffee."

"Lucretia—cut to the chase."

She sniffed. Nick hated the roundabout niceties that were supposed to cushion unpleasant things.

"Very well, Nick, if you must have it point blank at first dawn: I cannot have Miss Bowman with me any longer."

And this was what she most disliked about Nick: he yawned.

"Really, Lucretia? But it's been barely a month."

"The girl is impossible. You are wasting your time and your money with her, Nick, let me tell you," Lady Waynflete burst out in a rush. "Not that I can understand anything you ever do, but this caper positively defies comprehension. She has a mouth like a taproom bawd, she will not take advice, and no matter what she does, she has men hanging all over her every which way she moves. I tell you, Nicholas, I was fit to be tied last night, and all out embarrassed for the scene she made with those men. And all those lovely girls trying to get a word in edgewise, with their mothers pushing and trying to prise through the crowd . . . it was indecent, and so I told your Miss Bowman.

"You never did bring her to London to find a husband, and if you want to set her up as your light o'love, I would prefer if you removed her from my premises before that event."

"But," Nicholas interposed gently, "what exactly did she *do?*"

Lady Waynflete huffed. "She doesn't have to *do* anything, Nicholas Carradine. She just *is.*"

This was so exactly the case that Nicholas hid a smile. "Well then, what do you want me to do?"

"Find someone else to lend her countenance, of course."

"Lucretia, dear—it is too late now. You have pulled not only Jane Griswold into the plot, but Arabella as well. It would be more scandalous to turn Miss Bowman out than to keep her on with you for the next several months. It cannot do harm, and you may rest assured that by the end of July she will be out of your life forever."

"Well, yes . . . but what I don't understand is, what *is* the plot?"

And so like the ingenuous Lucretia to put her finger exactly on the case, Nicholas thought, hesitating a moment to consider his answer. Even he did not know at this point, because the fact was the elusive Miss Bowman had to provide *him* with some proof that his instincts had not been off the mark, and now she had been squired about to four different events, she had still come up blank each time.

"The point is," he said finally, "just what I told you: she is in my debt and I always collect."

"Smokescreen," Lucretia said roundly. "You have spent more to dress her in the first style of fashion than you can ever collect in the next ten years, and to what avail. Tell me."

Quick, sharp Lucretia, he thought: she and Jeremy might trip him up yet. Still, there was a point that he must teach Lucretia not to cross.

"I believe that is *my* business," he said coldly.

"*Not* when you bring it into *my* house and involve *my* friends," Lucretia retorted. "And *not* when the creature exudes such a magnetism that a man will look at no one else when she is—"

There was a knock at the door, and Jeremy entered.

"Mother—"

"My dear," Lucretia gushed, and then she turned to Nicholas. "In any event, Nick. You have to *do* something. Tell her not to *exude* so much . . . ah, Jeremy darling, how *are* you? Did you enjoy the Ottershaw party last night? And why didn't I see you for more than a moment?"

At that, it became a good morning. Nicholas did not leave. Jeremy arrived in time to have some coffee and was shortly followed by a host of his friends with whom he was going riding later that morning. And beyond that, she had made sure to send a brief little note to Miss Bowman, cautioning her to dress with care as she would be expecting callers that morning.

Indeed, following hard on Jeremy's friends' appearance, came Jane Griswold with the escort of her son, and soon after, Arabella Ottershaw, who refused to see anyone the day after her parties, preferring to hide out with old friends who would never gossip about her behind her back.

Jainee's indefensible tardiness was the only blot upon the early part of this day, and after a quarter hour passed, Lady Waynflete sent a discreet second note commanding her presence.

Marie delivered it and Jainee held it crumped resentfully in her hand as she paused in the hallway to check that her appearance was as it should be.

She resented Lady Waynflete's highhanded demands, but she knew she could not flout her wishes. The morning had been fraught with little things to put her in a bad temper: Marie's entrance into her room at dawn to find the bed in disarray and the blue satin strips entangled in the sheets; the first presumptuous note demanding she take particular care in her manner of dress that morning; Marie's knowing gaze as she impassively rolled up the satin strips and set the bed to rights. And then the second note, demanding her presence.

It was enough to make her scream, and that was over and above her regretful momentary feeling of tenderness for Southam, who had barely waited for the moment of her slumber to withdraw himself from her presence.

And Lady Waynflete's displeasure. And the fact she had as yet found no one who even remotely resembled the man she remembered.

It was curious that Southam had not questioned her last night, but then, she had chosen very carefully just how she would distract him—

And she meant from now on to wear the symbols of the night which had shown him clearly just who had enslaved whom.

She gazed at herself in the hallway mirror, and thought that her dress would pass muster with Lady Waynflete and her friends. It was a plain blue day dress from the collection of those she had brought from Brighton, the kind of dress in which she spent the mornings before she needed to dress for her nights at the gaming tables. Because of that, it had very little decoration, a plain front with a rounded neckline made to look like a vest over an underdress, long sleeves and black velvet bands edging the high waisted sash, the hem and the collar.

Nothing could be more innocuous except for one small meaningful detail: the sinuous cuff of blue satin wound around her wrists.

She patted her hair, which she had brushed into docile curls, smoothed the skirt of her dress, then turned and knocked on the parlor door.

It really was easy to get along with these well-to-do patronesses, Jainee thought from her seat to the right of and slightly behind Lady Waynflete. All she had to do was curb her tongue, restrain her dress, keep her hands folded in front of her and act awed and delighted that she had been lifted above her station by their beneficence.

It was hard; it was damned hard. She had not expected to see Southam there, nor Jeremy or Griswold and his mother, and she was especially shocked by the presence of Arabella Ottershaw, who ought to have been home receiving cards and thank you calls.

Still, Lady Waynflete treated her with that starchy, kind respect that paid obeisance to appearances, and welcomed her with a small degree of warmth, and invited her to sit beside her.

Nor could she evade Southam's black virulent eye, especially when he caught the lustrous wind of satin around her wrists.

She needed to do nothing. Everyone did it for her, asking her questions and answering them immediately, and greeting her as though she were some old friend, gently teasing her for joining them so late . . .

The scene was inevitably correct: the undercurrents threatened to swamp them all.

But she got caught up in it. She said pretty words of gratitude to Lady Ottershaw, and unexceptional words of conversation with Charles Griswold and Mr. Tavender. Here and there she replied to a rhetorical question addressed to her by Lady Waynflete as a means of including her in the conversation, and all throughout, she disdainfully avoided meeting Southam's eyes.

That was easy enough, but the heat she felt emanating from him almost fried her resolve. He was impossible, imperative, and utterly unending, and she couldn't conceive for a moment what he

250

could possibly want with Lady Waynflete this hour of the morning on a social call, especially since it had been borne upon her that he never aroused himself to do anything he didn't wish to do.

Yet there he sat, languid and smoldering, with perfect reserved manners, polite and attentive, speaking now and again with either Jeremy, Tavender, Griswold, Lady Jane or Lady Ottershaw, avoiding *her,* and aware with every fiber of his being every time she made one minute little movement.

It was a theatrical performance, a set piece where everyone knew his lines, scripted by years of precedence. There was not a false note anywhere, and yet the whole thing was a perfect illusion.

Her part was very small. A piece where she presented herself, said hello, and sat in the shadows until spoken to.

Perhaps it was best this way. Perhaps she needed to keep reminding herself that she was there solely on Lady Waynflete's sufferance and by the grace of her affection for Southam. It was a wonder she had not questioned his motives for asking her to do this great favor for him. Or perhaps that was the very thing which had brought him to the house this morning.

She felt a frisson of foreboding. What if . . . what if this morning's visit were the thing on which her future in London hinged? What if they had decided between them that—that what? She couldn't begin to think of a scenario that made sense. She only felt an imminent sense of danger and the presentiment that Jeremy had finally prevailed, and that Lady Waynflete would be perfectly happy to show her the door and not ask questions why.

Lady Ottershaw leaned forward toward her. "My dear, I must tell you—you must know everyone . . . even after you had gone—they wanted—well, they asked—and really, I couldn't tell—so of course I had to . . . well, that's one of the reasons why I'm—Lucretia knows . . . everyone was consumed with . . . well, Jeremy told them . . . so don't be surprised."

"As opposed to a dozen or two matchmaking mammas who will find their hallstands curiously empty of calling cards," Nicholas put in drily. "You made quite an impression, Miss Bowman."

Now he looked at her directly, and she had the grace to look away.

"So I was told by Lady Waynflete," she said. She couldn't resist the irony, and she was more than gratified by the dark warning look that passed over Nicholas' face.

"Oh, but who can blame them?" Lady Jane asked comfortably, even cozily, leaning forward to pat Jainee's hand. "You are so beautiful, my dear. Of course the men will fall all over you. But you have Lady Waynflete to show you the way of things, and I am sure that behind that wondrous countenance you have ample common sense and you will not let your head be turned by all the here and thereians who pressure you to make your acquaintance."

This wonderfully nurturing speech had the immediate effect of making Lady Waynflete feel a great deal better about Jainee. It was important to her that there be no misstep whatsoever concerning her sponsorship of Jainee and that no one feel that Jainee was trying to usurp that which rightfully was the purview of the families who habituated town every year during the season.

Even if it were true that Jane Griswold always tried to see the best in everyone and everything, it was also the case that she would be the first to censure any social solecism.

So it was even more gratifying that she had witnessed the events of the evening before and did not hold it against her protégée that the eligible bucks had chosen to chase after her rather than mind their manners.

And so she said, "You have put your finger on the very point of it, my dear Jane. Miss Bowman is the most level-headed girl I ever met, and I believe I can say she is the most plain-spoken. She knows exactly when to be candid and when to retire in grace, and I may say I am proud of how she conducted herself last night, despite all provocations."

Lady Jane and Lady Ottershaw nodded assent, and Lady Ottershaw said, "Oh, very prettily behaved . . . most impressed—all the men—how could you help?—never rude, very kind . . . no offense at all."

Thus sealing her approbation of Jainee's behavior by wholeheartedly agreeing with Jane Griswold, *and* in the presence of no fewer than four eligible gentlemen (including her beloved Jeremy) who would spread the word of how kindly her two friends had spoken of her protégée.

Lady Waynflete almost clapped her hands together in glee; perhaps the thing wasn't as bad as she thought, and perhaps she might get a bit of enjoyment out of it as she had envisioned in Brighton, when Nicholas had first proposed her undertaking the salvation of Miss Bowman.

And perhaps it all might fall apart in her hands, but this morning at least, surrounded as she was by friends and family, she felt secure in her decision, and even a moment's fleeting pride that she was chaperoning the beauty of the season.

The beauty, meanwhile, sat quietly beside her, hardly able to credit the deceitful *rodomontade* swirling around her. The play again, only the play, and the appearance to the audience — that was all that had any importance whatsoever, she thought acidly. It meant that Southam would not betray her, and neither would Lady Waynflete, so long as the rules and outward amenities were observed.

But she should have known that, she thought, and she should not have let Lady Waynflete's irritation daunt her.

Her part as Lady Waynflete's protegée was now part of the play and her circle had closed around her and they would not back down.

She was one of them now, and she felt a palpable sense of relief.

"Do not feel too secure in their sanction," Nicholas said suddenly, appearing by her side. "They will kill you as soon as embrace you."

"As opposed to those who would embrace me *and* stab me from behind at the same time? I prefer my betrayal in two stages, thank you, and I promise you I will never turn my back."

"You *are* too beautiful," Nicholas said, ignoring that, "and you will either be cut dead or lauded to the skies. There is no middle ground with this society, as you must surely have concluded by now. But I think it will be the worst for you because all the men will be on your side."

"Thank you, my lord," she said acidly. "I feel sure I can look forward to the rest of the season with that comforting reassurance."

"There is nothing comfortable about you, Diana. And no one will be comfortable around you except the legions of men who will follow you wherever you go. Take it as both a prophecy and a warn-

253

ing. And now I must mind my manners and give over my place to Tavender here, who is just salivating to speak with you."

She hated him, she really hated him and his steely barbs and his simmering black eyes that positively seared her with their malice. She hated him. Her hands clenched into fists as she smiled up at Tavender and he eagerly took Southam's place beside her.

She hated him, and she would punish him severely for his malevolent insinuations.

It really was quite easy, because he was watching her at that very moment with a proprietary eye, just daring her to make one misstep with the poor guileless Tavender.

In a way, it was too bad; she really had to mind her manners this morning because it was not only Southam's jaundiced gaze that was covertly watching her. Everyone in the room was observing her manners and her morals this day, and she could do nothing that would even remotely give rise to any gossip.

"Mr. Tavender," she said brightly, holding out her hand to him. "How very nice to see you."

It wasn't; it was excruciating sitting through a conversation with him and his well-meant, earnest compliments. But still, Lady Waynflete watched her with an eagle eye as Blexter brought in various tidbits for them to eat and pots of coffee and chocolate. Morning wore into early afternoon and everyone seemed loath to be the first to leave.

"Oh look," Lady Waynflete cried joyously, "we have more company," as Blexter handed her a card. "It's Dunstan. Dunstan has come."

A moment later, he appeared at the door, tall and elegant, bright-eyed and fit, his whole attention hewing to Lady Waynflete and no one else.

"Of course I've come," he said with a hint of snappishness which was either real or playful; no one could tell for sure. "I'm probably the only man in town who has not met your Beauty and I mean to remedy that this instant."

"Of course," Lady Waynflete said happily. "But you were nowhere around last evening, so of course you never met her."

She turned to Jainee, who was frozen in place.

254

"My dear, Nicholas' uncle, Dunstan Carradine. Dunstan, my protegée, Jainee Bowman."

She held out her hand; she wondered that she wasn't trembling from head to foot as Dunstan took it and held it in his own, tightly, warningly, and said, without batting an eye, "So charmed my dear. Lucretia, she is a raving beauty; all the reports were no exaggeration."

He turned back to Jainee. "You have taken town by storm, and the season has yet to begin. I owe you an apology for waiting so long to call."

She drew in a soul-steadying breath; she could not believe him, so aloof and collected he was, as if he were not as shaken as she. *You owe me nothing,* she thought viciously, as she smiled coolly up at him, hiding behind her gambler's face, the one that allowed her to stare into his with the same unemotional equanimity.

"Apology accepted," she said lightly, dismissively, as she tried vainly to reclaim her hand from the prison of his. *No, apology denied. The apology comes years too late—Father.*

Chapter Fourteen

It was inconceivable to her that no one in that room noticed the cataclysmic connection between them.

But then, why should they have? There was nothing about him that remotely resembled her: even his eyes, which she remembered as a deep sapphire blue much closer to her own, were nothing like her memory. They seemed faded, just as he appeared faded in the indeterminate way of someone grown older, different, far away.

His eyes were sharp, guarded, warning her, and the pressure on her hands was intense. She felt frozen in time again, she felt fourteen and she could, in her mind's memory, superimpose over this degenerated face the one that haunted her young girl's dreams.

She could hear his voice: *A moment, Jainee, a mere moment to take my son and be alone with him. Let me have my moment, child, because it may be forever before I see him again* . . .

A moment, she thought, her heart seized with rage as he held her immovable and some glittering conversation went on around her that she did not hear, a moment and then eternity; he had walked away with the boy and out of her life, and he had walked back into it just as cavalierly and expected her to breathe not a word.

He sensed her thinking: she could feel it, and she knew he could not read it in her eyes or the expression on her face. It was something in the tension of her body and the peculiar feeling of release once she had made the decision not to make the devastating announcement here.

Or not to make it, ever.

No, no—she had not thought that far ahead, but it was almost as if *he* had insinuated the idea into her mind all the while she had kept her eyes steadily on his face.

He was reading her eyes and she was reading his.

You would be wise to keep your counsel, daughter.

I have not decided quite how to handle it, but the story will be told.

I trust not. I hope you understand my warning.

But I have nothing to lose, father.

I will denounce you every bit as forcefully as you condemn me. Which of us do you think will be believed, tell me?

Still, when I fall, dear father, I will not fall so far as you.

When you fall, daughter, you may be dead . . .

She saw it—she didn't imagine it, the flash of pure murderous hate was there, gone in a blink, followed by the pacifying look of alternative reasoning: *you have no reason to tell—ever.*

And it was true, it was true: no reason except that it was a condition of her bargain with Dunstan's nephew; no reason at all beyond that, and her corroded need to confront him which had exploded in a way she had never dreamed all those years after he had abandoned them.

No reason ever if she wanted to stay alive.

"Dunstan, dear, you have monopolized poor Jainee unpardonably for this last half hour," Lady Waynflete interposed gaily without even a hint of subtlety. "The poor girl looks worn to a frazzle; I hope you did not bore her with talk of politics. No one is interested in politics this time of year."

Dunstan smiled ruefully. "Oh, I think not, Lucretia, but it is hard to remember every time I look at her face exactly what we have been talking about, is that not so, Miss Bowman?"

"I cannot see my face, so I am hard put to comment, sir," Jainee said testily, and she was startled when everyone laughed.

Lady Waynflete did not smile. "Well, I am never one to break up a delightful party, but it seems to me we are well into the afternoon and Jeremy and his friends will forego their plans for the day unless they depart now."

It was a signal, perhaps not so gracious as she might have been, but as she expected, Jeremy, Tavender and Charles Griswold immediately began making their excuses and taking their departure.

And as soon as they had gone, Jainee, in what Lady Waynflete thought was an unprecedented gesture of good manners, made her excuses as well.

What she didn't like and couldn't take was Dunstan, gazing deep into her protegée's eyes and murmuring, "We will see each other again, and soon."

She hated that. For one fulminating moment, she hated Jainee and she stood still as a statue as Jainee made her exit through the parlor doors.

Only then did Dunstan come to her and take her hands and suggest that they sit down together with Jane and Arabella and catch up on what had been happening.

And of course there was Nicholas, standing in a corner and glowering at his uncle, at Jainee, at Jeremy and his friends, to what purpose Lady Waynflete couldn't begin to understand.

The moment Dunstan made himself comfortable beside her was the moment Nicholas chose to take his leave.

Nicholas was *not* happy and she could not for the life of her figure out why when the truth was, *she* was unhappy and he should have sensed it, especially knowing how she felt about his uncle Dunstan.

But nothing mattered now Dunstan was sitting beside her and all cozy by the fire with Jane and Arabella; she never even noticed when Nicholas left.

And she quelled the jealous jolt of her heart when Dunstan put his hand over hers and began, "Lucretia, the girl is quite stunning. Wherever did you find her? You must tell me the whole story — every last little thing . . ."

She felt as if she had been struck by a bolt of lightning; for the first time in her life she could not conceive of what action to take. All she wanted to do was crawl into her bed, away from everyone, so that she could feel safe and warm.

There was no running, no hiding from the elemental truth of the matter: Southam's uncle was her father. The ramifications were appalling. It meant they were cousins; it meant they were blood. But

258

it did not negate all that had happened between them; the conjunction of their bloodline seemed so distant that it couldn't possibly be relevant. The worst part was, she could never tell him. And that was coupled with the heartstopping realization that her search was almost over, her promise to Therese fulfilled.

Her head whirled with the complications. Her practical self told her incisively, *run*. What sense did it make to remain in a place where there was such palpable danger? Why should she care about the boy? The boy was the boy; in all likelihood her father had never revealed his lineage — why would he have? It would only have linked him to the past he did not wish to acknowledge, and perhaps to something that would endanger his life.

How naive had she been not to assume that he would have planned for every contingency. A devious one, her mother had said, an aristocrat, a diplomat — and still she had not put the clues together to conclude she would be seeking a formidable opponent who would bring to bear every means at his disposal to rake over his past and cover every story.

Everything but one thing: the unexpected appearance of a daughter he never thought to see again.

What did a man do then, who had built a life for himself far beyond that one which he had chosen to share with the woman he had married?

She knew what such a man did: he dared her to wreck the edifice of lies he had built. He challenged her to try, and he threatened her life if she so much as attempted it.

And who was stronger? Who had every resource at his command to crush her and wipe her away as if she had never existed?

And who had not a particle of paternal feeling for a daughter he had not chosen to see in ten years?

She had no choices. She didn't know what she had except her obligation to Southam and the unexpected end of the line in her search for her father.

And the one was not compatible with the other.

For the first time since she had begun this adventure, she felt frightened, and she could not think of one solitary thing she might do to regain her momentum.

She could not even conjecture what might happen if Southam

were to appear this night. She ripped off the blatant satin wrist bands and buried them behind her pillows.

She refused tea and luncheon, and then forced herself to join Lady Waynflete for dinner.

The conversation was stiff with her unspoken resentment, and Jainee had no stomach at all for any contentious conversation with her patroness.

Nor could Lady Waynflete summon up anything to say to Jainee. She felt once again that the newcomer had usurped all rights, that her effrontery in permitting Dunstan Carradine such unlimited access to her person in public went beyond all bounds of good taste.

And she could not be fair about it; it was perfectly plain that Dunstan had come especially to see her—until he had caught sight of Miss Bowman.

It was just as she had concluded the night before: even dressed in the plainest of costumes and using no arts whatsoever to attract, the chit positively fascinated every man in sight.

There was no fighting it, obviously. She wished that Jane Griswold, who had championed Miss Bowman so eloquently, could take the jade into her home for just one week—one little week to see how Miss Bowman set everything topsy-turvy with her mysterious allure, and then she would see how understanding Jane would be, yes indeed.

And Dunstan, with his neverending questions about her; it made her blood boil just to think of his unwarranted interest.

In fact, both he and Nicholas had stirred themselves on behalf of Miss Bowman more than they had done in all the years she could remember.

She stared across the table at her and wondered why.

Miss Bowman, for the first time since she had arrived in London, looked totally fagged out. Her face was drained of color, and her eyes seemed preternaturally large in her face. She held herself limply, bonelessly, almost as if the fight had been knocked out of her somehow. She did not look feisty or at all attractive to Lady Waynflete at that moment.

Well, good, Lady Waynflete thought uncharitably. Why should the chit look forever stunning? Surely even beauties had days when they wished they needn't step out of their rooms. Perhaps this was one of Miss Bowman's days.

Perhaps the company had bored her to tears. Surely she would not scruple to say so.

Perhaps Dunstan had made a fool of himself in her eyes—oh, she certainly hoped so. Above and beyond everything, she considered Dunstan was *hers*. He had never married, never shown an interest in any woman that was not just a passing fancy, and in the end, he had always come back to her. *Always*.

A younger woman could not hold him, a man of his intellect and power of persuasion. A man like that needed a woman with a superior mind, a leavening of cunning, elevated social status and a wide circle of friends who could only be of use to him.

Jainee Bowman could do nothing for Dunstan Carradine except amuse him for a week, a month perhaps. And as evidenced by this evening, her beauty was not endless and forever. She could get tired, bored, annoyed just like any other woman, and all of her emotions would show in her face and etch away her beauty.

Lady Waynflete felt reassured by this, and by Jainee's unusual silence. Perhaps she understood that Dunstan was not permitted to be one of her conquests. Perhaps that was the thing rotting her soul from the inside and showing on her face. It would be well for her to comprehend that at the outset.

Lady Waynflete did not want to tell her. Lady Waynflete did not like scenes.

Marie looked at her closely. "Something is very wrong, mademoiselle."

"No, nothing." She denied it, knowing full well it was all written on her face and that Lady Waynflete had seen it as well.

"Something happened today?" Marie persisted, as she began helping Jainee remove her dress.

"No. Yes . . . I must think about this," Jainee said distractedly, taking the chintz robe that Marie held out to her and sliding her arms into the sleeves.

"Something has happened of importance," Marie said sagaciously, "and you know not what to do. Perhaps if you share it, mademoiselle, two heads might find a solution where one cannot."

Jainee sent her a speculative look. But Marie already knew the whole, or as much of the story as she had cared to tell. Marie was her ally, her quiet companion, ever grateful for having been lifted out of the backrooms of Lady Truscott's house and into the sumptuous life of the English aristocracy.

"I have seen my father," she whispered.

"Dieu," Marie muttered and crossed herself. "Sit down, mademoiselle, sit down; how shocking. How unexpected. You thought he was dead, I'm sure, for all your feelings to search for him — I believe you thought you would find he was dead."

Jainee nodded: it was true. She had thought — or maybe in the deepest part of her heart, she hoped that there would need to be no confrontation, no accusations, no recriminations.

And now — . . . *when you fall, you will be dead . . .*

"He is alive. I saw him," she repeated as if the words made him real and not the fact she had spent an hour in his sinister company.

Marie knelt before her. "Where? When?"

Jainee looked down into her kindly, ugly face, and shook her head. "I can barely believe it myself," she murmured, sloughing off the questions; she didn't want to answer questions, she wanted to *think.* But Marie wanted to minister to her; Marie shared her distress that the event had actually happened. She had seen him — he was alive.

But Marie did not understand the complications, and Jainee did not want to spell them out. "I saw him today," she said finally. "I just saw him today."

Marie patted her hand and rose to her feet. She took up Jainee's dress and smoothed the wrinkles in preparation to hanging it in the wardrobe.

"And did he know, mademoiselle?" she asked sympathetically, her voice muffled because her back was turned.

Jainee closed her eyes. On the stage of her mind, she could see the exact moment when Dunstan Carradine walked in the door, the instant she recognized him even before she saw him by his voice. "Yes," she said slowly, "he knew me."

"Mademoiselle must be on guard," Marie said suddenly, briskly.

"Look you, it must be true that he never expected to see you again, either."

"Yes, I have thought of that."

"We will take special precautions," Marie said.

"Yes . . ."

"Does Monsieur know?"

"No. Not yet."

"Does Monsieur come tonight?"

Ah, practical Marie. One always did what one must and when the thing was *fait accompli,* it was treated as the usual turn of events. Does Monsieur come tonight? As if she had been welcoming Monsieur into her bedroom forever, and nothing was unexpected.

She shrugged. "How can one know?"

"Nevertheless, if he comes, when he comes, I will watch. There will be no threat to mademoiselle in this house, in my care."

"Thank you, Marie." An idle promise that, but she could not tell that to Marie. If Dunstan Carradine wished to infiltrate a place, he would have the means to do it, and no rock solid peasant guardian would be able to stop him.

Look at how easily his nephew had penetrated the locked doors of the Mayfair townhouse.

Marie withdrew, and again she was alone with her thoughts and the pulsating desire to run.

Run where, with what? How many hundreds of pounds did she have secured in her trunk in the storage rooms of the house? How far would they take her and in what street in which city would she land, flat on her back, and no better off than she was now?

But her father would be nowhere around, her father would not search for her. In effect, she would be making a bargain with him: her silence in exchange for her life.

She could make the same bargain in London . . .

Could she? *Could* she?

An interminable series of bargains, one after the other, designed solely to protect her life after she had interfered in plans and schemes which had never concerned her at all?

She was a fool. If her father didn't destroy her, Southam would.

She groaned. Plans and schemes, and there was Southam, demanding she identify her father; how was she ever going to convince him that her phantom father was not in London so that she would not unmask his uncle?

Then again, she thought, he had taken a calculated risk bringing her to town and setting her up like this; she had not guaranteed that her father *was* in London. She had told him the fairy tale that Therese had related to her and he had chosen to make enough of it so that he agreed to the bargain.

After all, in two weeks or three, after she had made all the rounds he had proposed for her, it would have been likely she might not have seen him. And then what? What had Southam expected?

And if she told him, at the end of that time, that she could *not* identify the man who was her father, what then?

And why could she not decisively tell him now and end the farce?

He would have to take some kind of action—whatever it was, it would remove her from her father's sphere, and she could make some new beginning somewhere.

She hated trying to prophecy the future. To play games with trying to foresee what Southam or his uncle might do was worse than reading the cards. Nothing ever turned about the way one forecasted. It was as inevitable as the turn of the roulette wheel. Something always went wrong. Fate laughed. The gods were crazy.

She would *not* allow herself the lunacy of trying to predict what anyone would do. She couldn't. She would chain herself into an immovable lump if she tried to cover all of the "what if's" and possible complications.

No, she must deal, as she always had, with the event of the moment, and try to make sense of that. Perhaps fate had truly been kind. When she had lain upon Therese's dying body and made that promise to her, she had never dreamed that a year and a half later she would be in London and have met the man who was her father.

Everything was unlikely; nothing was set. A turn of the wheel, a pragmatic direction, and everything might change again, this time in her favor.

Was she not a gambler? Had she not risked everything on a turn of a card in order to accomplish her objective? And had she not made herself into the kind of woman who would always be noticed, and to whom men were kind?

She had planned it all and to the greatest extent, it had all gone exactly as she had mapped out. But only because she had not looked ahead, only because she had worked around the event of the moment.

And she had let nothing scare her, *nothing*, not even the thought of being bedded by Southam.

Edythe Winslowe had told her: one made one's moments, and it mattered not if she had been dealt a losing hand. Always there was something to work with; eventually, the cards would turn. She had only to take the risk and mind the danger.

Eventually she would draw the winning hand. Still, she could not fall asleep. Something had changed palpably in the atmosphere and she did not know how to define it.

She lay in bed, staring at the fire, watching the flames take on a life of their own as her thoughts went down wayward paths of their own.

. . . She must not show fear . . .

Southam would not come, not tonight: he was in a rage the entire afternoon as he watched her first with Jeremy's friends and then his uncle.

He thought Dunstan was taken with her . . .

. . . And Lady Waynflete, so cold and resentful at dinner, on her way to an evening of cards with friends, excluding her from the invitation deliberately, maliciously, even —

. . . Her voice, this afternoon, so cheerful, and yet, her eyes when Dunstan arrived . . .

. . . She was jealous of Dunstan's attention . . .

. . . No. How could it be, when Lady Waynflete was a widow and surely beyond considering another alliance for herself?

But why not?

She was inordinately fond of Nicholas, why not his uncle?

Had Dunstan ever married in England?

More layers. Her mind was sifting through the inconsequentials and upturning everything at the heart of the matter.

Now the complication of Lady Waynflete and her father . . .

No, she surely must be imagining that . . . But her father

had made a great show of sitting with *her*.

They were at stalemate . . .

He would do nothing if she did nothing . . .

If she were confident, if she were proud and did not let his presence cow her . . .

She would sidestep the question of her father with Southam and let him determine what the penalty would be . . .

Blood line . . . but no one was strict about cousinship in terms of preserving the patrimony — cousins cohabited, cousins wed . . .

For all she knew, she might be the daughter of some other man — Therese had never been particular. God — Therese . . .

She delved behind her pillows and pulled out the satin strips that she had buried there hours before and held them up to the firelight.

The key was Southam . . . Southam must be distracted, entertained, and bound to her as tightly as she tied the strips around her wrists so that he would be diverted from seeking her father. Yes, and just for as long as she could hold him away from the truth of it.

But the follow-up, the why of it — why did Southam seek her father? Yes — the key, the key, the why of it; their bargain had not been struck until . . . until what? Until in her distress she had called to him, she had said *"monsieur"* . . .

Her being French in some way contributed to his agreeing to their bargain . . .

But she could make nothing more of that.

Then Dunstan, back and forth to France . . . a wife and daughter — an illegitimate son abducted in the heat of a moment's peace before hostilities began again. He had no love for the boy, so why had he taken him? As a hostage? For blackmail? *Who? Who?* An emperor who was so far above the masses he would never even hear Dunstan's petition? It made no sense, no sense at all.

And if Southam did not suspect his uncle, then why had his interest been struck by the fact she was French?

Her head went dizzy with all the complications that crowded into her mind, and the questions, with odd alignments between her, her father and Southam.

"Ah, the queen of jades rests in her bower, preparing a new menu of tarts for common consumption," Southam's voice said from across the room.

Her head snapped up; she had fallen asleep, stupidly, indefensibly, unguardedly, for all of Marie's protestations of protection. And here he was, armed to the teeth with venom and stealth, and taking her by surprise once again.

"Oh no, don't move. You are a picture just as you lay, Diana, with your robe askew and the implements of your enchantment wrapped around your limbs. If only my lecherous uncle could see you now."

She knew it, she had guessed it; how perfect, how prime that he thought Dunstan wanted her. "He is an old goat, my lord, and he has no interest whatsoever in me."

"Oh, he is a goat all right, with poor Lucretia dripping honey all over him, and he will settle for nothing less than *garbage;* but he will not have *my* leavings until I am done with them, huntress. You will not go on the prowl for Dunstan Carradine and lure him into your satin toils, do you hear me, Diana? Do you?"

His anger boiled over; he could not bear the sight of her laying there as if she were awaiting a long line of worshippers, her body firmly and fully outlined beneath the thin material of the gown, the long length of her legs naked and entwined in the slithery erotic strips of satin.

For all he had known, Dunstan had come to her this night. He would not have put it past him after the fool he had made of himself with her; his uncle's inamoratas were legion, and he always went after the woman he wanted and got her.

He was in a rage, she thought: good. "You need not shout, my lord," she said silkily, watching him, attending to every shift of his diamond hard eyes and subtly maneuvering her body this way and that to reveal just that little bit more of naked skin to his burning gaze.

"So be it," he said, his voice calming down oddly. Already the hem of her gown had been lifted higher and higher on her thigh, and she had twisted her body ever so slightly so that the edges of the gown had parted and he could see the tantalizing shadow of her feminine curls.

She twisted the satin strip around her wrist and through her hair. She pulled it, watching him, down around her shoulders and between the partially revealed mounds of her naked breasts.

Down she pulled it, so that it lay enticingly between her legs, and down so that she could loop a length of it around her bare foot.

"I do not care about Dunstan Carradine," she said huskily, fervently; he had to believe that, he *had* to. She saw by the look in his eyes that he was hers, he wanted her, that Dunstan had become the furthest thing from his thoughts as he watched her play with the satin strips.

"Prove it."

She had not expected that; she had thought her delicious little seduction would work on him enough, but she could see that it had: his skintight pantaloons were stretched to the limit by his eager and responsive manhood. Now she must seduce his will, and that was the tenor of the game they played tonight.

She pushed herself into a sitting position and slowly untied her robe and slipped out of it. Now she was naked, in a pool of bright colors and blue satin, and she was rewarded by the fierce jut of his male root straining against the tight material of the breeches that almost could not hold it.

She did not know what to do next, what to contrive that would push him out of control to the place where he became hers and she became queen of his desire.

She picked up the end of one of the strips and wound it around her waist and crossed it over her midriff and then looped it around her breasts to compress them and push them forward, and then across her upper chest and around her neck. Her hands trembled, her body was edgy with explosive arousal just watching his response to her play.

She rose to her knees, like a naiad rising from the sea, inviting him, mutely calling to him, enticing him with her nakedness.

And there was nothing but the rock shelf of his manhood beckoning to her, and just the shadow of wetness at its very tip.

"What must I do, my lord?" she murmured, skimming her hands downward to adjust the strips of satin around the thrust of her breasts.

"You must show me there is no one else worshipping at the altar of your beauty."

"But I have revealed it only to you," she said poutily, wondering just where this game was leading. "I have kept our bargain."

"You have kept only what you wish to keep, and you dispense what you wish to dispense, Diana—witness today. It could be any other man standing here, surrendering to your nakedness."

"But it is you. And you have hardly capitulated," she said testily.

"Yes, it does make you sulky when your tricks do not work, does it not, Diana? I think you do not deserve such a feast of pleasure tonight, not after your siren call to every Jack-nasty in the whole of London. Perhaps you must learn that there is only one man who pleasures your body and owns your soul."

"And who might that be?" she murmured, slipping off the bed and brazenly confronting him.

There was no one like her, no one. She stood before him, arching herself toward him, all naked and luscious, gilded by firelight and streaming satin ribbon.

"Who must learn?" she whispered, extending her hand and touching the explosive tower of his erection. "Who would deny whom a feast of pleasure, my lord?" And she cupped him in her bold and questing hand. "Who stands before whom naked and offering a garden of delights?"

She stroked the massive bulge in his breeches. "Leave me now, my lord. Try to leave me now . . ."

He almost did it, almost—he wrenched himself away from her seductive hand, away from her lush breasts and stone hard nipples, but never could he tear himself away from the enslaving satin bonds that girded her body.

He tore away the impeding clothing that constricted his desire, and he reached for her, he hauled her up against his heat and his jutting hard length, and he held her against his body and whirled with her to move her against the bed, the wall, anything that would give him purchase to possess her instantly, immediately; he thrust his granite strength between her legs until he settled her nakedness against the door, and then, with one knee, parted her legs and covered her mouth and drove himself home.

She was floating on a sea of swamping desire, her whole world centered around the strength of him, the length of him and the thrusting force of his muscular possession. There was nothing else, not their mouths so furiously kissing, not their bodies so fiercely bonded together, not his words, a cadence in time with the rhythm of his thrusts eking life between his harsh hot kisses: "you are mine, you are mine, you are . . . *mine.*"

Nothing, nothing but the sole thrusting pleasure of *him,* ferociously claiming her, filling her, cradling her in a thousand lusty movements to prove his need and his desire.

His was the proof, hers the acceptance of his need; he had enslaved her forever by the virtue of this bond.

She drowned in a sea of pleasure, her body at the mercy of the virility of his. She felt every inch of his power, every relentless pounding thrust, all the heat and lust gathered in the carnal ramrod length of him.

And soon, in this maelstrom heat and explosive desire, he centered himself deep within her, finding the distended point of pleasure between her legs and working it, working it, thrusting and teasing it, pushing against it tauntingly, inviting her to close herself around him and find her glistening culmination.

Her body stretched against him luxuriously, seeking him, climbing against him, and finally settling and seeking that one elusive moment of recognition.

She bore down on him suddenly, frantically, loving the feel of her nakedness against the fine material of his clothing, loving that she was naked and open to him and that the fullest, most carnal part of him was serving *her.*

The cloth of his coat was rough against her breasts; the ferocity with which he possessed her elevated her streaming pleasure. It was moments, moments until the storm would break, moments . . . moments . . . it was coming — it broke, it broke, a shower of gold tingling all over her body, lightning, light, crackling through her veins; her body shuddered and shook with the force of her climax, reaching endlessly, mindlessly for the dark lush pleasure.

She rode it, rode with it, demanding more; her swollen mouth begged for his kisses as her spangling body calmed and the pinpoints of golden heat danced along the sheen of her moisture-soaked skin.

And from there it was but another moment until he gave in to his passion, to the lush call of her body, and finally to the grinding racking spume of his release.

And then he held her there, still tight, taut, deep within her, his hands framing her face, smoothing her hair, touching her kiss-stung mouth, suffused with the scent of their sex, the enormity of their play.

What was there between them? He could not comprehend anything but the driving need that centered him deep within her. Nothing more, nothing less. The feelings in his heart did not enter into it: there were none.

Women were born for betrayal: he had known it from birth, and he held that little bit of himself in reserve, waiting, waiting, waiting for the moment unearthed.

And she, she knew nothing but the throbbing need to bind him to her so irrevocably he could never get away. Men were born for betrayal, she had known it from her youth. She could only surrender and hope for the worst.

And when he finally left her, after carrying her to her bed, she felt a little prickle of abandonment, as if she could never contain him, and he would always leave her.

And who had capitulated to whom became not the point; the point was the swirling, opulent, swamping pleasure that swallowed them both and bonded them whole.

No other woman could serve him as well as she; she knew it, as she lay in her fertile pleasure bower, and he wanted her, and she would prove it to him . . . forever.

Chapter Fifteen

Everything seemed clearer in daylight. Even Marie's knowing look as she came to awaken her did not offend. There was something about a bright spring day with the sun streaming in the windows and a cozy fire by which to dress that made her feel as if she were overreacting to what were, at best, nebulous impressions of threats and plots and Lady Waynflete's secret yearnings.

These were the things that were real: her father had walked into Lady Waynflete's parlor and had turned out to be Southam's uncle; Southam wanted to use her to find her father, but for what reason she did not know—and now needed desperately to know. She could not tell Southam that Dunstan Carradine was her father because of Dunstan's singular unspoken threat on her life. She needed to buy time to try to find the boy.

Oh, the boy. The boy, the boy; somewhere in the shuffle the boy had gotten lost, and she really found herself wondering if she absolutely had to find the boy. She wasn't sure, even in her own mind.

She needed time to convince Southam that her father was nowhere to be found, or if he did not believe that, that her whole story was a hoax, top to bottom: a wager perhaps that she could twist even the dangerous and difficult Lord Southam around her little finger.

And that she had done with astonishing speed and thoroughness—except that his real interest in her lay in the story of her father.

And so she came back to Dunstan and the implicit threat her presence posed to him.

That was the reality, tempered by her suspicion that Lady Waynflete had been dangling after him for years with unrequited love, and she owed Lady Waynflete more than she could ever repay for her help and guidance.

There it was—a circle, a compass, with all the points meeting in her father.

She did not know what she was going to do.

"Dunstan has sent round a note that he intends to call this morning," Lady Waynflete said when she made her appearance for breakfast. "Perhaps you might tend to some shopping this morning?"

Such an off-handedly pointed little hint. "That sounds pleasant," Jainee agreed instantly, rather glad to have an excuse not to be at the townhouse when Dunstan arrived. Or had he thought he might come upon *her* in the course of paying a long overdue visit to Lady Waynflete?

He would be sadly disappointed, she reflected, but that was for Lady Waynflete to contend with.

"Very well, then. I will have a carriage sent around, and you will take Marie with you, and remember she *must* accompany you at all times. And I think . . . I think the Burlington Arcade has the most to recommend it. By now you must need to replenish some ribbons and the like. Hawkins will be driving and you may rely totally on him. Now, the air is very brisk this morning, Miss Bowman, so it would be appropriate to take your cape."

"Thank you, my lady," Jainee said meekly, refusing to rise to that pointed barb.

"You might spend the morning," Lady Waynflete called out to her as she was on her way up the steps to change into a walking dress.

You might spend forever, Jainee thought dourly; she might climb in that carriage and never come back, and for one dark moment, it seemed like a terrifically tempting thought.

But not without money, not without a plan, not without a final break with Southam, not with knowing what she knew about his uncle and doing nothing . . .

It was so good to get out of the stifling atmosphere of the

townhouse. It was perfectly clear to her that Lady Waynflete knew she neither wanted nor needed any refurbishments to her already extensive wardrobe. But still, the prospect of travelling alone through the streets of London had some merit and the novelty of adventure.

For the moment at least, she could enjoy the sights and sounds without feeling the pressure of Southam's demands upon her shoulders.

London was a city of movement; there was someone on his way somewhere every minute. The wonder was there were so many places to go. But then, she had done the morning rounds with Lady Waynflete; the fashionable world needed its occupations as well as anyone else.

And one of them was shopping in a massive mall filled with shops and fronted by palladian windows reaching fifteen feet to the ceiling. Inside its doors, shelves stretched floor to ceiling, stuffed and overstuffed with materials of every kind, color, pattern, thickness and delicacy. Stretched along the walls fronting these shelves were counters, hundreds of feet of them to display every manner of adornment from velvet trim to feathers, beads, gold and silver thread, buttons, braid, ruffles, lace, ribbons of every color imaginable, and thread to match.

It was easy enough to spend an hour browsing through the variety of goods here, and to select a length of ribbon, a set of black velvet bands to use for trim on a particular dress she had in mind, to choose a package of bugle beads for Marie to sew onto one or another of her lightweight shawls, and a package of needles for Marie.

What to do now? Not nearly enough time had elapsed since she had departed the townhouse, her purchases were made and duly tucked away in the carriage, and she had been warned by Hawkins that she was not to walk about with Marie, and the only choice she had was to put herself in his hands for a ride in Green Park before they returned home.

She was amenable to this, but truthfully bored by the prospect of going around that park drive yet another time. There was nothing new here; it was the same path and the same people, and she hadn't yet determined why this morning ritual was so revered.

But suddenly she sat up and took notice. Ahead of her, astride a beautiful, high-spirited mount, accompanied by a phalanx of admirers, was Edythe Winslowe.

She looked anything but bored: she looked entranced and enchanting, and as if she did not miss a thing.

She saw Jainee the moment Jainee saw her, and by an imperceptible movement of her stock, she motioned Jainee to meet her somewhat further on, beyond a copse of bushes where she knew they might have a moment's private conversation.

"Quickly, my dear. How do you go on?"

"Passably well."

"Nonsense—what have I heard about these past two weeks but the beguiling Lady Desire. You have made your mark. What? Had you not heard the name? Oh my dear, they speak of you everywhere, from the night of the Tallingers' party, at Lady Badlington's—forgive me, you weren't meant to know . . ."

And she remembered the whispers, the buzzing sibilant sound when she entered the Ottershaw home. Yes, Lady Desire, they were saying it, nodding to each other, pointing her out—clearing the way so that everyone could see her . . .

"Listen, my dear; we must meet. Come in twenty minutes: Covent Garden, twenty-five. Don't be late."

And she was off in a cloud of scent and galloping hooves.

"Mademoiselle—you need not go."

"Of course I need go, Marie, what are you saying? Miss Winslowe was my friend in Brighton. I will not cut her in London."

"Very well, mademoiselle. It is for you to decide," Marie murmured, but her disapproval was obvious, and Jainee did not know quite what to make of this reversal.

She honored her friendships, such as they were. Edythe Winslowe had predicted they might meet in London and that she would indicate how Jainee was to treat her, and she had done so: Jainee knocked on the roof hatch and Hawkin's face appeared.

275

"I wish to be driven to the address the lady Winslowe gave me," she said imperiously.

"Yes ma'am," he said, and inwardly, she felt relieved because she had been sure he would question her or that Lady Waynflete had provided him with strict instructions as to where he could or could not take her.

The only drawback, perhaps, was that though the carriage was not one of the more distinctive ones in the Waynflete carriage house, its driver, nonetheless, was known to be Lady Waynflete's man.

Well, it could not be helped, and the traffic here appeared lighter in any event. Probably it was not likely that the sticklers among the *ton* would be wending their way through Covent Garden at this hour.

The small rowhouse was easy to find, and luckily there was a carriage house behind so that Hawkins did not have to wait in front of the house.

Edythe Winslowe threw open the door before Jainee could even knock, and admitted her and Marie, whom she promptly dispatched to the kitchen.

"Tea will be forthcoming, and we will sit and have a cozy chat, and you will tell me how you are coping with your great success."

The rooms were smaller here than in Lady Waynflete's house, and everything much less grand, but still tasteful nonetheless. Edythe's admirers did not stint in their gifts, and she had been canny enough to demand not only clothing and jewelry. The house was hers alone and the furnishings within, and the day her last paramour abandoned her was the day she could retire in comfort and want for nothing.

"There, doesn't that smell good and *hot*. Sit beside the fire, Jainee, warm yourself. I'm sure that old witch Lucretia never thought to tuck a hot brick under the seats so that you would be warm while you travelled. No, no, you need not take off your cape if you are warmer with it. Take this cup of tea, that should help. Now, tell me everything."

Jainee sipped her tea, wrapping her hands tightly around the thin china cup and reveling in the heat. "But you know everything. The bargain was struck, Lady Waynflete took me up and I have made my appearance at several exclusive parties and have earned a dubious title into the bargain. The men are attentive, as you and I knew they would be, and I have made my moments, as you so rightly advised me, and I teeter now on the edge of success or failure. I have seen no one I could identify as my father, and so Southam will be bound to take me on or throw me out."

"Ahhh," Edythe Winslowe breathed. "Southam. How goes it with Southam, my dear?"

"He is intractable and impossible and hateful into the bargain."

"And how does he as a lover?" Edythe asked slyly.

Jainee hesitated. "I know not what you mean, madame."

"He beds you," Edythe said plainly. "I see it in your eyes, my dear. You cannot hide anything from a woman who has had the experience of men that I have had. And I have seen him. He is more reckless, less forgiving than ever. So—how does he as a lover?"

"He suits me," Jainee said briefly.

"Yes . . . he suited me as well," Edythe murmured reminiscently, and Jainee stared. "Oh? Hadn't you guessed? But no, you were too preoccupied with your own concerns. Yes, Southam did court me, but it was a short-lived affair, and it was he who abandoned me when I was perfectly content with what he chose to give me. I have never," she added, her face hardening momentarily into something awful and vengeful, "forgiven him. When I think how I groveled at his feet, begging him to take me back . . . only one time, only once. Never more than once when I really want a man. Never. But I have never forgotten the humiliation of it."

She pinned Jainee with her malicious gaze. "I swore I would have my revenge. The thought of it has sweetened the months since we left Brighton. And I have chosen you to be my instrument of reprisal."

Jainee almost dropped her cup. This woman with the malignant eyes was surely not the woman who had willingly aided her in Brighton just to amuse herself and stave off boredom. Or had *she* been naive at the very moment when she had been congratulating herself on her perspicacity in selecting the one right person to tutor her?

"I don't understand," she said finally, because she could not mesh her image of Edythe Winslowe in Brighton with the calculating brittle woman seated opposite her.

Edythe Winslowe smiled slyly. "By all accounts, you have learned well the lessons I taught you in Brighton. And by now you have also seen that illusion is more powerful than the reality. By the same token, what a woman's reputation appears to be is more important than what she does behind closed doors. You have gone fast and far in Southam's world and you've done it in a very short time. Part of your success is due to your uncommon beauty, and part is due to Southam's pushing you, subtly, behind the scenes.

"Of course, the astonishing part to me is that you have lasted this long. I fully expected Nicholas to be weary of the novelty of you before you even arrived in London. That does say something for your fascination, my dear, and it gave me the first inkling of how I might claim payment on your debt to me."

She held up her hand as Jainee started to protest. "No, no— don't read me some fairy tale about Lucretia Waynflete, please. I can read between the lines and I know very well how things stand. And so this is what you will do for me: you will ruin Southam."

The bold-faced outrageousness of that statement caught Jainee by surprise. But not for long. Already she felt an encroaching fury sweeping through her very vitals. How dared she! This woman, this friend for whom she had felt some affection!

Attack, attack—her mind geared into action almost instantly, defending her against an unspoken threat.

"I will not listen to this," she said with some heat, setting aside her cup, and rising as if to go.

"But of course you will, Jainee dear. You have no choice; you are walking tender ground here, and no one knows it better than I. You stand to lose everything if I bruit it about where you came from and how exactly you got here and how deeply Southam has had a hand in it—so to speak."

"You will look like a fool, and I will lose nothing."

"Do not wager on that assumption, Miss high-and-mighty Beaumont. Consider—Lord Ottershaw is a very particular friend of mine. Now were this to be the topic of discussion among the gentlemen of his set, it would only add to *my* luster as a desirable companion, and more men and more would want to follow his lead. However, the same would not be true if word got around about your liaison with Southam. No indeed, and in fact, the thing only has to be given life to make any one of your new-found friends doubt you.

"You could present a court-case of evidence that the inference was not true, and still you would be tainted. Your invitations would diminish, Lady Waynflete would politely disassociate herself from you, Southam would drop you faster than a winning card at *vingt-et-un*. Of course, as long as you were impeccably sponsored with the right credentials and nicely chaperoned, it wouldn't matter what the bucks called you behind your back: that would be considered delightful speculation as opposed to grim reality.

"So you see, I could probably pull you deeper down into the dregs than ever Southam could—or would. Gentlemen tend to buy off their mistakes; women destroy them.

"Think hard on it, my dear. You need never see me again. You have only to act, to seize the moment to somehow publicly humiliate Southam. It could take any form—from leading him into bankruptcy, to accusing him of forcing you into doing unspeakable acts . . . *I* do not care so long as you hang his laundry out to dry in public.

"Do you not, and I will see that you are washed down and thrown away with the bath water."

"I see," Jainee said through dry lips. "And how much time do you give me to accomplish this magic act?"

"Oh . . . it is April now—I should think that by the end of May you would have sufficient time. The season will be in full swing by then, and it is the last time and place you would want to hear *your* private affairs made public. It is the last gasp of the

279

season, my dear, positively fraught with every kind of social event and nuance possible. A perfect place to unleash the fireworks of a scandal, believe me.

"I promise, we need never meet again. From time to time, I will send you a little message to let you know I am thinking of you, and waiting in the shadows for that one divine moment of revenge.

"And when you accomplish it, my dear, you shall have a just reward. No good deed goes unrewarded in my world. I shall furnish you with the means to escape Southam's retribution."

"You are crazy," Jainee snapped.

"No, no, Jainee, only practical, the same as you. We are sisters under the skin; it is why you chose me as your mentor and tutor. And it is why I chose you. Think on it, my dear. When you are ready to acquiesce, I will know."

She rose up and pulled the bell-rope, and her servant entered. She snapped her fingers and a moment later, the servant returned with Jainee's cape.

Jainee wrapped it around herself with nerveless fingers; she couldn't find a single word to say to Edythe Winslowe's fantastical plan. Perhaps no words were needed: perhaps the thing would go away. But then she looked into Edythe's cold clear eyes, and she thought not.

Edythe walked her to the door. "Your maid has been sent round to the carriage, and it should be at the door just now."

And indeed, Hawkins was waiting, and ready to assist her into the coach. When she was seated, Edythe peered in through the door.

"Goodbye, my dear; I'm so glad I saw you in the park today."

And what if she hadn't, Jainee wondered as the carriage lurched forward. What if she had never ventured near that bedeviled park, had never seen Edythe Winslowe anywhere socially, would Edythe have found her anyway and issued her inconceivable threats and demands?

It almost seemed like some kind of conspiracy—that for the first time since she had come to London, Lady Waynflete expressly asked her to leave the house, and then this had happened.

But that was too farfetched. The correct assumption had to be that Edythe Winslowe had been watching and waiting and planning, consumed with jealousy that Jainee Beaumont had been successful where she had not.

And she was such a puny instrument of revenge, walking the fine thin line between Southam's will and Lady Wayneflete's fear of social ostracism.

She had no room to maneuver, she who was at Southam's mercy every which way. It really would be easier just to run away.

In the ensuing journey back to Lady Waynflete's townhouse, she thought of two dozen things she ought to have said to Edythe Winslowe, and the one she had not: *no.*

Two heart-stopping surprises in the space of two days were enough, she decided as the carriage drew to a halt. She would not even think about Edythe Winslowe's intolerable blackmail. All she could do was hope that Dunstan Carradine had departed and left Lady Waynflete in reasonably good spirits.

Distracted by her thoughts, she stepped from the carriage; she heard a thrashing in the bushes and the harsh yowl of a cat confined against its will. Simultaneously, she heard Marie shriek behind her: "A mouse! A mouse!" and she turned her head sharply as something scurried across her line of vision. Marie cried out again: "A cat—watch out for the cat!" and she swung her body around abruptly as something flashed out of the bushes after the mouse, and her foot stepped down, buckled under and her body toppled forward.

Her arms flailed out, reaching for something to hold onto, and there was nothing. She felt as if everything were turning upside down, and then she fell heavily on the ground, her head snapping backward to strike the ice cold marble of the lower step.

"Well, *was* it my fault?" Lady Waynflete demanded petulantly

281

as the doctor rinsed out another warm cloth and laid it against Jainee's forehead.

"It was not your fault," Jeremy said reassuringly, tugging on her arm to lead her away. "I sent for Nick. The doctor is competent, and you had better rein in your feelings of responsibility for something that was an accident, pure and simple, otherwise someone will begin to think there was something more to it."

"He was a present from Dunstan," Lady Waynflete said unhappily. "He was so repentant that he had not called for months; he wanted to make it up to me. So original. A companion for me, he said. Another man might have offered diamonds, but not Dunstan."

"Dunstan Carradine isn't in a fair way to affording the size diamonds you covet, mother," Jeremy said tartly. "Now come, Blexter has laid out tea in the parlor. The little monster is nowhere to be found, by the way. It's as if it disappeared into thin air, out and gone. But the doctor says Miss Bowman will recover and be right as a trivet within a couple of hours. You have no need to dress yourself with guilt."

"I wish I had never taken the chit in," Lady Waynflete said mournfully. "Dunstan truly only wanted to see her. The animal, that messy shedding cat, was only an excuse. And to what purpose? She was out, and so now he comes to dinner tonight. You *must* stay. So, for that matter, must Nick when he gets here. I don't think Miss Bowman will be in any condition to dine with us. But what if she is? What if she is?"

"Then she shall," Jeremy said practically, handing his mother her cup of tea which he had expertly prepared. "Rest easy, mother, it cannot be quite as critical as it sounds."

Lady Waynflete sniffed. "It can and it is. If she continues attending social functions with me, *I* shall be persona non grata because all the mothers will resent her beauty and the way men just buzz around her. Thank God she is not on the marriage mart, because I swear I would disown her before I would take her to the sanctum. No, Jeremy, this little affair of Nicholas' must end. I told him so the other day, and he sloughed it right off. But Dunstan hadn't come back then. Or actually, he had, only several hours after I told Nick . . . it doesn't matter. He's taken by her beauty and there is nothing I can do. *She* will receive diamonds, I would wager a hundred pounds on it. And I am left to explain to Dunstan how his lovely gift of hair and claws disappeared."

"I never did like the scheme to begin with," Jeremy said, "but we are left to clean up the aftermath, in spite of Nick's intentions — whatever they were. It positively destroys my faith in him."

"He was such a sad and lonely child," Lady Waynflete said. "I always think of that when I put myself on the line for him. But no more, no more."

They sipped in silence for a while, and at length, Blexter appeared, looking most serious. He bowed to Lady Waynflete and began, "I beg to report madame that we instituted a wide-ranging search for the creature and it cannot be found. All possible avenues were explored with no results. It would appear the creature wanted to disappear."

"Thank you, Blexter." He withdrew and Lady Waynflete turned to Jeremy. "Do you see? Not even Dunstan's gift wishes to find a permanent place with me."

"You are making much more of this than you need," Jeremy said blandly. "And now — here is Doctor Goodale. What news, sir?"

"The girl is awake and seems to be aware of herself and her surroundings," the doctor said briskly. "She took a heavy blow to her skull when she fell; there will be a lump, but she does not seem disoriented. Actually, she seems quite angry."

"Well, of course," Lady Waynflete said. "She will have to spend several days at rest, no doubt, and won't be able to go around exuding that beastly whatever she has to attract Dunstan. *I* would be angry too."

"Well, you are right on that charge, Madame. She must remain in bed for the succeeding several days, and perhaps take things a little slower thereafter, so we may be sure that neither her senses nor her equilibrium have been affected."

"Thank you, Doctor," Jeremy said quickly, before his mother

could put in another of her rash condemnations of Jainee. "What more must we do?"

"Watch for fever, dizziness. Let her eat — lightly — if she is hungry. Camomile tea for thirst. Barley water for fever. Some laudanum if she cannot sleep. But she appears strong-willed to me. The bump will recede in a day or two with continued application of a compress. If she changes for the worst, call me immediately."

"She won't," Lady Waynflete muttered. And then she remembered her manners. "Thank you, Doctor. And thank you for coming so quickly."

"No trouble, Madame."

Jeremy saw him to the door and as he drove away in his gig, Nicholas' carriage drew up and he was out the door, sweeping Jeremy into the house with barely a how do you do.

"What happened?"

"Ah, Nick, settle down; there is nothing critical here. Dunstan visited this morning and brought mother a fool cat that got out and scared Miss Bowman as she was debarking from a carriage and she took a fall. She's fine and feisty and the doctor does not believe she will stay in bed above five minutes, if we would let her."

Some of the tension drained out of him. "Yes, well — I must see to my investment, mustn't I?"

"Is that what she is?" Jeremy murmured. "Well, come; she is awake and ready to take on all comers."

She was awake, she wasn't sure she was alive, and she was drowning in a burning wetness which Marie kept assiduously applying for her forehead.

"Ah, Monsieur . . ." Marie breathed as Southam appeared in the doorway.

Jainee groaned. "Tell him to go away."

"Monsieur Waynflete accompanies him. I can tell him *nothing*," Marie whispered, and moved away from the bed as Nicholas came forward into the room.

284

And nothing would have stopped him anyway, she thought. His face looked as black as the night, and Jeremy Waynflete had already tactlessly withdrawn.

"Well, Diana, don't you look wan and fragile and delicious lying in bed. What kind of stunt was this? And who were you expecting to keep vigil by your bedside?"

She looked up at him balefully. "Your manner is most pleasing, my lord; it positively puts me on the road to recovery."

"Let us hope so before all your agitating admirers storm the doors and demand to be allowed to spoon feed you your medicine *and* their verbal swill."

"And may I say how *your* visit has refreshed me?" Jainee murmured, her voice dripping with irony. At that, perhaps it had: she felt tinglingly alive and combative again, ready to battle words with him or anything else he might choose as a weapon.

"What happened?"

"I fell," she said baldly.

"You are not clumsy."

"No. Something shot out of the bushes and distracted me just as I stepped from the carriage. It could have happened to you, did you arrive before me, my lord. There is nothing more to the story."

"Except that all will now express their intense desire to succor you in your hour of need; my mind reels with the possibilities."

"Your mind is deranged," Jainee said flatly, "and you are giving me a headache." She thought that sounded good, but she was sure she did not look as if she had a headache or even as if she had had an accident. She looked as if she were cozily abed, awaiting a lover, so of course his rage was out of all proportion with the incident.

"I will give you hell if my Uncle Dunstan walks through that door," Nicholas said darkly, and Dunstan's voice immediately rejoined: "Isn't that a little drastic, my boy?"

Nicholas turned and Dunstan entered the room with Lady Waynflete at his heels.

"Well, you can see for yourself, Dunstan, she is right as rain, no lingering after effects except for that awful rag on her head.

Marie will have her up and about in no time."

"Truly?" Dunstan asked, reaching for Jainee's reluctant hand.

"I am fine," she said tightly.

It was only a warning, his eyes said; his back was to Nicholas and Lady Waynflete—no one could see but her. *Heed me.* "I am pleased to hear it," he said, patting her hand. "Are you well enough to join us for dinner?" *I want you where I can see you,* his expression told her.

"I think not," she said, pulling at her hand.

"The doctor prescribed rest," Lady Waynflete put in. "Really, she ought to have some tea—I have ordered it for her—and a good long rest. Come, Dunstan, there really is nothing more we can do here . . ."

"Of course, Lucretia, you are right," he said lightly. "Perhaps I might call tomorrow, Miss Bowman, to see how you get on?"

"Yes, yes," Lady Waynflete said impatiently, "of course you can. Now come, Dunstan; Miss Bowman should not be forced to make conversation after such a potentially dangerous accident."

"As always, Lucretia, I bow to you. Nicholas . . . ?"

"Uncle."

It was like a dance. Step by step, they circled around each other—and her—trying not to appear obvious, each trying to gain some amorphous upper hand. She felt dizzy watching it; dealing with them sapped her strength.

By the time they left her alone, she was shaking with the enormity of her father's tacit confession.

It was only a warning . . .

A little diversion to send her tumbling to the ground, nearby a pristine marble step . . . that if she had twisted and fallen one way or another could have been spattered with her blood.

Her father had meant to kill her.

Chapter Sixteen

Dunstan's good humor was not at all overset by the fact that the feline had run away. "These things happen, Lucretia," he said temporizingly over dinner. "I would never assume you deliberately disposed of a gift that I gave you."

"Well, of course not," Lady Waynflete said indignantly, well pleased to be surrounded by three elegant gentlemen, one of whom was her heart's desire, and to have the new bane of her existence safely in bed a story and a half above her.

"The girl is astonishingly beautiful," Dunstan said, directing his comment to Nicholas now. "And probably up to no good. I'm really surprised at your foisting her off on poor Lucretia, Nick. You haven't a clue about her background or her motivation. It is not like you to be so imprudent. In fact, it is damned *un*like you."

Nicholas smiled grimly. "Whatever it is, she is here, and Lucretia has been good-hearted, if not patient, about it. The season will be over soon, and Miss Bowman will recede into distant memory. I daresay everyone will have forgotten her by the beginning of July."

"I would like to forget her now," Lady Waynflete said meaningfully, as the servants began to serve the soup course.

"Lucretia always knows what is important," Dunstan said.

And she was also expert at diverting the conversation, Nicholas thought, covertly watching his uncle. For the life of him, he could see no sign that Dunstan was smitten with the goddess, but Dunstan was as unfathomable as himself when it came to revealing emotion.

But neither had he mentioned their dinner of a month before when he had first revealed the existence of Miss Bowman and ill-conceived suspicions that Dunstan had summarily dismissed.

He didn't know quite what Dunstan's game was, but sooner or later, a clue would emerge. Dunstan was a little too lighthearted, a little too interested. A little too obviously making full use of Lucretia as a smokescreen for whatever his real intentions were.

Poor Lucretia, who had loved him so soulfully and so long. Poor Lucretia who had taken him under her wing and tried to nurture him the way his mother might have done had he allowed it, and had she lived longer. Lucretia would find no satisfaction in either of the Carradine men but she refused to believe that—yet.

He and Dunstan left together that evening, and Dunstan clapped him on the back as they stood waiting for their carriages to be brought around

"I never thought to see you fall, Nick, but I tell you, the only thing to do is take my advice: use her and lose her, or you'll be leg-shackled before you know it."

Or maybe you will be, Nicholas thought, glowering. *Or maybe she'll enslave us all and then run away with the first coxcomb who asks her.*

"And don't keep seeing plots where there are none," Dunstan added, in parting. "You can only fob off one nabob's heiress on society in a year, do you take my meaning?"

Nicholas waved him off and entered his carriage. On a whim, he glanced up at the second story of Lucretia's house where one window and only one was lighted up. The curtain moved and a woman's figure appeared, silhouetted against the back light; and the curtain dropped with heavy finality the moment Dunstan's carriage drove out of view.

* * *

She spent the ensuing two days staring out the window, almost as if she thought she could prevent Dunstan from doing anything as long as she could see him.

But of course he would never make so conspicuous a move. He would be subtle: he would unleash a cat, for instance.

There was no untoward movement outside the house for those two days, no suspicious loiterers. She felt as if she had invented a fantasy, and that if it were revealed to anyone, she would be condemned out of hand.

The bump on her head receded, leaving a faint bluish mark. She ate on a tray in her room, she drank quarts of tea and barley water, she spent hours drowsing in bed, trying to evade the truth of what had happened.

No one called, and no one came to see her, and she could have dropped out of sight forever, she thought morbidly, for all anyone cared.

Lady Waynflete gratefully left her alone and went off to one of dozens of myriad entertainments in the offing each night.

The streets were filled during the day with carriages and riders and gaily dressed people walking, walking somewhere, and she was bound for nowhere.

"Monsieur has been tactful these nights," Marie said to her that evening as she brought in the night's dinner on a tray.

"Monsieur has much to entertain him besides me," Jainee said trenchantly. But she felt lonely and isolated, suddenly, and at the mercy of a man who moved silently in the shadows.

She did not know what to do.

She could not pretend to be affected by her accident for the rest of the Season.

Nonsense. She turned away from the window on the third

morning castigating herself for her cowardice. But she didn't even know what her choices were any more.

Lady Waynflete bustled in. "Well, you look fit as a fiddle this morning, Jainee. I will tell you these last three mornings have been an absolute trial, with all your men callers leaving cards and demanding to know where you had been the night before. I won't answer for my patience if this keeps up. Do you feel well enough to go out and about today?"

She felt a profuse feeling of joy. "I believe so, my lady."

"Very well; the reason being that Dunstan has engaged a supper box at Vauxhall tonight and has invited us and Nicholas to join him for dinner, fireworks and who knows what all. I will tell you that his interest in your welfare puzzles me greatly, and I trust you are discreet enough not to encourage him in the least. Do I make myself clear?"

"You have always made yourself uncompromisingly clear, my lady. I have no interest in that quarter."

"I expect that will have to do," Lady Waynflete said grudgingly. "But none of your tricks, my girl: a plain dress tonight, if you please, something to withstand the cool night air. A cashmere shawl will do for a wrap. Perhaps a reasonable neckline will ensure some warmth?"

Jainee ignored her testy comments. It was enough to speculate on why her father was doing the conspicuous thing. Did he mean to shove himself in her face and fairly dare her to unmask him? Or was this sociable veneer a cover for the subtle warning he would continually issue for as long as she remained compliant—and silent?

She could not tell from anything in his manner when she and Lady Waynflete were escorted by him into the Gardens. He was ever the gracious host, familiar with the layout of the Gardens and certain of the box that had been engaged for him. It was a matter of a promenade on the Grand Cross Walk, a side tour to the two other prominent walks which featured displays which he was sure Miss Bowman

290

would enjoy and Lady Waynflete would like to see once more.

From there, it was a matter of nodding to acquaintances and to be seen as well as to see who was there of an evening before Dunstan led them to their supper box where Nicholas already awaited them.

Dunstan had already ordered the dinner, and while they awaited its arrival, they listened to the orchestra playing in the grove and spoke of mundane matters from Jainee's health to Southam's recent losses at White's, to Lady Waynflete's gossip about the dinner she had attended the previous evening.

This discourse was interrupted frequently by acquaintances stopping by and finally by the service of the food; Dunstan had not stinted in spite of the high prices and thin helpings of the meat, fowl and accompaniments. The presentation was lavish and included hams, chickens, fruits, biscuits, tarts, wine and, later, dessert.

"Now, at nine promptly, the orchestra will take a brief respite," Dunstan said, "and at that time, with your permission, I will escort Miss Bowman to view the wonder of the Cascade—which I am certain both Lucretia and Nicholas have seen enough times to last a lifetime. Now, do try the chicken; it *is* quite tender."

And he ignored Lady Waynflete's pained expression as she outlined his plan, Jainee thought. He did not care about her or how he hurt her feelings. If she had had a choice to refuse him, she would have, but soon enough the music stopped, and Dunstan indicated to her that they must depart.

Outside the box, he took her arm roughly and led her quickly away.

"You have been admirably reticent," he said as they joined a crowd of patrons gathered around a scene of a quiescent waterfall and some kind of mill.

"Where is the boy?" Jainee asked softly, hoping to shock

291

him, and to catch him off-guard. But it was a mistake. His expression changed into something dangerous, lethal.

"I'm sorry you remember about the boy," he said finally, and the tone of his voice did not change. "Look ahead, my dear. The waterfall begins and will turn the waterwheel below. It is quite the attraction here, but perhaps it will seem mundane to you."

"I remember everything," Jainee said fiercely.

"That is too too bad, my dear."

"My mother is dead."

"It grieves me."

"And now you try to kill me."

"You cannot prove that."

"You engineered that almost disastrous fall—"

"Nonsense. I was nowhere near Lucretia's house."

"Where is the boy?"

He gave a harsh laugh. "Safe, my dear. And that is all *you* need to know. Ah, the spectacle is over. I hope you enjoyed it. I hope you take to heart just how tenuous your position is. I truly cannot bring myself to threaten my own daughter with out-and-out violence, but please believe me, I will stoop to it if you cross me. If one word about our mutual past is bruited about, you will join your mother in whatever hell she occupies."

He took her arm again, tightly, ruthlessly. "Enjoy your Season, my dear. Put Nicholas through hoops: you would be the first woman in many a year to attract him so intensely. Take all you can get, and then get out. I trust you will take me at my word. You will be sorry if you don't."

They came in sight of the supper box nearby the Grove.

"This is the last warning you will get from me, Jainee. The next step is action. Ah, Lucretia, my dear, the Cascade remains the same frothing stage show it always is. You missed nothing, but your protegée was suitably impressed, weren't you, Miss Bowman? Oh yes, I see by your eyes, you were *very* impressed by the presentation."

292

* * *

The man was a chameleon, changing his appearance to accommodate whatever his surroundings demanded in coloration.

He would ever be Lucretia's hero, Jainee saw it plainly in her eyes, and he had become his nephew's nemesis, purely by his untoward interest in her.

And he was implacably her enemy, with no familial affinity whatsoever.

She could not sleep for thinking of all the things he had said and everything he had not said.

The boy lived — safe, he had said . . .

She felt tears creep out from under her eyelashes.

Join your mother — in hell . . .

Poor Therese, to have adored a man like that.

Poor Lady Waynflete, to be so fruitlessly in love.

And Southam, so silent and brooding, saying nothing, seeing everything, imagining the worst while Dunstan considered *him* negligible.

They had escorted her and Lady Waynflete home and had left to spend the remainder of the evening in deep play at Lady Badlington's gaming house.

Jainee's fingers itched to take hold of a card. She felt furious that she did not have the freedom of a man to go where she wished and do whatever she pleased.

The truth was, she was too jaded to partake of the innocent delights of a Season, and her background and status in Lady Waynflete's home precluded her receiving invitations to certain other events to which most marriageable young women looked forward.

But she was walking a fine line in some ill-defined middle ground, squeezed on both sides by the pressures from her past.

What she really wanted to do was call a carriage and drive to Lady Badlington's, wager her silver, and show them her mettle.

She walked to the window and looked out into the night longingly. Somewhere, there were still people at dinner, at parties, playing cards, playing with living.

And somewhere out there, someone lurked in the shadows, hiding behind bushes, skulking in the night.

She didn't know if she imagined it: she thought she had, but in the dim light of the street light, she thought she saw a movement, she thought she saw a man with his head turned toward her window and Lady Waynflete's house.

Her father was watching her; her terror ran deep. His threats were not idle. Once again, she could not sleep.

In the morning, Marie brought her a note which she unfolded hesitantly. "Monsieur will call today, formally, *downstairs*." She looked up at Marie. "I must be sure to dress appropriately."

"Bien, mademoiselle. We will make Monsieur take notice."

"Monsieur notices too much already," Jainee said repressively. "Something with long sleeves, I think, and one of those infernal waistcoat bodices. I do not feel like attracting Monsieur this morning."

Nor did he feel like playing games with her. Lady Waynflete had had him shown to the parlor, was mindful not to serve chocolate, and left him alone to await Jainee.

She arrived ten minutes later and shut the door briskly behind her. It was obvious from his expression that Southam was in no mood to bandy words.

"What do you want?" she asked directly, seating herself without a preamble and without the usual protocol from him.

"As usual, your plain speaking is disarming," he said, positioning himself opposite her. "I want to know how your search is progressing, Diana. And I want to know why my uncle has such an unholy interest in your welfare."

294

"I have nothing to report on either account."

"My dear Diana, Lucretia and I have taken you and thrust you into the highest circles, just as you enjoined us to, so that you could circulate and meet every possible prime candidate who could be your father. And you are telling me, there is not a one, not a familiar voice or face or mannerism of any person in the whole of London who reminds you of the man we seek?"

Oh, she would be lost now if she so much as moved a muscle. Dunstan's malignant expression flashed through her mind. Not a one, not a single solitary person . . . she could not fit the words to the tune. *I can't bring myself to threaten my daughter with violence . . .*

Yet. But he would, he would—she had seen it in his eyes and the feral expression of a man who would do anything to protect himself. He would.

And yet she had to give Southam an answer: he had *paid* for an answer, and in the end, perhaps, that was all that mattered: the answer—the right answer.

She lifted her head, her mind racing furiously. What was the answer to the man who was fast losing patience with her, and with himself?

"Not yet," she said finally, unequivocally. What was another lie heaped on the rest?

He began to pace around her, slowly, thoughtfully; there was no hint of temper in his attitude, only a kind of weariness, as if this were a game he was growing tired of playing.

"Perhaps the man does not exist," he said, his voice devoid of expression.

"The man exists," she said flatly, without missing a beat; and even he was nonplussed by the conviction in her voice.

"He may not be in London."

"He is *not* in France," she countered in that same flat tone. "But then, he may not wish to be found, my lord, and you may not wish to pay the price to buy the time it may take to uncover his whereabouts."

"Time is easy to buy, Diana. But what is the cost of credibility?"

"It has been but two months, my lord."

"Only two? It seems like years you have been having a grand time spending my money and acquiring a smarmu collection of coxcombs and court-cards, and with nothing to show for it but Lucretia's growing exasperation with your brassy mouth and your public displays."

Yes, Lucretia Waynflete had gotten to him, she could see that, and she had to wonder in that fleeting moment whether Dunstan had made any connection between them. Did it matter? How could things be worse?

She turned away from him abruptly and walked to the window that fronted the street and looked out. It was a fine sheltered life. Lady Waynflete lived in this beautiful home—she nursed her hurt feelings like an animal tended to its child, coddling them, protecting them, sustaining them to give her some hope of the future.

But she had no dreams to sustain her now: she had fulfilled her promise, she had kept her bargain, and when she would leave, she would have no life to return to, no hope to give her sustenance. She wondered if Southam had even thought of that. She was astonished that she, the ever practical planner, had not.

"And of course," she said dreamily after a moment or two, "there is always Lady Desire."

She heard a faint movement: her back was to him, and then he said impassively, "Oh, so you heard about that? You're damned lucky Lucretia hasn't."

"And if she does?"

"The games are over," he said brutally. "So I suggest you hone your senses for this last debut event before the Season gets underway, because after that, dear Diana, your name will be known, your reputation will be ruined and Lucretia will assuredly demand your removal from this house before the taint of your disgrace touches her."

Each word hit her with the subtle nick of a rapier. "I see," she said heavily, turning her face away from him. She wasn't going to cry, not her, but still, she had not thought there would be such an ignominious end to this adventure, really she hadn't. "I must produce results or my lord will cut his losses."

He came up behind her, stealthily, edgily. "A goddess can only turn a man into a fool for so long, Diana. And then one day he understands that it has all been a big cosmic joke for her entertainment only. I am not a fool, but you—you are a siren: you fascinate, you lure men to do your bidding, and then you abandon them, laughing at their puny efforts to please you. Yes, you must produce results, Diana. And this time, you must please *me*."

And what she had done, she realized, as her too-bright gaze skimmed the busy street in order that she did not have to look at him, was avoid planning for the outcome of this monstrous brainstorm of hers. She had never thought past the objective of getting to London. And she had never ever considered what might happen if she did not find her father.

What she had loved was outwitting Southam, but there was no reasonable way out this time.

Well, yes, my Lord, indeed I have found my father; he is your uncle. Why did you wish to know? . . .

Why *did* he wish to know?

Attack, attack, attack . . . She whirled to face him and was startled to find he was close beside her, watching her profile, inhaling her scent.

"Why *do* you want to find this man?" she asked bluntly—*touché, Monsieur . . .*

His black gaze seemed fathomless; he would never reveal anything to her, but she would not back down. Her eyes snapped with anger as he did not answer.

"My lord?"

"Let us say," he said finally, "that I have reason to believe that a man I am seeking and your father might be one and the same."

"And why are *you* on his trail, and how *could* they be the same person? *How?*" she demanded. It made no sense, none. Southam was a well-to-do aristocrat who had bowed to the great god of the cards: he did not work, he did not seek, except at night, roaming the city for a game and a tumble.

"That," he said roughly, "is none of your business. The man is a traitor, and with you or without you I will find him, and that is all you need to know. So—*en garde,* goddess. The day of your reckoning approaches, the day when all the idols with feet of clay shall be toppled from Olympus and become mortal once again."

Dear Lord, the man is a traitor . . .

She was hardly aware he had left; she turned slowly toward the window and leaned her burning head against the molding and the sheer curtain that framed the glass.

She could see the front steps and Southam marching briskly, angrily down them to signal to the boy who had been walking his horse to bring him forward. He mounted with a kind of suppressed violence; the horse reacted to his anger, rearing upward and to the side before he got control.

A moment later, his back ramrod straight, he headed down the street, leaving a retinue of Lady Waynflete's stable boys gawking in admiration behind him.

And one lone figure, dressed in fawn, edged his way furtively along the row of houses across the way, looking as if he were lost, the set of his body familiar, like the man who had lurked in the shadows the night before.

Yes, my lord, here is the truth of it: the traitor is your uncle, and he is my father, and somewhere in the bushes, he has posted watch guards to be sure.

To be sure of what? That she didn't leave the house?

That no one came in? To ambush her? To contain her?

This had become an unrelenting nightmare. At night, again alone in the house, she had kept watch by the window, certain Southam would never come, that Dunstan would not chance it even with Lady Waynflete gone, because the servants would know.

How cunningly Lady Waynflete had eased her out of the social scene. She was amazed at how quickly it could be done, how painlessly on the part of her patroness. The cards would keep pouring in, she knew, for another day or two or three, and then the gossip would start. Someone would pass the word: the beautiful Lady Desire was *persona non grata* with her mentor; Southam would abandon her. Jeremy would ask her to leave because Lady Waynflete was too kind-hearted.

And finally, her father would arrange for her to disappear altogether.

And Southam, with whom she had shared all those wanton nights of passion, would forget she ever existed, and he would lay in the arms of the milk-pail who would service him with all the imagination of a cow . . .

Never!

She could not bear to think of it — his high and mighty lord of lechery leering after that . . . person.

Surely he had more discrimination . . . ah, but men never had any judgment about strumpets whatsoever.

And that was not the point, either, she castigated herself, as she paced her room. Southam's ultimatum was the point. The man who might be skulking outside under her window was the point.

She edged her way to the far window, just beyond the point of light that illuminated the room.

The darkness was stunning, unrelieved by any light but a distant street light. Every shadow seemed to move and sway with the wind. Any shape could be a man or a tree.

She felt lost in it, as if she were the only one in the

world looking outward and seeing nothing. It made her feel insignificant, frightened of something larger than she that moved with all the patience of an unforgiving and slow-moving nature.

The blackness had no answers: it was impenetrable as Southam's eyes. One had to grope and feel one's way through it, and ultimately, surrender to it.

There was no other possibility.

She had to play the game Southam's way. It struck her suddenly as she stared into the blank darkness of the night that embodied all the threats surrounding her and crushing her: it was simple really.

All she had to do was find her father.

It didn't matter who, it didn't matter where. It just mattered that she found someone so that the bargain would be met.

She would figure out the rest later.

She wasn't at all surprised to see the movement: had she not been looking so intently, her eyes now accustomed to the dark, she would not have noted it. But it was there, muted, subtle, melting into the shadows now and again, distinct for a moment's verification that the light still flickered in her room and that she was still there.

She felt like a cat, hiding in the shadows, she felt like the huntress, sniffing its prey. Soon, soon she would pounce, and then she would seize the day.

It was Annesley's turn this time, this night, a small amusement for a bored constituency of friends and a jaded man about town who had very little to do until the seasonal horde descended to give him grist for his gossip mill. He liked to provide a prodigious dinner, some music, some dancing, and above all, in the back room, where it counted, a gut-wrenching game of cards to rival anything to be had at Badlington's or any of the clubs.

The party was just to provide a reason to lure his friends to the table and to provide the *ton* with something to talk about.

The exclusivity of the guest list made social climbers and aggressive mothers reel with despair; there was no telling how one got a coveted invitation, and only Annesley's closest friends knew that the eclectic mix of guests was served up solely for *his* amusement. He was like a man setting off fireworks and standing back to watch the resultant display, and he had coolly and calculatedly decided not to invite the desirable Miss Bowman solely on the grounds that she would distract the men from deep deep play. However, Charlotte Emerlin was another matter. He was rather taken with her bold transformation and her even more audacious pursuit of the ever more aloof Nicholas Carradine.

He wanted to watch her in action, without the tempting diversion of the beauteous Lady Desire. He wanted to watch Nicholas squirm, and he wanted the gorgeous Miss Bowman to know that her allure was based solely on the fact that others acclaimed it, and he himself had named it.

In short, he loved having control, and he watched with a disdainful and amused eye as his guests began arriving and looking around.

"Ah, Nick—you look utterly put out. Truly, you did not have to exercise yourself to come tonight. However, I thought it *was* diverting that Dunstan accepted an invitation. I left out Charles Griswold, he really is still too tender to jump into steep play. Now, what do you think of my table?"

Nicholas was in a foul mood altogether; he had lost at an exceedingly whimsical bet to one of the Prince Regent's intimates earlier in the day at White's and he was about to trowel in another several thousand pounds to Annesley's tables, and that on top of the exacerbating ultimatum he had given the intractable Miss Bowman.

His mood did not improve at the sight of Charlotte

Emerlin being towed into the reception hallway by her battleship of a mother; Gertrude was primed and ready for a good fight, he could see it in her eyes. She knew to a title who was to be present this evening, and Charlotte was dressed for combat, a willing extension of the blood lust in her mother's eye.

"Ah, Nicholas, how delightful to see you."

Conventional enough words, and he had come to expect the very obvious from Lady Emerlin, but the underlay of sarcasm had to be squelched immediately.

"The delight is solely on your side," he said dampingly.

But she would not be deterred. "Of course it is—that is why we are here. But enough of pleasantries; come, Charlotte . . ."

"Damn," Annesley said, "she got up a head of steam in the past year, didn't she? She won't take any guff from you, Nick."

"Yes, she probably thinks that her erstwhile servility did not serve the point, and now she means to be as abominably offensive as possible. It will be amusing to watch, at any rate. Will Lucretia be here?"

"She will, and Jeremy as well, and all of our crowd who are on strict notice to assemble in the card room at nine promptly. And of course, I've included Dunstan as a compliment to *you*, Nick, because I *know* you will make good his losses."

Something about that sly assumption did not sit well with Nicholas, but he resisted commenting and went off to find a tolerable slice of ham and a glass of port.

The incoming crowd swirled around him, heavy with the heat of gossip and innuendo, each and every one checking out who had been included on the guest list and who had not.

He heard the whispers as he circulated the room: "Where is Miss Bowman? He did not invite her? She did not come? Lady Desire, Lady Desire—cut by Annesley? Snubbed by the

302

top of the *ton?* What had she done? Why would he not include the most talked about beauty of the Season . . . ?"

And wave after wave of languid young men cornered Annesley: "Is that Incomparable, that one they call Lady Desire, is she to be here tonight?"

"Not tonight," Annesley would tell them, and after a time, he went in search of Nicholas. "I think I've created more interest in her by *not* inviting her, damn it. She is all they talk about, and I wish they knew that it was I who created her."

"Nonsense," Nicholas snapped, out of all patience with Annesley's indulgences. "She created *you,* Max. Could you ever picture hanging such a voluptuous name on Charlotte Emerlin?"

"My God, no," Annesley said, much struck by Nicholas' logic. By all rights, the chit ought to be here then, he thought, but it was too late to remedy the omission—unless he sent a special invitation to her personally, begging her forgiveness for the oversight of neglecting her.

What sight, he thought gleefully, the elegant and luscious Miss Bowman tripping in the door about midnight, just after everyone had been talking about her absence for hours. It was too good, too ripe to pass up.

He motioned to his butler, and he sent for some paper and a pen.

The man remained, blended into the shadows, and Jainee felt like a princess in a fairy tale kept prisoner by the ugly troll.

Lady Waynflete had gone off to some exclusive party, the details of which she did not need to disclose to Jainee; she was alone in the house but for Marie, Blexter and Lady Waynflete's retinue of servants.

And of course, the Watcher.

It came on nine o'clock and she had not moved. Neither

had her shadowy nemesis, and she wondered why she was standing, staring out a window at some unknown whose sole function was to keep her in a state of agitation.

Whatever happened, she could not remove him from his post; she could not blackmail Lady Waynflete's host into inviting her to the party; she could not rescind Southam's ultimatum of her father's threatening presence.

Attack, attack, attack . . .

She wondered what maidens of virtue did with their evenings when a finicky host or hostess removed them from the eligible guest list. Probably they spent the night crying buckets of tears and did needlepoint to while away the hours.

But she could not stand the enforced idleness. How many years had she spent in anticipation of a night's energetic play around her mother's table? Nothing had prepared her for a life of gentility: Southam's positioning her with the upright and morally correct Lady Waynflete had to be the biggest joke of all. No wonder they chafed at each other and Lady Waynflete could not cope with her waywardness. She was used to prim and proper young ladies who were thrilled at the thought of a Season in London, and chastened at committing any *faux pas* that would make them look bad before the censuring eyes of the *ton*.

Attack . . .

Her position any which way was tenuous at best: Lady Waynflete was ready to wash her hands of her; Southam would imminently give her her *congé;* her father watched her in order to intimidate her and perhaps do her bodily harm.

She knew what she was thinking. Deep down, deep deep down in that place where her soul had forever lived on the edge of disaster with Therese, deep down there she knew, she wanted action, she needed excitement. She yearned to vanquish her enemies with the ease that she had time and again defeated Southam.

304

All her enemies were at play; why should she not be?

Should she let the unknown watcher keep her immured in her tower of propriety when her reputation was steeped in the name of seduction?

She could not keep still a moment longer. If she hesitated, she handed the power to her enemy, to Southam, to her father.

She moved across the lighted window to the bell pull and gave it a violent jerk.

Marie came running.

"Tell Blexter I wish to have my trunk pulled out of storage, wherever that may be," she directed Marie.

Marie did not protest, although she knew that one of the footman would have to go to a great deal of trouble to unearth it from the attics.

Nevertheless, within the half hour, Jainee was opening the somewhat dusty case and rooting around in its contents, oblivious to Marie's avid gaze until she looked up suddenly and saw her hovering. "That will be all for now, Marie," she told her. "However, would you ask Blexter to have Hawkins bring round the least identifiable conveyance in the carriage house. I will be going out tonight."

"Surely not, mademoiselle. What if — ?"

"I am going out," Jainee said firmly and waited calmly and impassively until Marie withdrew from the room before she delved back into the remnants of her life in Brighton.

And here was that blue dress, and there was another gown, glittery with shot silver, and here were the plain, unadorned underdresses she had worn with each, and accessories, and a long hooded black velvet cape lined in deep sapphire blue silk.

All of these cherished dresses and items she removed from the trunk to empty it to the very bottom. And there, in a little secret hiding place which required that she prise open the floor of the trunk in a certain place and in a certain way in order to uncover the riches she had concealed there.

And hope that no one had been so suspicious of her when she had arrived that he had covertly searched her belongings.

But no . . . her hoarded cache of silver remained in place, glittering and cold to her touch, exactly where she had placed it. The gentility did not search for spies behind every corner and inside every trunk. The gentility went by appearances, and by what was said and who sponsored whom, and for the only time since she had comprehended that, she felt grateful that Lady Waynflete had taken her at face value and on Southam's say-so.

And now, spread out before her was a record of her life in Brighton, the clothing which Lady Waynflete had discarded in pursuit of more elegant attire.

She lifted one dress from the pile beside her, the beautiful tunic dress she had been wearing when Southam walked through the door at Lady Truscott's . . . an omen, perhaps? Who among the high-stakes speculators at the Lady Badlington's house would remember the gaming house hostess in Brighton of a year before?

Or perhaps she ought to disguise herself still further. The cape, over the dress, softened by a drift of blue silk wound around her head and across her chin to blur her features—cover her mouth, perhaps? Pulled down close to her eyes to give her a look of mystery, an aura of the exotic?

She must not be identified as Lady Waynflete's protegée, at least not yet, but as she surveyed herself in the mirror, clothed in the blue tunic dress with its embroidered bands of trim, she saw immediately she could not arrive and discard her cloak: everyone would know her. And even if she swathed her body up to her nose in cloak and blue silk, she was sure someone would recognize her startling blue eyes.

Ah, but the chance must be taken. She had gone a mile already toward the ravishing excitement of taking to the gaming table again. She could not stop now.

She found a pair of black gloves and added them to her

wardrobe, and a black velvet reticule in which to carry her stake.

She looked vaguely Egyptian, she thought, as she gave herself one last going over in the mirror, and checked that she had replaced the secret bottom of her trunk.

All was proper there, and as a final touch, she heaped the dozen or so dresses and accoutrements every which way into the trunk and just left it, open, yawning, inviting Marie or any of the house maids to explore its contents as they would.

And she—she was going to deliberately walk into hell in order to create her own little heaven.

Chapter Seventeen

The play in the card room at Annesley's house was deep and steep and rather bad-tempered. Beyond the baize door of the entrance to the room, they could hear the music loud and sweet, and the sound of laughter and conversation, the optimum atmosphere for a party.

It was just that the host was nowhere to be found in the public rooms, and time and again a servant came to the door requesting his presence or his direction, and on the whole the game was so riddled with these distractions that it became hard to tell who was up and who was down and by how much.

Except that it was clear that Southam was flat out, at *point non plus* with one of the Prince Regent's cronies who had deigned to play with them that evening.

"Ah, Nicholas, give over: you've had a bad run of luck for this year and more. No use repining. The thing's done and the only course is to try to recoup." This from Annesley who was gleefully counting his vouchers as he turned for the next deal.

And Dunstan Carradine, too, was five or six hundred to the good and he was being insufferably vocal about it, which Nicholas did not take kindly.

Over and above that, the port was flowing, poured by Annesley's generous hand, and every once in a while one or two of the eligible demoiselles who were audacious and on the catch made so bold as to join the gentlemen and hang over their shoulders to encourage them to recklessness in the course of the play.

It was a perfect opportunity for Gertrude Emerlin to push Charlotte forward once again; but she did not need much coaxing. After all, there were a half dozen delicious men half-foxed sitting around in one room tossing cards onto a table. Surely a little blatant femininity would be a welcome diversion.

She even liked the fact that the door was closed discreetly behind her. And the room was dimly lit, except for the table, and surrounded by a haze of smoke, and the faintly sweet scent of liqueur and wine.

There was a sideboard along one wall on which was the remnants of a variety of viands which had been served *en buffet*. Now and again, Nicholas or his uncle or Chevrington or Coxe reached across and nipped another morsel of meat or fruit and then returned to play. They continually argued about this card and that, sounding like nothing so much as children negotiating their play.

Perhaps that was the secret, Charlotte reflected as she eased herself into the room and behind Nicholas Carradine's chair. They were all little boys and they would respond to nurturing and discipline in equal amounts.

Dear Nicholas. She boldly touched his shoulder and then his severely cropped hair. Everything was straightforward and austere with Nicholas, from his dress right down to his deliberately acerbic manner.

But nothing would stop her now: she knew what was what, and what was where, for that matter, and it was only a matter of showing Nicholas that she was not the shrinking chicken-hearted virgin he had courted the previous year.

She boldly reached out her hand and stroked his hair and felt no rebuke when he shrugged it off. He was concentrating after all; Annesley had said he was down pretty far, and Coxe already held a handful of his vouchers in addition to a prime win on a bet they had made previously at White's.

He was not in a good mood, nor did he take his uncle's jabbing repartee kindly, even though none of this showed in his face or filtered through the expression in his voice. She felt it solely in the tension between his shoulders and the stiffness of his posture.

She was pleased to see Alice Cockburn wind herself around Annesley's shoulders as he continued his reckless play. Oh yes, and she whispered soft little nothings in his ear, delicious insinuations which cost her nothing, aroused him mightily and made her memorable to him.

There were smart young things parading around on the marriage mart this year, Charlotte thought, as she daringly ran her fingers around the collar of Nicholas' coat to graze the thin material of his shirt below the meticulously arranged neckcloth. They had been tutored well by mothers who understood precisely what was wanted in these days of tremendous competition among the newest crop of virgins who would supplant last year's eligible schoolroom misses (including herself) who had failed to catch a husband.

Of course one had to stand out. Look at that outlandish, flamboyant and altogether flagrant dasher they called Lady Desire. She popped onto the scene out of the blue; no one knew from where or who she was or her lineage or anything, and now everyone was talking about her and couldn't get enough of her, even Nicholas at the Ottershaw party, which had thrown her into a flaming rage.

Never again. No other woman would have Nicholas, she vowed, her fingers kneading his tight skin beneath the fine thin material of his shirt.

Only her. *Only her.*

She knew enough about it now, and she was watching at least three experts put these precepts into play: Alice Cockburn sliding her hand sensuously beneath the front of Annesley's shirt; Emma Acton already ensconced on Coxe's lap and stroking his face and hands; Sophia Spaulding with her arms wrapped around Dunstan Carradine's shoulders and cheek to cheek with him, alternately planting soft little kisses on his jaw and ear, and whispering to him those erotic little secrets that only she could know.

The clock struck midnight, and Charlotte was emboldened further by the fact that Nicholas had not removed her questing hands. If she could just slide onto his lap, she knew exactly the place to begin the sortie of pleasure which would melt his anger and reserve and leave him on his knees begging her forgiveness and her hand.

She had nothing to lose. He would never reject her fully and openly here, amongst his friends and their mutual acquaintances. The purpose of the privacy was to provide an intimate setting for just such happenings, if one wanted to make them happen. Annesley was always and ever attuned to the needs of his friends. Everyone understood that whoever of the fair sex entered that room was tacitly giving herself to anyone who was interested.

Of course they never were not interested, but everyone understood that going in. There were no preselected choices, nor was it prearranged who would enter the card room.

No one watched, but everyone knew, and no one ever gossiped about it afterward.

Nicholas went down again, and his mood turned perceptibly sour.

Charlotte reached around his shoulders with both of her strong arms and encircled his neck, crushing his impeccable stock. "Let me comfort you," she whispered in his ear as they heard a hubbub from beyond the door that sounded strangely like a cheer. The noise got louder and louder, and Nicholas did not respond, and Charlotte boldly took her chance and pivoted around the chair and into his lap.

It ought to have caused an instant and discernible response, something she could have worked with and coaxed into life. But instead, he ignored her, he threw in his cards, he wrote out his voucher and handed it to Annesley, and he acted altogether as if she weren't there.

And the noise grew louder, and Emma Acton seized on the distraction to begin kissing Coxe with sensual abandon; and Sophia Spaulding had grown so bold with her caresses that Dunstan Carradine thought he might explode.

"A thousand a point the next go-round," Annesley said loudly and firmly even though he knew two of his compatriots were occupied at the moment.

And Nicholas, looking as if some insect had alighted on him and he was loath to brush it off. God, and Dunstan, in the throes of a delicious moment of euphoria at the hand of Emma Acton.

And sweet salacious Alice Cockburn, hanging around his neck and whispering carnal nothings in his ear. And wasn't dear Charlotte trying hard to arouse some response from hard hearted Nicholas?

And the noise, louder and louder, almost as if the crowd outside were looking in and cheering them on to that final licentious moment of ecstasy.

Ah, it was too good—he moved his legs as Alice's long slender arm snaked down his chest seeking the thrust, the purpose, the point of the evening, and her delicate little tongue snaked right into his mouth and claimed him to the biggest burst of applause, and the sound of the clock striking at half past the hour, then one last stroke till the half hour, and—

The door swung open and the noise filtered into the room like the sound of a booming cannon.

They froze at this unheard-of solecism.

And then they all looked up into the cocksure and knowing blue gaze of the elegantly and minimally dressed Lady Desire.

The milkweed, she thought angrily as she watched the various couples disentangle themselves with a jaundiced eye. *She has wrapped her tentacles around my lord and utterly stifled him. But of course it must be what he wants, else why would he be here?*

God, Annesley thought, jumping up and pushing the door closed almost the moment she walked in. "You really must knock," he said gently, chidingly. *My God, that dress, that body, those eyes* . . .

"You really must be available to greet your guests," she retorted, not fazed one bit by his not-so-subtle rebuke. "My lord," she added, inclining her regal head toward Nicholas, "and Mr. Carradine. I have not had the pleasure of meeting the others, except, perhaps—" She looked at Charlotte. "Have we met?"

"Possibly in passing," Charlotte said silkily, "not worth remembering."

"My feeling exactly," Jainee agreed wholeheartedly.

God, the mouth on her, Annesley thought in awe. "Permit me, Miss Bowman: Mr. Coxe, Mr. Chevrington, whom I think you *do* know; Miss Cockburn, Miss Acton, and Miss Emerlin."

"I am pleased," Jainee said, but she was not pleased at all. The milk-wretch sat on Nicholas Carradine's lap like she had grown there and refused to move, not even to present the appearance of mannerliness.

She had staked her claim, quite obviously, and she was waiting to run the flag up the pole.

"Perhaps . . ." Annesley began, but Jainee held up her hand.

"I came only to pay my respects to my host," she said primly, quite properly she knew, "and of course I will now withdraw and mingle with your other guests. My lords—"

And she turned and opened the door and just walked out.

"Oh my God," Annesley breathed. "You know what they are all going to think, you know it . . ."

"They're all going to think she has been compromised by one of you," Nicholas said savagely, speaking for the first time since Jainee had come in the door. He pushed Charlotte Emerlin off of his knees and rose to his feet.

"And I'll tell you what else, Annesley, damn it. They're all going to be taking bets on it tomorrow at White's, and I will wager you someone will claim the win."

The rush of elation she had experienced earlier in the evening at both defeating her unknown watcher and penetrating the environs of Lady Badlington's gaming house dissipated as quickly as fireworks in rain.

She stamped back into the ballroom of Annesley's commodious townhouse in a fury. And it was not only Southam and that milk cow, it was also Lady Waynflete, rounding on her and accusing her of presenting herself where she had been most explicitly not wanted.

In truth, she had felt more than a moment's hesitation at accepting the rude and belated invitation to attend Annesley's select party. But she had decided for just that very reason: that the guest list was exclusive, and that Southam would probably be there, which would give her an opportunity to wag his tail with his friend's collusion and as much as say to him that his threats and ultimatums did not scare her.

And she had meant to turn the tables on Annesley as well, if he thought it would be a good joke to tweak her like this — pushing her away with one hand and leading her on with the other.

Well, that had all gone by the board: obviously the sanctum of the cards was euphemism for something vastly more expensive and carnal and she had barged neatly into the middle of it and shocked them all — except of course Southam, because nothing ever discomposed *him*.

But still, the whey-faced milkmaid was in place where she should not be and her hands were looking to *find* a place to be, and so be it: there were men who might faint at the touch of her hand as well.

She allowed herself to be drawn into the welcoming circle of them as she emerged from the card room. They plied her with questions, dizzying incomprehensible questions: "Who is winning? What were they doing? Is it true that Annesley hired the women who were with them? How far had they gotten? How far did they want to go? Was it true . . . did they really . . . undressed yet . . . ?"

And then the whole lot of them moved hastily aside as

Nicholas Carradine came storming through the crowd.

He knew exactly where she was: in the center of all the men as usual, *and* dressed in that flimsy bit of drapery she called a dress with every last contour of her body revealed to anyone who looked closely—which they *all* were doing, and worse, with that blasted strip of satin tied alluringly around her neck and her wrists over the elbow length gloves she wore.

And those eyes, that irritating smug, *come get me* smile: his hands itched, his groin ached the moment she walked in the door, the desired and uninvited guest. He could not begin to fathom how and why she had turned up at a function to which she had expressly *not* been invited.

That dress was an abomination—surely a year or two out of style; they didn't wear them quite so thin and clinging any more, with such low cut bodices and transparent fluttering sleeves . . .

He felt like shaking her; he had been sure he had scared her with his ominous demand for results.

Any other body would never have come flaunting herself publicly like this.

But any other body was *not* the huntress, he reflected grimly as he took her by the arm and wordlessly propelled her from the center of admirers to the outside hallway where the butler waited to serve the guests.

He disappeared in an instant at Nicholas' signal.

"What the hell are you doing here?"

As if he had a right to be angry with her! She could not believe his arrogance in the face of his own blatant pursuit of pleasure.

"Why, my lord, the same as you," she answered cheekily.

"Annesley issued you no invitation."

"But my lord, indeed—he had a change of heart, begged me to come and make his party into the event of the opening of the Season. Reams of prose about my beauty and affability and

315

how sorely I would be missed if I held it against him that Lucretia Waynflete had neglected to bring me. Truly, and Lady Waynflete does not remember a thing about it, and positively hauled me over the coals for coming where I was not wanted.

"But my welcome, apart from the brief rudeness of my host, has been all anyone could wish. I would have been so sorry to have missed this party."

She could see his rage fairly growing with each taunting word, and she went on, adding wormwood to gall: "I will save his note forever. So prettily written it was, a fair example of a man on his knees to make amends. Very instructive and entertaining reading, to say the least."

"You *never* say the least," Nicholas exploded. "And the worst thing you could have done was capitulated at the last minute. They'll be talking about it for weeks."

"Nonsense, no one knows, except you, Lady Waynflete and Annesley. And he is not your enemy, my lord. At best, he wishes he knew how to approach me, because he would like to be a particular friend—but not at the end of the line. So it is perfectly understandable." She loved it—jab, jab, jab, little hits, little pricks hard up against his shell of impassivity, outwitting him again just when he thought he had her subdued and submissive.

But she would show him—him and every other presumptuous and arrogant lord in the whole of England who thought he could make the rules and demand that *she* submit to them while he flouted them.

Yes, she felt a tremor of fine fury engulf her at the thought of that woman, that milk sop with her hands all over Southam mere days after . . .

"Annesley isn't at all particular," Nicholas said nastily, "and neither, it is clear, are *you*."

"While I must compliment you on your discrimination," Jainee shot back, "and your choice of the white-washed milkmaid as a partner in your pleasure this evening. Definitely a *most* particular taste, if looks are anything to judge by."

"At least she keeps her *mouth* shut," Nicholas ground out.

"And what does she keep *open,* my Lord? How convenient for *you.*"

He was going to throttle her, he really was, and right in front of several curious onlookers who were discreetly parading by the reception hall; no other woman in his life had ever spoken to him like this. He was going to—

"Oh, Nicholas—"

"Ah, the everlasting Miss Emer-milk . . . no, wait—Livermilk . . . ah, my Lord, the name escapes me, but it obviously does not you. It will be my pleasure to leave you in her hands."

"Dear Nicholas," Charlotte murmured, reaching for his arm, "the pleasure will be *mine.*" And she loved watching the strumpet turn on her heel to stamp away—but Nicholas shook off *her* hand and went after the bitch.

"I think not," he said softly, dangerously, grasping her arm and hauling her back to him. "Charlotte, you will just have to find someone else to play with."

She pouted. "But I like playing with you. And everything was perfectly fine before this dolly-mop barged in. Ah, Nicholas, what could be better than an evening of intimacy in the privacy of a friend's home? She's nothing but a fanfaron, and every other man here would fight to pander to any inclination of hers; you need not feel responsible for her here."

"I *am* responsible for her," Nicholas muttered, but only Jainee heard him.

"Indeed, my lord," she said through gritted teeth as she repeatedly wrenched her arm away and tried vainly to contain her fury, "I am strangely in full agreement with Miss Milk-curd."

"How lowering," Charlotte retorted. "I fancy however if you just dropped your neckline another inch, you would not want for attention that you could *milk* for all it was worth."

"My dear Miss Milkwort, I believe *you* are the one squeezing the most out of the situation. It is perfectly plain that Nicholas prefers even my abrasive company to any offer you could make."

"Ah, Miss Bovine—you mistake the matter: it is obvious he acts out of sheer courtesy and would relinquish the *chore* in a moment if there were but one *chivalrous* gentleman to take it on in his stead."

"Perhaps the more onerous task is returning to the sanctum with *you*," Jainee retorted, out of all patience with this rag-mannered doxy and Southam himself. It was just like a man, she thought virulently, to stand by and let women fight over him. He was probably enjoying it too, but he would soon regret that smug look in his eyes and the fact that he had said not one word in defense of either of them.

Charlotte laughed. "Then let him choose, Miss Bombast—let him decide."

"How kind of you to capitulate immediately, Miss Milkmouth," Jainee said silkily, "but do let Nicholas confirm it."

The bitch, he thought, his own feelings just on the edge of violence with her all over again. She was like a jungle cat, toying with her prey; huntress queen, the goddess pointing her finger and banishing the miscreant.

He wished he felt something for Charlotte Emerlin besides a vast well of distaste that was leavened with a curdling guilt that he had used her so badly.

For the first time it struck him how similar the two were in look and in height; but Charlotte was a pale version of the vibrant Jainee Bowman, who stood impatiently beside him radiating a positively killing heat, while Charlotte flexed the aloof *sang-froid* of the aristocrat.

So the choice came down to ice or fire, and either way, his fingers would get burned.

"Nicholas, Nicholas—" Annesley came galloping to the rescue just as a good host should, "leaving so soon; my dear boy? I can't bear it . . ."

"I think *I* can manage," Nicholas said drily. "Lucretia insists that I remove her, she has caused trouble enough tonight, and Lucretia has no stomach for either seeing her

318

home or even talking to her until tomorrow morning."

"What else can a good friend do?" Annesley agreed promptly. "And can you blame her? My dear, that dress is a scandal. No wonder everyone was applauding. But Nick—we'll miss you within. You had the devil's own luck tonight, and that side by side Dunstan's remarkable gains. It does make one wonder, doesn't it?"

He said a few more useless things while Charlotte fumed by his side, feeling as if she wanted to attack all three of them. And especially that smarmy bitch who just couldn't help that smug look on her painted bawd face. God, she hated the bitch, and she despised Nicholas for side-stepping a choice and taking Annesley's lead.

She would not be humiliated again. She would be bolder next time; after all, he had not pushed her away, or demeaned her with cruel words. All he had done was hang onto that breast-flashing harlot like she was his prisoner or something.

There was time. There was still time.

"Well then," Annesley said cheerfully, "come, Miss Emerlin, let me escort you back to the sanctum."

She looked up at him, startled. The sanctum? With Annesley? But why not? And possibly Nicholas would hear all about it, with that gossip Annesley throwing around the details like they were not supposed to be confidential. It might work very very well.

"Yes," Annesley said, smiling at her comprehension; after all, he had always liked a willing piece. What she looked like hardly mattered in the dim light and emotional heat of the card room. "Yes, perhaps we can uncover something of interest to occupy you. Perhaps you might sit in on a hand or two . . ." he suggested, unobtrusively leading her away. "Perhaps, you might even find a willing partner."

He ordered his carriage and the butler sent for their outer garments, which were brought promptly by a foot-boy who helped Nicholas on with his greatcoat and then handed over Jainee's blue silk-lined cape.

"How delightful, Diana," he murmured, swinging the cape around her shoulders and stroking the lustrous material of the lining. "So soft," he hooked the collar piece together. "So inviting to the touch . . ."

"And what would you touch, my lord?" Jainee asked caustically, watching the surety with which he fastened the hooks together. No clumsiness here, but something else, something burning deep behind his eyes as his large hands moved downward to the two edges that closed over her breasts.

The pretty little frill of material barely covered them; she knew it, she had done it deliberately; she had wanted to anger him and to tempt him at the same time. She saw his fingers tighten and she took a deep breath that swelled her upper torso and thrust her breasts forward.

"What you want me to touch," he growled, and he gave into the provocation of her bared chest, and under the cover of the all-enveloping cape, he reached for her and stripped the inch of covering material away from her nipples.

And then slowly he pulled the edges of the cape over her nakedness and fastened them together.

"I would like to think of you sitting like that, naked beneath your cape, your nipples caressed by silk and the excitement of knowing that I know that your breasts are bare."

And she felt it, instantly, arousingly, the soft firm graze of the silk against her turgid nipples, and the firm hard glitter in his eyes as he imagined it.

They walked out onto the steps as the carriage drew up, and she had no thought in her mind about secret watchers, only the secret arousal of her secret self and his surrender to his secret sight of her nakedness.

He sat across from her in the carriage, not saying a word. Everything was mirrored in his eyes as his carriage swayed past this streetlamp and that, and the flaring light filtered through the curtains at the windows.

Her excitement ran rampant as she felt what he was seeing in his mind's eye. Everytime she moved, the silk of her cape caressed the flush thrust of her breasts with the softness and tenderness of a lover's hand.

"Where are we going?" she whispered.

"Does it matter, Diana?"

It did not; she trembled with the need to have him touch her, but she knew he wouldn't, not yet, not now. She had nothing more powerful to wield than the thoughts running through his mind of how she had looked when he tore away the minuscule bodice of her dress. How potent was the imagination.

Even she, seated so sedately across from him, felt the stirrings of her imagination in the thought of his arousal at the knowledge that he had.

He would be thinking about those other times and the erotic pull and tug between them; and he would think about how she had looked the first time she wore the robe he had created just for her just to display her naked breasts. He would harden like a rock at the thought of her sitting across from him as prim as any virgin with her breasts bare beneath her staid black cloak. He would hate it that the silk could caress her and he could not.

And she would love it that he was aroused by the thought of her and could not act upon his need.

The carriage drew up before yet another townhouse but she was too focused on her excitement to notice it. The door opened; she moved automatically, feeling the sway of her breasts against thin silk as she debarked from the carriage.

She felt nothing but the tension of her arousal; she saw nothing but this tall austere figure leading the way into his house. She had no plans, no schemes, no plotted tactical diversions. She had fought for this moment and she had won, and she thought that her compliance was purely the nature of the conqueror parading her victory in triumph.

Nothing mattered but the moment: he had surrendered already by the very act of claiming her nakedness in public.

She entered his home as regally as any queen. A footman appeared and took his coat, but he motioned him away from her and instead indicated that she should go up the steep staircase that bisected the entrance hall.

She floated up the stairs. This was his home, *his* sanctum; this was the place, the time inseparable from him and divorced from any outside considerations. Here there were no threats, no ultimatums, no promises, no lies.

There was only the sense of being enveloped by all that he was and all, she realized with a brief little shock, that he might mean to her.

He paused before a door in the center of a long balcony which overlooked the reception room and opened it, and stood aside so that she could enter.

She stepped over the threshold into a huge room which occupied at least half of that side of the house and overlooked the gardens. On the far wall, a fire burned in the fireplace under a gracefully ornamented mantel. A richly colored landscape framed in gold hung above this, and beside the fireplace were two upholstered chairs with a table between them.

On the other side of the room, there was a clothes press and a wash stand with a pier mirror beside and in the center of the room, angled out from the wall and facing the fireplace, a huge four-posted bed dominated the rest of the room, sitting on a subtle-hued fitted carpet that felt plush and rich beneath her feet.

He closed the door and she could see various pieces of art either hung on the walls or statuary on the floor, and convenient sconces near the area where he dressed and washed.

Not an ascetic's room, she thought interestedly, but still the place of a man who had great restraint and still wanted to make a statement.

The size of the bed and its height, fairly overwhelmed her. The mattress was at least as high as her waist, and there was a three step stair pushed up against the siderail.

It was warm here, as if the fire had been going all day and

the heat had built up to the same fever pitch as the blood pounding in her veins.

"And now, Diana . . ." he murmured, coming around behind her and putting his hands over her shoulders so that he could unfasten her cape.

"And now . . . ?" she whispered, watching his capable hands uncouple each hook with unhurried studiousness.

The edges of the cape fell away from her naked breasts, and he whisked the cape away from her shoulders.

She reveled in the heaviness of her breasts and the tautness of her nipples. She could feel his eyes on her, she could feel the heat enveloping her, and the languid yearning for something more.

And he wanted it too, by the evidence of the granite length of him poking forcefully against the obstructing material of his trousers.

"And now, Diana — we play cards."

What? She felt as if he had doused her with cold water.

"Come by the fire, Diana, and sit across from me, and do not assume the evening is yours to command. *I* wish to play cards."

"But *why?*"

"Because you did not expect it, of course. Sit and let me admire your beautiful breasts by firelight, Diana. Surely I deserve that much reward for my restraint."

"I would not reward it *now,*" she muttered, throwing herself into the chair farthest from the door. "Am I to suppose that this was the mode of entertainment you would have provided that milkfish woman if you had chosen to be with her tonight?"

He removed a deck of cards from a drawer in the center of his side of the table. "But I would not have been with her, Diana. If a man has been with a goddess, how could he settle for a mere mortal?"

"What humbug," she said, but without heat. But now that the vibrant sensuality between them had diminished, she felt like covering herself up and donning her cape and just huddling by the fire.

"We will play *Quinze,*" he said meaningfully, "which is a game that has a certain resonance for me." He began shuffling the cards.

"It *was* your choice, my lord," she reminded him gently.

"It was a game in which the chooser became a beggar. But the rules have reversed here. The loser will be the beggar. One round, one article of clothing removed by the loser."

"My lord," she breathed, every nerve in her body leaping to attention. "You already have the advantage of me, and over all that, you presuppose that you will come away the winner."

"No, no, Diana. It is merely a means to challenge the goddess who feels she must forever be in control. Cut the deck."

She leaned forward and took the cards and the firelight molded a sensual shadow between her breasts. She separated the deck into two stacks and put one over the other and handed it back to him.

He looked at her once before he began dealing the cards and he felt a fierce rush of possessiveness at the sight of her in his fireside chair, her arms draped gracefully over the sides, her head back, her glittering eyes appraising him as forthrightly as he did her.

One round, one article of clothing removed . . .

One goddess, already stripped naked for his delectation, just waiting for the final subjugation.

She supposed he had thought it would be easy. Or perhaps he had also chosen not to remember just how skillfully she had outwitted him in Brighton. Or, barring that, it might have been that he had just wanted to add a certain provocation to the proceedings.

Whatever his reasons, he, by the end of the fourth round, had discarded more clothing than she and he was becoming testy as a bear.

"But my lord, you do forget I am schooled in these games," she pointed out reasonably. "And I am in no hurry to undress myself. In fact, I have felt that things had gone far enough as it was. But there—my turn to deal, is it not?"

She took the cards and laid them down before him, once, twice, three times until he held at twelve. She then placed a card face down in front of her and two more face up, set aside the deck, and overturned the hidden card.

"Ah!" She displayed for him to see her final score: fourteen—nine, three, two. "And so what will it be now, my Lord?" She enumerated what lay on the floor: "You have lost your stock, your jacket, and your waistcoat while I have only had to remove . . , a shoe. Well, your decision, my lord."

He removed a shoe, and reached for the cards.

One two three—stand: ten.

One two three: win at fifteen.

"Here is my other shoe," she said lightly and bent over to remove it, her breasts moving enticingly with the angle of her body.

And again. His ten to her eleven. He removed the other shoe.

Once more: his twelve to her eleven. She lifted her dress and slowly, slowly slid down the sheer silky stocking from her left leg.

Once more: her fifteen to his eighteen: he ripped off his shirt and the firelight and sultry shadows played all over his muscular naked chest.

She led: her twelve to his nine. He angrily pulled off a sock.

His turn: her fifteen to his twenty. He yanked off the other sock.

She took the cards, smiling that elusive cat-sure smile. Her thirteen to his fourteen. She lifted her dress once again and removed her other stocking, sliding it downward inch by agonizing inch until her foot was bared.

He dealt. His twelve to her seven. She smiled again and slowly unwound the satin tie from around her right gloved wrist and tossed it toward him.

It grazed his hairy chest and slithered downward to nest invitingly between his legs, and she smiled again and picked up the cards.

His ten to her nineteen. She unwrapped the satin tie from around her left wrist and let it slide to the floor.

"My lord?"

"A run of bad luck, Diana?"

"But I am still in my dress, my Lord, while you have only to lose your trousers. You had best beware."

He dealt. His fifteen to her twenty. Again, that knowing smile wafted across her lips and she began unwinding the satin tie which encircled her neck, and let it drift gently downward to caress her breasts and fall onto her lap.

"I make it even, my lord."

"How so, goddess?"

"I wager you are naked beneath your breeches."

"I *know* you are naked beneath your dress."

She felt that spewing excitement rush through her veins at the thought of it: that all she wanted was but a footstep away from her. She could lift her foot and touch it. She could . . . she stretched out her leg and groped for his foot, and reared back as she touched skin, hot naked skin that moved as tenuously as she.

She worked her foot forward again and this time, as she impassively shuffled the cards, she slid her foot against the living warmth of his, and then daringly, upward against the sinew and muscle of his hairy leg to the cushion of the chair.

The air between them became sultry, ripe with possibilities. She pushed her foot further, seeking the vee between his legs; she dealt the cards and she delved for it, snaking her toes inward, against the flat hard muscle of his knees and thighs until he gave into her and parted his legs to ease her way.

She wriggled her foot inward just a little further, and then she found the throbbing projection of his manhood and she sighed and rested the flat of her foot against his hot hard length and she dealt the next hand.

"I like the thought of imagining your nakedness beneath these clothes," she murmured seductively, as she turned over his cards. "Ten, ah, twenty, my lord. And I—make it . . . fourteen." She set down the cards. "My lord?"

He felt as tightly wound as a bowstring; somehow, she had vanquished him again—or had he conquered her? He would never be sure, and he was not a little piqued that she could have done it right under his nose.

But he couldn't even make a judgment about it; that erotic foot pressing against his erection drove everything crashing from his mind but his powerful need to possess her.

"I await the final disposition, my lord," she said somewhat petulantly. And why should she wait? *She* had played the game in strict accordance with the rules. It was now his turn to comply, to strip off the last vestige of the civilized gentleman and reveal his nakedness to her.

"Do give your imagination *full* play, Diane," he invited her, closing his hands over her foot and pressing it tighter against his hard heat.

"Oh no, my lord, our bargain is that I am to have something else with which to play." Oh, but his hands were so hot and she was sure she could still feel him elongating against the flat of her foot. That pulsating rush of excitement enveloped her as she waited, and heightened every sense to a fever pitch. "It was not I who made the rules."

No, it had been he in all his folly, pitting his wits against the cunning of the huntress. Slowly he relinquished her foot and moved back his chair. Still, she would pay for the grinding humiliation of having bested him once again.

He ought to have loved undressing in front of her, and he supposed he would have, were it not for the smile, the enigmatic smile that made him want to shake her, that made her bold and brazen and somehow able to turn things upside down in her favor. If it weren't for that, if she were more docile, compliant, if she were less blatant and flashy . . .

He shucked his breeches with one furious yank and kicked them aside.

Now he was fully naked before her, his rampaging manhood reaching for her while she sat there, arrogantly, a queen on her throne assessing him.

He was beautiful to her eyes, so perfect, symmetrical, so stone hard in all the places where she was soft, and soft in all the places where he needed to be tender. And the muscle and the strength of him: she marveled at the elegance of him and the knowledge that she possessed of his potency and his ability to pleasure her.

She wanted to reach for him, take hold of him; *know* the thing about him which was the least knowable. No tactile exploration of the thick hard length of him would provide the key to the virility of him. It just *was* and she openly worshipped him with her eyes and with all her capacity to *feel*.

But all he perceived was the insolence of the goddess who had thwarted him once again. And he didn't understand it, because the end result was exactly what he had planned, except that it was to have been her standing before him in abject nakedness and trembling with the excitement of what was to come.

He pushed aside the table and reached out and took her hand and pulled her to her feet. Yes, she was trembling; yes, her blazing eyes glittered with a kind of malicious knowledge. Yes, they were both aware of what they had come for.

She swayed toward him, her luscious naked breasts inviting his caresses.

He moved in front of her so that her pebble hard nipples just grazed the matted hair on his chest, so close that his jutting manhood pushed gently at the vee between her legs that was covered by the veil of her dress. So close that his mouth covered hers roughly, unwillingly, in torment and enslaved by the sheer naked femininity of her body.

She straddled the hard hot length of him, the sheer muslin of her dress draping over him like a curtain obscuring the backdrop of a play.

Who would know if he possessed her under the shroud of muslin?

And who would know that she had mounted him like a steed, her hips seeking the cradle of his and the fountain of his male root.

But he wanted her otherwise, under him, writhing and pleading for his tumultuous strength to take her, to ride her and pump every last ounce of his potent manhood deep and deeper still . . .

She clung to him, demanding his kisses, seeking the heat of his body. His hands tore at the skirt of her gown, grasping the hem and tearing it apart, bottom to bosom, and then he encircled her bottom and lifted her and carried her to the bed.

She heard the tear somewhere deep in her mind, and she felt him embrace her buttocks and heave her up off of the floor. He was so strong; her fingers dug into the inflexible muscle of his back and gave in to the implacable strength of him as he moved her to the soft cradle of the mattress and laid her down.

But he did not lay down with her; instead he pushed away the torn edges of her dress, and positioned her so that her buttocks were aligned with the edge of the bed and her legs dangled free.

He stood over her, male triumphant, his manhood thrusting at exactly the right angle to possess her just where she lay; it was perfect, it was the height of the bed combined with his fulminating need to see her, to watch her, to take the power back from her.

And somehow she knew it; her whole body was tense with wanting him, her eyes and mind filled with the arousing sight of him naked and poised to possess her. "Oh please . . ." she moaned; she knew somehow he needed to hear it. She needed not to command but to beseech.

He lifted her legs and braced them against his chest. Now her body was pitched perfectly to the angle of his first probing thrust.

"Oh please . . ." She loved watching him: his large hot hands holding tightly to her bare legs as if they were handrails and he was holding on for dear life; his face, streaming with the moisture of his intensity; the coiled strength of his body ready to unleash its power in the most primal way possible.

"Oh, yes . . ." as she felt the first firm thrusts of his maleness seeking her. *Oh yes* . . . as he suddenly reared back and drove himself deep within her; his hands slid hotly down her legs to cradle her buttocks and lift her tautly against his hips as he began the long fertile quest for her pleasure.

The play of the firelight cast his shadow as long and powerful as a god; but by this act, they were equal, and it mattered not that his was the power. His power was nothing without her pleasure.

And she did not withhold it from him. It glimmered in her face and skimmed a riotous course all over her body as he thrust and pushed and teased and lost himself in her. And she could see it in his eyes, and in the intensity of his expression and in his volatile possession of her: he watched her. He had the whole long exhilarating view of her body as she undulated against him. He could feel her response to his mastery in her complete surrender to his potency.

Her senses tingled with recognition in that one sumptuous moment when the thrust of his desire connected with the pure ravishing explosion of her need.

There, there—the voluptuous sweet spot deep within her ripe femininity, there—his rampant thrusts sending little spirals of feeling darting through the center of her being, little curlicues swirling downward and downward to the source of all pleasure, there—the gossamer ripple of something coming, swelling, welling tendrils of incandescent feeling expanding and billowing and coalescing into a fierce streaming spasm of culmination, fathomless, unquenchable, a torrent in her, a cascade of sensation in her: she couldn't stop, it was a fury in her, and he pursued it, relentlessly, forcefully, wringing it from her, demanding it, taking it with each savage thrust of his ramrod manhood until the last jolting spasm eddied away.

In that moment, he was nestled deep within her velvet heat and he felt the first coiling spurt of his own rampaging need.

She felt it too, and slowly, she raised herself up on her elbows so she could watch his inexorable drive to culmination.

It was the most mesmerizing vision: the goddess, her body half clothed, her breasts bared, her hair in disarray, her eyes glittering with the smoldering aftermath of her climax, her luscious body fused with his and that hot, knowing cat smile playing on her willful mouth . . . he clamped down on his unruly urge to spend his climax. He wanted to pump it for all it was worth, and he wanted her to watch him drain himself of every last drop.

The power of the mind and the draw of a woman's eyes . . . he saw her before him, naked and dressed, taunting and submitting, surrendering and triumphing; his blood throbbed with the lust of wanting her and his body responded in kind.

He became a piston of carnal motion, hot short blasting thrusts that shook him to his very marrow, focusing his force, tunneling it, through the tunnel, through the tunnel, into the light, into the bright white hot light, into the volcanic friction of the final convulsive release, and the final surrender to her elusive smile.

The party went on until the wee hours, and when most of the guests had departed, Annesley, Coxe and Dunstan still remained in the sanctum, playing cards and other more carnal games with the three self-designated ladies of the evening.

Three was the perfect number, Annesley thought: three vestals and three libertines; nothing could be better. And three eager and willing vessels of virtue who only wanted to be filled with the liquid of lust, and who plainly didn't care who was spewing into her at any given time.

331

It had been better than usual, an absolute round-about of satiation, with the prime surprise the knowledgeable and hungry hands of the newly retooled Charlotte Emerlin. She had been so furious with Southam, she had stormed into the room and taken on the first man she could get her hands on.

How delicious that it had been Dunstan Carradine who had been ready and willing to accommodate her right on his lap; and didn't they all avidly watch as she lifted her dress and straddled his naked member and bared her breasts in a frenzy and rode him remorselessly all the way to climax. And she wasn't done then—she wanted them all, and it was the wonder of a woman that while Dunstan was spent and needed a respite, she was able to come to Annesley next.

And what did that do to the other girls, who looked on in envy at first and then in anger that the Emerlin was sapping all the juice of their lovers. Ah, what a contest it became then between the three of them to arouse each spent and drooping member to new heights and new ecstasy.

And when they were exhausted, he and his friends played a desultory hand of something or other—he couldn't remember what for all the port and burgundy he had consumed, and within the hour, they were all ready for more licentious games in dark corners.

The clock had struck twice, three times, and sometime during this hedonistic night of pleasure, it occurred to Annesley that Nicholas ought to have been with them.

"Ain't that so, Dunstan?" he demanded, nudging Dunstan who had laid his head on the card table and was enjoying the ministrations of one or maybe even two of their willing partners beneath the table.

"Didn't it seem the game went all awry after Nick left? I mean, it's no fun at all to *lose* to your friends. What you need is someone who is your friend and a good loser and who has the money to pay his vowels. Someone like Prinny, or Nick . . ."

"Good man, Nick," Coxe agreed, his voice slightly wobbly

from excesses of drink and prurience. "Took that bet last night at White's, never blinked. Just handed over a fistful of blunt. Not like Prinny; doesn't hoard a thing, generous to his friends . . . good man, ain't he, Carradine?"

"The best," Dunstan concurred, picking up someone's half-empty glass and sipping it down. "Best boy . . . open-handed to a fault. Ah, Charlotte my dear, come sit here and let us talk about Nick. Tell us how much you love our Nick."

Charlotte wriggled her bottom to find the best position on his lap and felt his gratifying instant response. "Nick's a dear," she cooed, running her fingers through Dunstan's hair and slipping her tongue neatly into his drink-scented mouth. "I just love Nick," she added huskily, fitting her mouth to Dunstan's and demanding his kisses.

"Trouble was," Dunstan added when he came up for air, "Nick didn't love her—oh, but my beauty, *we* do, indeed we do," and he captured her hovering mouth this time and set her more firmly against his lap.

"Well, this is what I think," Annesley said with all the seriousness of someone about to make a portentous announcement. "I think . . . ohhhhh, I think Emma had better stop doing that . . . oh, *don't* stop doing that . . . Yes, well, this is what I think. I think . . . I can't think—oh, that's lovely . . . I think we ought to go and get . . . Nick. That's it—go get Nick."

"Nice idea," Coxe concurred, lifting his head from Sophia's breast. "Go get Nick . . ."

"Game's not the same without 'em," Annesley muttered, "Game's not the—same . . . go get 'im . . ."

"Don't wanna get 'im," Dunstan Carradine said, moving Emma's delightfully proficient hand where it could do the most good.

"We'll get 'im, soon we'll get 'im," Annesley promised. "Can't have a card game without Nick . . ."

Charlotte slid off Dunstan's lap and pulled down the hem of her dress, smoothing it over her knees. "It's a perfect idea," she murmured, straightening her dress and patting her hair. And then she planted a thick arousing kiss on Annesley's mouth. "Do that for me, Max. Do it tonight. Let's go get Nick and bring him back — tonight."

They were a merry group, all except Dunstan who groused about leaving their sanctum of gratification for some harum-scarum idea, and what if Nick were asleep or with some doxy and didn't want to play cards anyway?

The clock struck four as their carriage rumbled down the empty and echoing streets to Berkeley Square.

But they didn't notice; they were too busy stealing kisses from whoever was closest.

Black shadows moved beneath the grey-black dawn, and nobody noticed; they were too busy sliding their hands up the nearest knee and feeling for their partner's bushy mound of Venus.

And the carriage drew to a halt and they never noticed; they were all in the throes of evanescent pleasure.

Annesley awoke to the fact they had arrived first.

"Here we are — go get Nick . . . Gotta summon Trenholm. Trenholm will let us in and we'll just go on up to Nick's room and make sure he can't say no."

He clambered unsteadily out of the carriage and weaved his way up the steps, leaving his companions to find their way as they could. There was a bell which had a clang he could hear even on the street when he pulled on it, and he was satisfied that Trenholm at least would not leave them standing outside.

Everyone crowded around him, waiting for the acknowledgement, and it took a good five minutes before the door finally opened.

"Mr. Annesley," Trenholm said, his voice betraying not a shade of shock to find him standing on Nicholas' doorstep.

"GottagetNick," Annesley said by way of explanation. " 'Scuse me, Trenholm old fellow, but we need Nick. Game ain't been the same without 'im. We all came to get 'im. I'll just make my own way up the stairs."

And up he went before Trenholm could protest or even try to reason with him, which would have been an utter waste of time given how foxed he was—they all were—Trenholm thought dourly, and he watched them ascend with no little certainty as to how Mr. Nicholas was going to contend with six sodden nobles bursting into his room.

But Mr. Nicholas was used to Mr. Annesley's excesses. It wouldn't be the first time he had done something so outrageous . . .

They paused at the bedroom door, all six of them, bobbing and weaving to varying degrees as they tried to get their balance after climbing the steep staircase, and tried very hard not to look down over the railing of the balcony.

And then Annesley pounded on the door and shouted: "Nick, Nick, we've come to get you. We need you, old boy. The game ain't the same without you. We need your money, old man. Open the door and come out. We'll have a game down in the parlor; you don't even have to leave the house. Nick—Nick—"

Nicholas yanked open the door. "Annesley! What the hell—"

"Came to get you old man; sorry for barging in like this. Need your fine tuned hand, Nick. Game wasn't any fun without you. We'll just set up in your room . . ." And he pushed his way past Nicholas, with the five others following, like an inexorable wave about to crash on the shore.

And he stopped. And he sobered up very rapidly. "Well, damn, Nick old boy: you bedded Lady Desire."

Chapter Eighteen

The ramifications were appalling: and they all got a quick lecherous look at Jainee's bare breasts before she snatched up the bedclothes and burrowed under them.

"I told you he was with a high-priced harlot," Dunstan said, his voice hard and rather menacing as his glittering eyes met Jainee's without a trace of feeling.

"But God, she is beautiful," Annesley breathed. "Tell you what, Nick old boy. Dress her up and bring her back to the sanctum and we can all have at her."

"Wish we'd known," Coxe said mournfully. "A waste not to share those bosoms, Nick. You are *not* a good friend."

"Of course we could remedy that *here*," Annesley went on hopefully. "I mean—four hot mares and three lusty stallions—what an equation, eh, Nick? What do you say? Take Charlotte, you would not believe the change in her. Or Emma—wonderful hands, wonderful. And Sophia—twice as large as Miss Bowman on top. And always ready to offer her wares. God, Nick, you wouldn't have believed it: Coxe on one side and—"

"I will kill you if one word of this gets around," Nicholas said, his voice dangerous, deadly.

Annesley stopped in mid-sentence. "Nick—*never*."

"Not a word," Coxe swore solemnly, transfixed by the sight of Jainee, wrapped in sheets and coverlets, her hair tumbling down her white shoulders, sitting cross-legged in the center of the bed. "On my honor, old man."

Charlotte swept to the forefront, her eyes blazing, her body shaking with anger at Annesley's betrayal and offering them all up for Miss Bowman's entertainment. "I will tell everyone," she said viciously. "This bitch has had it all her own way since the minute she came to London. It's fitting that Miss Bowsprit got caught in the bed that she made: now I'm going to make her lay in it. I'm going to rub her nose in it, and no one can stop me."

And she wheeled around and stalked out of the room, her blazing pale eyes daring the other two women to stay with their lust-fogged lovers.

They didn't know the difference anyway, she thought. They were mindless animals, grabbing for any pleasure they could get, now they were considered on the shelf. But not her, not her. That should have been her laying languidly in Nicholas' bed, sated in the aftermath of carnality. Dunstan Carradine was no substitute: he was only the closest relative available on the spur of the moment.

Had she known that Nicholas was going to fornicate with that whore, she would have followed him home and pulled him away from her bodily.

Well, now he must pay. Now he had gone too far in the year and a half with which she had been involved with him, either directly or peripherally. Heretofore, there had never been any gossip attached to his name, save his reckless attitude at the card table.

And she hadn't cared, after she had jilted him, what he had done or who he had done it with. But now she was experienced, now she knew what she really wanted, and when she had just decided to go after Nicholas and win him again, he did *this* to her. Now she was going to make him sorry for everything he had done to her.

She was going to make him *beg*.

"Tell *everyone* you know," she instructed Emma and Sophia, having commandeered Annesley's carriage to take them to their respective homes. "*Everyone*. It's time that virtuous whore got what's coming to her. Ha! Lady Desire. Whoever bestowed that name knew what he was talking about. I just wonder how other many men she's lured into her bed. Damn her, damn her. Stupid, gullible Nicholas—I will make him pay—I *will* . . ."

And Emma and Sophia patiently listened and then Sophia said

plaintively, "But why did we have to leave? I thought we could stay and have some more fun."

"Oh, we're going to have fun," Charlotte said viciously. "Lots and lots of fun watching Nicholas Carradine squirm and twist and finally crawl on his knees to me and beg for mercy."

"God, Nick—just look at her sizing us up. I mean to tell you, my sizer is about ready to explode. She wants us, old man. Why don't you stop talking for her and let her give the word."

Nicholas turned and looked at Jainee, and she thought she would never want to see such a look again.

"*You* are a pig, Mr. Annesley," she said succinctly.

"God, what fire," Annesley breathed. "Let me show you what a pig ruts *with,* my imperious darling."

"Get him out of here," Jainee exploded. He was unbelievable, with all his talk of mares and pigs and having at her. And Dunstan, just standing there looking evil and daring her to spit out one word. And Coxe, half falling down from drink and who knew what else.

Damn Nicholas for just standing there and literally saying and doing *nothing* when the milkmaid was about to pump her udders and spray the whole city with the tale of them barging in on Nicholas and guess what delicious morsel they had found *him* nibbling on.

"Waintree," Coxe mumbled suddenly, groping for a door or a piece of furniture to lean on. "Got to offer—"

Dunstan leapt on it. "Nonsense. Listen, Nicholas my boy. This is *not* irreparable. Lucretia doesn't enter into it. We agreed the bitch is disposable. And Charlotte is obviously hot for revenge. It seems to me you could solve two problems with one solution."

"You are cracked, uncle."

"Ah, but you weren't with her tonight. It is a new and improved Emerlin, my boy, and I tell you, she is as brazen as any whore but her money and lineage are a damned sight more seductive. She was incredible. So think about it. Just think about it. You don't have to do anything tonight but pay the little twitch-tail off and

338

somehow get her back to Lucretia's without anyone seeing her. Do it, Nicholas. This is *not* the moment for spur of the moment decisions."

"I hope," Annesley spoke up, "I hope you are finished prosing, Dunstan, because I'm ready for a hot hearty taste of what Nicholas has been sampling while we were wasting time with those drabs."

He started for the bed and Nicholas moved directly in front of him.

"I think not, Max."

"Ah, Nick, we talked about a man's getting his hands deep into *her* pockets. What's the difference?"

"The difference is, she's Lucretia's protegée, and Charlotte is going to make enough trouble—maybe even for you if you put your poker in the wrong fireplace."

"Oh God, I never even thought of that," Annesley groaned. "She *is* a vicious piece. Damn—a man can't get an evening with a *discreet* tart these days."

"But it's interesting," Dunstan said. "There *is* one solution that makes it right for everyone: you save your whore's reputation *and* you effectively shut up the Emerlins *and* make a splendid match at the same time. Nick, it's made for you. Last year, I would have said no. If it were any other trollop—who cares. But this is a touchy one, what with her being involved with Lucretia. However, an offer for Charlotte would necessitate your getting rid of her altogether, but I don't think that would be a bad thing."

"Waintrue," Coxe muttered, sliding to the floor.

"Are we quite finished?" Nicholas said, having listened to this whole discourse without saying a word or moving a muscle.

"You know, Nick," Annesley interposed, "I don't care about the Emerlins. It's ridiculous to think she would expose herself to gossip and ruin you as well as *me*. Besides, she wasn't that good anyway. Or—" he amended, catching Dunstan's angry eye, "rather, she was fantastic, but *my* tastes are a little extreme. I like a feisty one, like—"

"Are *you* done?" Nicholas interrupted him before he enlarged on that theme.

"Just *think* about it, Nick," Dunstan put in.

"I am thinking about it," Nicholas said impassively. "Now both of you take hold of Coxe and get him out of my bedroom, and I hope you remember it was your imprudence that caused this mess in the first place."

He slammed the door in their faces and turned to Jainee. "Now you—"

"Dear God, if anyone else calls me a thing, a you, a whore, I will *attack* him," Jainee said heatedly.

"I'm sure you will," Nicholas said calmly.

"Gentlemen—their games, their lewdness—it goes beyond comprehension . . ." she muttered angrily. "You are no different, my lord; you just choose to take your pleasure in private."

"And so do you," he retorted.

"I have never heard the like of what goes on behind closed doors when men play cards," she said indignantly. "It is inconceivable. It is—typical. A man thinks with his loins—it must be so. How could a man with any discrimination even *think* of exposing himself publicly with such a one as the cow-cud. It defies imagination—"

"Are you finished, my lady of the flimsy dresses and invisible undergarments? You cannot repair that dress. I will take it with me."

"What?"

"Yes . . . and your stockings and shoes and your cape. Just to insure you remain where I leave you, Diana. Just where you are right now, right in my bed."

"But—Lady Waynflete—"

"I am not taking you back to Lady Waynflete's house just yet. You will stay here. And you will speak to no one, and you will do *nothing* until I return."

"But I have no choice, my lord," she said viciously. "Unless I put on a pair of your breeches."

"Or these," he murmured, picking up the seductive satin ties and tossing them onto the bed. "Especially these."

She picked one up and defiantly wrapped it around her neck and around her sheet-shrouded breasts. "No different

340

from my dress, my Lord; I believe I might pass."

"Oh, you might get three feet, Diana, but you certainly are welcome to try if it is so onerous to stay here for an hour or so. Please."

"I refuse to bow to your hallowed god of illusion, my lord. You can track over reality all you want and veil it with every manner of whole cloth, but you cannot disguise it, and that milk cow will do all she can to discredit us both."

"I am sure she will," Nicholas agreed calmly. "Your word you will stay here."

She sent him a simmering look.

"I will lock the door."

"I will jump out the window."

"That is foolish, even for you, Diana, although I suppose a goddess must feel she is indestructible."

She took a deep angry breath. "What are you going to do?"

"Repair the damage, of course. Seamlessly, I hope, and with whole cloth. Now, swear you will remain in bed until I return."

"I don't trust you," she said peevishly.

"Nor I you," Nicholas said stringently. "That should be enough to assure you that I will do my best to extricate you from this predicament."

The moment he closed the door behind him, she leapt out of bed and reached for the doorknob—and heard the ominous click of a key turning in the lock.

She felt a fine seething rage envelop her as she paced to the window, naked, oblivious to the light and whether anyone could see her.

He was there, the misbegotten son of a—she could not think of a word *low* enough to describe him as she watched him mount his horse, speak a word to Trenholm and gallop away into the night.

And the shadows moved behind him.

Her heart pounded wildly. The shadows moved . . . someone—something on foot, running swiftly and gone a moment later beyond the lights from the house.

Her heart felt like it would leap out of her chest.

She imagined it . . .

It was late; she was all emotional with the events of the evening. Southam was making her crazy.

She scurried away from the window and into the safety of the bed. Covers were for hiding, she thought frantically, for pulling up over one's head and shutting out the world. What else could she do now while Southam was off who knew where, and that milk person was probably already fueling the fire that she had been so eager to ignite.

She hated inactivity. She hated leaving the decision about what to do in his hands.

She couldn't sleep.

She felt exhausted.

She would just put her head down for a moment and calm the thudding of her heart. And she would not think about the shadows or the recriminations . . .

She slept.

But it could not have been for more than a half hour, an hour at the most, because before she knew it, someone was shaking her awake, and none too gently either.

She opened her eyes groggily to find Southam by her bedside.

"Well, even a goddess must sleep," he observed prosaically. "I expected you to be fully awake, plotting and planning your next conquest."

"I wish I were all-seeing and all-knowing," she said waspishly, annoyed that he had pulled her out of a deep and very satisfying dream, "because I *never* would have walked out of the house yesterday and we would have avoided this tangle."

"Then you will be reassured that I have taken steps to *untangle* this dilemma," he said as he arose and moved across the room. He wanted to be as far from her as possible now. And he wanted to look his fill of her incandescent beauty in the midst of his disheveled bed.

There was just no hiding all they had done there earlier in the evening, no toning down her vibrant sensuality and the flush of satiety in her face.

She looked like a nymph, rising from the frothy backwash of the sea. She looked fragile and she looked indomitable, and he didn't know quite how he was going to let her leave his bed.

"I am not reassured *yet*," she said pointedly, folding her arms across her chest.

"It is very simple, Diana. You will marry me."

That shocked her; the very words sent her senses reeling. He was mad, he had to be.

"Are you *deranged*? I *thought* you had agreed to the solution of milking the cow."

"I did no such thing, Diana. I merely said I would think about it. About thirty seconds' worth during that morass of inanity that Annesley inflicted on me. It is really quite simple—if it is legal, there cannot be a scandal. Lucretia is protected, you are . . . well, let us say I will have you where I can keep an eye on you. Charlotte cannot touch you; I do not have to ever think about offering for *her*, and Dunstan will be unhappy for about a month. On the whole, a quite elegant solution, I think."

It wasn't elegant at all—it was rag-bag solution, pieced together by a man who was desperate to save a friend's stature among her peers; it had nothing to do with his wants or needs, or hers.

"Men have married for less cogent reasons," Nicholas said. "Did you not forecast a love affair and a probable marriage?"

"Did I?" She was startled that he remembered.

"And I called it a fairy tale; I think rather that everything you have ever said to me is a fairy tale, Diana, but that is neither here nor there right now. What is to the point is that Lucretia awaits you downstairs, with a minister. I have obtained a special license and we will be married from this house today, with Lucretia as our witness."

She shook her head: she could not yet comprehend that he meant what he said. There were so many things to consider . . . the blood . . . Dunstan . . . his motives, her own if she were to acquiesce.

343

"I swore on the grave of my adoptive mother that I would protect Lucretia if her taking you in would cause a scandal," Nicholas said quietly. "I would never cause her any grief, but if word gets around that her unknown protegée was caught in my bed, her honor and credibility will be stripped away from her before the sun rises. But if she can say that we were married this day and that she witnessed the ceremony, then the burden devolves on us to provide the proof and corroborate the truth of the matter. No one is going to ask what *time* we were married, Diana. Neither will Lucretia offer the information. It suffices that *this* day, the day that my alleged friends broke into my house and found us, *this* day we were married by special license."

Her head was spinning. He was marrying *her* to cover for Lucretia Waynflete's bad judgment. No, to cover himself, really, for foisting her on Lucretia. She could not put it all together, what it would mean if she agreed to this most foolhardy plan. He truly should have offered for the milk cow. She would be the perfect society matron.

Dear lord—nothing made sense. If she agreed, it put paid to Edythe Winslowe's blackmail, it put her beyond the reach of Dunstan's threats, it gave her time and the wherewithal to continue her search for her half-brother; it gave her Southam and his mercurial passion forever.

Had he said *adoptive* mother? She couldn't quite sort through it all—she had missed some of it, surely not something as important as that—*adoptive* mother, he had sworn something . . . and she, she had forecast a probable marriage: how wicked the cards were. Or perhaps how wicked was she.

"Lucretia is waiting with an appropriate dress for you," Nicholas said. "It will answer, Diana, and perhaps far better than doing nothing because I never would have offered for Charlotte Emerlin. Once was enough. Twice makes me look like a fool."

"And yet you have not even asked *me*," Jainee said, thinking that here he was ordering everything and not even considering her wishes whether she had them or not. She didn't, but this was such a havey-cavey way to go about it.

"I don't make pretty speeches," Nicholas said. "You under-

344

stand the practicality of the arrangement. And time is passing."

Jainee felt like stamping her foot. The fool did not want to tidy it up any more than the actual event, she thought resentfully. An arrangement. Nothing to do with fanciful things like the fortune cards and perhaps his warring feelings about her. Oh no, not Southam. Preserve the stone-face. Get on with the business.

"What is in it for me then?" she asked, spitefully she thought, but he deserved it, really he did.

He gave her a quirky smile. "I will forgive your debt. I will send Lucretia to you."

But of course his room was the last place Lucretia wanted to go. She thought he was mad too.

He leaned over the balcony railing and signalled to Trenholm who went to fetch her from the parlor where she was keeping company with the minister.

"I can't tell you how I feel about this," she whispered fiercely as she passed him on the stairs. "I would rather endure the scandal."

"I would *not*," Nicholas said succinctly and turned his back to her. But after all, she had said much the same thing on finding him mysteriously in her room in the dead of night, demanding that she dress and come back to Berkeley Square with him.

"You have gone round the bend, Nicholas. Your mother would be appalled," she grumbled as she groped her way around her room for a candle and dressing gown. "What is to do that you had to rouse me at this ungodly hour and however did you gain entrance to the house without Blexter admitting you. *What* is going on here?"

His explanation was quick and concise and neatly omitted how he had gotten into her house, but it didn't matter, because she fixed her attention directly onto Dunstan's reasonable suggestion and nothing else, not even the fact that Charlotte and two other ladies had been with Dunstan and Annesley.

"Dunstan's solution makes sense, Nicholas. It solves everything. Charlotte is only after attention from you anyway. You don't have to love the girl. You just have to get an heir with her and then you can go your own way. What is so difficult about that? *If* you really want to protect me from this shameful episode."

"Charlotte bores me to tears; Miss Bowman does not. The end effect is the same, except I wind up with the woman with whom I was in bed. Perhaps Dunstan should marry Charlotte since they seemed so cozy with each other last night."

Lucretia froze. "Never say such a thing, Nicholas. They were *not*. Dunstan played cards all night and had just a bit much to drink. His suggestion is eminently sensible. I won't be a party to this nonsense after all."

"The only person Charlotte has ever wanted is me," Nicholas said curtly. "She retrenched a year ago and mother Gertrude took over and made her into a trollop of the first water, and while her excesses seemed to enchant Coxe and Annesley, they arouse nothing in me but extreme dislike. And guilt, I might add, for the shabby way I was forced to treat her the brief months we were engaged. But that is *not* enough to make me to offer for her to save the situation. And once I am wed to Miss Bowman, nothing you can do will alter things. I would much rather you bear witness and lend us your countenance. But—you must do as your conscience dictates."

Her expression softened just a little. "I can bear a little scandal, Nicholas."

"*Not* over a stranger whom I coerced you into sponsoring. No, you would not soon recover from that, whereas I would not be tainted at all. They would say it was just like a beautiful woman to gull an ascetic like me. But Lucretia should have known better. They will say that you should have seen through her the moment you met."

"Yes," Lucretia said thoughtfully, "indeed they will."

"So, like it or not, Lucretia, let us take the brush and paint the thing over with whitewash and let them say whatever they will."

"I do not like it," Lucretia said roundly, "but I will do it."

And she was doing it; she laboriously reached the top of the steps, with Trenholm but a moment behind bearing a trunk with a suitable dress and accompaniments for Miss Bowman to wear.

He smiled sardonically at the thought that the goddess might open the door stark naked—but she was cleverer than that, he was sure of it.

He made his way to the parlor to join the minister, a man he had known since his youth, a man of discretion and no little understanding of the impetuousness of a lover. And he was prepared, for a handsome remuneration, to defend the marriage to all comers, whatever their motives. He and Southam understood each other perfectly.

It was a matter of several moments while the Reverend Maynard filled out some forms and obtained as much information about his intended bride as Nicholas knew — which, he realized, was not much.

He himself had changed into formal clothing for the wedding and he had commandeered Trenholm as both the caterer for a celebratory repast after the ceremony, and a witness.

And he had taken great care that no one else would be involved, not friends, acquaintances or even servants, barring his most excellent and discreet butler.

He wondered what Lucretia was doing up in the bedroom with Diana. More than that, he was drowning with curiosity about what she was saying.

"I detest the scurrilous way Nicholas has chosen to remedy this situation," Lady Waynflete was saying for perhaps the second or third time, and to herself while she draped the folds of Jainee's dress around her slippers and helped her hook and lace up the back.

But Jainee had had enough of that. Lady Waynflete was a most grudging maid, resentful of having to do the thing, fretful because she was aiding in what was essentially an elopement by special license, and positively enraged that Nicholas had chosen to marry *her*.

"So you have said, madame, twice now at least. Tell me, why then are you here? After all, it is solely my lord's desire to protect you."

"And *you*," Lady Waynflete reminded her trenchantly, as she stood back and admired the effect of the dress, one of perhaps two or three that had been made up in white silk and muslin. "Yes, that will do."

"It's very plain," Jainee said, adjusting the neckline.

"Your maid is not here to redesign it," Lady Waynflete snapped.

Jainee stared at her through the looking glass, which distorted her figure slightly because Lady Waynflete was standing slightly behind her.

"Why do you dislike me so?" she asked curiously.

"I do not dislike you," Lady Waynflete said staunchly. "I disapprove. You are too fast, your clothes are too flashy, your mouth is too brassy. I don't know who you are or where you come from. You have said nothing about your parents or your past, and you have gone out of your way to fascinate every man who crosses your path—and Nicholas is no exception, whether he knows it or not."

Jainee nodded. "You have the right of it, my lady, and I have been grateful for all your kindness, however reluctantly it was offered."

"Ah—see! You have done it again. Such plain speaking and yet a body does not know whether you are expressing your gratitude or being churlish under the cover of a compliment. I do not like not knowing where I stand—with anyone."

"And yet you would support Nicholas' decision," Jainee murmured, refusing to elaborate on what she had meant.

"Oh yes, my girl. I support it. And why, you may ask. I will tell you. Because it makes no difference to me whether he would marry Charlotte Emerlin or you or do nothing at all. However, his taking you provides me with several advantages: it dislodges you from my house and my responsibility, and it removes you from the circle of available men who seek to pursue you. You may conclude that that circumstance pleases me very well."

"I have never sought to attract Dunstan Carradine," Jainee said levelly.

"My dear, you do not need to *try*," Lady Waynflete said cynically. "But Dunstan is honorable, and has great respect for family. He would never try to pursue you once you are Nicholas'

348

wife. And so, for those reasons, I will lend countenance to this marriage. Now tell me, what do you wish to do with your hair?"

The clock was just striking six, the dawn just rising outside the window when Jainee made her way downstairs, followed by a faintly exasperated Lady Waynflete.

Nicholas sat with his back to the parlor door as she paused on the threshold, and it was the Reverend Maynard who saw her first, and rubbed his hands together. "Ah, the bride . . ."

Trenholm, who had been laying out a buffet table, ceased that operation and immediately came to stand behind Nicholas as he rose to his feet and turned and saw Jainee standing in the doorway.

She was heartbreakingly beautiful in a simple gown of Indian muslin which was banded with ivory satin and swirled out in a little train behind her. The sleeves were long, the shoulder line slightly puffed, and she wore gloves, and a sheer gauze veil pinned to the circlet of pearls she had wound through her hair.

Her color was high, her eyes unnaturally large and blazing with emotion. In her hands she clutched what looked like a bible.

Behind her, Lady Waynflete stood like some avenging fairy godmother, her expression resigned. As Jainee moved forward slowly into the room, she followed, and the look in her eyes changed imperceptibly to one of complacency.

Dunstan was safe from the toils of the temptress: Nicholas had been right—marrying her was the only thing to do.

Jainee glided to Nicholas' side, and she and Trenholm took their places slightly behind.

The minister asked several questions, all relating to Jainee's birth and parentage, and Lady Waynflete was shocked to hear that her father was English and her mother French. But it was probably that the chit had been raised in some godawful hovel somewhere in the country, and of course she had wanted to dispense with such a humble background. They had invented a much better one for her in Brighton.

The Reverend Maynard began his sonorous reading of the marriage service.

Jainee could hardly keep her eyes straight ahead. She was insane, she could think of a hundred reasons why she must not allow Southam to ride roughshod over her and coerce her into this marriage . . .

"Do you, Jainee Bowman, enter into this marriage of your own free will and volition?"

The words stuck in her throat.

"I do," she whispered.

"And do you, Nicholas Carradine, Lord Southam, enter into this marriage of your own free will and volition?"

He did not hesitate. "I do."

"And do you, Jainee Bowman, take Nicholas Carradine, Lord Southam, to be your true and lawfully wedded husband, to love and honor, to cherish and obey . . ."

She hardly heard past that dreaded word: "obey." She almost said no.

"I do."

"And do you, Nicholas Carradine, Lord Southam, take Jainee Bowman to be your true and lawfully wedded wife, to love and honor, to cherish and protect . . ."

"I do."

"And now if there is anyone who knows of any just impediment to this marriage, let him speak now . . ."

Jainee was sure Lucretia Waynflete would say something just at the last moment. But there was only silence, and the Reverend Maynard continued:

"And so, having exchanged vows and pledged your life and your love to each other, you will now exchange rings as a symbol of the vows you have taken together. Nicholas . . ."

Amazingly, he produced a ring, and he took her hand which forced her to lift her eyes to his, and he repeated the words after the minister: "With this ring, I thee wed . . ."

His eyes glittered with unreadable emotion, equal to hers in intensity and reverence for the moment.

"Jainee . . . ?" the minister asked gently, breaking into her awed sensation at the feeling of this ornate and heavy ring encircling her finger.

She felt a hand on her arm, and she turned to find Lady Waynflete at her elbow, her hand extended, offering a wide-banded gold ring.

She took it, she took his large hand in her own, and she tremblingly repeated the minister's words: "With this ring . . ."

"And now," Reverend Maynard beamed, "it is my pleasure to pronounce you husband and wife. Congratulations, my dear," he added, reaching for her hand and Nicholas' simultaneously, and joining them.

Husband . . . the word sat uneasily in her mind. . . . *wife.* What *was* a wife? She did not know the first thing about "doing" a wife.

"My lord," she murmured, her eyes downcast and focused on the sight of her hand swallowed up in Nicholas'. And the ring: the thick gleaming gold band that seemed to rightfully fit Nicholas' finger. How? *Whose?*

What had she done?

Nicholas relinquished her hand to take two glasses from the tray offered by Trenholm, who, after his part as signatory witness, began to serve the celebratory breakfast.

Her own ring looked strange too as she curled her fingers around the goblet and took a sip of champagne. *Whose* ring? Weighted on her finger, it was, like a statement of intent.

She felt a tremor of apprehension because she could not picture what her life was going to be like past this next fifteen minutes. She was Nicholas Carradine's *wife.*

She was Lady Southam . . .

"I must be going," Lady Waynflete said abruptly, breaking away from her conversation with Reverend Maynard. "Congratulations, Miss Bowman. You've done excellently well for yourself. I trust you will rise to the occasion. I will send Marie with your belongings before the morning is out. Nicholas, my dear, I cannot imagine what your mother would think of this situation. No doubt *she* would find some saving grace. Good afternoon, Reverend."

Jainee watched her depart with mixed emotions. She

351

was not an enemy now: she was a conspirator in a face-saving marriage about which only four people knew the truth.

It had just gone seven o'clock when Southam's carriage drew up before Lady Waynflete's house.

She still was in a state of bemusement as she inserted the key into the door and swung it open. It was inconceivable that Nicholas had finally been caught in the parson's mouse trap, and by that cunning adventuress. Oh, she should have taken Miss Bowman's facetious remark for true: for look at where it had got her—right in the arms of one of the wealthiest and most eligible and least gullible men in all of London.

The girl was a wonder, she thought helplessly, and she could not but think that somehow she had engineered the situation to force Nicholas into taking action.

Was she *really* that clever?

She faced that question as Blexter came forward out of curiosity and met her in the hall. "Never mind, Blexter—let us say I took a morning constitutional."

Better than nothing, she thought dolefully, when she had never exerted herself in the least in all her life.

And then Marie: "Madame, madame, mademoiselle has not returned to her room; her bed has not been slept in. Where can she be, what shall I do?"

And Lady Waynflete thought how ironic it was that Miss Bowman's maid would be the first to hear the news before anyone of the *ton*.

"Rest easy, Marie. Nothing has happened. Miss Bowman and Lord Southam eloped tonight. She is at his townhouse and you will have the goodness to pack her clothes and be ready to proceed there before the clock strikes noon."

Marie's mouth fell open. *"Dieu,"* she breathed, and clapped her hand to her lips.

She recovered in an instant. *"Bien,* madame, I will be ready."

No questions, pure acceptance, Lady Waynflete noted. Perhaps it was so with maids and footmen; they were so used to obedience.

So she did not notice that Marie did not head directly upstairs to begin packing as she made her weary way into the parlor where Blexter was in the midst of brewing tea and a footman was laying a fresh fire.

Nobody saw Marie as she edged down the long basement hallway and scuttled out to the stables behind the house.

And she hid in one of the stalls, waiting, waiting. In this she was taking a chance: there were any number of stable boys in and around the carriage house in the morning. But she was waiting for a particular one, in the hope that he had not been tapped to exercise Mr. Jeremy's stock this day.

How much luck, how much? That mademoiselle had run off with Monsieur and successfully brought him to point was a stroke of sheer genius on *her* part—all unknowing, of course. And now it was merely a matter of notifying Robert, a certain stable boy who had been clever enough to get himself hired so that he could be directly on the scene when she needed to transmit her messages.

It took a while, but the luck held. Robert was the first of the pack into the stable, leading one of the carriage horses.

"Robert," she whispered over the clatter of the horse's hooves. "Ro-bert . . ."

He heard her then, and he searched the stalls until he found her crouching behind one of the partitions. She pulled him down beside her and put her finger to her lips.

"Only listen," she said in French, her voice barely above a breath, "la Beaumont has married Monsieur and I leave for Berkeley Square tonight. Nothing, *nothing* could be better. Listen, listen: she has found her father. She now has the protection of Southam's name. She will find the boy and all shall go as planned. Tell them that all is proceeding *better* than planned. We will find the boy now, with Southam's help, and I promise—I *swear*—I will kill him. Tell Murat . . . tell her that . . ."

Chapter Nineteen

The news exploded all over London like fireworks going off in forty different directions.

Southam married! The luscious Lady Desire out of circulation!

The dog—

Such secrets!

From one house to the next, one servant to another, friend to friend, making early morning calls instead of early afternoon, the news spread and magnified and expanded into stories of such deception and derring-do that even had anyone known of the fiasco at Southam's home the evening before, that story would have gotten lost in all the fairy tales.

The news put Gertrude Emerlin in a rage, and sent Charlotte into her room in a fit of fury that could only be vented by smashing things.

It made Annesley fall off his chair laughing at the sheer gall of Nicholas to have countervented gossip in such a daring way.

Coxe didn't remember any of it, and Dunstan was the first to call on the newly wed couple.

"Uncle," Nicholas greeted him warmly. "Come join us at breakfast with the Reverend Maynard, who was kind enough to call."

He ushered Dunstan into the dining room where Jainee sat side by side with the Reverend Maynard, dressed in gown of Indian muslin which was tied around her body with a long lustrous stream of satin material.

Damn him, Nicholas has thought of everything, Dunstan thought, holding out his hand to Jainee. His daughter, his niece by marriage.

She read his murderous displeasure in his eyes. Her head lifted, her eyes sparkled dangerously. *"Uncle?* Do join us."

He could do nothing else and he ungraciously settled himself in a chair opposite the minister. "I suppose it could be said that you took my advice," he commented acrimoniously.

"I was sure you would wish me happy," Nicholas said imperturbably. "Have some coffee—or some eggs and smoked *tongue.*"

Dunstan shot him a suspicious glance. "I believe I will."

Nicholas smiled. The minister said, "I must be going," and Nicholas rose to see him out.

Jainee's food suddenly stuck in her throat.

"Well my dear, aren't you the one," Dunstan said, as he neatly cut his meat into small manageable pieces. "How did you convince him? Or did you think that your marriage would remove the threat of violence against you? Oh no, my girl. Nicholas could be a widower in a fortnight, and it would be better for me if he were. He cannot protect you if you choose to be foolhardy. Perhaps you have made the most short-sighted choice of all. Ah, Nicholas, do you know? I really am not hungry; I only came to wish you well, and to say that we must talk, and soon."

"As you wish."

"Dinner then?"

"Name the day."

"I will send round a note after I consult my calendar. Tell me, will the new Lady Southam feel slighted if it is just we two alone?"

Nicholas turned to her. "Will she?"

Jainee smiled, that smile that made his hackles rise and, he suspected, Dunstan's. "Nothing *you* could do would upset me—uncle," she said pointedly. "We have all seen a wonderful example of what happens when men get together and dine alone. Do as you will. I can certainly keep myself occupied."

Neither of them liked that statement of mischievous intent.

Jainee smiled. "Thank you for coming, *uncle.*"

"Welcome to the family, Jainee," he answered in kind.

Nicholas saw him out and when he returned, he found Jainee pacing the room.

"This will not work," she said agitatedly. "It just will not work."

"The thing is done," Nicholas said calmly. "Why do you not like Dunstan?"

How perceptive of him, she thought, unable to calm herself or stay still. "I like him well enough," she said diffidently. "Do you?"

He ignored that. "The word has gotten around. You may thank me for thinking of resurrecting last night's dress so that callers did not find you in your wedding dress."

"I am ever so grateful."

"And you must write a note to Lady Waynflete to express your appreciation of the loan of her dear deceased husband's ring so that we could complete the ceremony. Dunstan did not need to know that, and neither did the minister."

"Of course, I will do that," she murmured, much chastened. They had not had a moment to talk since the ceremony. Trenholm had laid out the breakfast immediately, Southam had sent her upstairs to change and the Reverend had stayed to celebrate afterwards.

She fingered her ring. "This is a beautiful ring."

"It was my mother's."

Of course, she should have guessed, but how could she have guessed? And his tone, when he mentioned his mother—so reverential, so . . . sad.

"I thank you for it," she said gently, and she was stunned to see a flash of pain in his eyes.

It was gone in the blink of an eye. "Despite what Lucretia thinks, and she was my mother's great good friend, I believe my mother would have liked you very well," Nicholas said, "but—" he added as the doorbell pealed urgently, "she would have hated this circus. Ah, Jeremy—what's to do?"

"Are you out of your mind?" Jeremy demanded, storming into the room ahead of Trenholm, and totally ignoring Jainee's presence. *"Are you crazy?* Were you drunk? Honest to God, Nicholas—Miss *Bowman?"*

"Ah, yes—Miss Bowman. Permit me, Jeremy—may I make you known to my wife, Lady Southam?"

"Damn—I beg your pardon . . ." Jeremy muttered with ill grace. "My apologies, Miss Bowman. *Nick*—" he added meaningfully.

"You can speak frankly, Jeremy; I don't think you have failed to make your feelings known to my wife before this."

"Yes, well—"

"Have·some breakfast, Jeremy; it will improve your humor."

"The *only* thing that will improve my humor is if you tell me straight out this thing is all a hum."

"Have some coffee, Jeremy," Nicholas said, seating himself and pouring a cup that he did not want.

"Damn, Nick—it's all been a plot, a scheme. She has been after you, your money, and she put herself in a place where she could get it. I never in my life thought you would be *gulled* by a piece of Haymarket ware, especially when you could snap your fingers and have any eligible heiress in *England*."

"The coffee is quite tolerable," Nicholas said, sipping his with remarkable *sang-froid* during this heated harangue and forbearing to look at Jainee's expression. But Jeremy had raked her over the coals the moment she set foot in Lucretia's house, so none of this would surprise her. And perhaps it *was* best she know just where she stood among his intimates because he was damned sure he did *not* know where she stood within his life. "And the ham," he added, proffering a dish.

"You can be mute as fish all you like," Jeremy went on, ignoring Nicholas' interruptions, "but I think your upper story's to let if you think this clanker will pass muster with the *ton*. Your reputation won't withstand it."

Nicholas shrugged. "Frankly," he said lazily, "I don't care."

"Ah, Nick . . ."

"You're making more of this than needs be. The end-tale is simple: Miss Bowman and I were married by special license directly we left Annesley's party."

"Ah, but Nick—never a word or a sign . . ."

"Surely *never* a word," Nicholas said satirically. "I wonder why you thought I lifted her out of Brighton."

"I thought you were three sheets to the wind," Jeremy said

dampingly. "And I blame mother as well. Who should know better than to become embroiled in one of your schemes. She is prostrate, Nick."

"Yet, she was here," Nicholas reminded him cuttingly. "*And* provided the loan of a ring," he added meaningfully, and Jeremy froze. "So what you must do, Jeremy mine, is merely corroborate that I am married and I am a happy man."

"Annesley don't say that," Jeremy said, because he could not push the disapproval of his mother a step further.

"Well, Annesley appeared last night at a very inopportune time and let no grass grow before he began turning my bedroom into his sanctum and proposing to turn my wife into his abbess. *Please,* Jeremy—that viper is the least reliable witness on earth and a downy one at that. He mixes trouble and innuendo in lethal doses, but I warn you, neither I nor my wife will sip from his cup of scandal broth. Nor do I recall asking him advice on the how and about of my marriage. He knew nothing, he invaded my house with great incivility at four in the morning, and I leave the rest to your imagination. Are you clear now on that sequence of events, Jeremy?"

"As glass," Jeremy said ungraciously. "And the shock of it reverberates all around London. This ain't a secret to keep between the teeth, Nick. They're going to be on your doorstep, imagining the worst."

"Are they not already?" Nicholas asked, with a nod toward Jeremy himself.

"It's obvious you don't care a farthing for my opinion, Nick. I can take the hint. I hope you ain't headed for a come-down, but that *is* your lookout." He rose from the table and bowed stiffly to Nicholas. "Nick." And he turned to Jainee. "Lady Southam."

Nicholas began languidly buttering a piece of toast. "How kind of Jeremy to favor me with his company on our wedding day. He does like to air his vocabulary."

Jainee roused herself finally over this disingenuous understatement. "Nonsense, he rang a rare peal over you, my lord, and from all indications it is nothing to what is to come."

"It is nobody's business," Nicholas said, and there was a steely

358

note in his voice which caught Jainee like the scrape of a knife against metal.

"Well then, my lord, perhaps you might tell me just what follows next?" she asked caustically.

Nicholas bit into his toast. "Do you know, Diana? I haven't the faintest idea."

It was all of ten o'clock before things calmed down. Coxe popped in, and Mr. Chevrington, and Charles Griswold, all quite curious to see the how of it: Coxe and Chevrington swearing that when they had separately left him the evening before, Nicholas Carradine was not a married man.

"I believe no one ever gave me a chance to make the announcement," Nicholas said chidingly. "Annesley was in his cups and full of fantasy about what he wanted to do with my wife, and the wonder is, gentlemen, that I did not throw him down the stairs. Please pay your respects and remove yourselves so that we may have some peace this morning."

They at least were chastened by Nicholas' unequivocal assertion that they had been married on the heels of their departure from the Annesley home.

Annesley was another matter altogether.

"If you ain't awake on all suits," he said admiringly, clapping Nicholas on the shoulder and gallantly kissing Jainee's hand. "But you can't fool me, Nick. I was there. You just let Dunstan prattle on and on and then you made your choice for the second go-round."

"My dear Annesley, can anyone stop Uncle Dunstan when he is having a chin session? Especially when he's disguised? Let us leaven this bumble-broth with a spoonful of reality, Max. I left your party with Miss Bowman, as you well know. Indeed, I quit the game early, did I not? Yes. And, if you recall, there was a plausible, if not entirely truthful excuse as to why *I* was escorting Miss Bowman, and not Jeremy or Lucretia. The rest, my friend, is none of your business except that you were impossibly uncouth that night, and discourteous, uncivil and rag mannered, and frankly, Max, I truly didn't think you deserved any explanation for what you found there."

This gentle and rather flaying speech only slowed Annesley down a step. He smelled blood: Nicholas was too talkative, too disdainful.

"Don't try to turn me up sweet, Nick. You know damned well you had not thought of tossing the handkerchief until Dunstan put it in your head."

Nicholas shrugged. "Or perhaps it had already been done, Max, and what was the point of arguing."

"I don't believe you," Annesley said.

"You may ask Dunstan if the Reverend Maynard did not pay us a wedding day call."

"Oh God, Dunstan here already? Came running, did he?"

"To wish us well, of course," Nicholas said gently.

"Ah, Nick—this is a smoke-cloud if ever I saw one, and just to protect your lady-bird against the slings and arrows."

Nicholas got up and walked over to the table by the parlor door, picked up a piece of paper and tossed it negligently right into Annesley's lap.

He read it and for a fleeting second he stiffened and then he flung it down on the sofa beside him. "You can't fob me off with paper, Nick. I know what's what."

"If a man can't read what's before his face, he must be drunk as an emperor, and at ten in the morning. I don't know, Annesley. I think I would advise you to think about marriage yourself. And Charlotte Emerlin would not be a bad choice."

"Oh, you've got starch, Nick, I'll say that for you," Annesley said angrily. "But I promise you, I have more than one string in my bow: I'll get to the truth, damn if I won't."

"But why must you?" Nicholas asked gently.

And Annesley turned to stare at Jainee, who was huddled in the corner of the sofa opposite where he sat. His face was set and he reached for his hat.

"I'll tell you why, old son. Because I wanted her for myself."

She was exhausted. It was not yet noon, and Marie had not arrived, so she could take no relief in changing her clothes so that she could at least move around in company. No, she must sit primly in the corner minding her manners and tamping down on her temper and wondering exactly what she had gotten herself into.

Had she truly felt she had had no choice in the matter of saving Lucretia's reputation? Or had she just been swept away by the event of the moment and the force of *his* conviction?

Whatever it was, she was leg-shackled for life. Or she could disappear just like her father and never give it a second thought.

Lady Southam: so well known now that no one could sneak up behind her in the depths of the night with murder on his mind.

So well known now that even her father must pause to consider the consequences of such an action. So well known that the haunting shadows that moved in the night would totally disappear.

Who had gained the benefit from this marriage, she thought ruefully. Southam was stuck with her while she harvested the advantage from his protection and his name. Therese would have been proud of her. *The best way to love them is to strike a bargain with them . . .*

Or perhaps that stricture had been knit into the fabric of her being before she had ever been aware of a father and her disillusioned mother.

Whatever it was, it was true, for despite all the gains on her side, Southam was still free to do as he would and there was no way she could stop him.

It was ever so with a man, she reflected as she watched him stare into the fireplace from her corner of the sofa. The next party might well find him ensconced in another sanctum with another knot of willing women by his side.

That was marriage; her duty was to get him an heir, and she understood very well all about that.

She narrowed her gaze speculatively as Southam picked up their marriage lines and stared at the paper as if he had never seen it before.

Yes, things were different now. Her life would be subject to the will and the whims of Nicholas Carradine and she could have no say in his own: he might go anywhere and do anything he pleased.

Well, we shall see, she thought, we shall see. She still held an ace in hand—the liberating symbol of the Lady in Black, whom she had thought never to resurrect again. But maybe, she thought, just maybe—depending on how closely Southam meant to confine her—she might spend that card again.

And finally, Marie arrived, just in time to save her from falling asleep on the sofa.

"But which room?" she asked in bewilderment as she caught sight of the long wagon train of trunks and suitcases strung along the steps to the second floor.

"My mother's room connects with mine," Nicholas said, hiding his dismay at the generosity Lucretia had displayed with his largesse. "You may closet your wardrobe in there, but you will sleep with me."

She saw immediately why she had noticed no door in his room: his clothes-press was backed up against it, and it had to be moved before the trunks were brought to the adjoining room.

This operation required three footmen under Trenholm's direction, and a subsequent rearrangement of the bedroom furniture in order to accommodate the clothes press, which then usurped the space taken by the washstand, which necessitated the bed being moved to find a place for it.

In the end, the clock had struck two by the time she and Marie were able to unpack the trunks. Marie was so excited, she could barely hold a dress steady to hang it.

"Mademoiselle—madame . . . my lady: such news, and to be among the first to hear it! How clever you are, madame, how subtle. All will be well now, eh? You need not fear for anything and your search will go on."

Her search—yes, her search. Her father was found, she knew she had confided that much in Marie, but the rest . . . oh, she was so tired, so drained from taking this irrevocable step.

Southam would make no demands on her: somehow she knew it. She climbed into the beautiful gilded bed that had been his mother's and drifted off to sleep.

He awaited the morning newspapers, thankful that she was occupied elsewhere. He had the peculiar and unconscious sense that everything was fixed now, ordered, and that she could never leave him now, no matter what the provocation.

But her presence in his house did not engender a sense of peace; rather, he felt edgy, prickly; she was not a comfortable woman. She was one about whom he would always be wondering what she might do next.

She was a one who would twist circumstances to her need. Clever. Apt. Daring. All the things that had made the jaded bucks of London want to fall at her feet. And all the reasons he had wanted to contain her.

"My lord?"

Trenholm, bearing a tray full of papers: *The Post, The Chronicle, The Times* . . . he made sure they were all there, and he lifted out *The Chronicle* and began to read.

The columnists were not kind. The news had spread in a minute; the wonder was, there was that much detail.

What much-courted nobleman, favored by the gods from childhood on, has now taken fate into his own hands and secretly wed the Fashionable of the moment and precipitously snatched her from the hands of her devoted admirers? A marriage of convenience? Of love? Or of expediency? Only the parson knows for certain. Suffice it to say that my Lord has never come up to scratch heretofore. So, why now?

That was *The Chronicle*, condescending as ever. But *The Post* was no better.

The elusive lord and the fast and flashy arriviste: a match to be reckoned with between the pages of a lurid romance novel, but surely not as the first on-dit of the Season. Town is agog with the news of the secret alliance between his evasive lordship and the bedizened "lady" whom all men desired. The wonder is his lordship fell for it—or perhaps he was tripped?

He threw the paper aside and reached for *The Times,* but the informant, whoever it was, had not gotten there in time. The sole item of interest surrounded speculation about the mysterious lady who had attended the evening at Lady Badlington's and had played impressively and with skill.

And of course, there were the requisite several lines about Annesley's party and a coy reference to the games behind the scenes, which had been omitted from the previous two papers.

Annesley would be *green* that his party had been relegated to five lines in one column. But that it had been mentioned was enough: the tit-tattlers were everywhere, and if they could not sell to one paper, they would take some silver at the next.

And they were sharp: nothing got by them—which meant that he must see to returning Lucretia's ring before someone noticed. And he also must send a formal announcement to *The Times.*

There were invitations to reconsider, although he rather thought he would receive notes remedying that and including Jainee, even at the last moment.

Above all, he thought, he must not forget his primary objective with her: this marriage did not negate the quest which he had undertaken two years ago. A traitor existed, and he played among them and was considered one of them, and he had sworn to root him out.

It was the one thing of which he must reassure his uncle. Nothing had changed. The marriage would not interfere. It would be as if nothing had happened. The game would go on.

"At long last, a moment alone," he said whimsically as he seated her at the long dining room table and took a seat directly across from her rather than at the other end of the table.

"Surely you have some engagement or other tonight," Jainee said tentatively—or was she hoping? She could not imagine what would happen next. For the first time she felt tentative and awkward. The ring constricted her finger, reminding her, taunting her—she had made another bargain, and this time she might not come away the winner.

She did not know how to share with another human being. She knew how to take care of and she knew how to take action. She knew nothing of a life of leisure and grace where the days were filled with pretty pursuits and gossipy visits with friends, and parties or theater at night.

"Not tonight," Nicholas said. "I have sent round notes cancelling tonight and one other engagement later on in the week. We dine à deux and we will talk, nothing more."

"But there is nothing to say: Lady Waynflete's reputation has been saved, yours has been ruined and mine has been elevated to heaven," Jainee said testily. "And now I must learn how to . . . to—"

"To be a Lady Southam," he interpolated, "as opposed to lady anything else. Dear Diana—it is time to be mortal."

"All in aid of preserving appearances," she put in stringently. "And now look where we sit."

"But nothing has changed, Diana, except that now you are with me and Lucretia can no longer complain."

"And so I will be a target for every disappointed virgin in the whole of London. Yes, I should say nothing has changed."

"Exactly my point. The only difference is that you cannot go around tempting all your former acolytes."

"Indeed?" she said coolly. "What may I do, pray?"

"I have not thought so far ahead as that."

"But I have, and the future looks dismal."

"Then I shall have to keep you entertained, Diana. Perhaps the ongoing search for your father will occupy some of your time. You have now had another go-around in the upper strata whose behavior is more like the lower orders; is there nothing to report?"

Was there a little flicker of acknowledgement behind her eyes?

"Nothing," she said firmly, on sure ground now because the ultimatum was obviously negated. "And what of your threats and promises, my lord?"

"Oh, I daresay the punishment fits the crime, Diana," he said as Trenholm entered, followed by the first footman bearing a loaded tray. "We *are* married, are we not? There is a prison if ever there were one."

There was a different kind of tension between them now: they were distant with each other, polite, wary. The powerful sensuality between them became tempered by a kind of circumspect circling of each other, as if they were sniffing out weaknesses, misrepresentations, lies.

They had had their wedding night, Jainee thought ruefully as she tucked herself into the bedroom of his mother yet another night alone. And he had done everything up just right: she could not cavil.

He had sent the formal notice of their marriage to *The Times* so after that first flurry of disbelief, no one could gainsay him.

He had given her the wherewithal to replace Lucretia's ring with one of her own choice which she had presented to him solemnly and with unusual formality.

He had taken her to visit the patronesses of importance: Lady Ottershaw and Lady Jane Griswold; they who had championed her to begin with would continue to observe the niceties if she only played her part, he told her.

She did not know how to be meek, but she did understand how to be gracious. They could not comprehend how Lucretia thought she was brassy or unsuitable.

They went to the theater and to Bagnigge Wells. He bought her a subscription to the lending library and took her on rides around the park so they could be seen, but never did he suggest they go one foot near the place she most wanted to be: Lady Badlington's gaming house.

Sometimes Southam would disappear for an afternoon or an evening and she would feel like screaming in frustration at having to contain her energy and remain at home.

But she had stopped looking for shadows and she had started planning how she was going to circumvent this town life of boredom. It almost seemed as if he were filling her days so she would be exhausted at night. Nor did he make any effort to claim her, and she wondered, when he was away from the townhouse, whether he had fixed his interest elsewhere.

Oh, but what did it matter? The thing was done. She didn't care about him. She had everything she had wanted when she had first conceived this luckless plan: it didn't include having his lecherous lordship at her beck and call. No doubt it was true that once a man was married he lost interest in the object of his pursuit.

But her interest in returning to Lady Badlington's had not diminished: it had intensified in tandem with her frustration.

It remained only to arrange it somehow, and through the offices of Marie who was friendly with one of Lady Waynflete's stable boys, she procured a carriage and arranged for it to meet her a certain night — the night that Southam was to dine with Dunstan. So when he left her, she donned her disguise, and as stealthily as the shadows that still pursued her, she slipped from the house and melted into the darkness in search of excitement.

Chapter Twenty

Dunstan was not pleased. Dunstan felt as though he were losing control, and he eyed his nephew with no little apprehension as he seated himself at the table.

"Marriage agrees with you," he said caustically, indicating that Nicholas should help himself to the wine.

"It might well agree with you too, uncle."

"Ah, no. I watched my father and mother live together in the same house barely speaking for twenty-five years. And then there was poor Henry, unable to conceive children. Oh no, the energy of all that drains a man, turns his power into sap. I would rather fast and feast than nibble on the bone for a protracted period of time. You're a fool, Nicholas: you had the whole of London at your feet, any woman you could ever have wanted, and a commission of interest to keep you occupied. And what must you do?" He shook his head despairingly. "I will never understand. That wanton, that gutter piece. How on earth she tricked you into bringing her to London I will never know. Can you get an annulment?"

Nicholas shrugged, not affected one whit by this diatribe. "You know the answer to that, Dunstan. Why ask?"

"Because I still don't believe the marriage lines were signed before the event."

"But it matters not what you believe; the papers are signed, the ceremony performed before two witnesses and an annulment is out of the question."

Dunstan stared at him. He sounded so adamant, but the thing was early days yet. Surely the bitch would disillusion him. She was just the type. Hadn't she sprung from his loins? Her cunning was disconcerting; her plan had been perfect. Lady Southam, as well known as any society beldame by the mere virtue of the name and the gossip that would precede her reputation. It was a master stroke.

It left him hanging: his pursuit of her had to be subtle, almost invisible. He would never know before the fact what she would choose to reveal. He could not visit Nicholas more often than was usual in order not to arouse suspicion, and that was without the complication of Lucretia, who for some reason felt she had a proprietary stake in him, and hung onto him like a leech.

The wonder was he could be kind to her. Maybe he felt a little pity for her; more than likely he thought he could use her somehow. Who would have guessed her mysterious protegée would turn out to be his daughter.

Fate was laughing at him: the adoptive son of his brother married to his daughter.

And now all he had worked for could be lost in one *grand guignol* gesture by either one of them.

It was unbelievable, and he didn't know quite what to do.

"Well — you seem quite obdurate on the point to be sure, but one never knows just what is around the corner, does one?"

"How philosophical of you, uncle. Now what had you in mind?"

"A report merely, and perhaps some indication from you as to how you plan to go on."

"Nothing will change. I will make my rounds with the usual regularity. I lost extensively to Coxe about a week ago and that was most satisfactory to him. But I cannot point a finger at him or anyone in particular, uncle. It almost seems like a conspiracy among them to goad Prinny into every excess they can dream up in an evening. There is just nowhere, yet, to fix the blame. But they do not question my presence and they have accepted that my pockets are as deep as theirs, and in Coxe's case, a veritable ocean by comparison. They do welcome me with open arms. A pocket full of silver is the best introduction in the world."

"Cynical and wise," Dunstan murmured in agreement. "Oh, what a weapon the government has in you, my boy. You do me proud. You really do me proud."

* * *

She loved the crackling sense of excitement she felt as she entered the portals of Lady Badlington's house in Russell Square. Everything about it was right, from its understated elegance to its location on the fringes of a burgeoning fashionable district. No one ever felt shoddy entering these doors. Instead they felt welcomed, as if they were visiting a centuries' old club which catered to their every whim.

She heard the whispers instantly: *lady in black — she's come — that lady in black . . .*

"Madame?" The well-trained butler assumed nothing, nor did he make judgments. He merely asked expressionlessly whether she wished to remove her cape.

She waved him away, seeking to speak as little as possible. They all knew who she was, anyway. She had made an impact, and she had known it. She had chosen to be distinctive and there was a price to be paid for it: this persona could not remain anonymous.

Lady Badlington came to greet her and took her gloved hands. "Welcome back, madame. I wish you good fortune this evening."

"Grazie," Jainee murmured. "You need not trouble."

"No trouble, madame. You know where to find what you wish."

"Indeed."

She glided through the rooms, watching the hostesses and croupiers, trying to decide who looked beatable and who was on the watch. It was easy when you knew, and she was less vulnerable than most. She understood the language of the body, or a contortion of the face. Ah, she had lived with it so long, she had played with it herself.

She favored faro and *vingt-et-un;* she thought she might try the roulette wheel this night. She bought a large number of counters, chose a table, and settled in for the evening.

Across town, at a house in Portman Square, the Earl of Amesbury was hosting a ball for Margaret, his one and only daughter, who, Max Annesley thought, had as little chance of making a favorable match as Edythe Winslowe.

The chit was as innocent as snow with no countenance to recommend her or offset her rather limp personality. It was all her father, beefing up the rolls of invitees, scavenging for any remotely eligible male in town, planning the most advantageous time of year, just before the hordes descended and Almack's became prime. Oh yes, he had treated it exactly like a campaign and he was going to lose the war and win the battle: everyone who was anyone was here, and everyone assiduously avoided Margaret of Amesbury.

He sighed. It was a boring lot as well, with the exception of the presence of Charlotte Emerlin. She was drawing all the men away from poor Margaret, who had little or no conversation in addition to her unremarkable looks.

If only her suitors knew what he knew about the pouty-lipped Charlotte; God, they would die for a piece of her. *He* might bow down for a piece of her as well if nothing better turned up.

He supposed that was why he had accepted the invitation in the first place. Or had he hoped that Nicholas would bring his juicy bride and let them all salivate over his good luck. No, Nick wasn't like that at all. Nick was possessive and obsessive to the extreme. He would never share. He had always departed five minutes sooner than he needed to at every card game in order to avoid the fun and games that succeeded the serious betting.

No, there would be no Lady Desire tonight. But he felt his male root engorge at the mere thought of her. The picture of her lounging in Nick's bed all disheveled and naked under those covers was positively seared into his brain. If she had been in his bed, she would have shared—he *would* have.

"Good evening, Max."

Ah, here came Charlotte, having learned the lesson of the good loser and what to do to make a man grovel at her feet. Gertrude Emerlin had obviously invested instantly in a flashier wardrobe with less subtle sensuality. Charlotte's breasts were very much on display and encircled round the bodice with all manner of frills and sparkle to call attention to them.

And he remembered them well. There was something to be said for a compliant woman who was secretly wanton *and* indiscriminate as well.

Perhaps, he thought, he ought to begin his campaign with her right at this moment. "My dear Charlotte, ravishing as always.

And the dress—it positively makes you look naked."

She smiled insolently. "Thank you, Max. I am amazed that I am coherent enought to go about town tonight. How angry I was at this clandestine marriage. And what must you have thought, one of Nick's closest friends, to not have known a thing about it."

"It was gizzards and gall with me," Annesley said candidly. "And I tried to trap him on it, and he was cool as cucumber. But you and I know what we know, don't we, Charlotte. We were there. He did not talk of marriage lines or anything else."

"Well, hardly," she said with some resentfulness. "You were so busy discoursing on the heat in your sizer . . ."

"Ah now, Charlotte. Truth to tell, my sizer has an ache in it as long as your arm. Wouldn't you like to relieve the strain?"

"I might think about it," Charlotte said consideringly, "if you could come up with some good way that we could strike back at Nicholas. I want to *kill* him. I want to step all over him and mash in that proud, aloof face of his, I want to—"

"Oh my dear Charlotte," Annesley murmured consolingly in order to harness all that spewing passion for himself. "Why don't you come step all over me? Let me be the vessel through which you vent all that delicious temper. I promise you, we'll find a way. Let me devise the way and I will avenge us all."

"Oh yes," she breathed, "that would be perfect."

"Come with me. We will leave for the hour and no one will ever know. I haven't forgotten the night of my party. I've been thinking of you a lot, dear Charlotte, and how ripe and willing you were for me. Come . . ."

He led her away, a little repelled by how easy she was, but when push came to shove, and he had her on her back in the coach of the Earl of Amesbury, those considerations went right out of his mind in the wake of his seeping pleasure in her fertile and responsive body.

And she knew just how to revive a man from his labors. After, she was full of little pets and kisses and tricks to incite his drooping manhood.

He remembered it well, and enjoyed it copiously as she played with him and demanded that he service her insatiable need.

He did his best creative thinking then, as he stripped away her clothes and carried her to climax once again, while the most fertile idea took root in his brain.

It was the scent of chocolate that got to him.

He returned from his uncle's house rather late, and everything was in darkness with the exception of Trenholm, the ever vigilant, and his branch of candles to guide his way to the stairwell.

He paused and looked questioningly at his butler, and Trenholm said, "My lady is awake and asked for a pot of chocolate."

He took a candle and lighted his own way upstairs to his bedroom, curious as to why Diana was still awake on a night when she had fallen sound asleep so early.

The scent was like perfume, drawing him on, and he entered his bedroom where, in accordance with his wishes she had slept quietly by his side this past week, enveloped in cotton gowns of no great sensuality.

But she was not in the room, although the tray with the pot was set invitingly beside her side of the bed.

He put down the candle and went looking for her in the adjoining room — and paused in the shadows at the threshold to watch her from afar.

She was dressed in one of those curious underdresses over which she wore tunics or gowns of netting or silk, and she was rummaging through the wardrobe there, looking for something.

Three robes lay on the bed there, none of which he recognized. Marie was nowhere in evidence to aid her. It was the goddess alone, seeking the elusive.

The idea aroused him: had he not futilely been searching to solve the mystery of *her?*

And then she removed the gown he had given her, the one she had not worn for him for many weeks; the one with which he had been bent on enslaving her and had been trapped himself.

"Put it on, Diana," he said commandingly from the doorway.

She whirled, holding it against the flimsy underdress which concealed nothing. "My lord . . ."

"Put it on." He wheeled away from the doorway and left her alone to change.

She bit her lip; he was a complication she had not expected on this night of further triumph for the lady in black. It had been but a week ago that she had been moaning in his bed: it seemed like a year, and that this man was a stranger.

But still — she shrugged, she knew the power of her body and the potency of the robe. She had but to slip it on and fasten it beneath her naked breasts and she would feel as wanton as any fancy piece, and ready to command.

And why not? She could never take the chance that this marriage would unite them beyond the piece of paper that now resided in his desk. She had wanted to enchant him, to bind him to her with every means she had at her disposal, and perhaps it was more necessary now that his honor had bound them in a more permanent way.

She examined the robe, she remembered the thrill of wearing it, the sense of her femininity and his surrender to it. She was a goddess when she wore the gown, ravenous to wring everything from him, and beyond.

Oh, the robe . . . she stepped out of the underdress, naked, and thrust her arms into the sleeves of the robe. She felt a storm of excitement possess her as her trembling fingers hooked the edges together to compress and lift her naked breasts. Her nipples hardened instantly in the caress of the cool air. Her body streamed with an intoxicating sense of her power.

She had only to add the one note of the erotic satin strip wound around her neck, and she would be ready to subjugate him all over again.

She stood there, just inside the doorway, as if she expected he would kneel before the throne of her femininity.

He turned his back, and motioned her to enter.

"My lord?" she asked quizzically, never moving one pace from where she stood like a pagan goddess.

"The imperious Diana," he murmured, moving toward the side of the bed to the chocolate pot. "Come to me, Diana, for I will not go to you."

"Who commands and who obeys," she said softly. "Such a hard game when the rules keep changing."

374

"Oh no, Diana, nothing has changed: the bargain is the same, except that the barter has become my name instead of a pocket full of silver. It is still in your best interest to obey, Queen of the Moon, and feast on the memory of what awaits you."

She moved, a step at a time, into the room. "I must be absurdly forgetful, my lord."

"No doubt all the adulation has turned your head, Diana. But a woman must be ever careful to guard that precious part of herself from all who would consume it."

"And you, my lord? Do you wish to consume it?"

"Why should I, huntress? I *own* it."

She stiffened. Here was truth, disguised as a game. *He owned it . . .* he owned *her* and nothing else counted.

By design or by plan, she was his to command for as long as time. She bridled at the thought, her eyes blazing at the challenge.

Attack, attack. He would never *own* her, but by God, she would possess *him.* She would fill him up with the essence of her, and make him crawl for more. She would dominate his desire so that he would want no other woman, and then—and then he would see how much of her he would own.

She veered away from him in her slow steady pacing into the room and went to the opposite side of the bed from where he stood waiting for her to obey him.

"Owning me and making me do your bidding are two very distinct things, my lord. And if I do not wish to come, I will not come. Perhaps that will compel you to come to me."

"Oh, I think not, Diana. I think we will always disagree over who has mastery over whom. You will always be the willful postulant."

"And you will always be the willing teacher," she finished with the intonation of the student who has learned her lesson. She touched the bed which he had covered with a lush overlay of velveteen, and she sent him one of those cocksure *make me* looks, and she climbed right up onto the bed.

"Here is the middle ground, my lord, and here I await you," she said insolently, arranging herself for the best effect. A twist of her body here so that her breasts were displayed to their fullest advantage; a crook of her leg there so that the robe fell away from her lower extremities and revealed her long legs encased in their deli-

375

cate sheer stockings, and her naked thighs and belly and the tempting thatch of her waywardness.

This was right, with the glittering challenge in her eyes, and that soft treacherous satin tie around her neck. She looked as wanton as any *fille de joie,* and she did it deliberately, knowingly, intentionally to incite him and win the point of power.

She was luscious, laying there like some *odalisque,* a faint pouting smile on her lips, waiting, waiting, shifting slightly, pushing her breasts forward, running her hand lightly down her thighs to tug gently at the stockings that seemed to just want to slide down her legs of their own volition. And of course to do that, she had to spread her legs slightly apart to get purchase to lean forward and insert her fingers beneath the frothy little garter so she could pull. And when she was done, she crossed one leg over the other so that the lush crown of her femininity was hidden from view, and she rested her arm on her hip and played lightly with the edge of her robe.

He waited; it seemed to him that he was pushing himself beyond that which any man should have to endure, particularly a *married* man. Ah, there, something was wrong with the toe of her left stocking, and she angled her leg once again to give him a good full view between her legs.

She was the consummate temptress, he thought, girding himself to fight her to the ultimate moment. She knew exactly when to tease and when to entice. She revealed everything and left him panting when she withdrew for just one palpitating moment.

The arrogant look in her eyes challenged him, goaded him, commanded him to bend to her, and he swore he would never bow to the imperious queen of predators. She would eat him alive, and what he wanted, as always, was to devour her.

He poured himself a cup of chocolate, ignoring her blatant provocation, and lifted it to his mouth. The scent of it and the lingering taste shot him back to the first time in London in Lucretia's parlor, to the taste of her and the texture of her kisses.

He felt the treacherous desire in him rise like steam, enveloping his senses, fogging his judgment. Through the haze and the throb of his pounding heart, he saw the slave of his desire and the subtle little undulations of her body beckoned him like a siren call.

He wanted to drown her in chocolate and feed on her forever.

There was no middle ground, there was only the heat of his volcanic passion flowing like lava all over his soul.

She held his eyes, her body in languid repose, her leg still angled to reveal as much as possible, her smile still playing lightly, arrogantly around her lips as if she could see the very war within him and she was enjoying every minute of it.

Perhaps she was; perhaps she thought he would finally break and come crawling on the bed to her, but he knew he was stronger than that, stronger than she and that the power lay in the way one wielded it.

In a sudden panther-like move, he reached across the bed and grabbed her foot, and with one herculean tug he pulled her body toward him until she was laying flat on her back before him, and open to his every desire.

"Here is the middle ground, Diana. It lies on my side, in my hands."

She was angry now, her eyes sparkling with vindictiveness as she struggled to sit up. "Indeed, my lord. Your handling is all that could be desired."

"I expect it is," he murmured, holding the cup up to her lips. "Drink."

"The elixir of power," she spat. "I have no need of it."

"But I do," he said with a small predatory smile, and he tipped the cup and poured the thick clotted chocolate all over her breasts.

The liquid molded against her like a sheer fabric, surrounding the contour, dripping over the hard tips and puddling between her legs.

"Lay down," he commanded as she made a movement of protest. He pushed her and she fell back onto the soft lush velvet. "Don't move."

"And what would you do?" she demanded snidely.

"Don't beg the question, Diana. Just enjoy my lust."

Oh, but was it lust, or something deep and carnal driving him? He ripped aside the encroaching fabric of her robe, and poured another cup of chocolate all over the lower part of her body, along her belly and down around her mound, on her thighs and down her legs. And her naked body soaked up the sweetness as if it had been waiting for this all her life.

He shucked his clothes, a matter of tearing off his shirt and removing his breeches. Naked and elongated to bursting, he climbed over her and began to drink.

Just below the knee, and gently lapping at the sensitive places behind them, above them, working his way up, sucking and licking and running his tongue along the sweetness of her body creamed by the chocolate; along the flat of her belly and in the cradle of her hips, his tongue pursued the sweet clotted taste of her to the very taut tips of her breasts where he suckled the sweetness until she almost exploded from the wet pull of his mouth.

He eased away just in time, just in time, his body winding itself around her with the hard granite length of him between them, and he settled his mouth unerringly on hers.

The taste of her was endless, fragrant with chocolate and promises to come.

He reached behind him for the chocolate pot; he wanted to envelop her in this sweet smear of his greed to possess her, and he poured it again, without looking, all over her, all over him, and he let go the pot and began massaging the thick clot of it into her skin.

His manhood yearned to taste her, but not before he had drunk his fill. He moved to her breasts again, lapping at the luscious sweetness of her hard nipples one after the other and back again as she thrust them willingly into his mouth.

Her hands reached for him but he wouldn't let her: her body wet with the fragrance of chocolate and passion was his to command. He worked his way downward, with thick slurping kisses, and light little suckings across her belly until he reached her chocolate-perfumed bush.

And here, and here . . . he straddled her now to face her feet so that he could meet the sugar fragrance of her womanhood. He buried himself in it, sliding his arms under her and lifting her into the carnal kiss of his exploring tongue.

She had never felt anything like this in her life. The taut point of his tongue possessed her as tightly and neatly as his manhood. She reached for him, as rivulets of liquid feeling streamed through her veins. She could just reach him, and the thick ridged tip of his thrusting maleness, she could just hold it and stroke it while he worked the magic of his mouth against the lush open center of her.

She rolled slightly to one side, so she could hold him, she could kiss him, she could contain the whole of his maleness in her hands; she could bear down on that singular wet point of pleasure deep within her core. She could give herself to it and take him with her as well.

She undulated against him, and pushed herself into that point, and then she was there, with her mouth positioned above the rock hard thrust of him, angled in such a precise way that it seemed as if he were made to be caressed by her mouth.

She grasped him with both hands and brought him to her kisses, surrounding him with the wet heat of her willing mouth. She could not get enough. She wanted the whole, and the gods did not make it possible for her to possess the whole the way he possessed her.

But it was enough, enough: the intensity of her feeling for it aroused her to a fever pitch. She held the essence of him in her hands, in her mouth. Her tongue explored the thick hard muscularity of him, with a heat that reacted to every last lapping convulsion he pulled from her.

It was coming, once again, it was coming, and the newness of this way of coupling heightened the keen thready sensation that wound its way downward to his greedy mouth and erupted into a starburst of shimmering pleasure that exploded every which way.

She bucked against him, reaching for the feeling, her lips pulling and tugging against his ramrod length, sucking the very essence of him into her as he convulsed against her rapacious mouth.

And then, as always, it slowly eddied away, subsiding into a buoyant feeling of triumph, because both of them had won.

"I knew you were the one to come to," Annesley said complacently as he lolled in Edythe Winslowe's massive tent bed with Charlotte Emerlin, his arm around her, idly fondling her while he waited eagerly for Winslowe to begin some of her erotic little tricks. "This is perfect, Charlotte, perfect."

"It has been perfect," she cooed, her hand stroking his as he reacted to Edythe's amusement as she watched their by-play with a

379

patronizing little smile. She loved the feeling of shaping Annesley in her hands just like potter's clay. How malleable he was, how urgent.

"Well, that she-bitch thinks she has won," Edythe said poutily, "but little does she know. She thinks Southam's name will protect her, even against me, and I suppose, in a way, she is right. No door will be closed to her certainly, but there are subtleties which come into play, aren't there, you big luscious man, and that is why I am so glad you came to play with me."

"It was obvious we must join forces to defeat her," Annesley said, smirking as Edythe's avid gaze focused solely on him.

She smiled at him, a slinky knowing little smile that promised untold delights to come; he smiled back, aware that her sensual pull was much more intoxicating than Charlotte's: *she* was the courtesan, and Charlotte was the acolyte, and he was the most fortunate of men to have them both at his disposal.

"Yes . . ." she murmured, "we will spread the nasty rumors in just the right places." She reached out to touch him. "How she plotted — ah — and deliberately . . . um . . . set out to ensnare the poor innocent ascetic Southam. Ah, what man can resist — " she sent him a sidelong look of pure knowing lust, "a pair of blue eyes and such a blatant bosom? No man can, Max, isn't that so?"

"That is so," he growled, taking sensual advantage of her words and the invitation in her voice.

"Exactly. Now, this is how we play: we do *not* start to spread rumors with the Griswolds or the Chevringtons — there is too much support for her between them. However, the Ottershaws are another matter, *and* the mothers of all the girls whom she cut out this season who were on the catch for Southam. I truly believe that is all one has to do: just the most intimate little disclosure that she was a gaming house doxy on the edge of penury looking to trip up any man with money. And I know, because I advised her just what to do, my friends. Did you not know? Oh yes, I was there, I told her when Southam came and I told her exactly how to get him."

"Brilliant," Annesley breathed, coming to life once again at the thought of the lady-harlot being tutored by the lady-whore.

"True," Edythe avowed. "There need be little else but innuendo in just the right ears and they will snub her for the next twenty years, and no one will be the wiser. And I will start with the chubby Lord Ottershaw and set things in motion."

The thought of Ottershaw and Edythe in bed amazed, amused and aroused him, yet Edythe had dropped his name in such a matter-of-fact and commonplace way, and was already on to the next part of her plan.

"Your mother, Charlotte, your mother is the person to take this information and do the right thing with it."

"You can be sure," Charlotte said dreamily, her imagination liquid with the image of the bow-legs standing in the midst of an elegant room with all backs turned to her and facing dead silence. "It is wonderful. Just wonderful: Lady Southam, the cynosure of London and no one speaking with her let alone inviting her anywhere she does not have to be. It is perfect, just perfect."

"Then we agree," Edythe said complacently. "We will set the thing in motion tonight."

"So soon tonight?" Annesley murmured insinuatingly.

She met his lust-fogged gaze. "Perhaps not *so* soon tonight, Max," she agreed huskily, and coquettishly, she allowed him to lure her into bed beside them with kisses, caresses, and the amorphous promises of a willing conspirator.

Chapter Twenty-one

It was a sensual war between them, and a state of being which shut out everything else. He sent back every invitation with his regrets; he wanted no one else to have her.

How inventive she was in enticing him. He was consumed with the thought of possessing her night and day; she wanted only for him to claim her whenever he would.

Every word between them became an invitation. He took her everywhere: on the dining room table after the servants had removed the service; in the reception hall at night, on the steps and in the parlor and while Trenholm waited outside their bedroom door.

He dressed her and undressed her, and wound the satin strips around her body and possessed her. He entered their bedroom one evening to find her naked on the bed, the strips wound around the posters, and her hands grasping them for purchase, awaiting the moment when he would come to claim her.

She had Marie alter some of her clothing to make her gowns more revealing to seduce him still further. The lowered bodice, the subtle slit in the skirt, the back of a dress lowered until it nestled on the curve of her buttocks, still another gown altered to display her breasts much like the robe he had given her, compressed and thrust forward to invite a man's caress.

She remembered the exact day she had worn it for him. They had planned to attend a party, she had promised him that she would be dressed and waiting for him. Her excitement was uncontrollable as she put on the dress and adjusted the bodice. She loved the thought of it, for here she was fully dressed, from stockings and chemise to jewelry and gloves and the contrast of the feeling of being thoroughly gowned against the feeling of her naked breasts pushing out against the frame of the bodice was positively voluptuous.

She was only awaiting his voice as she stood poised at the window, her back to him when he finally entered the bedroom.

"Diana . . ."

"My lord," she said breathlessly, turning slowly to face him.

He would never get used to the sight of her naked breasts against the fullness of a dress; it had been his fantasy, his dream, and she acted upon it time and again to please him. But perhaps not tonight?

"Is something amiss?" she asked gently, a faint tremor of excitement coloring her voice.

He couldn't keep his eyes away from her and her taut tight nipples. "Not a thing. Come look at yourself in the mirror and tell me if we do not make a handsome couple."

She walked slowly toward him, letting him look his fill of her exposed breasts in the brightly lit room.

She came right up to him and pressed her breasts against his chest and offered him her mouth for a kiss. And the kiss went on and on and on until she felt weak with languor and he eased away gently and murmured: "We must be going."

"Yessss," she breathed.

"Look at us," he urged her, and gently pressured her to turn and face the mirror.

"We do well together," she whispered, awed at the sight of the dress and the voluptuous fullness of her breasts defining it.

He slipped behind her and reached around to cup her breasts. "We must go."

"Whenever you are ready, my Lord," she murmured, loving the look of and the feel of his hands on her.

"Am I not ready now?" he wondered, nudging her buttocks with his hard hot resolution. "Your nipples beg for my caresses," he whispered as he encircled first one and then the other taut tight tip.

"But we must be going."

"But are we not embarking on something now?"

She caught her breath as the first crackle of sensation jolted through her. Her body sagged against him, and she arched herself

383

against the sinuous feeling of his fingers playing with her and the visual glimpse of it in the mirror.

It was the most erotic sight she could imagine, the two of them standing there, bonded body to body, his hands to her breasts, caressing the nipples in full view of both of them.

She felt the flowing connection between them as he stroked and squeezed just the very tips of her nipples into stiff tight points of pleasure from which there was no escape.

Her body writhed against him as the molten flow of honeyed pleasure began the slow inexorable slide to her very vitals. She had to get away from him, she had to: the flexing pressure of his fingers on her nipples was both joy and pain; she had never dreamt that her body could respond this way, spewing forth this shuddering glissade of sensation that took forever to settle deep in her womanly core.

And that was the whole of it, that his hands could evoke those sensations that needed nothing more, and the newness of it and the faint chafing of her nipples when the pleasure had subsided and the molten flow had gone.

"And now, Diana," he murmured, swallowing her breasts in the palms of his hands, "and now . . ." as he held her against the tautness of his body and the thrust of his desire which would temper itself for another time, "we must prepare to go."

She swallowed hard and put her hands over his. "Yes," she said, the light back in her eyes as she watched them in the mirror. "See how I will make the change to respectability." She pushed away his hands and took up a length of satin from the bed and wound it around her shoulders.

"And now, my lord, you will see the first vestiges of modesty: I will tuck the ends in and around my breasts and no one will be the wiser. Only you, my Lord, who will know what lies beneath this swath of satin around my neck. Only you will have the memory of my naked breasts to carry with him throughout the night. Only you will be able to strip away the pretenses and caress my nipples again this night."

She was so clever, so adept at arousing him at every turn. They went out together into the night to the party of the evening and as he sat opposite her in the carriage, he thought of her body beneath

384

the dress, and he thought of the response of her nipples beneath his caress. So clever, so sly. Diana on the prowl again, with her husband as prey.

He did think, that night, that it was the first time she had been complimented on her restraint, and he smiled arrogantly because he knew that Diana had no prudence whatsoever, and as she intended, only he was aware.

He almost could not walk through the company alone for the burgeoning size of his erection every time he thought about her.

She would smile at him from across the room and he would know what she was thinking; her eyes would flicker downward, and he would know what she wanted. She would brush by him in passing in the thick of the crowd, and he would feel the intensity of her ardor in the caress of her hand. She would arch herself slightly forward as she would be conversing with someone, and he could see the outline of her nipples against the soft lustrous pull of the satin material.

Always satin with her, always, for its creaminess, for its feel—he wanted to take her into some dark deep corner and feel to his heart's content the treasure that lay beneath the satin.

She was so luminous that night, they said, as she glided through the room, talking with this one and that.

Annesley was there, and Charlotte Emerlin too, looking like two conspirators, mouth to mouth, body to body, whispering secrets which no one could share.

"Just look at her," Charlotte hissed at one point during the evening. "She has nothing on under that bodice, *nothing;* shameless bitch—and Nicholas positively salivating every time she waltzes by."

"I know someone else who has nothing on under her dress," Annesley whispered, taking advantage of the press of the crowd to slide his hand down the curve of her buttocks.

"That is different. Quality can do as they like. Brighton bitches should remember where they came from," Charlotte panted as his caress became more intimate. But who would notice in the crush of people surrounding them that he was fondling her so brazenly. She didn't care. She hoped Nicholas was watching and regretting what he had missed. She wriggled herself closer to him and began massaging him beneath his breeches.

But Nicholas never noticed Charlotte. He saw nothing but the huntress prowling the ballroom, gracious and taunting by turns, making every man crazy and hopeful by turns.

"This will be the last party that strumpet can enjoy in peace," Charlotte swore, as Annesley began inching up her dress to find her bare skin. "Bitches in heat should couple in the barnyard."

"And quality," Annesley muttered, as he found her wet warmth and inserted his fingers there, "quality can do as they like."

"The man-crazed bitch. Look at her . . . Max—" her voice wavered as she capped a swift culmination with the thrust of her anger, "God, I can't wait to bring her down. I can't wait . . ."

And then she came near them and Annesley froze exactly where he was, until she went by with a brief cold nod to him. "Jade," he spat after her, removing his hand from the torpid intimacy of her body. "Lick and spit, that's the Bowman doxy, and better than she should be now she's got Nicholas. It will do, Charlotte, it will do. We'll get her, never fear. In another three weeks, she'll be gone from here."

And when he could not stand it a moment longer, he prised her away from yet another knot of admiring swains.

"It is more than time to go."

"I was waiting for your command, my lord."

"Get your cape, Diana."

By which time he had had the carriage brought round, and that with unusual expediency because they were among the first to leave.

The evening stretched out ahead of them, long and luxuriously.

She climbed into the carriage and placed herself across from him.

"I have thought of nothing but your breasts all night."

"I wanted you to think about my breasts, my lord."

"*Everyone* was thinking about your breasts, Diana," he said darkly.

"But you were the only one to know I am naked under this dress."

"Show me your nakedness, Diana."

"Oh, I think not, my lord. Not in such a public way," she murmured, deliberately coy.

"I want to possess you in a very public way, Diana; right here, right *now.*"

"Does my lord command me?" she asked coquettishly.

"I demand it," he said roughly, on the edge of grabbing her and pulling her to him by force if nothing else. Word games had never made him feel so frantic before. The whole evening had been building block upon building block to this awful need to possess her instantly, however, wherever he could.

He heard the faint rustle of her dress as she raised it to facilitate her movement across the space between them. He heard the soft pluff of her cape falling to her seat, and he felt the tight grip of her hand as she held onto him as she moved across to his lap.

He was ready for her. His renegade manhood jutted out toward her, begging for the surcease of her moist haven. She straddled his legs, seeking him; his hands grasped her buttocks, guiding her slowly slowly downward until his potent manhood kissed the crown of her velvet fold.

And then with one swift undulating motion, she took him, and it was enough, it was enough: he could not suppress the endless spew of his culmination, spasm after spasm engulfing him and crashing him against the stone hard shore.

And then it was done, gone as suddenly as a summer storm, and he remained nestled within her, rocking with the motion of the carriage, and his face buried in the artificial thrust of her breasts, his hands cushioning his manhood, stark and still strong.

She could feel it, she could work with it, and in opposition to it. She could feel the unfurling in the stormy eddies of his male juices. It could come, it could come. Gently, against the sway of the carriage and the feel of him deep within the center of her being, she began her own tumultuous drive to completion.

And when they arrived at the house, she was back in her place, her cloak wrapped around her, her eyes bright with promise.

When they debarked, she was not looking for shadows, but as she waited for Nicholas to ring for Trenholm, she turned and looked out into the dark of the night and she saw — she thought she saw — she could not believe what she saw.

Her whole body began to tremble top to bottom as Nicholas let her in the house, and she went racing upstairs to their room and to the front windows to ascertain what she had seen.

But there was nothing out there, no movement, no strangers, no black caped man lurking in the shadows with the well-remembered features of that murderer, de Verville.

She ought to tell Southam, she thought edgily as she paced the room early the next morning while Marie laid out her clothes.

"Madame," Marie said consolingly, "you cannot be worried now. Monsieur will protect you. Nothing can hurt you, and yet you are like an animal in a cage."

How could she tell Marie? "I am bored," she snapped. "I believe the only affair on my calendar today is a trip to the lending library where I will choose some ornately written romance or poetry that is a great deal less interesting than my own life."

She let Marie help her slip into blue muslin morning dress which fastened at the back. "It is enough, Marie, thank you," she added as Marie began fussing with the drape and the fit and the tendrils of hair that curled beguilingly down her neck.

Good enough to go to the library and take a turn around the park to while away the morning and perhaps a little of the afternoon.

Not enough to calm her nerves, which were still shaken by the apparition she thought she had seen. de Verville — never! In London, after all this time? It was unthinkable, insupportable. It made no sense, so obviously it must have been a trick of the shadows, or one of the ones who skulked in the darkness at the whim of her nemesis.

Well, yes my Lord, here is the whole of it: your uncle is my father and the man who murdered my mother and seeks the boy has been lurking in the shadows, and of course your uncle is the traitor, which must explain why I never told you . . .

But it explained nothing, least of all her horrible feeling that de Verville's presence was more ominous than anything else.

If it *had* been de Verville — but her mind must be playing tricks on her. The man could not be in London. The possibility was as remote as . . . her becoming Lady Southam.

But there was no one in sight on a bright spring morning as she stepped into Southam's curricle for her dash around town with Mr. Fogg at the whip and Marie by her side.

The purity of the day made her fears seem irrational and groundless. There were no threats, no father who wished she had remained in France lest she reveal some potent secret, no subtle pressures to contend with, nothing.

She was Lady Southam, out for a morning's foray into the pleasures of Town, appropriately accompanied by her maid. Nothing could possibly be unbalanced. Everything was right and fine.

But still she watched for anything that seemed suspicious practically every foot along the way, and she could hardly think about a book she might want to read when she knew her evenings would be spent as covertly as possible staring out the window.

And the ride around the park — she was distracted and unaware: but Marie noticed — no one seemed to care. It wasn't that she was ignored; it was merely that no one was looking in her direction to see her — deliberately.

But even Marie could not countenance that — that every single one of her lady's acquaintances had turned his back.

Ah, perhaps it was a trick of the morning, she thought, forbearing to mention it to Jainee, who was wholly preoccupied with some distant thoughts. Perhaps she had misunderstood.

The campaign began in earnest on the weekend. That Saturday was the night of the Northington rout. Everyone had been invited and everyone made room on his calendar to attend.

Even Lady Waynflete had come, having somewhat recovered her countenance after Nicholas' marriage. She had spent a forlorn three weeks hiding in her house, waiting for the hatchet to fall. But the only recriminations she heard were from Jeremy, who derided her part in the affair, and criticized her roundly for lending away his father's ring.

"And never mind it was returned to you promptly and with a

pretty note," he said angrily. "You never should have let that piece of Brighton brass get her hooks into Nicholas."

"It is done," Lady Waynflete said tiredly, "and I am sick of wasting away in my house waiting for my friends to call. I have not heard from Nicholas nor Dunstan and I mean to beard them both and demand explanations."

But Dunstan's welcome to her was so effusive she forgot anything she had to say of a critical nature and basked in the glow of his attention. Perhaps he had missed her, she thought. Perhaps he was coming to see that chasing after chits was child's play compared to what he could have.

However, Jainee Carradine, Lady Southam, did not look like a chit when she and Nicholas finally were announced and walked proudly through the door.

She looked as regal as she ever had, and a compliment to Nicholas as a wife in her beauty and her bearing if nothing else.

She saw Lady Waynflete and came directly to her. "My lady. My apologies for having been so reclusive," she said softly, "but my lord and I are still in the first blush of newlywed days."

"I understand, I assure you," Lady Waynflete said graciously, and held out her hand to Nicholas. "You dear boy, how do you go on?"

"All is well, Lucretia, how could you think otherwise?"

They turned to make their way through the crowd, but this time Jainee heard none of the underlay of whispering that used to accompany her appearance. This night, the hum of conversation was low, and almost furtive, and as she began to make her way through the crowd, she saw erstwhile acquaintances barely nod to her and then turn away.

And then the whispering started.

"They say . . . they say . . . a trollop in a gaming house — took him in completely . . . no better than she should be . . . who is she to have Southam when no one else could snare him . . ."

"It was Edythe Winslowe who told me . . . do you know she was there? I heard it from Ottershaw. Gertrude Emerlin is prostrate over the matter . . . he could have had Charlotte . . . she had to be tutored in the art of trapping a man . . . they say she was as coarse as the gutter — couldn't speak decent English . . .

men are fools . . . what did he see in her?"

"Winslowe . . . Winslowe . . . Winslowe—she told her what to do, can you picture this? She told her how to dress and to change her name, and she told her Southam was the one to catch . . . and that strumpet did it—somehow the bitch did it . . . what *is* her secret?"

Jainee did not flinch; she could not hear the secrets they were whispering, but she could tell they sought to snub her, and she could not imagine why.

Nicholas saw it too, he felt it in the air, he heard the innuendo all around him, the rise and fall of the conversation as the *ton* closed rank after his wife had passed.

Annesley was in a corner just enjoying the sight with Charlotte by his side. "It is delicious to see," he said gleefully. "She doesn't know which way to turn—just *look* at her."

"Nicholas will rescue her," Charlotte chimed in resentfully. "He won't let her sink alone."

"Not yet, my dear, not yet. But wait. This is but the beginning. Ottershaw and your mother have done their work well. Ah! There he goes. Nicholas is nothing if not masterful. He fairly lifted her off of her feet and carried her away from the crowd. Of course, he never cared about this sort of thing, but when a man has a wife . . . well, it makes all the difference in the world. I tell you, Edythe Winslowe is an absolute genius at revenge. The erstwhile lady of desire must be prostrate with anxiety."

But the cuts did not send Jainee into nervous spasms. She was furious, blindingly, arrogantly furious that someone had spread a rumor vicious enough to make a public spectacle of her in this way. "They think I am the milkmaid," she raged at Nicholas. "They think I will go into hiding and never come in public again. But they know nothing of me, *nothing.* I will become more in the public eye than ever and I will make them all crawl with apologies for treating me so badly. You will see, my lord. You may even wish to immure yourself away from the scene of the battle. But *I* will persevere, I promise."

He had to admire the way she sailed right back into the ballroom and continued on with the events of the evening, despite the out and out snubs of people who had once avidly sought her company.

The worst was Lady Arabella Ottershaw, which distressed Lucretia Waynflete terribly; and her most surprising ally was the proper and correct Lady Jane Griswold.

"Scandal-mongers all," she said roundly when she had a chance to speak with Jainee. "Nothing to do but jaw over people's indiscretions, as if their own linen were as pure as the snow. Arabella's a fool, but it's that husband of hers . . . well, we won't speak of where he is dropping *his* linen these days. We won't speak of anything, if you don't wish."

"I was naive, not stupid," Jainee said, "and I will tell you that the body of the rumor has truth within it. However, Miss Winslowe was remunerated in fair coin with the fruits of *my* experience as she played the tables. She, however, entertained false hopes about Southam, and when he dashed them, she swore revenge, and chose a convenient medium through which to pursue it. She must have been crushed to hear of the marriage, why else would she come baring her claws?"

"And how many other women are enjoying your social ruin?" Lady Jane murmured. "Yes, I can see the case, although the details are murky. She went down to Brighton because it was necessary in order to avoid a scandal herself. And probably because she knew Southam would be there, since he had started playing very deep with Prinny and his set. Yes, that I see. But you, my dear? How came you to be embroiled in this?"

"My mother was an inveterate gambler and I found I was exceedingly good at the games; I had learned them at her knee, after all, when she had taken it up to support us after my father left us. When she died, I promised to try to find him, and I made a bargain with a wealthy gentleman who had the kind of connections I needed in order to pursue this dream of my mother's."

"And did you find him?" Lady Jane asked curiously.

Jainee looked past her to a place where she knew Dunstan was standing and conversing with Annesley and a few other of his friends. "I begin to believe he never existed," she said finally. "There is no one the like of the man I remember in the whole of London."

* * *

They went everywhere, just to be seen: to the theater in an open box in full view of the lower stalls and the more exclusive seats. They rode in the park, they strolled the malls, they attended an exclusive card party at the home of Lady Jane who was tickled that Jainee was experienced at gaming, and who made sure word got around.

"Why would you champion me?" Jainee asked her.

"Why should one's past impinge upon the present? Whom have you hurt, besides all the disappointed mothers who would have seen their daughters married to Southam—in their dreams? If Nicholas cares for you, that is all that matters to me."

But Nicholas didn't care for her: Nicholas didn't quite know what to do with her except try to subvert her nature by directing her toward more sedate pursuits . . . during the day.

"But I wish to go to Lady Badlington's," she charged him one early evening after they had exhausted all the social venues and had received much the same treatment at each.

"I think not, Diana—it is an explosive combination, the cards and you."

"So much the better."

"Nothing will quell this scandal this season," Nicholas said.

"And neither of us really cares," Jainee pointed out.

"Except for the odd awkward moment, I suppose that is true."

"The gaming table is one place they cannot ignore me," Jainee argued.

"Isn't it rather that you hate to be ignored?"

"That too," she agreed, "but is it not true that money is a great equalizer? I could play at the tables with Lord Ottershaw and he wouldn't give a whit for scandal if he thought he could win a hundred from me."

Hadn't he said much the same thing to Dunstan?

"I resent the fact you have the freedom to do this and I do not," she added irritatedly when he did not respond. "And why should you? Why are you gambling away your assets when you have absolutely no reason to? They were all talking about that wager you made at White's, and the amount you turned over to Coxe on the mere whim of what a man will wear on a given day. Yet you would

393

deny the same pleasure to me and I have the talent and skill and knowledge to play on an equal footing with any man. It is incomprehensible, my lord, especially when women are welcomed in all of the gaming establishments."

"But not my wife," Nicholas said darkly.

"Then your talented wife shall have to go alone—or find someone to take her. It is the last best place to squash the scandal."

"By doing exactly what they claim you were doing: playing the cards and playing to the crowd?"

"Yet it is fine with them when my lord does it. No scandal attaches to *him*. The woman must be his downfall."

"It was ever so, Diana."

"The siren who leads him into every kind of hell."

"The story is as old as the bible, Diana. Nothing has changed."

"I am not ashamed," she said fiercely. "But perhaps my lord *is*."

"It is as simple as this: *Lady Southam* does not frequent gambling dens."

"As opposed to all the other high-born ladies who do?" Jainee inquired sarcastically. "Or play cards for cutthroat stakes when their husbands are not around? What is the difference?"

"The difference is, it is *my* money you would be gambling away."

"But *you* are gambling it away anyway, and I most assuredly would win."

"But you will most assuredly stay away, no matter how much visibility you believe it will give you."

"Will *you*, my lord?" she asked craftily.

"I don't have to, Diana," he reminded her disdainfully. "You do tend to forget who is in debt to whom here, and who ought to exhibit more gratitude for her position."

"Oh, so we are back to that, my lord? It seems I have no position, if your friends are to stand in judgment."

"You never back down."

"No, my lord. I only get back up."

And he saw the truth of that as they attended this social gathering and that and the response to her presence was almost uniformly the same.

Moreover, the marriage crimped his plans as well. It was impossible to make excuses night after night in order for him to make his

394

rounds amongst his intimates, and that hampered the progress he had already made.

He saw the season slipping away and with it, the easy access to those who were propelling the country into monstrous debt. And he saw the winter, when they were squirreled away in the country, as a stretch of time out of hand, where nothing would be accomplished.

Or was it just that he would miss the excitement?

The folly of his irrevocable gesture came home to roost: she would never be a lord's proper wife. Nor would he have the peace to fulfill his commission until she were somewhere safely out of the way for the rest of the season, and the search for her mythic father suspended.

One night, after the theater, when he knew Coxe would be abroad at Lady Badlington's, he left Jainee asleep in his bed in the satiety of their lovemaking, certain she would not be an impediment to his gaming this evening.

But the minute the door closed, she sat bolt upright.

"*Dieu*—it is ever so with men," she muttered, sitting with her arms crossed, waiting to hear the tell-tale clip of horse hooves before she rang for Marie.

"I am going out," she announced when Marie appeared. "The tunic dress will suit me fine, the diadem, pearls, the blue gloves and silver bracelets. The velvet cape—*hurry!*"

She had no idea where Southam was headed, but he might very well be on his way to Lady Badlington's. So be it. She needed to present herself at Lady Badlington's too—not as the lady in black, but as herself, the woman who was the equal of all the hypocrites who had turned their backs on her in all their fancy salons for the past two weeks.

Chapter Twenty-two

It was merely a matter of mentioning her name, haughtily of course as if she had expected she would be instantly recognized since she *was* the talk of London: "I? Why, I am Lady Southam," was all the introduction she needed to gain entry to Lady Badlington's.

Even so, she furtively glanced around before she walked through the portals because she was sure she had been followed. And then she handed her cape to a footman, and followed him into the reception hallway.

Lady Badlington wafted forward to greet her. "You are?"

"Permit me—I am Lady Southam, of course."

"Ahhhh . . ." Such a speculative and long drawn out *ahhh*, as if she weren't quite sure, what with the lady's reputation, and then had reconsidered in light of the enormous sums which Southam had left deposited in her house.

"You are welcome, of course," Lady Badlington said. "Tell me, what is your pleasure?"

Her pleasure was to find Southam and roundly tell him what she thought of him sneaking out on her. But necessity overrode that need almost instantly when she contemplated for a moment how much money she had already pocketed as the mystery lady in black. Almost enough to buy back her debt to Southam, she thought. Almost enough to buy a new life.

"The card table beckons me tonight, Lady Badlington. Faro or perhaps *vingt-et-un*. But did you say my lord was here tonight?"

Lady Badlington's eyebrows rose a fraction. "I had supposed that was why you had come."

Jainee smiled nastily. "But no, my lady. As his time is his own, so is mine. I never like to see talent wasted, do you?"

Lady Badlington left her then and she wandered into the main room and exchanged some silver for a stack of counters before she sat in on a game.

It was child's play, and the reckless desperate ones were easy to spot. And the ones who had maligned her, they were all here: Ottershaw, Chevrington, Annesley, Dunstan Carradine.

Annesley strolled over, a snide look on his face. "Dear Lady Southam. What nerve you have, showing your face in public."

She hated him right then, virulently and violently, because he was everything an aristocrat was supposed to be—and he was less, and he didn't care who knew it. "And what nerve have you, Mr. Annesley? Would you challenge me on *my* terrain?"

He was taken aback by her direct attack. She amazed him all the time. He had expected that she would retire into Southam's house until the end of the season after the first set-down, and what had she done but flaunt herself all over London on Southam's arm and win Lady Jane Griswold's approbation into the bargain. She was not an easy piece, but he was never a man to refuse such a challenge.

He bowed stiffly. "Your servant, Lady Southam."

"Your choice of venue, Mr. Annesley."

And now everyone was watching them, and Jainee wondered just where Southam had got to, if indeed he had come this evening.

"Piquet would suit me," Annesley said cautiously.

"Lady Badlington should be able to provide us a table. Set the stakes, Mr. Annesley."

He hated her, he absolutely hated her; everyone was all ears, listening to her imperious commands. Across the room, neither of his so-called friends made a move to help him; Chevrington had already moved out of the line of fire.

But the stake could be limitless, he thought, what with Southam's backing—and why shouldn't he bankrupt the bastard after the way he had treated *him*? Dunstan would understand perfectly, if the expression on his face were anything to go by. He

397

could swear Nicholas' uncle hated the bitch, but that seething contempt in his eyes vanished in an instant, and he came forward to join them, playing the part of the voice of reason.

"My dear Jainee—surely you don't mean to . . ."

"Of course, uncle. I would never have suggested it if I did not mean to . . ."

"But Nicholas—"

"My lord has nothing to do with this," Jainee said sharply. "This is between myself and Mr. Annesley, for the gaming room is *my* salon, and here there is no distinction in station."

No one misunderstood what she meant, or what challenge she had issued to Annesley. He looked, in fact, excessively uncomfortable in spite of the fact he was certain he would come away a winner.

"A table has been made ready." This was Chevrington, sent expressly by Lady Badlington to announce she had prepared a space for them to play.

"Mr. Annesley . . . ?"

He had to lead the way, which meant he could not look at Jainee's face or read what was in her eyes. But she was a damned cold-blooded bitch if she could agree to his terms and coolly allow him to turn his back on her.

God, wait till Southam heard she was here, he thought as they entered a small and secluded alcove in the back of the house, away from the main card room.

"This will do nicely," Annesley said, as he pulled away a chair for Jainee and then seated himself. Ottershaw and Carradine pulled up chairs around him, and he felt as if he had girded for battle.

But he hated the fact she looked so amused, so calm, so *certain* as she removed the requisite cards from the deck and shuffled the remaining thirty-two.

"Your cut, Mr. Annesley."

He cut.

"You may have the deal," she added, setting the deck in front of him.

"As you wish, Lady Southam. Let the game begin."

* * *

There was a point at which Annesley began to be glad that they were playing in relative isolation. He did not like the pile of counters on her side of the table, markers for the points he had lost which enumerated silver and honor.

Ottershaw had gotten disgusted and left, and sometime later, Dunstan had disappeared as well. So there was no one to witness his outrageous downfall but the capricious and smug Lady Southam, who gathered her counters and waited for him to determine the end of the game.

Or maybe Dunstan had gone to find Nicholas. He *hoped* Dunstan had gone to find Nicholas; it was just the thing a man's friend should do in this situation, especially when the bitch was enjoying her revenge.

Assuming she even knew . . . ?

It was her smile more than anything, that slight curve of the mouth that never changed and kept him completely off-balance. That smile said that she knew exactly what she was doing and that *he* didn't.

He hated that smile. Every time he took the trick from her, he felt like smashing the cards right into her face. That smile said that his win had been pure luck and that *she* would win *capot* next time, and he had better beware.

"All that they have said about you is true," he muttered, as she dealt the cards, laid out the stack and considered her first discard. She laid in three cards and replenished with three from the stack.

He discarded five and removed five more and they began the order of declarations.

"I begin," Jainee said. "Point of five."

"How much?"

"I make it eleven."

"Good."

"Tierce."

"Equal."

"Jack."

"Good."

"Trio."

"Equal."

"Ten."

"Jack."

She scored her points, the last of which she had lost to his superior card, and led with her first suit.

"How perfect, Diana—queen of hearts."

"My lord?" she said equably, not even looking at him.

"I believe it is time to leave."

"Never say so, my lord; we have yet to commence the game. Mr. Annesley?"

He looked at Nicholas and he played a card: she took a trick, announced the point, and led the next.

The play went fast and furiously after that; she routed him with nine tricks to his three in the first deal of the six they had agreed upon.

She took the deal and they began again; she never took notice of Southam lounging in the doorway, coolly waiting for the outcome of the duel.

Annesley was perspiring, but it was his custom never to reveal a weakness. Only a friend who knew him well could see that Diana, queen of clubs, was beating him thoroughly at his own game.

Nothing about her had changed since the first time he had seen her presiding over the tables. She still wore that faint amused smile; she still focused on the game to the exclusion of everything else. She was still a player with a rapier mind who could spontaneously turn the advantage.

She still was dangerous.

"*Pic, repic* and *capot,* Mr. Annesley," she said at last in triumph as she counted her points. "I believe my point is proved."

"You will accept my vowels," he said stiffly.

"With pleasure."

He reached into the drawer of the table and pulled out a draft and a pen and a bottle of ink which were kept there just for that purpose, and wrote out the amount, signed it and handed it to her.

"Thank you, Mr. Annesley."

"Your servant, Lady Southam," he muttered, bowing to her and Southam and tactically withdrawing.

She handed him the draft. "I have covered your losses, my lord. I do believe we might make an excellent team in this manner—if you feel you must keep losing so disastrously all the time. I must say, my lord, that your friends all took great pains to apprise me of that fact."

She pushed in her chair and a thought struck her. "Or perhaps I might finally repay *my* debt—that would be most refreshing to me. Are you coming, my lord? I believe I would like to try the faro table next."

"You have already tried my patience past the boiling point, Diana," he said roughly, grasping her arm and pulling her back. "It is time to leave and to stop making a spectacle of yourself."

"I?" she asked, horrified. "How so, my lord, when I distinctly saw Miss Callaway and Lady Codrington engrossed in loo in the first salon. Can they be more respectable than Lady Southam?"

"*They* were never hostesses in a Brighton gambling den, my lady, and I think their reputations will *not* suffer on account of it."

"What a pity: I play so much better than they."

"And so you have shown them this evening, and what do you suppose Annesley will do with that?"

"He will *not* boast that he lost to *me*."

"No, rather he will smear your name all around town that you are exactly as the gossip portrayed you," he said angrily.

"And you are *not*, despite the fact you visit this house regularly and drop monstrous sums in the laps of men with half your intelligence. So we return to the original point, do we not? And yet, I was not that man's inferior across the table, and it did not matter where I came from or what I had done four months in the past. All that mattered is that I controlled the cards."

"All that matters is that you want to control *everything*."

"Is it not just, my lord? I am much more sensible than everyone else."

"You are reckless, troublesome and dangerous in your innocence, Diana. And if I had thought about it—"

"But you didn't, and neither did I. I never dreamed that I would be so stifled and constrained in my actions. It never occurred to me that women of impeccable reputations could gamble with impunity, but a woman with talent and intelligence and year's experience behind the tables could *not*. I bow to your point, my lord. You have taken on a woman who is less than docile, and I have bargained myself into a life of confinement and suppression. If you had thought about it, my Lord, you never would have offered to protect Lady Waynflete."

Perhaps I chose to protect you.

The thought hit him like a lightning bolt, thundering through his mind, his heart. But it didn't matter—he had chosen, and the choice had bound her to him: the reason didn't matter. "I need to protect you now," he said finally. "It is too much: the talk, the snubs, and now *this*. I want you away from here."

She felt a coldness envelop her heart, her hands. "Away?" she murmured reluctantly. "Where?"

He guided her out of the alcove, toward the lights and the people so that she could not protest his decision in so public a place. "To Southam, of course, and I will join you next month."

She balked and he pressured her forward. "I will not go."

"Of course you will go, Diana. The memory of the *ton* is notoriously short: some new sensation will overtake it within a week. But meantime you will be out of the line of fire, and by next season, your escapades will have diminished into anecdotes and you will have been labeled an Original."

"I am sure that is satisfactory to you, my lord, but I do not wish to leave London."

"You do not wish to leave the gaming table either, but that is of no moment." He signalled to the butler as they came into the reception room.

All eyes turned toward them.

"I am more at home here than ever I would be at Southam."

"But it is *not* necessary to show that to every manjack in the whole of the city."

"And it is not necessary to hide me away as if I had some disfigurement," she snapped, catching the edges of her cap as it was laid across her shoulders.

"This is worse: it is a distortion of your past and a stain on your reputation."

"*Your* reputation, you mean," she shot back. "And thus does the disdainful Lord Southam bow once again to the great god of appearances."

"I genuflect to the god of disappearances—get into that carriage."

"Umph," she said roundly, as he pushed her in.

"Nor do you know when it is best to be quiet," he added stringently.

"*Never!*" she hissed.

"I expected no other answer. And so—we are going to Southam."

Annesley, sulking in a corner, had avoided company for almost the whole time that Nicholas and that lady strumpet were in the house. He had not yet thought of a way to minimize his losses at her hands, and he would be hard put to make good the debt. But that ignominy paled beside his fulminating desire to pay her back in her own coin.

"What do you think?" he said to Chevrington who had come by to inquire whether he wished to join a table at *vingt-et-un.* "I just had the most unholy thought."

"My dear Annesley . . . do tell."

"She was an absolute bitch at the cards."

"So rumor said."

"Well—*think,* man: has there not been another woman of equal skill and success patronizing this house of late?"

"*No,*" Chevrington breathed. "Do you think?"

"Why think?" Annesley said nastily. "Who not just—*say?* We'll top scandal with scandal. Surely it's possible. Did not Lady Badlington say the woman in black played like she had read all the chapters in the devil's books? I tell you, it's as likely as anything else. And even if it ain't so, I mean to get the bitch back for tossing me tail over top tonight. Cold-bloodedly she did it, Chevvy—and I will *never* forgive it. Out to prove something, the little drab from the gutter. Well, I'm going to prove something to *her:* she can't rout a man at cards and expect to get away with it."

Nicholas saw the item first, in *The Chronicle,* the very first paragraph:

The Woman in Black and lord's lady in blue—one and the same, or a separate two? One's face was covered, the other's not; one was so cool, the other was hot. Born in the same place and at the same time, could they be sisters of the same clime? One lord's low-born lady, seeking noto- riety and fame, not content to sit home—cards are her game. This on-dit speaks with words that are true: The Woman and The Lady are the same one—not two.

And it was all he needed to read.

"Trenholm! *Tren-holm!* Start packing my bags—we are going to Southam, *today!*"

Chapter Twenty-three

So—Annesley had spread his poison, she thought savagely, and now *she* must be removed from the lights and delights of London and made to rusticate in some far-off place that Southam himself had not been to in years.

And didn't that work out deliciously well for *everyone* concerned?

Southam could continue to pursue his course and squander massive sums of money on making himself agreeable to those fat aging buddhas who attended the feckless Prince Regent.

The women of London could rest secure in the fact that she would not be around to tempt their husbands or usurp their daughters.

Annesley had got his revenge in the nastiest way possible, and neatly put her out of the way so that he could discharge his debt at some later date.

And over and above that, her father would be ecstatic that Southam had immured her away in some fairy tale castle, away from witches, trolls, elves and magical princes—and the temptation to reveal secrets.

They were going deeper and deeper into woodland as they left London behind. She toyed with the idea of trying to escape him at the layover which was two-thirds of the way there by his calculation, and a day's ride when he travelled alone.

So it didn't seem likely she could abscond when she could not ride or handle a team, or even know which way she should go.

He had sent word on ahead by a groom that they would be arriving on the succeeding day and that all should be in as much readiness as possible, but he had not been there in years and subsequently did not even know the state of the house.

"So you will enclose me in ruins and go off to London to your heathenish entertainments, my lord. It does not sit well with me at all."

"And yet you sit still for it because you know there is no choice."

"I know nothing of the sort, and I was going on perfectly well at Lady Badlington's before you intruded."

"And as a result, a new scandal erupts and the rumor that you had been playing the tables long before you appeared there as my lady wife. How much money, Diana?"

"Perhaps it was not me."

"The coincidence is glaring."

"*You* are glaring, my lord; I have done nothing of which to be ashamed. And you will have me back down and they will all titter and talk behind their hands that every word of the gossip was true."

"Or they will forget about it in a day and take up some new sensation."

"Yes, such as your losing some other deranged bet with Coxe or one of his ilk; or Charlotte Emerlin winding up under your feet one morning when you have drunk too much with your 'intimates' in the back rooms of whatever hells you frequent. Oh no, my lord. You are removing an obstacle from the path of your comfort, pure and simple."

He refused to be drawn by that challenging statement. "It is spring in the country, Diana—the perfect environment for the huntress."

"And what shall I chase, my Lord? Deer? Rabbits? Gameskeepers?"

"Your conscience?" he said grimly. How like her to bring a *man* into it. Or was it that he would never be able to trust her. She was no passive lady, dependent on her lord for everything. She had shown everyone she had no need of anyone else, and that with her own skill and ingenuity she could take care of herself.

He had counted that pile of markers on the table beside her: he knew how much money Annesley was in debt. She could walk away from him tomorrow with it. She could disappear forever and never be in want so long as she was clever with the cards.

He hated it. Everything else was secondary to that. She must not go; scandal-mongers and boredom must not influence her to leave him. It was a matter of a month. The stories would die down, the season would be over, everyone would retrench and she would, in retrospect, be applauded for her resourcefulness and her candor.

And she would be *his*.

But his statement, to her, meant that he had not forgotten any of the mistruths she had foisted on him. She could never feel secure, she thought. The lies, in one form or another, would come back to haunt her. And the only thing that had kept Dunstan from keeping his threats was that he knew she could not reveal his true identity to Nicholas. But he trusted her not: all the moving shadows were Dunstan by surrogate, waiting for the least little misstep on her part.

All the little shadows would follow her straight to Southam and finally call her to account.

She felt her whole body grow cold with dread. What if it were true? What if it were possible that Dunstan was following them even now?

As they drew in to the courtyard of the inn, she surreptitiously looked around to see whether there were anyone suspicious following the two carriages. But that too would be so obvious, and Dunstan Carradine was never obvious.

The likelihood was, he had no idea that Nicholas had decamped for Southam in the wake of the tittle-tattle in the morning paper; there wasn't even a stowaway hanging on under the carriage bearing the luggage and the servants, and Jainee felt foolish in the extreme for allowing her amorphous fears to let her imagination run away with her.

It was early evening by then, and the landlord, by virtue of having been informed by Southam's groom, had a fire going and dinner awaiting them.

"This is country hours," Nicholas said as they sat down to a hot meal of mushroom soup, chicken, sweetbreads, sauced tongue, vegetable pudding, peas and a dessert of almond custard.

"I'm sure I will get very used to them," Jainee said coolly.

"You are not being put in prison," Nicholas snapped.

"No, a mere vacation for my shattered nerves."

"Everyone in London is aware your nerves are made of shiny shiny silver, my dear. Stacks of it, as you bore your way through the pocketbooks of London's wealthiest men—including *me.*"

"Ah, so we come to that, do we? Well—I did very well at the tables when I went as the *Incognita,* my Lord, and I am perfectly willing to repay you for all that you have expended on my behalf."

And that was what he hated about her the most: she would never beg, never bend. She had the wherewithal as well as he, and when it came down to it, hers was the more admirable stance. She had, in effect, earned her money, and he had had it handed to him on a silver salver.

"And how do you calculate the energy, the invitations, the near ruin of poor Lucretia . . ."

"Pooh—Lucretia Waynflete would have survived that little tempest, my Lord, as would have I."

"How little you know of society, my dear. How very little you know. Lucretia would have closeted herself at Tazewell for years over this ostracism, and they would not have let her forget it, either. When one of their own commits a gross folly, it truly is unforgivable, because it means any of them could fall from grace as well. And were Jeremy to try to contract an alliance, Lucretia's solecism would taint his chances as surely as any lack of fortune or patrimony."

"And so my noble lord, with one mighty stroke of his mythical honor, has made all right with the world for Lucretia Waynflete and saddled himself with the burden for the rest of his life."

How did he answer that? He did not know how to answer it, nor did he wish to point out to her that she could vanish from

408

his life forever if she chose to do so. He felt a gripping terror at the thought, and more than that, a desperate urge to constrain her somehow, because the vast spaces in and around Southam would not be enough to impede her if she truly desired to go.

"There has been but a month since the wedding, Diana. I would not invalidate the union quite yet."

"This is not a *union,* my Lord," Jainee said grimly, "this is a *battle,* and one that I am determined to win."

But when she slept, she looked like an angel, with her hair in wild disarray all over the pillow, and her body boneless and fragile and heavy with dreams.

He was taking her to Southam, where he had not been since his mother died. Always, he had lived in town and wintered over on the smaller estate that he had occupied until the death of his father. He had not wanted to go back there ever again, lest he hear the echoes of the child and his endless yearning.

He had buried the child when he interred his parents.

He had given the house over to the care of the servants, on the massive pretext that he did not care about it himself.

It was the first place he had thought to take the woman he had made his wife when the need arose to protect her.

She moved restively in her sleep, almost as if her body could not acclimate itself to the earlier hour of retirement. He wanted to put his hand on her and calm her. He wanted to mount her and claim her. He wanted to run as fast and as far from her as he could go and he wanted to stay with her forever.

The goddess at rest . . . He felt a coiling sense of possession: he had found her, he had named her. No one else could have her, *no one.*

And if there were nothing else between them but that raging ongoing battle for control, he would fight with her and for her to eternity.

He got up to poke at the fire; this small and cozy room seemed barely big enough to contain the both of them, with its large bedstead and washstand and a chair by the fire. But the room was warm and drenched with his emotions, dredged up from the place where he had hidden them for so long. And all because he had chosen to return her to Southam and nowhere else.

She stirred again, pulling at the cover, stretching and turning finally to face the other way.

How innocent her face was in the depths of her sleep; how strange it was to be with her in silence.

Without words, she was a vulnerable child, as scared of the night as he. Perhaps she even used the words to fill the night, to give shape and sound to an emptiness that could be conquered no other way.

He had welcomed the night and the oblivion of losing himself in the restive world of the bored and the disenfranchised aristocrats all and looking for communion.

And he had found it in the least likely place.

He bent over and touched her face, compelled by the thought, the second one that had come from a place and a feeling he did not know he had.

She awoke in an instant. "My lord?" Her voice was sleep-fogged, almost drowsy as if it were the aftermath of another kind of awakening.

"You have never called me by my given name, Diana."

"Nor you me," she muttered, a little disconcerted by this soft side of him. "Or perhaps you have forgotten it."

"More likely it is not how I perceive you, Diana—you have never been Jainee to me."

"And you will always be 'my lord' to me," she said, prickling up instantly.

"I cannot envision a lifetime wherein you address me only this way."

"I cannot imagine a lifetime we might spend together, my lord. It is merely until such time as we agree that we will go on our separate way."

"Imperious Diana—ordering things around again to suit her whim. There has been no talk of this union dissolving."

"We have gone through this, I thought. I did make myself

410

clear on the matter," she said, struggling now to sit up so that she would be in a more aggressive position. It was purely impossible to argue with the man when she was prone. She was wide awake now and *listening*.

He would not stop trying: he wanted in the worst way to make her docile and biddable. Lifetimes! Who would ever think in lifetimes but a man who expected a woman to become a servant and be at his beck and call.

He stared at her rebellious face for a long time, his eyes flicking with the emotions his heart would not admit. "There will be no dissolution of this marriage."

She gave him a knowing, rather snide look. "You will soon reconsider that, my lord."

"What would you do if I chose not to?"

She felt it instantly: this was the crux of the conversation and instinctively she knew her answer was very important to him. And it could not be born out of her natural combativeness or any urge to have at him.

"I do not know, my lord," she answered finally, and it was as honest an appraisal as she could give.

But he knew: he would bind her up so tightly in those blue satin strips she would never get away, *never*. The ferocity of his feelings were like a firestorm in him, sweeping, burning, devouring, unbearably hot.

"Say my name," he demanded in a voice rough with emotion.

"My lord?"

He put out his hand and touched her lips. "Say my name, Diana."

She felt the heat rise between them, catching like tinder. "As you wish, Nicholas."

His fingers followed her lips as they shaped his name. "Say again."

"Nicholas," she said painstakingly, her body heated instantly by his touch. It didn't matter where, or how: the conflagration ignited immediately and totally at just the scent of him so close to her and the simple act of his placing his fingers on her lips.

"Nicholas . . ." she whispered and it seemed like an admission, that when she voiced his name, he then became real. And when he was real, he was not the enemy she was fighting with her very soul.

His fingers moved, feeling the texture of her lips, the sensation of his name in the sound of her voice, testing the pliant shape of her mouth. He bent toward her as he moved his hand from the exploration of her mouth to her strong-willed jaw; and he cupped it, and raised her lips to his.

Ever so slowly, he fit his mouth against hers, slowly, slowly he claimed her, gently, so gently sliding his tongue into her mouth, feeling for her, stroking her, feeling her melt under his hand, under the heat and lush possession of his mouth.

He had kissed her before, but never had he kissed her like this, with no acrimony between them, no duel of provocation, with the light so low and tender, and somewhere, caught between them, the definition of his name and the burgeoning of something tenuous and strong.

He lowered her downward so that his weight became a part of the connection between them, welcomed, cradled, sought just for the feeling of pressure of body on body.

He melted into her, his heat defining her, his hands entwined in her hair; she strained against him, she wrapped her arms around him and pulled him into her sensual essence.

And still they kissed, hungry for each other in this other place where there were no boundaries, no strictures, no ties. Here was a place, time out of tide, where no one was watching, no one need know. The fire was tender, the embers burning low, banked like the passion between them as he explored with kisses the honey sweet recesses of her mouth.

She ached with his kisses, wine-hot kisses lush and ripe, arousing her body, seeping into her soul. Ever many kisses, endless, unbroken, wet, promising . . . perfect.

The feel of him so tightly and intensely *there,* content to nestle against her, made her weak with longing.

And when he began finally to untie the ribbon on the neckline of her one virginal nightgown, she felt like hurrying him on.

But this was slow, sweet love; she had never had this—the leisurely loverly exploration of her body with the sole intent of arousing her, feeding her desire, fanning her passion. Slowly, sweetly, over, under—she needed to do nothing, for he would do it all.

He put her on a lush cloud of feeling, he made her queen, he kissed every inch of her as if he had never touched her before; he took her with reverence and with feeling, and at long slow last when he had done with her, and had removed his clothes and come back to her in all his naked glory, only then did he possess her in the fullest most meaningful sense of the word.

Slow, slow—he probed her, he entered her welcoming fold: she was ripe for him, ready for him, melting at the first firm thick fulfillment of her.

She surrounded him, she pulled him tightly against her, reveling in this lucid perfect joining; she never wanted to let him go.

He moved, so lightly at first, softly, the faintest twitch, a thrust, a sigh deep in his throat as she answered the movement with a squirming of her hips. And again, that thick twisty thrust, and again, with more momentum this time, as if he were seeking her concurrence that the time had come to surrender to this thick hot passion that enveloped them.

The time was past—in a minute, the movement of her body turned from teasing to urgent, pulling him on, demanding, goading him with the rocketing gyrations of her hips.

He drove her and he drove her; he could not stop the wild and furious thrusts, he couldn't contain his overpowering desire to utterly permeate her body and her mind with the drenching residue of his passion.

The heat, the closeness in the room enclosed them, their own private cave, primitive with their passion, explosive with the moment of climax.

He reached, she thrust, pounding the fragile cradle of her hips voluptuously against him; again, again, again, the thick steady driving force of him pushing her, commanding her—"yes, yes, yes . . ." the words sibilant, guttural in her passion urging him on, "yes—"

It was coming, it was coming—always it felt like it started in some nether place, building from a little nub of feeling deep within her center, stretching, elongating, expanding into infinite possibilities, always molten, crackling like lightning, breaking all over her body like a wave, sunlight dancing in pindots all over her skin all the way down to her toes.

A wave it was, pounding and crashing, and sunlight heat, coursing and flaring all over her, streaming and shimmering all over the pure power of his utterly drenching release.

"Never fear, Jeremy," Lady Waynflete said with some contentment the following morning. "Nicholas has some discretion: he has spirited the doxy out of town and I don't expect we will see her again until next spring—if ever."

Jeremy paced the floor indignantly. "You know what this means."

"It means *nothing,* my boy, since Nicholas had the sense to tie her up in marriage before the scandal could rub off on me. So there is no use repining. He said he would protect me, and he did."

"And at an unimaginable cost," Jeremy muttered. "It defies everything."

"The girl is resourceful and clever. She got what she came to get, Jeremy, and she fooled all of us into the bargain, Nicholas most of all. Well, it will be last year's news as of tomorrow: your friends will find some other gabble-babble to blow out of all proportion in order to entertain themselves."

Blexter scratched at the door. "Mr. Carradine, Madame."

Lady Waynflete jumped up and immediately reached for her hair with one hand, and to smooth her dress with the other. "Why did he not send a note? How do I look, Jeremy? The man will never—Dunstan, my dear. Good morning, come sit. How delightful of you to call."

"A minute's stayover only, Lucretia. Don't bother with the amenities for me. Tell me, do you know where Nick has got to?"

"Certainly: he has gone down to Southam."

"To *Southam?* Are you sure? Not Timberlake? The boy hasn't

414

been to Southam in years; in fact, I don't think he's used Timberlake either in all that time, but surely he would be more likely to go to—Southam, you say? Well—I suppose he did the right thing. After that last item—indecent, that woman, barging into Lady Badlington's and walking off with all that money, and then, in public, she hung Annesley out to dry—" He shook his head. "Shameless, that woman. How Nick ever got caught in her toils I will never know. Southam . . ."

"Well, I know," Lady Waynflete said comfortably. "Do you remember how we said for years he ought to . . . but he never did. You went down once, I remember—in aught two or three—and you said the place looked like a ruin. How do you suppose he means to keep her there if everything isn't up to the nines?"

Dunstan didn't move a muscle. "I was there? Was I? Back then? Such a memory, Lucretia—" Too extensive, he thought, too obsessive. "Well—I must have told Nicholas what was to do and he made repairs. He must have. I just would have thought the memories . . ."

"But his mother and father have been gone this age. That cannot signify, all those old feelings. He's gone past them, surely."

"Nick was ever close one. Who would have thought he would spring a marriage on us?"

"Well, the betting goes that it is all a hum," Jeremy said. "It's gone down hundreds of pounds he'll get rid of her now. You wouldn't believe the book at White's."

"I might take a flyer on that one myself," Dunstan said. "In any event, dear Lucretia, you must excuse me. Nick absconding is one thing, but Nick at Southam is very hard to conceive."

He turned at the door. "Does one know whether Nick will return to town to fulfill several engagements he has at hand?"

"Indeed," Lady Waynflete confirmed. "He will return for the next month at least. He did say he especially wanted to go to—Dunstan! Where are you going? That man! He can never be held in any one place for any length of time."

It was his besetting sin, she thought, because otherwise he would know that every time he walked through her door, he had come home.

* * *

She saw Southam for the first time through a parade of trees down a long winding driveway, awash in sunlight that surrounded it like a halo.

Here was Southam, the manor where Nicholas had been raised and come to manhood, which stood as testament of time and the strength and will of the Carradine forebears.

He felt it himself, the sense of history with which he was connected and which he had resisted for all the days of his life. He could have reached out and embraced it, and he had chosen instead to retreat and withdraw and fight a useless fight he never had won.

It stood, battered and stately, three stories tall and four square, towered on equal sides of the third story, and waiting, always waiting until its master chose to return home.

The elegant entrance was as inviting as ever, a double staircase leading up to the pedimented door inside of which was . . . home.

A house, he thought, as Mr. Fogg urged the horses onward and the carriage moved forward, was a place of patience: it sheltered and enfolded and eventually it let you go. It held no grudges, it stood its ground, and it welcomed you whenever you chose to return. It was eternal, it always remained.

It was huge. Jainee could not encompass the whole of it as the carriage slowly approached the gravel oval in front of the house where it would pull in and stop. It was breathtaking. She felt as though the house might swallow her whole, that she could get lost in it and never be found for days.

The carriage lurched to a stop. Mr. Fogg jumped down and immediately set out the step to facilitate Nicholas' descent.

He stood, arms akimbo, in front of the door he had entered a hundred times in his youth, and the one he had slammed in finality some ten years ago, after his parents died and long after he had taken up residence elsewhere.

He felt like a boy again, without the same frantic pain engulfing him in resentment.

416

Jainee stepped down beside him, pulling her cashmere shawl more tightly around her as if it could protect her from something unseen.

The door opened and a man stepped out who was as stately as his surroundings. "My lord?" His question was uncertain, his voice as rich as the color of the bricks on the house.

"Exeter." Nicholas tucked Jainee's hand into his arm and led her up the long flight of stairs. "This is my wife. Jainee, this is Exeter, who has been running the house since my departure and my parents' death. He will see to all your needs. All is in readiness, I take it?"

"Indeed, sir. The apartments on the first floor are thoroughly prepared for your use, and several rooms above have been allocated to Madame's maid and whichever of your staff will be staying over."

"Excellent. Come, Jainee. Come into my home."

The words reverberated: *my home*—and the house had grown smaller since he had run. Surely the hall was overpowering when he was a boy, and the rear salon totally intimidating. The library, stacked to the ceiling with unread books now crumbling from disuse, had been a chamber of horror for him who had not been bookish. And the reception room, which encompassed the entire right wing of the house, had been a place he had not been permitted to enter.

The house had diminished with his memories. He felt nothing discordant now—only a calm, clear sense of place.

Their rooms were located in the wing opposite the reception room, accessible through a transverse hallway which ran the width of the house.

These had been his parents' rooms, and he had been given the bedrooms directly above. He had felt lonely, banished, isolated, he had never reveled in the monstrous amount of room and freedom that they had given a little boy.

It would be different with his sons, he thought. He would keep them close; he would move heaven and earth to contain them.

His sons . . .

"Mr. Nick!" A voice from the doorway, delighted, cheery, old.

417

"Mrs. Blue."

"And you remember me. Ah, my boy, so good to see how well you've turned about. Your mother would be proud," Mrs. Blue said, bustling into the bedroom without an invitation and taking one item and then another and setting it just where she thought it should be.

More words, echoing across a lifetime . . . *Mother, mother—pretty lady would be proud* . . .

He should not have come. He felt the past grip his entrails and twist them tightly with guilt and remorse and the knowledge he could never undo the sorrow he had caused her. . . . *Mother* . . .

"Ah, me, and your beautiful bride—we will be the best of friends for the weeks you go away; never you fear, Mr. Nicholas. We will find much to do, much to talk about. She will never miss you, but *you* will pine for her, I can see that you will. You have started already. Come, a luncheon has been made ready in the dining room, just where it always was, overlooking the drive. Didn't your father love to sit in of a morning, reading the paper and waiting for callers? Those were the days . . . those were the days."

Those were the days, long ago and gone, irretrievable, irreplaceable, carved like a marker post into his heart.

They explored the place the rest of the day; she was particularly taken with the long elegant reception room and its pairs of corinthian columns framing each of two entrances, from the hallway and the drawing room. The ceiling was frescoed with streams and wreaths of flowers picked out in gold and a faceted glass chandelier hung suspended from a rosette in the middle of the room. On the wall, directly under, was a fireplace, and opposite, on either side of the floor to ceiling windows, were thick tufted sofas. There were Aubusson rugs scattered along the floor and chairs everywhere to insure seating for everyone.

Beyond this room was the much less formal drawing room, and across the hallway the dining room. The rear salon had been given over to family entertaining and it was hung with enormous gilt-framed portraits and scenes of everyday life and furnished in a more informal manner.

The library, down the hallway and adjacent to their rooms, contained bookshelves built into every wall, floor to molded ceiling, a scattering of comfortable chairs and a sofa by the fireplace, and a fitted rug to give it a more cozy aspect.

The kitchens and work and storage rooms were in the basement, and the stables and barns were a quarter of a mile beyond the house, out of sight of any of the rooms but the upstairs.

It was a smaller house than Jainee had imagined from the outside, yet it was large enough to be intimidating to her; she had been used to the neat two-story house of her mother which had had three rooms on each floor, nicely arranged for convenience and comfort, and no more than a soul needed, surely.

She had hardly said a word to Nicholas on the plan of his leaving and they went to bed soberly and quietly, almost as if the ghosts of his past could not let them find each other in the dark. In the morning he was gone, everything left unspoken, thick as the air with emotion and ties unbroken.

Chapter Twenty-four

"Ah, there is so much to do," Mrs. Blue assured Jainee as she wandered back into the house looking forlorn and lost. "Listen here: we will want to tend to the gardens and do some riding and driving about. You can spend your mornings writing letters and leave the care of the house to me. And that great big library with all those books just begging to be read — ah, cheer up, my lady. He will be back, sooner than you think."

But she didn't know what to think. Here, so far away from London, where the sky was an unearthly shade of blue, she felt so close to heaven she could have touched it, and that all earthly concerns had no reality in the world of Southam Manor.

It was enough to just spend a morning walking about, down faintly laid out tracks and then suddenly come upon some whimsy, something unexpected: a pool, a folly, now in ruins. A birdbath. A little garden still growing wild in the wind.

This had been the sum and substance of Nicholas' life in the years when Dunstan Carradine had been the devoted *chevalier* of her mother and called himself Charles Dalton. No wonder Therese had discarded his name and retained her own. Had she known of his perfidy even then?

But there were no shadows surrounding the manor house. There was only clarity and the first days limned by her sense of a first step taken and something irrevocably bound.

The accidents began to occur in short order, one right after the other, and nothing suspicious — not at first.

There was the dish of macaroni pudding that made her sick to her stomach. And a fall she took down the outside steps because she tripped on an untied lace. There was the buggy ride she took one morning, her hands confidently guiding an old mare that was easy as a baby, so said Mr. Finley, who cared for the horses. Even he could not understand why the old girl just upped and whacked away like that, toppling the cart and leaving Jainee shaken and not a little afraid to step foot into one again.

A pile of books fell on her head while she was browsing in the library—an accident, surely, and she did slip and fall on a sliver of soap that had been left by the washstand floor—pure carelessness on her part, no other explanation.

A glass broke in her hand at dinner one evening, but she must have been clutching it too tightly; blood smeared her palm and stained the pristine white table cloth.

Mr. Fogg, who had stayed on at Nicholas' instructions, drove her to Hungerford, the nearest town, and she was nearly run over.

Another time, a crowd surged against her, pushing her into the oncoming traffic.

Accidents all, spread over the space of a week and a half, some her fault, she was certain; she was clumsy in her new surroundings, and the burden of wearing the name Lady Southam wore on her mightily.

She was alone; she did not know who among the servants who had lived on the place was her ally except for Marie, who hovered close to her now and watched her every move.

Mrs. Blue dismissed it as coincidence. "But send a note to my lord, if you feel you must. Fogg will take it, or Finley or one of the grooms."

But how could she even explain it to Southam when every retelling brought the accidents into the perspective of them possibly being her fault; either she had not looked, or she had not tied or she had dropped the soap or pressed the glass too hard because for some reason she was edgy dining alone.

She pricked her finger arranging flowers; a stand full of ink spilled all over her papers, her desk, her clothing.

She fell out of bed.

She felt evil swirling all around her. She didn't know who, if anyone, was her friend.

The portraits in the salon intrigued her and one afternoon she persuaded Mrs. Blue to sit with her there and talk about the two who had been Nicholas' parents.

"Well, there he is — Lord Henry, he was, and there she is — lady Eliza . . . such a wonderful woman, she was. Mr. Nicholas . . . well, he broke her heart and he raised it up to heaven, he did. He came tumbling down this very chimney one day, did you not know the story, my lady? And they was so yearning for a child for themselves, they bought him away from that slug who had made him a slavey, and they raised him like their own. And poor Mr. Nicholas, crying for his mother; he was all of four or five and he didn't know. But he never stopped wanting her, even when Lady Eliza held him in her arms and tried to comfort him. The boy was so unhappy; they never could find who was his mother and how he ended up in the hands of that scurrilous Mr. Slote. They did everything for him, and it seemed like he mourned his lady mother forever. How beautiful she was, my lady, do you see?"

She saw: such fine eyes, filled with humor and a sad wisdom that must have come from so futilely loving the child she had wanted so much. She knew nothing of Nicholas' life at all, barring that he had not been the natural son of his parents. She felt a pain in her heart for the child who had gotten lost. She wondered about childhoods and parents and whether anyone could grow up pure and untouched in a world that was so sullied.

She, who had a father who had come and gone like the seasons, and a mother who needed a mother herself, and Nicholas, in the throes of yearning forever for the mother who had abandoned him.

And somehow, they had found each other and her father had come to life as his uncle.

The Fates were surely laughing.

"He got away from here as soon as he could," Mrs. Blue went on. "He was going to search for her, he said. He said, he thought she was a great lady because she had had all the fine things that great ladies had, and if he were invited to enough places and met enough people, he was sure he would find her . . ."

"He never found her," Jainee said, because she knew the end of that story. His cynicism, his need for control, his reputation for utter callousness, these were the tools of a man seeking to immure himself in a hell of his own making.

"No, my lady. And he abandoned Southam Manor much as she had abandoned him, and we soon fell to wrack and ruin. He heeded no one's pleas to save us until Mr. Dunstan, Lord Henry's brother that is, came for a visit and saw the whole, and he was as shocked as can be that Mr. Nicholas would destroy his legacy this way. And that's when he took a hand—but he never came until this day."

"I have met Mr. Dunstan Carradine," Jainee murmured, thinking furiously. Something struck her about the fact that Dunstan had come back to Southam Manor when the house was untenanted and falling into disrepair. "It must have been so long ago that the house had deteriorated the way you say; it is so beautiful now."

"Oh yes, many years ago—eight or nine at least. Of course, Mr. Dunstan was never a frequent visitor to begin with. He was always off somewhere doing something for the government, and I know Lord Henry could never quite figure out what. And after my Lord and Lady died, you never saw him for dust either. But then he came—he had come from someplace where the Manor was closeby and he thought he might take a look. I remember the day because when I showed him around, he was properly shocked at the state things had got to."

Jainee's heart was pounding like a drum. The boy was safe, he had said. The boy was safe . . . and he had come to Southam Manor about the time he had abducted the boy: the peace had been on then, short-lived, but long enough for plots and plans and uncommon visits to places he never originally frequented. And Nicholas had been gone by then . . .

What did it mean?

"Tell me about Lady Eliza?" she said, to cover her confusion and the frisson of horror that swept over her as her mind leapt from connection to connection with no logic, no proof whatsoever.

"Oh, my lady . . . so dear she was; I came to this place myself when I was but a girl, you know. She was so good, so caring. So strong in her way. Like silk, you know. So fragile but it holds up under any circumstance. Always smiling the kind smile, always interested in things, in people. Mr. Dunstan loved her, I think."

"What?"

"Oh yes, my lady. Part of the reason Mr. Dunstan stayed so much away. He loved Mr. Henry but my lady—oh, I think she was his queen. And maybe he thought the fault of her barrenness lay with his brother and that he could have carried on the line. It is just a feeling I had, my lady . . . nothing personal. I thought you would like to know the whole, and who to tell you but me?"

"Yes," Jainee murmured, "the family retainers always know the secrets, do they not, Mrs. Blue?"

"I want to see Mr. Nicholas happy before I die, my lady. And children surrounding him and making this house whole again."

"Yes," Jainee whispered, seeing a vista of the lineage of Nicholas Carradine carried on by her, perpetuated by him.

"The Lady Eliza—she would have lived for this day did she but know it was coming."

Jainee looked up at her portrait, at the sad wise eyes and the faint knowing smile that played over her firm lips. Like silk . . . warp and weft and tightly woven. Loved by two brothers; had he been a traitor then? Had he already gone to France and successfully courted Therese Beaumont and made the child who was herself? Had her rejection turned him into a traitor of everything he had ever known?

She breathed deeply, dismayed by the wealth of secrets, the motivations and family intentions that no one ever knew. Questions cracked in her mind like little electrical bolts. Had Lady Eliza loved *him* and chosen Lord Henry?

424

Sad wise eyes—who did you love? Who did you want?

How different, how flamboyant and gaudy Therese must have seemed next to the memory of *her.* Had he deliberately sought that difference? Had he ever even cared?

She felt a chill, thinking about it.

What if all of this impacted everything today?

She sliced her finger with a knife as she cut an orange. She moved while Marie was altering a dress, and Marie stabbed her with a pin.

The candles by the window caught the drapes on fire and the whole room could have burned down, except that she awakened and had the quickness of mind to beat them out with the covers from her bed.

"I do not like the country," Marie said once, twice. "It is too quiet. Nothing happens. There is so little to do."

But everything was happening; her clumsiness made her feel stupid. Her father's story was reeling in her mind.

She went for a walk to escape—not a long walk, she wasn't sure by that time she could trust herself not to have some kind of incident; a short walk, one that took her around the house and out toward the back gravel drive which led to the stables and the outhouses. Mr. Finley would be there, should she need aid or succor. There could be no trouble, no reason not to go.

She visited the stables and rubbed the nose of the old mare who had toppled her from the cart, all at Mr. Finley's insistence, and because she did not wish to offend him or remain so scared.

Attack the problem—attack it. Action was the key point; never let the enemy see you down.

The mare nickered and took a piece of carrot from her hand. She stopped trembling and perceived the sweetness in the old horse's eyes.

" 'Twas an accident plain and simple," Mr. Finley said. "This old lady would never hurt a fly."

She walked out of there toward a grove of trees that led to the little pond, her heart pounding furiously. The mare was as gentle as a baby and yet for some reason, she had gotten spooked and toppled the cart.

. . . Her father might have been in love with Lady Eliza . . . he had come to Southam Manor mysteriously some eight years before after having avoided visits for so long . . .

There was nothing to connect those two things together, *nothing*.

. . . He had been returning from somewhere close to the Manor. He had just been in France—she knew it, she knew it . . . how could it not be? He never would have taken the boy back to London. That would have been sheer folly for a man who was a confirmed bachelor and held in esteem by his peers . . . to appear with a baby in his arms? To claim it was his own by some serving wench somewhere—how could he explain that when in higher circles it was well known he was on diplomatic mission to France?

It had to have been—he had been there on a legitimate mission and chosen Therese, beautiful Therese, to be his light of love. She had gotten pregnant, maybe he had consented to marry her, maybe not—which would surely explain why she had never used his name—and sometime beyond that, she had caught the eye of the emperor because of her friendship with Caroline Murat.

And when the baby was born a boy, he returned. *Why had he returned then? Why take the baby if he were returning to England?*

Her mind teemed with stories, with possibilities; her heart ached for her poor mother. Her concentration was focused solely on understanding all the pieces and parts of the puzzle in her hands.

She wasn't looking, and so it was the same explanation as it always was: she just wasn't paying attention, and when the shot rang out, she was caught squarely on the shoulder and she fell, heavily, like a sack of flour, into the grass, screaming.

"You was careless, my Lady, and that's all there is to it." This from Mr. Coolidge, the gameskeeper, who had been hunting rabbits or quail or something—she couldn't keep it quite straight in the heat of the pain in her shoulder hours later, after the doctor had come and gone and everyone was trying to understand how it could have happened.

"Always have to be looking in the grass on a spring afternoon, my lady. *Always.* I'm surprised Mr. Nicholas hasn't told you. And if I saw something move, it ain't my fault if it was you," he said firmly, "though I *am* sorry as can be, my lady."

She dismissed him, and chased out Mrs. Blue and her gallons of broth and warm cloths with which she intended to bathe her forehead, her hands, her neck. Marie hovered, her hands fluttering helplessly.

"I have to think," Jainee said with some spirit, but she felt so weak, so disheartened.

Nicholas had just gone off and left her, after that keening swelling night of love, and all this had happened.

She didn't have a story to tell him that wouldn't somehow destroy that little knot of tentative trust.

She thought there were no shadows at Southam Manor. Now she felt them all around, and they were reaching for her, sweeping over the evidence with a tide of accidents which could solely be laid at her door.

She knew how it looked, she could hear how it sounded, and a terrible fear took hold of her; she had nothing but her ultimate secret between her and Dunstan's threats.

London was empty without her.

It took him a week—less—to understand that the moment he had brought her back home with him, he had added an unexpected symmetry to his life. And it was something that went beyond the games and the words.

It was her presence, her drive, her guile.

The house was empty without her.

He went to quiet dinner parties, the theater, to White's. No one dared outrightly question him. He dutifully lost money with good grace and had meaningless conversations he could not remember.

Dunstan was nowhere in sight; Annesley avoided him. And Charlotte Emerlin had set her sights on a new target: Jeremy Waynflete.

Edythe Winslowe was more in evidence than ever, in the wrong places, but now she had her hooks firmly into Lord Ottershaw, who had never been able to stand his wife's indecision, and liked a woman with more stuffing who understood the niceties of obligation as long as he supplied her with the niceties.

Nothing had changed—and everything.

The Chronicle's gossip column said what everyone was thinking:

> *What hotly pursued lord has returned to town sans the baggage with which he left? Good news for the ladies, particularly one whom, we hear, is not quite the lady she seems—but perhaps she has found ways to interest another party? Lady Badlington, at least, can breathe a sigh of relief, and welcome his lordship's custom with open arms.*

So they were talking about Charlotte and Jeremy, he thought, throwing the paper onto the floor. And they never stopped talking about him.

It didn't matter. It seemed a world away from his ineffable discovery at the inn that he was finally ready to go home and hold one certain woman in his arms.

At the most now, she took a chair and sat out on the parapet of the steps to the front door of the house.

It was a good place to sit: it was sunny and warm and gave a good prospect over the drive and the bower of trees just beyond that led to it.

Here, she was hiding in plain sight so that her mystery nemesis

428

could not get her. Here she was so obviously visible that should something occur, it must be seen too.

And here, she could think and fit the story together in some way that made sense as she had been trying to do ever since Mrs. Blue had told her of Nicholas' childhood and Dunstan's inconstancy.

But why the boy? It was the only point that didn't fit.

The boy, she thought about the boy—the baby he was when her father so precipitously and charmingly took him from her arms and walked away to England with him. In aught one? Two? Easy to do. Peace at hand between France and her nemesis. Visits back and forth. She could not remember that year without feeling Therese's desperate grief at the loss of the baby and the truth of the father who never was. A devious one, Therese had called him, her eyes hard and far away. An aristocrat . . .

Born into it, in fact, and a second son, and the consequences of being one were severe. Passed over on every account. Usurped by a ruffian who fell down a chimney just when he might have thought it was too late for his brother to conceive an heir.

And loved his brother's wife. Pursued her, perhaps. Joined the ranks of the foreign office after she rejected him so that he did not have to stay in England, perhaps?

Sent to France—and then, and then Therese: lovely, laughing, lighthearted Therese, who was always willing to strike a bargain with the man she loved.

And then the boy.

He had been gone a long time by then.

She tried to remember. No, he had not been around by then for perhaps a year, maybe two. They had gone to live at court then, she did remember that, probably as a result of the emperor's uncommon interest in the lady who laughed so much, and flirted and thought a lot of herself, and could not, initially, by his importuning, be breached.

She had stayed with Murat while her mother sashayed around court and played with the emperor's sensibilities and Josephine fumed. Oh yes, Murat had been gleeful at the thought of Josephine's anger at discovering this new petticoat which had attracted the emperor's interest.

It had lasted, what? A week? A month? Had Therese lived there or with Murat then? She couldn't remember. All she knew was at one point, the excitement of being a part of court abruptly ended.

They were given the neat little house in which she grew up, and nine months later, Therese gave birth to a son.

Yes, that all was fitting. He had gone, her mother had won the emperor's heart for perhaps five minutes or five months, and the end result was the child.

And months later, Dunstan reappeared, charmed his child and took the boy.

The emperor's blood . . .

Who had said—deVerville had said over the body of her mother while the house lay in smoking ruins . . .

Why the boy?

"Horseman is coming, madame," Exeter said at her ear.

Her heart leapt: Nicholas had returned!

She posted herself at the stairwell ledge, her hand shading her eyes and looking out toward the tunnel of trees.

A solitary horseman emerged from the shadows in a gallop and rounded the gravel drive like a man in urgent haste to return to a loved one.

He drew up, the horse reared and she gripped the stone ledge. Dunstan!

"Well, my dear—I had heard that Nicholas had imprisoned you at Southam Manor, and so I decided to come and keep you company. Are you not delighted to see me? Call the groom—I'm here to stay."

"This is a *dull* evening," Lady Waynflete said mournfully as she looked at her cards, assessed the likelihood of her taking any tricks—which was nil—and set them down disgustedly. "I haven't seen Dunstan in a fortnight; he is probably chasing after some fancy piece again, and my patience will be strained to the limit once more."

"You have no reason to believe . . ." Lady Jane Griswold said gently.

Lady Waynflete sighed. "No, but I have ever hoped he would one day realize . . ." She stopped short as Gertrude Emerlin returned to their table.

"So lovely: Charlotte and Jeremy together in the parlor. They look so well together."

Lady Waynflete said, "I had rather hoped . . ." and broke off as Lady Jane signalled to her.

But Gertrude Emerlin had no scruples about asking the questions that everyone wished to know the answers to. "So where has that disgusting Nicholas Carradine gone to these days?"

"Why, he is in town," Lady Jane said, gathering up the cards. "And I believe Lady Southam is enjoying the spring at the Manor."

"Horrible how he jilted my poor girl and flaunted that creature in her face when Charlotte wanted to make amends. It would serve him right if Jeremy just swept her out from under his nose," Gertrude said righteously, taking the deal and flipping the cards to each of the women with the expertise of a born gamester.

"And why Nicholas has come back to town I will never know," Lady Waynflete said. "Just the other day, Dunstan was asking about—" She stopped again. And there it was, that niggling little feeling of unease she always had when Dunstan had been attentive and then suddenly disappeared.

He had asked about Nicholas. *He had asked if Nicholas were to come back to town.* She had said . . . she had said—oh, a month at least he was due to stay. One enormous month when that creature would be alone in the country with no company in sight but the servants; wouldn't she welcome a *familiar* face, a face that was kin, a face that had fawned all over her while she had been under Lady Waynflete's roof.

Her cards fell from her hand and she pushed her chair away from the table. "I must leave you, my dear," she said to Lady Jane. And to Gertrude: "You will excuse me."

She rushed out into the parlor where the guests at this select

431

dinner were playing games and dancing to the music someone was playing on the harpsichord.

Jeremy was nowhere in sight; Lady Waynflete gave a cursory search among the guests, and with her mother's eye, noticed that Charlotte was missing too.

It didn't matter. She would send word to Jeremy. If he knew her plan, he would try to stop her anyway. He would never allow her to belittle herself by chasing Dunstan Carradine all the way to Berwickshire and Southam Manor.

"Don't even tote up the losses," Dunstan had advised him those many years ago when he had recruited him for the task of rooting out a traitor. "It is nothing compared to how much he has drained from the treasury of England by goading Prinny to excess. One of four, one of five, we don't know, we can't tell. We need someone who can play deep and impress them with his cold-bloodedness.

"And we can't do it fast. We have to insinuate you into the set where money is king and the prince is a loser. I thought it all out, and although your spotless reputation is a hindrance, it still may work to our advantage. Tell me what you think."

But he had recorded the losses every time, and he knew to a farthing how deep he had cut into his fortune.

The stiffer price was having to use Charlotte Emerlin as a pawn in the game, despite the fact she was thoroughly dislikeable and just as virginal and precious as she could be. That had changed, of course, although had she done during the months of their betrothal, it would not have made a difference.

The plan was the plan, to be adhered to with no deviation whatsoever.

He was to offer for Charlotte and then jilt her after regaling her with stories of his supposed exploits that were not fit for un-sullied ears.

It had worked. He was the aggrieved lover who had been spurned; she cried buckets of tears and her mother hauled her off to their country estate for lessons, obviously, on how to

432

please a man and the ultimate irony of her cavorting with Dunstan in the most licentious way possible and then taking up after Jeremy in a match which was beginning to look more and more likely every day.

And he had played his part well: he had set a little bet here and there everyday, just to add interest to things, just to forget. And the bets got bigger, the subject matter wagered upon more outrageous.

Everyone wagged their heads and their tongues: he was totally gone over Charlotte Emerlin. Had never been the same since she cried off. A man had to drown his disappointments somehow. Lady luck was a better wife than a woman. Lady luck consoled you, smiled on you, rewarded you and every once in a while reminded you that you were alive when she kicked you when you were down.

And the more money he played, the higher the interest of the feckless four who surrounded the Prince. The wager at White's was the culmination, and his first step into the secret room of the inner circle.

But all that had changed.

Jainee . . . he breathed her name, her real name, her euphonious name, the essence, the name who had surrendered to him unconditionally without contesting her supremacy in a cluttered little inn halfway to home and had made him whole again.

Jainee . . .

He wondered why, when his mind and heart were so full of her, he was maundering around London, keeping engagements that didn't matter, fighting a battle for Dunstan that had no foreseeable termination, when he could be down in Southam Manor learning about Jainee.

No other woman in his life had ever offered to win back that which he had lost. How Dunstan would have laughed at that.

What couldn't she do, with her strength, her practicality, and the wisdom of her plain-speaking?

Jainee . . . goddess no more. Woman incarnate, forever *his*. What sane part of him had had the sagacity to bind her to him for the rest of his life?

He would never know, but by early morning the next day, Dunstan's plots and plans be damned, he was going to Jainee and straight on into his future.

Chapter Twenty-five

"So, my dear daughter, tell me what you would like to know," Dunstan said affably as they sat at the dinner table and waited for a footman to come in and clear the table.

"You know," he mused, "I have always loved this house. It is so much more intimate inside than you would expect from without. The rooms are not too big and overwhelming, and there is such a sense of being welcomed into its center when you walk in the door . . ."

He trailed off as a footman entered with a tray and began to clear the table. "We will have brandy — and coffee? in the library, unless you would prefer otherwise, Jainee?"

She shook her head. The night would be long: he had come all this way to kill her, she thought, and she must push herself to stay awake, despite the threat, despite her aching shoulder and her head which was thrumming with the tension of the revelations to come.

"Excellent. Come." He rose up, came to her chair, helped her out and offered his arm with all the good will in the world.

"I am quite proud of you, you know," he said as they strolled across the hallway to the library where a fire was blazing and the atmosphere was as intimate as if lovers had sought its refuge. "You are very beautiful, and you have your mother's wit and guile *and* her peasant practicality. Never in a lifetime would I have thought you could track me down. Such intelligence — absolutely from my side of the family. Have a seat, my dear," he invited, and she sank gratefully into a chair by the fire and he took the opposite. "Ah, the brandy, and coffee. Excellent. Thank you so much."

He held his snifter to the light and admired the color. "Henry was ever a man to keep a well-stocked cellar. This is luscious. Where were we?"

"My intelligence, from your side of the family," Jainee said rudely.

"Yes, yes. Quite a shock. Tell me how."

Jainee looked at him, totally unable to connect him with the father she had known. What she saw was a man puffed up with importance, with a lean feral look to him because something in his plans had gone awry. He had built a life here, and what had happened in France had been set aside like losing his place in a book he was disinterested in. And now she could topple him whole, right off the pedestal society that had permitted him to occupy and ruin everything.

"It was the boy," she said finally.

"The *boy?*"

"She got greedy, she asked for more than she was entitled to, and they came, and in exchange, they wanted the boy. She had no boy to give him. She had her grief and guilt, but she didn't have the boy. So they killed her. And they thought they had killed me, but they hadn't. And she lived long enough to exhort me to find the boy because they most certainly would kill him too."

"Extraordinary," Dunstan breathed. "Just unbelievable. Poor Therese. Poor Jainee. On the streets, alone, no money, no soul . . ."

"Murat took me in," Jainee said, her voice expressionless, "out of kind feeling toward mother. And because she wanted to sell *me* to the emperor as well. He is desperate to get a child—any child with anyone, and Murat was determined to prise that woman from the throne. Events you had no control over, *mon oncle*. Including her talking her brother into sending her husband to Italy. I went with her and she eased my way to England from there. A year later more or less, I had the fortune to meet my lord, and the rest you know."

"What a story, *what* a story. You gulled Nicholas as neatly as everyone else."

"One tells the truth by omission, as you must readily know. I told my lord I was seeking my father."

His heart constricted. *What else did Nicholas know?*

But that was jumping the gun: Nicholas would be here if he thought there was any threat to this woman or to his inheritance. Nicholas knew nothing. Nicholas trusted him. He always had, and this jade would not come between them, not for anything.

It would be her word against his, and whose had to be the strongest case?

"And for that, he married you," Dunstan said finally, shaking his head. "Amazing. I *am* amazed. The folly of men. The determination of women. It is ever fascinating." He took a sip of brandy. "And Fate—so fickle and always amused by the puny efforts of men. It does give one pause. Why don't you have questions for me, Jainee?"

"I have one question," she said carefully. "I think I know the rest."

"And children," he murmured, "always believing there is nothing new to be learned. Ask your question, daughter."

"Why the boy?"

"Ah, the boy . . ." He seemed to sink into deep, deep thought and she felt a flare of resentment that he might not answer her questions. She had waited so long, but he looked like a man of infinite patience, sitting there and staring into his brandy and the reflection in its deep color of the flames of the fireplace.

"The boy . . ." he said at last, his voice far away. "The boy was insurance on certain promises the Emperor made to me. It is as simple as that."

She felt something within her deflate. All the anger, all the guilt, all the crying and recriminations because a man wanted to save his skin and wring something additional for himself into the bargain.

It was monstrous. But he could not have had any idea how the abduction would destroy their lives, and somewhere in the shire there was a little boy, innocent of his heritage and the trail of

437

deception and murder which had followed.

"You are the traitor whom my lord seeks."

"Indeed yes, and it was I who set him on the trail in order to divert any suspicion from me. So you see, the intelligence does come down this pathway, Jainee, and not your mother's. You and I—we are devious, but we go after what we want, and we use any means to accomplish it."

Oh yes, oh yes—he was right: she had told herself that so many times. Any means, any way.

"And in the process, of course," he added, "I convinced him to gamble away the Southam fortune. Now tell me, that isn't clever? At some point, my dear Jainee, I will begin to wonder about his sanity, and perhaps I will pull him up into a court and demand to be made an executor on the basis of Nicholas' destructive behavior. And they will put him away, and I will finally have Southam—which should have been mine all along."

Monstrous . . . heinous . . .

"You were in love with the Lady Eliza," she said baldly, and his head shot up.

"No one ever knew that," he said, his voice deadly.

"People knew it," she said, allowing that certainty into her tone. Oh, he would kill her now just to erase the knowledge from memory. "She married Lord Henry, didn't she? She did not want the younger son. So you set about ruining the child to pay for the transgressions of its mother."

"If they had not adopted Nicholas, all this would have been *mine*. If she had married me, I would have given her the earth."

"Even if you were married before."

"It was another country, another time. It had nothing to do with England—or *her,* except that I accepted the commission to get as far away from her as possible."

"And so you found Therese—who was as unlike her as any woman could be."

"She had nothing to do with Eliza, and she was *there.* And then—so were you."

"And the boy."

"And the boy," he agreed.

"Where is he?"

"Where I told you, Jainee. Safe."

"Nearby?" she hazarded.

He shook his head.

Shee took a deep breath, shifted her aching arm and plunged into the uncomfortable question. "Is he dead?"

"My dear daughter . . . are *you?*"

"Not yet. *Did* you try to kill me?"

"Let us say the little accidents were . . . warnings."

She felt cold. His eyes were remorseless, and he was looking at her, and she was his *daughter.* "Here, too?"

"I thought I was very clever, actually. Nothing that seemed amazingly unusual — in the house . . ."

"In . . . ? Everything?"

"My dear, what does everything mean? I caused a stack of books to fall on your head . . . I made you fall out of bed, and of course the candles. Excellent work on my part. Nothing that didn't seem in the normal course of events except for a little carelessness."

"And the rest . . . ?"

"The rest too, my dear: the cart, and of course I followed you to town and tried to both run you over and push you under a carriage in traffic. Yes, of course. The shooting was the easiest: I was behind Mr. Coolidge. You know I was here for two weeks before and followed everyone's schedule. It was too easy."

And the other things? Not him? The glass, her fall, the ink — not him?

She had an enemy *in* the house, and her enemy sat beside her, and she would never get out alive, never.

"No other questions?"

"Why don't you just get it over with?"

"There's time, my dear. There is time. I had thought I would spend a day or two with you to get to know you, but I saw immediately how fruitless that would be. There is just no way I can trust that this story would never come out, no way. Of course, I understand how hard it would be to tell Nicholas that his traitor is both his uncle and your father. I appreciate fully the conflict

439

you have had over this situation. But here at Southam Manor, Jainee, you are alone with yourself and nature. Confidences flow; see how we have aired our secrets with barely a nudge from one to the other. What wouldn't you have said to Nicholas over the course of time? He would be astonished—and angry, but eventually he would forgive you, and he would have come after me.

"No, Jainee. This is the wisest course. You were warned and you chose to stay in the race and now your horse must stumble and you will get caught on the turf. You are victim of war, my dear, long fought and hard won—but only by me."

"You have such contempt."

"My dear, I have manipulated everyone from an emperor right down to my own brother and his adopted son. Everything would have worked out fine had you not appeared on the scene. I daresay Nicholas would have expended a lifetime of income within the succeeding two years keeping up with Prinny. A brilliant stroke, don't you think? He never would have looked *my* way; the secret is that everyone must trust you and that you never must show that contempt."

"You could not sell him away from marrying me."

"If only I could have, Jainee. This story might have a different ending. The fates again, I'm afraid. Laughing, turning everything slightly askew. God, I can still feel the sensation the first time I saw you at Lucretia's. My blood ran cold."

"And mine," she said grimly, lifting her arm yet again to relieve the pressure on her shoulder.

He ignored that and got up from his chair to look out the window.

"It's so dark, Jainee. This is a night of mystery and of death," he murmured, wheeling around to face her with a pistol in his hand.

She started. She had not expected it quite so soon. Her father was a man of many surprises, not the least of which was that he would take her life as calmly and cold-bloodedly as any murderer.

Her father was desperate. No one had ever threatened his

440

comfortable existence before; no one had ever tapped into his plots and plans and secrets.

Of course she had to die. There was no other choice. Then he would go on as he had before until the time he could take action to ruin Nicholas and destroy *his* life.

He paced closer to her, his hand steady on the pistol as he held it by his side.

It was a curiously beautiful instrument, brass barreled and chased in silver with ornate designs inlaid into the burnished wooden stock. Just a lovely thing that he would point at her and do away with her lovely life.

Closer and closer as she sat, she couldn't move, she couldn't speak. There wasn't a servant around; they had all retired for the night. It had to be one o'clock, perhaps two. How long had they talked?

She knew everything now, but what was the point of knowing everything if within a moment or two she would know nothing.

Her thoughts raced furiously through her mind, disconnected, desperate.

She could never beg, never. Perhaps that strength in her stopped him for one silent moment. It was as if he could not quite bring himself to lift the pistol—not yet.

Daughter, daughter . . .

She had no filial claim . . . what was he seeing as he looked at her so intently. Dear Lord, she had faced a pistol once before, the specter of death twice in as many years. . . *Maman, maman*—Therese was behind her, with her: *come to me, Jainee, I wait for you . . .*—her voice in her ear, shutting out the buzzing, the singing tension, the ache in her arm—everything, everything but Nicholas' face and *her* voice, crooning softly, *come to me, come to me—I wait for you, I yearn for you . . .*

He lifted the pistol and took aim at her head.

. . . It is painful but a moment, maybe two, and then we will be together, me and you—

She thought she heard the click of the cock, she thought she heard noises and the voices of angels—

A shriek from somewhere behind Dunstan as he took his

441

sighting . . .

"Dunstan! Don't you dare touch that girl . . . !" And the diminutive form of Lucretia Waynflete hurtled herself at him and caught his arm a moment before the pistol went off and they fell in a tangle of legs and arms, her smaller bulk leeched onto his lean frame, the pistol beneath him, a heartbeat away from discharge.

The shot was deafening, a roaring in her ears in a wave of pure terror so intense she was sure she had died.

And then there was silence, a thick numbing fear-soaked silence in which she realized she was still alive, and she was hearing a suppressed sobbing sound, muffled against something thick and muted with unbearable pain.

She opened her eyes slowly, almost fearfully, afraid of what she would find.

Beside her, on the floor, Lucretia Waynflete lay on top of Dunstan Carradine's motionless form, her face buried in his morning coat, her tiny frame heaving with the force of her weeping, a river of blood streaming out from under his body.

And then she looked up, and there was Nicholas standing in the door.

Chapter Twenty-six

Dunstan was buried two days later on the grounds of Southam Manor.

"And now," Nicholas said mordantly, "it belongs to him; he will never leave it and he will never again sin."

Lucretia sagged against Jeremy, who immediately put his arm around her to bear her weight.

Nicholas dropped a handful of dirt gently on the casket and turned and walked away, Lucretia's sobs a chorus to his grief.

Jainee stood as still and tight as a statue, her face blurred with tears and a sense that her grief would never spend. She waited until Jeremy had left, supporting Lucretia's spent body as he took her back to the house. And then the servants, and some of his friends who had made the trip up from London to attend the burial—Coxe, Annesley, Chevrington, Charlotte Emerlin and her mother. Lady Jane Griswold with her kind eyes.

They had all come the night before and were to depart directly after the funeral. And, she thought, if she stayed very still and never moved again, she might not have to face the end of what was to come.

She could be the marker on her father's grave, the goddess turned to stone in reverse of the myth. She wished she were stone and hard and unmoving and without feelings.

She was shocked she had feelings and a sense of deep, irreparable loss.

Some time passed, she couldn't tell how long: it was marked by the sound of carriages crunching down the drive as they began the journey back to London; and voices, distant, muted with goodbyes and sorrow.

Soon she could move, soon. The gravediggers waited, and waited, as she stood by the coffin and stared at the fields beyond. From here, from the little family cemetery, Dunstan's grave would overlook the little pond that she had discovered, and the riotous carpet of wildflowers that swept to its edge.

The only man I ever loved . . . Lucretia's wail when Nicholas finally got to her and pulled her off of Dunstan's inert body. *The only man* . . . as she immediately leaped on Jainee, tearing and clawing at her dress, her face.

Horrible, terrible to see Lucretia fall to pieces like that, inconsolable, utterly devastated, her whole body awash in anguish that could never be assuaged.

She felt a chill, and she moved: she took one step forward and another and forced herself to leave the graveyard, and her father to his final rest.

A man was a fool, Nicholas thought, who spent weeks ruminating on all he had missed and all he might have lost; a man should have known that dreams were fleeting and the cost was too high. It had taken one tender moment for him to fall victim, and one tender betrayal from her to fall from grace.

He was waiting for her in the library, for whenever she would choose to come. It didn't matter. He had been standing in the shadows and he had missed not one scurrilous word.

"You heard the whole?" she had said when she saw him.

He nodded. And there was nothing more to say. She hadn't told him and he had found out this way, just when he was ready to hand her his heart. The perfect perfidy.

It was well that the room was dark, with just the play of firelight over the tall stacks of books. The darkness comforted him, as it always had, inviting him into its embrace.

He had remained thus since his guests had departed and Jainee had returned from the graveyard. Mrs. Blue had brought food and he had waved it away.

He waited for Jainee.

He thought he had no questions, that he would just tell her that she had to go.

But he found, sitting by the firelight, that he had a dozen or more questions, that he did not understand the how of it, and where Jainee fit into the story. Not entirely, not completely. And he thought if he knew any more, he might kill her himself.

She entered the library at a moment when his gaze was focused on the flames in the fireplace, and he was not watching for her.

"My lord," she murmured, and he looked up, startled, and then motioned her to the seat opposite which had been moved from the place where Dunstan had fallen.

She didn't even know where to begin. Apologies seemed superfluous and she knew there was no way she could make amends.

"You know everything, my lord," she began tentatively, unsure whether she should even try to explain. The tortured expression on his face told her not to try. Her words made no dent in his anguish.

The silence between them lengthened, broken only by the crackle of the flames as another log fell into the ashes.

"When," he said finally when he could make himself speak, "when did you know?"

She swallowed and took a deep breath. "When he came to Lady Waynflete's house for the first time, I knew." *And he threatened to kill me,* she wanted to cry, but that was the most unbelievable thing of all, that this smooth and oily man had even threatened her and then gone on his social rounds and treated her like an equal.

The words hit him like blows. "For so long."

"How could I tell you?"

"We made a bargain."

"It did *not* include turning over your uncle and branding him a liar, a cheat and a traitor. You would never have believed me," Jainee said desperately. "You *never* would have believed it."

He didn't know—he just didn't know. If she had told him: "he's my father, he is the man you seek"—he didn't know. The

445

point was, *she* had known.

He didn't know what to do about her, either.

"Who is the boy that Dunstan kept talking about?"

"The boy," she murmured, hugging a thread of hope. "The boy is my half brother—the illegitimate only son of Napoleon of France.

"My mother was killed because Napoleon wanted him and Dunstan had abducted him away. Don't you see? You must see, my lord—it is a chain of circumstances with Dunstan at the lead, maneuvering everything. We were all his pawns, all. You could not have deduced it. No one else had, not even those with whom he had worked. Not even his closest friends. How so the nephew he had only latterly come to know? *Think*, my lord, *think*. He tried to dissuade you from this marriage. He became so much more attentive to Lady Waynflete when he became aware I was living at her house. Who could have known his motives and machinations."

"You did," Nicholas said starkly. "Only you."

"Yes, the guttersnipe from the gaming house. My credibility exceeded my debt, my lord? I think not. You would have thought it some kind of ruse, pure and simple. And beyond that, he had threatened me did I tell you. You heard: he tried to kill me. Even in London. Small fragile accidents that might all be my fault. He said it, everything. Why can you not understand?"

"I heard."

"He loved your mother, you know."

"I heard him." He couldn't bear it. For want of a love, a kingdom lost . . .

"I swore I would find the boy," she said suddenly into the silence. "I swore to my mother on her deathbed."

"And so—another lie?"

"An omission, my lord. Only my father knew where the boy was."

"And he did not tell you?"

Jainee sighed. "No. What do you wish me to do, Nicholas?" And this cry for clemency came from her heart.

"I don't know," he said, and he could find no emotion within

446

him to reach for her. The silence lengthened until she could do nothing else but leave the room and leave him to his thoughts.

He would never forgive her, she thought, as she lay awake long into the night, aware that Nicholas had chosen to take his rest someplace upstairs and away from her.

It all came down to that: she had known and she had not told him. Whether it would have sounded plausible, whether he would have believed her, that didn't matter. Only that she had known.

He could not see the case for the facts. He could not look at circumstances or motivations or the untenable position in which Dunstan had placed her. He would not credit Dunstan's threats or the actions he had taken against her.

What he saw was she had made him look like a fool.

She had sought to protect them all.

She supposed, in hindsight, she had not given a single thought to the outcome. How long could Dunstan have borne up under the strain of knowing that *she* was in London and could have instigated a scandal that would ruin him? And when his subtle threats started, and her sense that she was being followed and watched, how long would it have been before he had taken some comprehensive action?

The danger had only become real to her after she had come to Southam Manor, not before. Perhaps she had thought she was safe in the fickle crowd of Dunstan's society friends.

Or else she had been just plain naive. The threat had always been there, from the moment she identified Dunstan as her father. She had just thought herself invincible, untouchable, and the thing would remain unresolved.

But the accidents when he had finally got her alone at Southam Manor . . . too clever . . . nothing that would not seem in the normal course of events, and everything laid to a moment's carelessness on her part.

Except for the glass, the ink, the pin prick, the treacherous fall . . . and her thought that someone in that house was against

447

her—someone else wanted her out of the way.

But now Dunstan had died, she should feel safe, but instead she felt uneasy as if there was something she had missed, something she had overlooked.

The other accidents—they had to have been her own fault, through her own carelessness, except that she was never negligent, nor was she clumsy. But perhaps she was thinking too much upon the incidents. They were such inconclusive, inexplicable little mishaps.

Nothing to worry about—except that they were coupled with the larger more direct and lethal attacks of her father.

She felt so disquieted. Dunstan's death had shaken her up more than she had ever expected. She felt a flat emotionless sense of loss of something forever irretrievable, she felt an incalculable sadness for Lucretia who had loved him so futilely, and she felt a faint glowing feeling of pride that she and her mother had been able to live without him.

But for the boy, there would have been no quest for her father; there would have been nothing of the chain of events that had led her to this moment and the ultimate end to his one act of greed.

If he had not stolen the boy . . .

She might still be in France, squirreling away money so that she and Therese could make ends meet. There would have been no Nicholas, no outrageous wagering, no Lady Southam. It made her head spin to think what there would *not* have been.

The boy . . .

He was the only component of the story which had no explanation. He was the mystery, the cipher, the cause. Everything had happened because of the boy.

And if she gave up the search for him, then everything that had resulted would have been for naught.

But he had been a baby when Dunstan had come, and seven or eight years old now. How would she know the boy? She had no clues, except the unexpected visit of Dunstan to Southam Manor in 1802, nothing more. The boy could be anywhere—here at first and then perhaps her father had removed him to London where he could better oversee his upbringing.

Or the boy could still be here—within walking distance, or shouting distance of the Manor. Within a mile or two or three. Or living with some family in Hungerford Village. Or . . . a futile chore to investigate all the possibilities?

She had to do *something*.

She had lost Nicholas. Perhaps she could find the boy.

Nicholas had gone on a round of visiting his tenants, with whom he had had no contact for these ten years.

But he had left instructions to restrict Jainee to the house.

Immediately, she wanted to disobey him and carry through a host of unformulated plans that included scouring the countryside to see if anyone had gotten wind of a child in some unusual circumstance.

But that also would alert anyone who might be hiding him, and she thought that Nicholas' limiting her to the house would have the positive effect of making her think and plan carefully exactly how she was going to approach this quest.

"Monsieur was quite put out this morning," Marie commented as she arranged Jainee's hair after Mrs. Blue had delivered the news of her confinement to the house with her morning chocolate. "Up all night and stamping about. His uncle's death has deranged him, and he will take it out on you."

"He is merely shocked by the turn of events," Jainee said calmly. "All will soon be back to rights."

"Monsieur is angry with you for hiding the truth, madame. He will not change the course overnight."

"I don't expect him to."

"He might confine you here forever," Marie said and there was a note in her voice that made Jainee look at her.

"Does this trouble you?"

"I have said, I do not like the country. Always I have been in the great cities and with the courts of the great rulers. Here I am restless, madame, and if I may say—bored. I ask you to consider whether you might return me either to the court of Murat in Italy or back to France."

"How is this? You have not aired your discontent but once, Marie, and now it is a month and you still feel the same?"

"I do not wish to remain here," Marie said.

"But we won't be in the country forever."

"I want to go back to France, madame. I ask only that you consider my wishes in the near future."

"Yes," Jainee said; what could she say? Marie was her last link with France and with the life there. Marie was efficient and had been so properly grateful to have been sent with her—and now she was bored. But then what did she have to do but mend her dresses, do some ironing and—what else? As her maid, she was not responsible for anything else. A girl from the town, skilled with a needle, could do as much, including hook up her dresses and arrange her hair. "Yes, I will certainly think about what would be best to do. Perhaps a trip into town in a day or two would alleviate the monotony."

"My gratitude, madame," Marie murmured, and left her alone with her chocolate.

And now the first consideration of the plan: she must talk again with Mrs. Blue.

"There was nothing unusual, my lady," Mrs. Blue said when Jainee invited her back to the salon to tell her some more about the time of Dunstan's visit in aught one or two. "He had come many times but not on a regular basis when my Lord and my Lady were alive, less when they took in Mr. Nicholas, but certainly as much as any kin who lived away and was in diplomatic service. We knew that. Didn't think anything of it when he came by and said he was back from a mission and passing this way. Seemed natural to me, it did."

"Did he stay over?"

"There was barely a bed to offer him, what with the roof leaking and all. We lived in the main part of the house back then because there was nowhere else, and we couldn't bear to leave the place to maunder away to the rats and the rain. Yes, my lady,

450

he did, he stayed — in Lord Henry's bed, just for the night."

Wanting to feel what it would be like to be master of the Southam fortune, Jainee thought trenchantly. There was no end to her father's resentment over that deal of the cards.

"And had he said where he had come from?"

"Oh now, my lady, I couldn't remember if he did. It was that long ago, and the only reason I remember even so much is that he reported back to Mr. Nicholas and immediately, workmen were ordered to begin to repair the place. So it was fortune smiling on us that he came."

And fortune smiling on him that no one had noticed the coincidence — but no one would have known there was even a reason to question Dunstan's presence in Berwickshire in aught one or aught two.

And so he had come, she thought, from any direction and he could have left the boy anyplace. But he must have had some place. He could not have planned so carefully to abduct him and then just hand him off to any peasant woman willing to take him.

There had to be *someone,* if indeed Southam had been his destination on his return from France.

Someone . . . and she had to deduce somehow who that someone might be.

When Nicholas entered Southam Manor two days later, Jainee barreled into him with no sign of remorse or sorrow or anything. "My lord, you *cannot* keep me confined in this place for another day. I must go to town tomorrow, and if you do not remove this stricture on my movements, I shall have to sneak away."

"Well, Diana," he said coolly. "You are ever goddess-like. You play with people's lives, you wreak destruction and then you just go on your way as if nothing had happened."

She quieted instantly, feeling the pure pain of futility knife through her. "No my lord; it is merely that your keeping me inactive does nothing to resolve the fact that I kept from you an important piece of information — which you would not have believed anyway. And since there is no way to determine whether you are right or I am, I see no reason for you to imprison me here when I might accomplish something if I were allowed to move about freely."

"Indeed? And what might you possibly accomplish *here*, Diana? There are no foolish fops to adore you, no parties for you to attend to shine like a jewel. No neighbors to visit. No charities in which you wish to involve yourself. What could there possibly be in town that would be so urgent that you must take yourself away from Southam Manor?"

Oh, the question—here was the test of her, of everything. No truths with omissions. No lies. No stories. And yet, how could she confess her tenuous thinking about the boy. He would reject it altogether.

But he had rejected her already. She had nothing but her search for the boy to hold onto, almost as if it would prove the truth of what she had told him did she find him.

She took a deep breath. "I search for the boy."

He had not expected that. She might have said she wished to leave him—but he would never countenance that. She might have said she wished for a change in the monotony of her days, and he might have believed that.

But never this. "The boy must be dead."

"I think not."

"It doesn't matter."

"I want to know," she said desperately.

"And why, Diana? So you can go carousing around the countryside making yourself conspicuous as usual. Do you think some brazen cow-handed country bumpkin will rescue you from me? I would kill him first and you would not get five miles beyond the village limits. There is no rhyme or reason to this, no matter what Dunstan said. *If* he took the boy and brought him to England. He might well have left him in France. He seems to have left a string of women wherever he damned went, and the person who should be the last to believe his lies, is the first to want to uphold them."

"I want to find the boy, nothing more. I believe he *is* here because Dunstan was here in '02, and probably after he returned from France. Why would he not bring him here if he wished to use him as a pawn to coerce the emperor? If he kept him in France, he would not have access to him, because he could not be sure the peace would last longer than five minutes. And look at what happened: war broke out again the following year. The boy *must* be here or Dunstan would have been desperate. You *must* let me search for him."

"You will not leave Southam Manor," he said roughly, and she saw he refused to consider this possibility as well. She hated his stubbornness and his blind eyes. She could not wait until his sight cleared. She could not sit still long enough.

Mr. Finley was dubious, but he also still felt a little guilty about that one little accident that was so perplexing. And yes, he knew that my Lord did not wish my Lady to be gadding about the countryside, but he also wanted to prove that his dolly-mare was as gentle as a lamb because the Lady had not volunteered to step foot into the cart since the mishap.

And here she was this early in the morning, desiring to take the cart and the mare, and very pretty about it too, she was, and he was torn between wanting to obey his Lord and impress his Lady.

In the end, because she promised not to go further than the boundaries of Southam Manor, he agreed to hitch up the mare and show her again the trick to handling the reins.

As he watched her go off, he was reassured as well that she had taken her maid with her. There was nothing to it: my Lady merely wished an early morning drive and so he would tell Mr. Nicholas—simple as that.

But it was not simple for Jainee. The cart, which had two wheels only, wobbled and turned every which way and she was sure she would overturn the thing at any moment. Moreover, Marie sat disapprovingly beside her, never saying a word. Which was just as well: she needed every ounce of concentration to keep the mare in check. It also took some doing to find the main road. Only after they turned into it and found a sign for Hungerford did Marie venture to comment. "You have not said why you rush to go into Hungerford, my lady; surely not solely on my account?"

"I will not let that man dictate what I can do or cannot do," Jainee said through gritted teeth, every ounce of her strength and wit focused on keeping that gentle mare on some kind of even course. "I cannot sit in that house a moment longer and not do *something*. My father is dead; my lord has abandoned me. The story is ended but for the question of the boy."

"And so *now* you seek to find him?" Marie asked, her words wobbly from the bounce of the cart. "Why now, why here?"

"Because there is nothing else I can do," Jainee said unhappily, pulling on the reins with all her might as they came to a crossroads. "And which will be the best road to go—I do not know."

They came to Hungerford as the sun rose high and the road became clogged with wagons heading for the village.

Jainee did not know what to expect when they finally entered the village limits, but it was not nearly as big a place as she had hoped. Still, there were several shops lining the one winding main street, and there were vendors come to sell their produce and their wares, and there was a bustle and a vitality to the proceedings that was very pleasing, and which gave her hope she might somehow stumble on a clue.

She did not even know what she intended to do or say, and as she maneuvered the cart into the traffic and along the serpentine main street, she took mental note of the places at which she might inquire and formulated several questions which would seem innocuous enough on the surface.

The last problem with which she had to cope was what to do with the cart and the mare, and the simplest solution to that seemed to be to leave it somewhere nearby, could she find a place, and put Marie in charge.

This was not accomplished quickly, but after a time, she was able to secure a space toward the bottom of the street from the shops in which she wished to visit, and she left Marie there.

The walk up the winding street was somewhat arduous, and she had not prepared well for that with her flimsy kid slippers and thin paisley shawl which did not stand up well against a stiff spring breeze.

However, there were several likely shops and how she was dressed was of no moment in comparison to the possibility of discovering some piece of useful information within.

In very short order, she visited the dressmaker's, a pastry shop, a bootmaker, the booklender's, the tea shop and the shop which sold all manner of wares from material to trimmings to furniture. In all of them she asked one of two questions: was there a school nearby; or, she was looking for a relative she had not seen in many years, someone who had reportedly moved in or around Hungerford and had had with her a baby at the time who was probably a boy of seven or eight now. Did anyone know of such a person, because she had come to deliver some very good news after everyone had given up hope of finding them.

There was no school nearby, that she established very quickly and it dashed a very significant hope she had that the child might have been sent to one to be educated as would befit someone of his lineage.

In the second case, she was met with either blank stares or questioning of such depth and pure malicious nosiness, that she could not bear to continue the charade. In any event, there had been four or five newcomers with babies within the last seven or eight years, but unless she came forth with names and details, she found that these close-mouthed country people were not going to discuss one of their own with a stranger.

Marie was sitting patiently as a buddha when she returned to the cart. "Ah, madame. Have your efforts proved fruitful?"

"No. Perhaps." Jainee took the reins from Marie and sat holding them loosely in her hands. "No one will talk, except to say there are a half dozen families with young children who arrived in the time period which is most likely. No names, no details." She cracked the reins and the mare moved forward.

455

"But we must find out something more definite then," Marie said.

"They will not talk."

"Perhaps I—?"

"You?"

"You are too beautiful, madame. I am one of them. Let me try, my lady. It could not hurt."

Jainee agreed, and Marie debarked and went along the street, accosting strollers and several of the produce workers who had set up along the way and in the market square at the top of the street.

She was back within fifteen minutes. "They are uniformly a close-mouthed lot," she said disparagingly as she climbed into the cart. "They tell nothing unless you find the proper question or the correct story. *I* came upon the right story and so I have found out some names. There is the family Brooke, the family Goodstone, a Mrs. Colethorp . . . each of whom are fairly newly come. So there is no time to waste, madame. We must seek these people out immediately."

Jainee snapped the reins and the mare moved forward. "I am amazed at your luck and your cleverness, Marie, but surely there is no urgency to begin the search today. It will take some inquiries to discover their direction in any event."

"No, no, madame. We will find out today. We are so close—so close."

"And it is also likely that it is not any of those people, despite your excellent discoveries."

"I think we should ask at the dressmaker's, madame. Whatever the make-up of the family, a woman always needs a dress."

Jainee felt suddenly as if a stiff wind were buffeting her around, but it almost seemed ill-tempered to argue when Marie only sought to aid her in her search. "By all means, inquire at the dressmaker's."

She halted the cart and Marie stepped down and walked briskly up the winding street and disappeared soon into the shop. She reappeared very quickly looking disgusted and annoyed and when she stepped up into the cart, she turned and spat on the ground behind her.

"These English! So stiff, so reticent. Ah! They have heard of the family Brooke only, close-by Southam Manor, two miles in the opposite direction. So we must go there, madame, and begin the search."

"Why so?" Jainee said, lifting the reins again. "Already you have made more progress than could ever be expected, and all in the course of a couple of hours. My father is dead; there is no urgency about proceeding today. Tomorrow will do."

"Oh no, madame, there is great necessity."

Jainee stiffened as she felt something dig into her ribs. "Marie!"

"I have in my hand the pistol, madame, the very one which killed your father, and with which I would not hesitate to kill *you* if you do not heed my instructions. We will find the family Brooke—today."

Chapter Twenty-seven

She lifted the reins slowly and whapped at the mare's rump. Marie pressed the barrel of the pistol even more tightly against her ribs as the cart lurched forward and the mare started into a fast trot.

"Keep your hands tightly on those reins," Marie instructed, her voice emotionless. "You do not want the mare to run away with you again."

Jainee bit her lip and hauled back on the reins to get better control. Marie was not jesting: the gun barrel was aimed upward and just under her breast and painfully jammed against her.

She quelled her fear, she had to. "I don't understand," she said when she felt she could be coherent—and commanding. She slanted a covert look at Marie's implacable expression. "Explain it to me. Marie—"

"Concentrate on the road, madame. It is your only hope."

"Hope for what? What are you doing? What is this all about?"

"Madame talks too much," Marie said with relish, almost as if she enjoyed being rude to Jainee after all these months of posing as the perfectly obedient maid. "There is nothing mysterious, madame, except for your blindness. It is the boy."

"The boy? You have some connection to the boy?"

"Not I, madame—*watch the road*—not I: my mistress, the Murat of Italy. Did you not know? Such an innocent young thing you are, thinking that my mistress had allowed you, yes— *allowed* you to come to England when she had planned for the emperor to bed you to try to lure him away from Josephine once more and divert his attention toward her husband as his possible successor. And then you had to mention the boy. She had forgotten all about the boy. A child with the blood of the emperor might have first claim on him, certainly a claim above a brother-in-law.

"So, my lady, my mistress allowed you to come to England to find the boy, and she gave you myself as an agent of the King. My orders were to find the boy and to kill him."

"Dieu," Jainee whispered.

"You took so long, madame, and all that sparring and fighting with Monsieur when you could have been on the trail of the boy. I am not a patient woman. Two and a half years, and messengers coming, and agents to help with the surveillance of Monsieur's townhouse and to follow you wherever you went. A boy in the stables, lest you got past me somehow.

"And phut—*nothing*. Little accidents, to make you think that someone was after you, and to frighten you into pressing forward with your search lest you be harmed before you found him.

"Did I think I would have to compete with Monsieur's uncle? Never. I so wish you had told me he was your father, madame; it would have saved some trouble. Because just when I think there is no point, that the secret has died with him, and I must compel you to return me to my mistress as soon as possible—you begin the search anew.

"And so now I must complete the mission, madame, and as soon as possible. So we drive to the family Brooke and we find the boy."

Jainee grasped tightly onto the reins with her icy hands. All these months . . . Marie a traitor, a killer, a step away from destroying her. She could barely comprehend it. It wasn't possible; Marie was her confidante, the one person in the whole of England who was from home, who was a link . . .

"Do not slow the cart," Marie said harshly.

They were the last words she spoke. A shot rang out, she fell forward, and the mare, startled, kicked up her heels and went hurtling down the road, overturning the cart and dumping Jainee and the mortally wounded Marie onto the track.

459

She had left him.

It was the inescapable conclusion, and Nicholas paced angrily in the library as he went through the events of the day yet one more time with the poor distracted Mr. Finley.

The facts did not change, even in the tenth retelling: she had come to the stable early with her maid. She had wanted to use the cart, to prove to herself she was not afraid after that almost disastrous spill. She meant only to drive it within the limits of Southam Manor. She had gone off around eight o'clock. She had not returned.

It was midnight by then and he had already ridden the miles between the Manor and the village and the roads all around looking for some trace of her. He had found nothing; she did not want to be found.

But curious things stood out: she had taken no luggage. She had left no word with anyone. She had no money, at least that he knew of, although her mythical winnings as the lady in black had to be taken into account. But he had seen no sign of money, not on their journey, not in her room.

He and Mrs. Blue meticulously searched her possessions and came away with nothing. She had worn her shawl and a plain round gown with a waistcoat bosom. Nothing to attract attention. Nothing flamboyant, almost as if she had a reason for dressing plainly.

Not like Jainee at all.

Mrs. Blue testified she had asked him many questions about Dunstan and he recognized the details as the parts of the puzzle she had outlined to him.

Which meant — what? That she had gone to follow the slender thread of a trail Dunstan had left in Berwickshire eight years before? But she would have gotten nowhere; her surmises were patently guesses with no basis in fact, and she should have been home by now.

. . . Home . . .

The manor had suddenly become home?

He felt a sense of ballooning urgency and a spiralling anger that she had done this to him. He had not wanted her to leave, and she had given him no time to come to terms with her suppression of the facts.

He didn't even know what it was yet: he didn't like *betrayal*. It made the deed unforgivable, and he wasn't sure, when he was thinking clearly, that Jainee was not right and he would not have listened to any such fairy tale about his uncle.

Probably, he would have berated her for trying to manipulate him with specious stories to try to distract him from her duplicity.

Damn her and damn. He held on tightly to the tenuous connection they had made the night before they came to Southam Manor. Such a gossamer thread of hope and burgeoning affection.

He had thought he had dreamed it, except that when he had been in London, it had pulled at him as tautly and tightly as any hemp rope hauling an immovable object from one place to the next.

He saw himself as the object, and the rope as the one rough, interwoven strength between them.

She could not have left him.

He felt like a child all over again. He felt that wave of loss and longing, inexplicable, and bound now with memories of the past and the urgency of the present.

He felt inconsolable. He felt he might drown in his tears forever. He could not go into the main salon because he did not want to look at the portraits of his parents. He felt them pulling at him, commanding him. He felt as if every secret were contained in Lady Eliza's sad wise smile.

He resisted it; in his mind, he spoke to Lord Henry: *And so see what things have come to; did you know, did you? that Dunstan was so full of rage and retribution? Did* she *know?*

And oh, if she knew . . . he didn't know if he could get past that either. The beautiful lady. The woman whose hands had soothed every hurt, whose ears had listened to his yearning for another woman, whose tender words had blunted the pain.

461

She could not have known. He just could not believe it of her. The portraits beckoned from the darkness of the room.

He paced the hallway, reconstructing for the hundredth time the scenario of Jainee's flight from Southam Manor.

Mrs. Blue came by to assure herself that he was all right. "Perhaps you would just like to take this branch of candles into the salon, Mr. Nicholas, and visit with your parents."

"Mrs. Blue . . ."

"They have waited a long time for your return, Mr. Nicholas. They only saw you a moment when you brought Lady Southam around. They want to know you've come back to them."

"Mrs. Blue . . ." he protested again, but she would not listen to him. She gave him the candelabra and pushed him toward the room. "Go on, now."

He moved across the hallway, propelled by her certainty.

The room was in utter darkness, its beautiful brocade furniture covered with sheets. Winding sheets, he thought mordantly, to bury the soul who thought he could come to life in this house.

He walked slowly toward the mantel and held up the candles. The flame heightened the facial part of the portraits and made them almost pop out against the darkness of the backgrounds.

I've come home . . .

The words formed in his mind before he could contain them. *Father—*

Lord Henry had been easy to call father; even in the portrait, his face reflected a genuine kindliness that was tempered by an underlying steeliness. Nicholas remembered how many times he had tried to butt against his father's elegant sense of righteousness, and how many times he had fallen and Lord Henry had picked him right back up again.

Strange he should remember that in the depths of his sorrow.

He turned to the portrait of Lady Eliza—beautiful forever in her gilded frame, just as he remembered her from his youth. *Beautiful lady . . .* the words formed again instantly, unpremeditatively. He could recall the scent of her perfume, and the softness of her hands as she would stroke his head when he was troubled. And her hands were firm, commanding, in charge

462

those many times he had gone hell for leather and injured himself. She was always there, she always listened, she rarely criticized, she was much beloved by everyone around her.

Except me . . . The words stamped in his mind hard and harshly against the sweetness of his memories. "Except me," he whispered out loud, holding the candles higher.

Beautiful lady . . . Her love knew no bounds with him; he could do no wrong, and whatever scrape he got into, whatever his needs or his wants, she always championed him.

I love you . . . her sad wise eyes seemed to say, as if across heaven and earth the substance of that love could never change.

He felt remorse grab his gut so tightly it could have been a stab wound to his heart. He felt the tears. *I always loved you* . . . her eyes seemed to say. . . . *Nothing you ever did changed that* . . .

Nothing . . .

Nothingness—

"*Mother,*" he whispered brokenly. *Mother* . . .

She heard him, he knew it, he felt it like a benediction: *she* was his mother, purely and simply, alive or dead, forever and always. "*Mother* . . ."

She knew it—she had always known it from the moment she had deemed he could stay. It was in her painted eyes, and in that wondrous accepting painted smile.

And through his tears, he looked at her more closely, and in her sweet knowing smile, he saw the smile of Jainee.

She awakened with a start, utterly unaware of where she was, conscious somehow that time had passed and that she was in strange surroundings.

It was a room, plain, unvarnished, with a bedstead on which she lay, a window with a pulled shade, an ember fed fireplace, a sputtering candle on a nearby washstand, and a man sitting in a chair opposite the bed watching her.

"Mademoiselle Beaumont," he said cordially as she bolted into a sitting position at her realization she was not at Southam

Manor. *"Bien.* I have waited a long time for your sleep of the dead to wear away. Time is wasting, and we must get down to cases."

Her eyes widened. "Where is Marie?" She knew the voice, oh how she knew the voice: it haunted her dreams, and it said the same words that he uttered in response to her question.

"Where is the boy?"

She saw him running through the sweet little house she had shared with Therese and her mother quivering at gunpoint the moment before she was caught in the crossfire between him and his associate.

"Where is the boy?"

The question brooked no lies, no stories. He held a pistol in his hand aimed directly at her heart. She couldn't move one way or the other without a bullet smashing right into her.

"I don't know. Tell me where is Marie, M. deVerville?"

"Ah, such a long, long memory, Mademoiselle Beaumont. I am flattered and if there were time, I would be interested. But I have travelled long and hard and at great risk to get the boy, and I will have him."

"He is not to be had; no one knows where he is, least of all me."

"A very nice story, Mademoiselle, but tell me, who was nose to nose with her father the traitor all these months? How could you not have discovered his whereabouts?"

"You may as well shoot me," Jainee said angrily. "He never told. The boy's whereabouts remain a secret from me and from the emperor as well."

"Indeed, it is the one thing we do not want: the boy must be presented to the Emperor and soon, or else it will be too late. Now, Mademoiselle—"

"I cannot tell you what I do not know, Monsieur."

"You would not tell me, you mean. Of course. Of course, in that case, I have only two choices: I can force you if I do not believe you. Or I could kill you, just as I eliminated your troublesome mother, who was costing my mistress so much pain and money."

464

He had not forgotten then, and neither had she. But the curious use of the word "mistress." She could not factor it into her memory of the event or why it should be the money of the mistress and not the emperor of which he spoke.

She needed to buy a moment's time. There was nothing likely in the room she could use as a weapon except perhaps the candlestick—and her wits. She didn't understand anything. She sensed more hours had elapsed since she had left Southam Manor, and she was certain something awful had happened to Marie.

The mare had reared and just taken off: the cart had toppled over—there had been a shot . . . Marie had slumped over—the cart had toppled and she had hit her head. Yes Marie . . . Marie could be dead.

And now deVerville and more threats. "Who is your mistress?" she said finally because she could not think of a single thing to say in the face of her imminent death. He could do nothing else: she could tell him nothing.

"My dear Mademoiselle Beaumont, surely you knew that your mother had very craftily applied to the empress to take care of her wants and needs rather than the husband. What a hold to have over Josephine—the Emperor's first blood. My mistress desperately wanted to protect it to use it for herself when the need arose and now the time has come. The emperor seeks a divorce and an heir, and my lady can provide him with the one to save herself from the other. You will provide me with the boy."

"And if you kill me—"

He smiled, a taut, evil smile. "I will find him anyway, Mademoiselle. I will tear up this countryside, and I will toss everyone to the dogs. The boy *must* be found."

So there was no hope anyway, she thought desperately. He didn't need her; his search might be more efficient without her. She could sense already that he was losing patience with the game of trying to coerce information out of her. She had to move, she had to *attack*. Soon . . . soon.

"Then you must find him," she said brazenly, her heart screaming with fear that she was deliberately goading him.

Immediately, he rose up, looming over her and shoving the nose of the pistol right into her face. "I think not, Mademoi—oof!"

She pushed him, she pushed him hard, with an upward thrust of both of her hands and he went down heavily, futilely as the pistol went off and she simultaneously jumped off of the bed and reached for the candlestick.

She had one moment—a moment in eternity as he began to pick himself up and she, fool that she was, flung the candlestick onto the bed and ran for the window.

She heard the whomp of the flame catching the bedclothes and deVerville's scream as he attempted to cut across the room and catch her.

She dived out the window, not knowing if it were ten feet above the ground or one. The flames roared like a waterfall behind her. She fell through space like an angel, secure of her place in heaven.

At dawn, she crept away from the copse of trees and bushes in which she had found shelter for her battered body.

At dawn, she could just see the charred ruin of the house where deVerville had imprisoned her. She did not know if he had survived the fire or had perished within. She was certain Marie was dead, but at dawn at least, she could see where the threats from her enemies were coming from.

She felt as if she had no vigor within her; she could have liked to have just put her head down and gone to sleep forever, in the forest, alone with the angels.

But there was Nicholas—and the boy.

She found a road and began walking, tiredly, dispiritedly, with no hope, no hope anyone would come along anytime soon.

A kindly farmer picked her up several hours later, distressed by the hopeless sag of her shoulders and the frailty of her frame, curious about the torn and slightly burned hem of her fashionable dress.

There was nothing she would explain. He agreed to take her to

Southam Manor somewhat dubiously, and only on the promise of some reward.

"You live around here?" she asked him after a while.

"Certain, ma'am."

She felt a pinprick of interest. "I was looking for a boy," she said suddenly.

"Lots of boys hereabouts, ma'am."

She smiled faintly. There wasn't much more to distinguish him from lots of boys hereabouts but his age. She felt a disheartening sense of futility.

"Perchance has he got a name, ma'am?"

A name? A name? A *name* . . . how had she not thought about a *name?* "His name is . . . Luc," she said hesitantly, "and he is seven or eight years old."

"Luke . . . Luke . . . ummm—Luke. You don't have the surname, ma'am?"

"The—" she said faintly. *Whose* name? Not Dunstan's. Perhaps her *father's?* Her heart began pounding. What if it were—what if? "I believe the name is, it's Dalton . . ."

"Ummm—Luke Dalton, Luke Dalton—sounds familiar ma'am. Maybe it's the Goodstones' boy—they took in a boy a long time ago, or Mrs. Colethorp's boy—she lives over Hickham way, beyond Southam Manor in the other direction. One of those would be your boy, I'm thinking."

One of those . . . your boy . . . your boy . . .

She fell into Nicholas' arms and into a deep exhausted sleep, and there was nothing anyone could do about it except thank the farmer and pay him handsomely.

She slept, and three days later, she awakened to find Nicholas by her bedside and Mrs. Blue hovering nearby.

"My lord?" she said dangerously, and it seemed to him that she had never gone away. "We have work to do. Mrs. Blue—I am so hungry. I need a wash, a fresh dress. I have much to tell my lord. Hurry, hurry."

She smiled faintly as Mrs. Blue scurried from the room, and

then she turned to Nicholas. "Listen you, we must find the boy, and I think perhaps I have a clue . . ."

"My dear Diana," Nicholas said exasperatedly, "I don't give a damn about the boy."

"Of course you do, my lord. I will tell you the whole in time."

"I want the whole now, huntress; you were reeling in hell when the farmer delivered you to the door."

She nodded. "I myself cannot comprehend: I went for the boy and Marie came with me, and what does it prove but that she is seeking the boy too—just as my mother predicted," she added darkly. "She is an agent of the Murat, and now, I am confident, has paid with her life for her sins. The man who killed her is the very man who murdered my mother and followed me, as he must have done, to England to also obtain possession of the boy. They all wanted the boy, Marie to kill him, and deVerville to return him to France, and the empress who would use him to secure her place as the emperor's wife and provide him with an heir.

"And so—the rest is inconsequential, except to say they both made the mistake of thinking that because I had tracked down my father, I knew the secret of the boy's whereabouts. I did not—then. Perhaps . . . perhaps I do now."

The important thing was the boy—he could see that, but he felt absurdly disappointed that she did not wish to resolve the problems concerning them.

It could wait—it *could*. She had returned, and he would not question it.

He knew his mother was smiling.

Chapter Twenty-eight

"Mrs. Blue, you must tell me—do you know of a family Goodstone or a woman named Mrs. Colethorp?"

"The family Goodstone . . ." Mrs. Blue mused, pleased to see Jainee had indeed gotten dressed and removed herself to the library where she had settled in a comfortable chair by the window with a cup of tea and some buns.

"Umm . . ." she said finally. "Yes—they are new ones, lately come, five years or more along. They live down by the Hungerford mill. Now the other—the other—yes, I know *of* her, my lady, and why do you wish to know?"

"Why do you not wish to tell me?" Jainee asked curiously, her interest piqued by Mrs. Blue's peculiar phrasing.

"Mrs. Colethorp is not a lady, my lady."

"I see." Better and better, Jainee thought. "Perhaps you might just tell me what you know about her."

"She lives alone, with her son . . ."

Yes! Jainee thought wildly, hardly able to contain herself. "Go on, Mrs. Blue."

"And they say she derives an income from certain favors she granted his majesty, the king, in the time before his illness overset him. She does not mingle, my lady. I know nothing more about her."

"It is enough," Jainee murmured. "And her direction, Mrs. Blue?"

"Over Hickham way, my lady."

"I am so grateful," Jainee whispered, hugging the information close to her heart.

469

"We have come to the end of the story," she said as Nicholas guided the barouche through the town and on to the road to which he had been directed.

"We have come to nothing," Nicholas said dourly. "This may well be a wild chase. It is based on no pertinent information and a clutch of unsubstantiated guesses—and your faith, I might add. You will be sadly upended if the boy does not prove to be here."

"One must try," Jainee said philosophically. "See there—that must be the house. How modest a living for the courtesan of a king." She felt a spurting excitement as though every answer awaited her beyond the door of the half-timbered house a hundred feet beyond.

But what if there were nothing there but the disappointment of her life? She refused to think about it and determinedly climbed down from the carriage before Nicholas could come around to help her.

"This is the place," she said firmly, and knocked on the door.

A moment, two moments later, it swung open and Jainee looked into a pair of bright blue eyes, so similar to her own.

"This is the boy," she whispered, and reached out her hand. *I have found him for you, Therese. He is alive—he is loved.*

"Who are you?" a harsh voice demanded, and Jainee looked up.

The woman was not visible—she was just beyond the door, lurking in the shadows as if she did not wish to be seen.

"I am Lady Southam," she said resolutely and stepped inside the door.

She knew Nicholas was behind her. The boy had moved backward to accommodate the fact she was moving forward, and the room, contrary to what she expected, was flooded with light. The woman, who was not young, was bathed in a halo of sunlight.

She saw all this—and the boy reaching for the comforting hand of his mother to ward off the threat of the strangers—and

470

she had a fleeting impression of the elegance of the surroundings, before she heard Nicholas' voice behind her, harsh, bloodless and utterly devoid of emotion.

"Well, Diana—let me make you known to Mrs. Colethorp—the woman who is *my* mother."

It wasn't the house—the house had been someplace else in that long-ago time. It was the scent and sense of the things with which she lived, the enfolding homecoming he felt when he walked through the door, and then the rage of comprehension that she had always been so close.

Dunstan had known.

Presumably, Lord Henry had known.

Her face mirrored her fear, and perhaps a little relief as well? He couldn't tell, he didn't want to know.

He looked at the boy and he looked at Jainee, and he saw nothing but the eyes, and the firm true face of a youth who knew nothing but the comfort of his life with his mother.

But so had he done—just not with this woman.

She knew him—she almost stepped toward him, her hand reached out to him as if the touch could span the years with which he had lived without it.

He made no move toward her and her hand dropped to her side. Her eyes implored him to be kind, and flickered away to Jainee, who stood shocked and helpless, with no words to assuage the wounds.

"Please sit down," the woman finally said because she had to do something, and she watched with a mother's eyes as Nicholas moved sinuously into the room and prowled around it as if he knew every inch of it, every piece of furniture, everything, *all*.

Oh, my mama has pretty silver things like that . . .

—Like that . . .

. . . and that—

—and that . . .

He paced them off like a treasurer in his counting house, laying the memory against the weight of the years lost and his

471

child-self diminished, and there wasn't enough silver in the house to pay the price of what he had lost.

"It is time for Mrs. Colethorp to tell us the story," Jainee said finally, seating herself by the window where there were several chairs set around to provide a spot of intimacy in the large room. "Nicholas . . ."

He heard her speak his name from afar.

"Nicholas—you *must* listen. Please sit down. *Please.*" God, the bitterness in his face, she might never be able to wipe it away.

He sat, poised like a lion on a pedestal on the arm of one chair.

Mrs. Colethorp drew the boy with her and sat down in one of the others.

"Since you found the boy," she said, "you must know as much as I can tell you."

"Dunstan brought him to you."

"Yes."

"It was no accident," Nicholas said suddenly, angrily.

Her body sagged. "No, it was no accident. But it was not immediate either, Nicholas. You must believe me. Your parents had no idea where you had come from until many years later, and then it was most imperative that we hide the origin of your birth from you, most urgent. Your father agreed, we *all* agreed, Nicholas, that it would be for the best. You know why. You must know."

"I know nothing," he said, his voice raspy with anger. "Tell the whole, madame. Lay everything out on the table that I might understand why I was so precipitately abandoned by you."

Her face seemed to dissolve before his eyes. She had been so pretty, and on her better days she was well able to maintain that imperious air of a well-loved mistress, proud that she had been retired to the country, and willing to live in the background now her sovereignty was over.

But anguish bloated her face now, and the creamy skin was mottled with sadness, her firm lips turned downward with guilt, her black eyes so like his own sodden with unshed tears.

She was a slender woman, too, but his sudden appearance

added weight to her shoulders that made her body seem as if it were sagging from carrying a burden too heavy for her to bear.

Only the boy stood by to comfort her: he had known no other care.

"It was an accident, Nicholas. You wandered away in spite of all caution, and that demon Slote got hold of you. And we were all so scared, for we knew he had been out and about and stealing unencumbered children. I will never know if you were a direct target or if he happened upon you, but when we finally realized you were gone and raised the alarm, it was too late. No one had seen you, and Slote could have been fifty miles beyond Dorcombe by then.

"I can't tell you," she said beseechingly to his hard, hard face, "how I cried, how I searched: We had dogs, we had friends, we had spies trying to track down Slote, and he was too clever to be found because he had snatched ten little boys that day. *Ten*, Nicholas. Ten mothers bereft of their reason for living. Ten! Oh, it was unbearable, unbearable . . ."

She began to cry, and the boy handed her a handkerchief. "In a while, however, after you had been with your father for several months, he began to be curious about your parentage, and he began making inquiries. He was just highly enough placed so that he could gather some information, and some gossip and add the sum together, and soon enough, he found me, and he told me he had you, that his Lady Eliza had fallen in love with you when you toppled down the chimney and they meant to keep you and raise you as their own.

"How could I protest? What had I in comparison to Lord Henry, except a reputation and a son who would be considered baseborn in spite of his blood. He had paid me the courtesy of telling me, but he did not expect me to contest his decision. He wished only that I would remove all tell-tale objects from the house in the unlikely case you might find me and recognize them.

"I do not know whether he confided in Dunstan, or whether Dunstan found out himself, but by and by, he came around to me and we were friends. He moved me closer to Southam Manor

473

that I might watch the progression of your youth, and years later, he asked me to take the child. Lord Henry never knew that I was as close as Hickham, and Dunstan never told me where the child was from. I was only to take care of him, to raise him as my own.

"It was like getting another chance with my son. I love the boy, and I have never stopped loving my son. But my son will never forgive *me*," she ended, tears staining her voice once again.

"Your son must think about it," Jainee said unhesitatingly. "There is so much to understand, and so little time. The boy could be in danger. And it is the reason I have sought him out. I am Jainee Beaumont, and I am his kin. Dunstan was my father. My mother bore the boy who is in much the same position as was Nicholas when he was a child. And now you must listen, as carefully as we did to you . . ."

She was not helpless at least: Nicholas was cogent enough to understand they were not fighting some nameless Slote — it was something bigger this time, and something that required bold action.

"For it is still not clear if deVerville lives, nor did I see the body of Marie with my very own eyes," Jainee pointed out. "We must protect the boy."

That mandate, at least, was clear, and there was only one way Jainee could think of that met her requirements.

"We must remove them both to Southam Manor."

"No."

"You will of course reconsider."

"No."

She did not know if they had any time or if they had all the time in the world. "Mrs. Colethorp is willing."

"How could she not be?" Nicholas said bitterly.

"We will do it," Jainee said firmly, ignoring him and enlisted Mrs. Blue and Exeter to help.

It was done in a week, the whole of the house removed to Southam Manor and room made on the upper floors to incorporate all the pretty silver things he remembered from his youth.

The boy, so placid and adoring, the boy was himself thirty years earlier, and the woman, his mother, had finally come home.

Her cottage burned to the ground mysteriously one night. The authorities laid it to a smoldering fire. A body was found in the ruins, burned beyond recognition.

"It is deVerville," Jainee said grimly, "trapped by his own blood-lust and misplaced loyalty. It *has* to be."

But she kept watching the shadows—and none of them moved. Still, it was not enough to hope that both Marie and deVerville had perished.

So they stayed on through the month of June to be certain, to sustain that hope, and so that they would not have to face what lay between them.

But everything now had changed. There was a boy in the house, and the story of his mother.

But she is not you . . . he spoke to the portrait, *she could never be you . . .*

His mother seemed to smile at him.

His mother gained strength as she became accustomed to the luxury at the Manor and the thought that all the secrets need no longer be contained.

She talked endlessly with Jainee while Nicholas and his servants roamed the woods and made sure that the paths were free from threats.

The boy bloomed as he learned to ride a horse and shoot a gun, and was taken up by Mr. Finley because of his love of horses.

The boy could have been him, Nicholas thought, he could have been the boy. And he was what he was because of the unflinching love of his *beautiful lady,* as the boy would be what he was because of *his* mother.

And so he learned that he did not have to choose,

that the past was over and irretrievable, and the only place he could go was forward, step by step, into his future.

By July it seemed there was no longer anything to fear. And so in July they returned to London, and it came almost as a respite from the fraught and emotional weeks preceding it.

It was a relief to leave the Manor, not because Nicholas had not grown to love it, but because he needed now to find his way with Jainee, and nothing could be resolved until they were alone.

They were hardly ever alone at the Manor.

But he became increasingly aware of Jainee as the tension eased between them and they both almost literally set aside that moment of truth about Dunstan which was so painful and sought almost simultaneously to begin again.

Jainee was very good at beginning again.

It wasn't as if he could identify the very moment when he understood that her looks had intensified, that her dress had become more sensual, that her words sometimes had double meanings. That her mouth ached to be kissed and there was not one private place in the whole of Southam Manor save the bedroom, and they were not as yet sharing that.

Did she brush against him once too often?

Or lean over as she was intently choosing a book from the *lower* shelf in the library?

Were those meaningful glances which touched the private place in him and revealed how much she remembered and how much she wanted?

Jainee—goddess of the moon; Diana, on the prowl again.

He wasn't sure a month was enough time for all the wounds to heal. On the other hand, a month *was* enough time to watch her in action and how she was with the woman who had borne him, and how she cared for the child, and how she treated the servants, and how everything interested her and she took great enjoyment in pursuing and knowing everything about everyone

476

that she possibly could.

She was born to the Manor even if she had not been raised in one.

He felt a great stirring of need deep in his vitals. She was *his*, she had always been his from the first moment he saw her, and their fate was bound inextricably together.

One night, she read them the cards: his mother first, then the boy, then himself.

Such fortunes she told, all full of happy portents and good things to come. He forebore to point out she could tell the cards any way she chose.

"See here, my lord—an unexpected journey, and here a house. Oh, a woman, wonderful, everything lovely that you have ever wanted. The cards smile upon my lord tonight. But then, you will have to be patient for your dreams to be realized, but here is a pleasant surprise . . . and . . . ah, my lord—a good marriage—"

"Enough of this nonsense," he decreed exasperatedly. "We will go to London."

London was hot, steaming, the streets were crowded with the same number of carriages and the same number of bucks and beauties seeking recognition.

The papers were full of the same gossip, most notably the desirable connection between Lord Jeremy Waynflete and Miss Charlotte Emerlin which was being touted in every column.

"He might not have even offered for her," Nicholas commented, "but now he has no choice."

Trenholm was waiting, the door to the townhouse thrown wide.

"Blessed peace," Nicholas murmured. "Holy silence."

Jainee ran lightly up the steps ahead of him and disappeared into the house.

When he entered, she was nowhere around, and then he felt the soft drape of her perfumed shawl settle on his head.

He pulled it off and looked up to the balcony outside his bed-

477

room door and there she was, laughing, bending over the railing suggestively, mocking him. "No peace, my lord," she called down. "Not ever." And she darted into the bedroom.

Slowly, holding her shawl to his face and inhaling her scent, he mounted the steps and climbed inexorably to the point of no return.

Everything else—apologies, explanations, declarations—could wait until tomorrow. This would be his reality tonight.

She awaited him exactly the way he had always envisioned her: the goddess, naked on his bed, clad only in her stockings and a streamer of erotic blue satin, the sultry blue glow in her *make me* eyes challenging him to finally and irrevocably claim her passion and her love.

FEEL THE FIRE IN CAROL FINCH'S ROMANCES!

BELOVED BETRAYAL (2346, $3.95)

Sabrina Spencer donned a gray wig and veiled hat before blackmailing rugged Ridge Tanner into guiding her to Fort Canby. But the costume soon became her prison—the beauty had fallen head over heels in love!

LOVE'S HIDDEN TREASURE (2980, $4.50)

Shandra d'Evereux felt her heart throb beneath the stolen map she'd hidden in her bodice when Nolan Elliot swept her out onto the veranda. It was hard to concentrate on her mission with that wily rogue around!

MONTANA MOONFIRE (3263, $4.95)

Just as debutante Victoria Flemming-Cassidy was about to marry an oh-so-suitable mate, the towering preacher, Dru Sullivan flung her over his shoulder and headed West! Suddenly, Tori realized she had been given the best present for a bride: a night of passion with a real man!

THUNDER'S TENDER TOUCH (2809, $4.50)

Refined Piper Malone needed bounty-hunter, Vince Logan to recover her swindled inheritance. She thought she could coolly dismiss him after he did the job, but she never counted on the hot flood of desire she felt whenever he was near!

Available wherever paperbacks are sold, or order direct from the Publisher. Send cover price plus 50¢ per copy for mailing and handling to Zebra Books, Dept. 3794, 475 Park Avenue South, New York, N.Y. 10016. Residents of New York, New Jersey and Pennsylvania must include sales tax. DO NOT SEND CASH.

WAITING FOR A WONDERFUL ROMANCE?
READ ZEBRA'S

WANDA OWEN!

DECEPTIVE DESIRES   (2887, $4.50/$5.50)
Exquisite Tiffany Renaud loved her life as the only daughter of a
wealthy Parisian industrialist. The last thing she wanted was to
cross the ocean on a cramped and stuffy ship just to visit the un-
civilized wilds of America. Then she shared a kiss with shipping
magnate Chad Morrow that made the sails billow and the deck
spin. . .

KISS OF FIRE   (3091, $4.50/$5.50)
Born and raised in backwoods Virginia, Tawny Blair knew that
her dream of being swept off her feet by a handsome nobleman
would never come true. But when she met Lord Bart, Tawny saw
at once that reality could far surpass her fantasies. And when he
took her in his strong arms, she thrilled to the desire in his searing
caresses . . .

SAVAGE FURY   (2676, $3.95/$4.95)
Lovely Gillian Browne was secure in her quiet world on a remote
ranch in Arizona, yet she longed for romance and excitement.
Her girlish fantasies did not prepare her for the strange new feelings that assaulted her when dashing Irish sea captain Steve Laf-
ferty entered her life . . .

TEMPTING TEXAS TREASURE   (3312, $4.50/$5.50)
Mexican beauty Karita Montera aroused a fever of desire in every
redblooded man in the wild Texas Blacklands. But the sensuous
señorita had eyes only for Vincent Navarro, the wealthy cattle
rancher she'd adored since childhood—and her family's sworn enemy! His first searing caress ignited her white-hot need and soon
Karita burned to surrender to her own wanton passion . . .

*Available wherever paperbacks are sold, or order direct from the
Publisher. Send cover price plus 50¢ per copy for mailing and
handling to Zebra Books, Dept. 3794, 475 Park Avenue South,
New York, N.Y. 10016. Residents of New York and Tennessee
must include sales tax. DO NOT SEND CASH. For a free Zebra/
Pinnacle catalog please write to the above address.*